Eldin of Yashor

Jacqui –

It has been fabulous seeing you again & meeting your twin cutie pies. I can't wait to work with you.

You Rock!!

Love always,

E. Tyler Storm

Eldin of Yashor

C. Tyler Storm

LANGDON STREET PRESS

Langdon Street Press
212 3rd Avenue North, Suite 290
Minneapolis, MN 55401
612.455.2293
www.langdonstreetpress.com

ISBN - 978-1-934938-54-6
ISBN - 1-934938-54-8
LCCN - 2009936443

Book sales for North America and international:
Itasca Books, 3501 Highway 100 South, Suite 220
Minneapolis, MN 55416
Phone: 952.345.4488 (toll free 1.800.901.3480)
Fax: 952.920.0541; email to orders@itascabooks.com

Cover Art by Julie Bell and Boris Vallejo
Typeset by Peggy LeTrent

Printed in the United States of America

Acknowledgements

For Sharon (thanks for believing in me from the start), Angie 'n' Vanessa (for being the quarters in my pocket, I know I can always pull you out when I need to call someone who cares), Lila (for your unwavering friendship for the last gazillion years), Donita (I'm so proud of you!), Liz (I miss you), Honey Anne (great observations), Janine 'n' Trisha (the best kiwi mates ever!), Momma Maria (I miss your cooking), Ms. Kimmy (I miss our Germany adventures!), Christy 'n' Michelle (for inspiration in my life and wonderful friendship), and Allison (long talks, feeding me such great food, and your friendship). Thank you all for your love, and support. I truly feel blessed to have people like all of you in my life! The best things in life are free...

A special thanks to Ms. Kay Dragoun for going above and beyond to help a lost little tenth-grader believe in her talent. You are an exceptional teacher.

I'd also like to thank my editor, Laine. Your observations and insight were invaluable. Thank you for helping me fine tune Eldin. I loved working with you and hope that we may continue to work on all of my projects together!

About the Author

I was born 31 December 1966 in Amarillo, TX, to a 16-year-old girl by the last name of Wolf. She gave me up for adoption at birth, and I was transplanted to Enid, Oklahoma, by my adopted parents. They are wonderful parents with questionable taste in hometowns! In the fourth grade, I wrote my first novel, *Double, Double Stole and Trouble*. I believe my parents still have that handwritten mess of a manuscript locked up in a file cabinet somewhere. As a sophomore in high school, I won a citywide essay contest with the first essay I ever wrote. After that, I wrote for the school newspaper. I conducted a telephone interview with Leslie Evans, the information director with the new *Women's Sports Magazine* for an article on the lack of women's professional team sports. Because of that article, I was offered a cub-reporter position with the magazine to cover the 1984 Summer Olympics in LA. Due to a parental decision, I was unable to accept. Being young and immature, I decided that I would "learn them a thing or two," so I quit writing. Of course, the only one it hurt was me.

As an adult, I have lived an incredible adventure thus far. I have served in the US Army overseas. I have explored much of western Europe. I've camped in the Alps, swam in the Mediterranean Sea, and repelled off the Trier Bridge in Germany. I've ran my fingers through the grooves inside some covered bridges in the German countryside left by General Patton's tanks. After I was discharged, I attended the University of Connecticut, where I found a passion for rugby and reignited my passion for writing. I have traveled the world and left footprints on most of the continents. I have twice jumped off the tallest building in New Zealand for fun (630 ft free-fall), swam with the dolphins in the Bay of Islands, been blackwater rafting in the Waitomo caves, and scuba-diving off the coast of Kauai. I fed and played with a pair of eight-week-old tiger cubs. I've seen so many incredible places; I know I am truly blessed!

I am lucky to still have both of my parents with me. My father is a retired cattleman, and my mother is a retired RN. I have an older brother who is an MD and married to another MD (thanks, bro, for having all those kids and taking the pressure off me and SJ to have more "grandkids," you are the best!), and a younger sister (don't believe that stuff about D being the best…you know it's you), who is working for the US Dept. of Commerce in Foreign Relations (trade relations and embassy stuff). I have one spoiled rotten kitty-kid, Kia Ora, who is far too smart for my good, and one real adopted daughter who has made me a "g" word far too young as she has had a son and daughter of her own while in her early twenties. She is currently attending nursing school, and I am very proud of her!

Preface

Drakknia had always been a utopian society...until evolution chose women as its champion, and they grew bigger and stronger than the men. There was a coup, and society fractured along gender lines. The matriarchal society of Yashor began a bloody never-ending war with the newly patriarchal society of Drakknia over ideological dominance. Eldin, a young, brash 23-seasonmark-old captain in the Yashor Sword Corps, has several small storms in her path. She has to try to win a war that she doesn't believe in, keep her inexperienced younger male-child sib alive on the battlefield, and protect the beautiful young healer she has lost her heart to from the equally beautiful but deadly soldier with whom she shares her body. If that wasn't enough to drive her totally mad, Elrik, the legendary general and Eldin's mother, has just taken her last ride and left the fate of Yashor in her hands. But what Eldin doesn't know is that an even deadlier storm looms on the horizon. One that threatens to destroy everything that Eldin loves—her country...her family...even her heart.

1

Thick clouds of churning dust choked out the sunlight as the two armies clashed in a fierce battle over the blood-soaked ground. Eldin's sunburst-blonde mane whipped about her face as she slashed another opponent. Horror-stricken, the soldier watched as his belly opened and his vitals poured out. Eldin knocked the dying man to the ground and surveyed her immediate surroundings for her sword's next challenge.

Seeing her sib, Seldar, across the battlefield, Eldin made her way to him, felling several soldiers whom were no match for her skill. Nudging Seldar with her shoulder, Eldin grinned. He spun in her direction and swung his sword wildly. Realizing that he was going to attack at the contact, Eldin feigned left while countering his stroke and was able to stop his blade's momentum before it was able to inflict any damage.

"How fares thee, Seldar? Are you making much sport today?" Eldin greeted her sib as she plunged her sword into another unfortunate opponent with effortless skill.

"I am making much more sport than you, Captain," Seldar answered, using his older sib's rank.

Seldar avoided a well-timed thrust from the Drakknian in front of him and nearly lost his balance. He was not used to the savage pace of combat yet, but he reveled in the chance to make his hero, Eldin, proud of him. Seldar would gladly give his life for the chance to be recorded in the Scrolls of Yashor. Only the bravest of Male-children ever made the skins of the sacred scrolls. Normally, the Scrolls of Yashor were reserved for fallen Amazon Warriors. Every hero's name was transcribed onto a scroll; when the scroll was filled, it was moved to the Great Temple's crypt for safekeeping. At the Season's Mark, every name was read aloud, and a prayer of thanks was given to them all by the High Priestess. It was the greatest honor a male-child could achieve.

If he could just prove himself worthy to Eldin, Seldar would be happy with that accomplishment. He knew that Eldin had made it possible for him to get out of his serf training to join her district's army, despite his being the best cook in the entire district. Pain engulfed Seldar's shoulder and served as a reminder to focus on the battle.

Eldin blocked a stroke from her enemy and easily pushed his sword away. The frustrated soldier tried to counter but lost his balance and lunged toward Eldin. Eldin's massive muscles rippled gracefully as she used the doomed man's momentum against him and knocked him to the ground. She kicked him in the side so that his body rolled face-up toward her before she plunged her sword deep into the soft flesh of his neck. A clean killing stroke, the soldier neither felt pain nor suffered, for his death was almost instantaneous. Eldin caught Seldar watching and risked the moment to instruct him on Amazon fighting laws.

"As a member of the Army Sword Corps of Yashor, you must never strike an opponent from the back. That is the ultimate act of cowardice and punishable by death. No, at least give him the respect of facing his death like a woman," Eldin explained quickly.

Seldar nodded his understanding and turned just in time to see a Drakknian swinging his sword at him. A heartbeat before the blade would have opened his head and ended his short life, Eldin's sword stopped the blade's momentum and offered Seldar the chance to defend himself. At twelve hands, four fingers, Seldar was getting fairly tall for a male-child, but he still had not "filled in" his frame with muscle yet. His sib Eldin was an imposing figure at seventeen hands, two fingers, with massive muscles that created a body built for the rigors of army life.

Seldar was matching his enemy's sword stroke for stroke. He focused intently on the swinging steel and found it difficult to match pace with his opponent. With each swing, Seldar was losing confidence. The Drakknian soldier was superior to Seldar, and he knew it. Suddenly Seldar's scream pierced the air, just as the slightly dulled blade of his opponent pierced the flesh of his leg.

At the sound of her sib's pain, Eldin flashed rage at the source of Seldar's wounds. The young Drakknian soldier did not stand a chance against Eldin's far superior skill and fell from a barrage of blows meant to inflict great pain as well as death.

Seldar fell to the ground, his sword still gripped in his hand. He felt the gush of bright red blood that spurted from his leg like one of the great fountains in the Council of Nine's courtyard. His head felt light, and the stench of the dying filled his nostrils. As Seldar lay in a pool of his own blood, his mind slipped back to his childhood. Eldin would return home from schooling, and she would sneak him out of the kitchen, away from the monotonous "male-child's work." They would run into the woods that surrounded the small keep of their mothers, Elrik and Dinyar. Eldin would find a sandy area next to their favorite fishing brook and show Seldar what she had learned that day. It was a dangerous thing to do. The law strictly forbade teaching a male-child anything outside of basic serf or soldiering skills. Anyone caught doing so would be tried by the Council of Nine for high treason. Eldin did not care. She risked her life and all the lands of then-Colonel Elrik to show Seldar the wonders of a Yashor education.

The black veil of unconsciousness gripped Seldar's mind like a vise just as Eldin picked him up and placed him over her left shoulder. His grip finally easing around the hilt of his sword, it fell to the ground, a silent marker of where Seldar had fallen.

Eldin fought through the chaos toward the edge of the battlefield. Her mind racing with fear for her sib's life, she sliced a path of death through the Drakknians. Steadily, Eldin made her way to her huge roan stallion, Thunder. Carefully, she mounted the magnificent warhorse while balancing Seldar over her shoulder. Once comfortable in her saddle, Eldin managed to slide Seldar off her shoulder so she could balance him in front of her as she held the reins. Eldin tapped Thunder's flanks, and he bolted as if he were a flash of lightning toward the healer's area. Thunder's hooves tore through the ground with each powerful stride.

The healer's area was just over the rise, and Eldin silently thanked the Goddess for the speed of the beast beneath her. Instinct told her that every heartbeat was precious to her sib. Now all she had to do was convince the healer that a male-child was worth the effort of saving. *Goddess, it probably will be no small task either.*

Kiya spotted the rider galloping toward her and caught her breath. The unison between the rider and war steed was magnificent. As they drew nearer, she gazed for the first time at the woman who commanded her district's army. Thick shoulder-length blonde hair framed a strong, compassionate face. A deep, authoritative voice interrupted Kiya's thoughts.

"Ho, fair Healer. I know that he is only a male-child, but I am verily attached to him. If you could find it in your heart to share your gifts with him, I would forever be in your debt," Eldin petitioned the beautiful young healer.

Kiya was in awe of the young captain. She had heard mention of stories about Eldin's ice-blue eyes setting hearts afire, but she had never actually believed them...until now. Eldin was the perfect picture of Amazon strength and beauty. She was the most handsome woman Kiya had ever laid eyes upon. Even blood-soaked and dripping in gore, the warrior was nothing less than breathtaking. *Blood-soaked...wait a heartbeat, there is something...*Kiya shook her head to clear her thoughts. Eldin mistook Kiya's silence for disapproval.

"I would gladly give you my essence, if it pleased you, in exchange for my sib's life," Eldin solemnly offered her body to Kiya.

Kiya subdued the sudden flames of desire that were coursing through her body. Her cheeks burned as she realized what the handsome captain had just offered her.

"By the Goddess, no! That will not be necessary, Captain Eldin. To anyone that you deem worthy of my gifts, I will gladly give my attention. Here, help me get him into the wagon," Kiya replied as she reached for the young boy in Eldin's care.

Eldin gently lowered Seldar into the healer's wagon and watched intently as Kiya began her ministrations of mercy. She wrapped a torn piece of cloth around Seldar's leg halfway between the wound and his hip. Seeing what she needed, Kiya reached out and claimed a dagger from Eldin's bootstrap sheath and twisted the cloth around the hilt until the pressure caused the bleeding to stop. Next, Kiya took a sheepskin bladder bag containing water that had been boiled of all imperfections and poured it over the wound.

Kiya was glad that the boy was unconscious, because she had to scrape away the dead skin and remove the dirt from the hole in his leg. The procedure was necessary, but it was also extremely painful. Why, she had grown women who found it difficult to deal with the pain, let alone a small male-child. No, it was much better that his mind would sleep through this.

Eldin watched from the relative comfort of her saddle. *Goddess those blades hurt.* Eldin absently rubbed her side in sympathy pain where an old scar stung. She watched as Kiya produced a pouch of medicinal salve and rubbed it into the clean wound. She used some treated catgut thread to repair the bloodline and to sew closed the gaping hole that the sword had left in its wake. Afterward, she released the pressure of the cloth wrapped around his leg.

"Now I must pray for the Goddess to smile upon him and to heal his soul," Kiya explained.

Eldin's left eyebrow shot up at the comment; it was widely accepted that male-children did not possess a soul. It was also widely accepted that the Great Goddess would only smile down upon the female race, and you were blessed to be born in Her divine image. Despite her initial fears, Eldin was beginning to like this healer.

Kiya took Eldin's strong calloused hands into her own and felt the depth of the woman's soul. She embraced the courage, the fear, and the passion that was Eldin. Kiya mingled her energy with Eldin's. It was warm, inviting, and oddly familiar. Kiya was drawn deeper into that core essence that was love. Alarm bells tolled in her mind. It would be unethical to go any farther, no matter how familiar the essence seemed. No, she must only touch that which was necessary to affect the prayer.

Eldin gasped at the feeling of Kiya's energy deep within her. It was compassionate, loving, and adventuresome. It was as if she had always known the healer. Slowly, Eldin felt Kiya withdraw after the completion of the prayer. Kiya held onto Eldin's hands just a few precious heartbeats more before reluctantly allowing them to slip from her grasp.

Eldin regained her composure and bent her head in a wordless tribute of thanks. Before anything more could pass between them, she spurred Thunder into action. They were off, galloping back to the battlefield. Eldin pulled back on the reins suddenly and circled Thunder at the top of the rise for one last look at the healer. She smiled as she realized the healer's beauty for the first time. *Now there is a woman worth going to war over!* Eldin spurred Thunder again, and they headed back to battle.

Kiya watched them disappear over the ridge and felt the unfamiliar pang of loss when they were no longer in sight. Recognizing a potential weakness of the heart, Kiya tried to control her new feelings for Eldin. She must dowse the sparks of attraction or risk losing her heart to the all-consuming fires of passionate love. It could not work, a healer and a warrior, she admonished herself. *Still....*

* * *

Back in the middle of the battle, Eldin could see that many of the lesser-conditioned Drakknians were beginning to grow weary. Even when you are fighting for your life, there comes a point when your flesh will betray your soul and leave you helpless at the feet of Death; a merciless Death whose voracious appetite for the living is never satiated. If Eldin's troops could hold out a little longer, the Fates would judge in Yashor's favor.

Two more blood-drenched candlemarks the battle raged before Drakknia sounded the retreat. Eldin's troops began cheering her name in a mantra of exultation. Eldin fought the urge to run from the adulation, for she never quite felt deserving of such love from her soldiers. A few candle-drips later, Eldin had quieted the joyous victors. She gave out orders to set up a perimeter watch and clear the bodies of the dead from the field.

Once Eldin was satisfied with the perimeter defenses, she rode out to visit the wounded. Her district had suffered heavy casualties, and she must visit each of them regardless if they were awake or trapped inside their own mind. It was a responsibility that Eldin took very seriously. The sergeant of Eldin's elite honor guard met her at the edge of the healer's area and took Thunder's reins. She held him for Eldin's dismount, and then she led the horse to be fed, watered, and brushed down.

Eldin approached the first wagon and silently prayed to the Goddess for the strength to help her wounded. Three mortally wounded Amazons lay in the first wagon, and Eldin climbed in beside them. She took the closest warrior's hand into her own and bent forward to speak softly into her ear.

"Ho, my precious warrior of Three Rivers. How fares thee?" Eldin inquired.

The young woman labored to inhale enough breath to reply. "I do not know, Captain. I fear that I shall not see the dawn. I cannot feel my legs, but the rest of me is on fire."

Eldin felt a lump in her throat. This one was barely sixteen seasonmarks old, yet her eyes looked like those of a wise old crone. Her innocence and youth had been stolen, replaced by blood, fear, and death. Yes, Death was eagerly waiting to get his claws into this one; it was almost a certainty. She had been hit with a flaming ball of pitch and severely burned over most of her body. The fire had consumed her flesh, leaving nothing but charred muscle, bone, and excruciating pain in its wake. At least her head and neck had been spared.

"You will live in the pages of the Scrolls of Yashor forever, young hero," Eldin comforted her. "Is there anything you wish me to tell your loved ones?"

"I am an orphan, Captain. There shall be no one to mourn my death," she replied, stiffening her jaw against the pain at the reality of her own words.

"I will," Eldin assured her, tenderly stroking the injured woman's forehead in the manner that she remembered her mother, Dinyar, often doing to comfort her in her own periods of illness.

The young woman looked into Eldin's eyes and then labored in another breath. "By the Goddess, if I am to know only one kiss in this lifetime, then I am honored that it is by your lips that I travel to the Hall of Judgment, Captain Eldin."

"Are you ready then, young hero?" Eldin inquired gently.

Attempting to be brave, the youngster nodded. Her display of courage didn't fool Eldin; she still saw the fear. It was enough to rip at her heart. Reluctantly, Eldin had to finish this and move on. She bent down to administer the "kiss of release" to end this needless suffering. Eldin's lips gently caressed the young soldier's lips in an attempt to convey the love and gratitude of their nation for her sacrifice. As she finished kissing the dying warrior, Eldin placed a large drop of hooded snake venom on the warrior's lower lip. This was offering her a chance to cross over peacefully since she was beyond a healer's help. All of the mortally wounded gladly licked the deadly poison and traveled to the Hall of Judgment to be free from pain until the time when they would walk the earth once more. This youngster was no different, and Eldin stayed with her as she breathed her last.

The young warrior struggled for breath, clutched at Eldin, and said, "Remember me!"

A tear silently slid down Eldin's cheek; the panic at the very end made her wonder if this tradition was truly "compassionate."

"Be well, little one, and save me a place at the banquet. I shall light a candle for you at the Seasons' End Feast," Eldin whispered as she covered her with a funeral cloak.

Eldin checked on the other two warriors in the wagon. They had already been claimed by Death, so she placed cloaks over their bodies and prepared them for the funeral pyres that would be lit later in the evening.

* * *

Kiya looked up from the body she had just covered and watched Eldin in silent scrutiny for a few candledrips. She had never known a leader as devoted as this one seemed. Hopefully, Eldin was all that she appeared to be and did not have some dark hidden agenda. A broad smile lit up Kiya's face, despite herself and her initial reservations. Her cheeks flushed a deep red with embarrassment as Eldin looked up and their eyes met. Eldin grinned a lopsided greeting, which only added to her charm as far as the healer was concerned. Kiya quickly resumed her work.

* * *

What was it about this healer that made Eldin smile when what she had wanted to do only heartbeats before was cry for her lost warriors?

"She is a Demon Shamaness. Sure, that has to be it," Eldin rationalized under her breath.

It took several more candlemarks to finish seeing everyone, and although Eldin was exhausted and sickened by the sight of so many wasted beautiful lives, she still would not accept any food or mead until she was ready to visit her sib. The sun had set, and even-feast had been over for at least a candlemark when Eldin finally accepted a bowl of stew from the healer. Even then, it was only under threat from Kiya to pull her off the fighting scroll if she did not eat and get some rest that Eldin finally relented. Having been outmaneuvered, Eldin silently took the bowl of stew and found Seldar. *Demon Shamaness*!

Eldin found him lying in a wagon close to the healer's own tent. Kiya had placed the boy on a mattress of straw-stuffed cloth. Unusually nice accommodations for a male-child, she noted. Eldin climbed into the wagon, taking care not to spill her stew, lest she incur the wrath of the Demon Shamaness, and sat down next to Seldar. He was sleeping peacefully. Goddess, he looked so vulnerable, but then wasn't that nature's defense system? Didn't all youngsters look too cute to harm?

"You scared ten seasons out of me today, Seldar. I am going to be an old crone by your next seasonmark if you keep this up! Goddess knows I do not know what I would ever do if I lost you. Not that I blame you, of course. No, you were fighting most bravely, just as I always knew you would. Hades' fire! Whatever am I going to do with you?" Eldin asked herself.

Eldin shoveled a spoonful of the warm meat stew into her mouth. She allowed the mixture to flood her taste buds. It was spicy, thick with greens and root vegetables swimming in rich gravy, and positively delicious. In no time, the mound of stew was consumed. She took a quick survey of the surrounding area and, upon seeing no one, triumphantly licked the last of the gravy from the bottom of the bowl before placing it aside. She stroked Seldar's sweat-matted dirty blonde hair. He would live, Eldin was sure of it. In the future, she would assign one of her elite guardswomen to watch over him in battle, and Eldin herself would drill him until he could match swords with the best of her Amazons.

Despite the archaic laws concerning male-children, Eldin loved her sib dearly. She shuddered against a sudden chill night breeze and covered Seldar with her cloak to keep him warm. Just a few more candledrips and Eldin would head for her own tent. She just wanted to relax with the night breeze and her sib. Eldin stretched and yawned. She would just rest her eyes for a heartbeat.

* * *

Kiya smiled at the sight of Captain Eldin asleep, sitting next to the wounded male-child. Quietly, she pulled herself into the wagon and made her way to Eldin. Gently, she shook Eldin's shoulder. Kiya yelped out in pain as the startled warrior's fist connected solidly with the healer's nose and sent her toppling out of the wagon.

"By the Goddess, are you all right?" Eldin asked rather sheepishly as she fully woke and realized her violent reaction to the healer's touch.

Sparks of pain flew haphazardly behind Kiya's clenched-shut eyelids, paying tribute to Eldin's strength, while blood trickled freely from her injured nose. Her voice sounded muffled and tiny behind her hands, which involuntarily cradled her injured nose.

"I think you broke it," Kiya managed to voice audibly.

Eldin leaped from the wagon and helped Kiya to a sitting position. She took Kiya's hands away from her nose so that she could survey the damage. Eldin produced a clean cloth from inside her belt pouch and tenderly wiped the blood from Kiya's lips.

"I think it is just bloody. It isn't twisted or anything," Eldin tried to reassure the healer.

"Are you always so disagreeable in the morning, Captain?" Kiya deadpanned.

A fresh wave of pain washed over her when Eldin applied pressure to stop the bleeding.

"I am so very sorry, honorable healer…" Eldin began.

"Kiya! My name is Kiya," she interrupted.

"Please excuse a battle-weary warrior who has not felt a kind touch in far too many moons. I am sorry, Kiya." Her name rolled off Eldin's tongue as though she had been saying it for a lifetime.

Eldin gazed into Kiya's panther-green eyes and felt drawn by an irresistible urge to press her lips against Kiya's. She bent forward slowly, awkward in this unfamiliar urgency. Was this just battlefield lust? No, this was much more frightening. This felt undeniable, unstoppable; this was…*need*.

Kiya's breath caught in her chest as she realized the handsome young captain's intentions. She searched the depth of Eldin's eyes. They were ice on fire. Her body was being assaulted by waves of Eldin's intensity. Kiya could not block out this much energy even if she had wanted to; it permeated every cell in her body.

Eldin felt desire on a level that she had never known existed. Her heart started beating fast and hard, as a tribal drum summoning the dancers to join in the celebration. Eldin could feel Kiya's breath hot against her lips as they were almost joined.

"Excuse me, Captain," a voice ripped through their web of lust, causing them to jump away from each other like two schoolgirls caught kissing behind the stables. "The Drakknians have been spotted along the eastern ridge in attack formation, and it appears that they have reinforcements."

Eldin tore herself away from Kiya's charms, and her voice was low and husky from unspent desire. "I am sorry, Kiya. I must attend to this."

Eldin stood and cleared her head. *Goddess, was that ever close. Whew, disaster avoided!* Eldin and Maric left Kiya to her day's work.

Kiya brought her fingers to her lips as she watched Eldin stride purposefully toward the other side of camp. A small sigh escaped her throat as her fingertips did nothing to quench the deep ache to have her lips caressed by another set of soft, yielding, commanding…*Kiya! Stop this! You have wounded to attend to*, she admonished herself.

* * *

Demon Shamaness, Demon Shamaness, Demon Shaman…

"Captain!" Maric all but shouted as she lightly backhanded Eldin's arm to gain her attention.

Eldin snapped out of her silent mantra and looked over at the sergeant of her elite guardswomen.

"Sorry, I was just thinking of someon…thing…something. I was thinking of something," Eldin attempted to cover her slip-up.

"Captain, what are your orders?" Maric prompted.

"Orders? Oh, right. Sound the general assembly and have the archers divide into two groups along the north and south ridges," Eldin explained as they walked quickly back toward the warrior's camp. "When we have lured them into the center of the battlefield, I will call a retreat. I want the archers to begin raining arrows on the Drakknians as soon as my warriors are clear."

Maric placed her right fist over her heart and bowed her head in salute to her captain. "As you command, so shall it be done."

When they were safely out of earshot, Eldin clasped Maric's shoulder and said, "Thank you, my friend."

Maric looked at Eldin as if she had three heads. "For what? Delivering bad news?"

"For saving me," Eldin answered.

"From the healer?" Maric still did not quite understand, for Kiya was a fiery beauty.

"From myself," came the reply.

"You know, Captain, you can't hide behind a sword forever. One day you will find yourself in love again. No matter how many swords, shields, or ghosts you try to use as bricks in your wall, love will find you," Maric shared her opinion with a reluctant Eldin.

"I do not 'wall myself away.' I share myself with Delyn, as well you know," Eldin retorted.

"Ha! You may share your bedroll with her, but you do not share your soul with her. You have acted quite dead since…" Maric started.

"I know perfectly well of *when* you speak, so you need not ever speak of it again. Now do your duty, Maric, and leave my heart out of your affairs!" Eldin boomed and quickly spun on her heels to walk alone to her tent.

Maric knew better than to push this issue with her friend. She would let it go...for now. Besides, she had work to do to prepare for another battle. Soon, perhaps they would get a respite from all the action along this border. One could only hope.

* * *

Thunder stamped nervously in front of the Amazon Army. His nostrils flared when a sudden breeze brought with it the smell of death from the previous day. Eldin held him with a firm hand and confident seat. She could feel him strung as tight as an archer's bow in anticipation, so she allowed him to prance the length of her troops and back again. Eldin calmed the magnificent steed with a soothing stroke of his neck as another breeze blasted across the open field. It smelled of rain as well as death. At the slight touch of Eldin's spur, Thunder shot like an arrow toward the middle of the field.

Eldin could see the black and red armor of the Drakknians advancing on them like a sea of pestilence. Horses' hooves and warriors' boots kicked up billowing clouds of dust that made eyes sting and breathing a chore. Eldin was always amazed at the lengths an army would go to just to capture a piece of barren land and at how many lives Yashor was willing to lose in order to keep it.

Eldin did not have long to ponder that paradox, for Thunder was already reaching the first of the Drakknians. Eldin gave Thunder his rein and allowed him to choose his own path into the brewing carnage. Thunder sidestepped a swordsman as he slashed at the steed. Eldin leaned over in her saddle and sent the unfortunate soldier's head flying from his body with one mighty swing. Thunder seized an open opportunity and charged through two soldiers, sending them both crashing to the ground. They were quickly pounced upon by Yashor foot soldiers, and dispatched.

Tynka was among the first Amazons to engage the enemy. She landed one rage-fueled blow after another in search of the kill that would satisfy her need for vengeance and restore her shattered soul. Sweat streamed down her bloodstained face and stung her eyes. These male-children would know the wrath of Tynka, firstborn daughter of the legendary warriors Tyndon and Katuk. They would feel the fury of her sword. They would pay for killing her love. Her dark eyes blazing with hate, her jaw set with purpose, Tynka swung again. They would know her wrath; then they would die. More blood splattered her face as yet another male-child fell to her blade. Goddess, it hurt!

Lieutenant Delyn smiled at the music of war. A symphony of clashing swords and curses echoed across the battlefield. Nothing compared to the exhilaration of cheating death. However, being ravished by Eldin did run a close second. Delyn's opponent tried to thrust his sword into her side, and her blade broke from the intensity of her counterstrike. Seeing what appeared to be an open opportunity, the man thrust again.

"Oh no you don't!" Delyn stated as she pivoted, avoiding the blade, and grabbed his wrist with both hands.

She ducked under his armpit and then pulled his arm back toward her. The inexperienced soldier's reactions proved to be fatally slow, as he could not release his sword before it had lodged six inches deep into his midsection.

"You don't mind if I borrow this, do you?" Delyn asked sarcastically while she held him helpless with one strong arm and used the other to grab the hilt of his sword.

The Drakknian cried out in pain as the sword sliced completely through his midsection. Death would follow shortly, and the doomed man fell to the ground when Delyn released him.

"Quit your crying and take your death like a woman, you weakling!" Delyn sneered, already stalking her next victim.

A tear slid down the dying man's cheek. His young wife would be raising their two children alone, or worse, the state would take custody of his family and a stranger would raise his children. A stranger would take his wife. It was not fair! If only he had not been so swayed by his father's opinion about serving the "Great Nation of Drakknia." This war was stupid, and now he would never hold J'pei in his arms again. God help them. God help them all. His vision got dimmer, and he gave into the great sleep, to wake no more. As he died, Delyn was already sending another man to accompany him in the journey of death.

Now that the enemy had fully committed themselves, Eldin whooped the signal for retreat. The Amazons gave final blows to their enemies and then broke away from their swords' engagements to run back toward their encampment.

Stunned, the Drakknians stood looking at each other and their unchallenged swords. Here they were, lathered in sweat, ready for a fight, and the Amazons run? This was not like them. Amazons had always been ferocious fighters who welcomed death over retreat. What would suddenly cause them to run? This had an uneasy feel to it. Finally, the Drakknian field marshall raised his sword in victory. He started yelling curses at the cowardly Amazons. Slowly his troops followed his lead. They were ecstatic in their easy victory.

Suddenly, on both sides of the ridge, the archers revealed themselves. Arrows bearing the flame of Amazon vengeance rained down upon them. Screams of pain and panic rose from the Drakknian army. The Drakknian officers tried in vain to keep the men together, but they broke ranks and started running for their lives. Many men were simply trampled to death in the ensuing chaos.

Eldin rode over to Lt. Delyn, who was watching intently as the archers loosed another wave of flaming death. Men fell all around the battlefield when the arrows pierced their flesh, and the pitch burned through to the bone. Her eyes gleamed and a slight smile played across her full lips. What exquisite joy, what carnal ecstasy played out before her. A sigh of contentment escaped Delyn's throat; it was good to be an Amazon.

"Delyn, I want you to take a group of volunteers to chase the Drakknians out of Yashor territory. Then go through the battlefield to find me a couple of prisoners whom you believe will survive their wounds. Kill the rest by order of the Council. I will send you some trainlings to assist in scouring the dead, if you like. I think it would be good for them to learn firsthand just from where the spoils of war come," Eldin conferred with her second-in-command.

"Aye, Captain. I think it will open their eyes to the real nature of the battlefield. Besides, they shall see it sooner or later, and I would just as soon it not be in front of a crazed Drakknian Hades-bent on killing them. You know, just in case they should lose their stomachs," Delyn replied.

"I know the first time I saw a dead body, my mid-meal revisited me," Eldin recalled.

Delyn placed a hand upon Eldin's knee. "Well, you always were a bit soft in the middle, Captain."

Eldin grinned at her part-time lover's remarks. "Here, all this time, I thought *that* was the part you liked. Hurry on now, before you lose the kill."

Eldin tapped Thunder into a comfortable canter, while Delyn turned back to the soldiers. A light rain began to fall; they would have to hurry or lose the tracks to the approaching storm. Tynka's sword was above her head before Delyn finished explaining the mission. She would chase them to Hades and back for the chance to avenge the death of her love. Poor Cindic, she should have been there. A tear made its way down Tynka's blood-caked cheek. She wiped it away with the back of her hand, the blood of her kills smearing from her cheek to her hairline.

Delyn quickly organized her volunteers. Once assembled, they moved swiftly out of the valley. Eldin watched them pursue the enemy until they were out of sight. Perhaps she would give Delyn a visit this night. After all, it had been a long time, and the Drakknians were on the run. She turned back toward their encampment and continued to keep Thunder at a slow pace so he could cool down.

Outside of her tent, Eldin handed Thunder's reigns to the sergeant of her elite honor guard. Maric bowed her head and placed her battle-scarred right fist over her heart in salute to Eldin.

"Ho, Maric. Where are our trainlings?" Eldin inquired.

"They are arguing over who gets to brush down Thunder for you. Most of them are in the horse tents trying to be available for when he arrives," Maric answered, a smile of amusement on her weatherworn face.

"Why would they be arguing? Thunder is just one of many steeds that our district has issued to us. True, he is a magnificent animal, but I just don't see..." Eldin began.

"Captain, it is not your horse's attention they seek...it is yours," a bemused Maric explained.

"My attention?! Whatever for? I am an old, tired, and cranky soldier," Eldin protested.

Maric's rich earth-colored eyes danced with glee at the captain's embarrassment. Once even she had considered Eldin as a mate, but then Eldin had gotten close to…well, at any rate, she had forced her feelings for Eldin to fade like the scent of freshly picked roses set out in the summer breeze. It was for the best, really. Eldin was her friend, and she would never know the true depths of Maric's feelings.

"Captain, you have an entire gaggle of fourteen- and fifteen-season-marks-old trainlings who see you as the most handsome, debonair, and daring hero that ever walked among the Amazons. They are falling over one another to do something…*anything*…to get you to notice them. Why, they would crawl across the mountains of fire on bare bellies for a word, a wink, or just an embrace of their shoulder from you. The funny thing is, you never notice. This tends to drive them a bit mad." Maric could no longer contain her laughter, and it rumbled from the depths of her soul like a low-pitched staccato thunder. "Why, sometimes they are even distracted from their sword training when you happen by."

Eldin was aware that the clouds swirling overhead made it impossible for the sun to be responsible for the bright crimson coloring that had invaded her cheeks. Surely, Maric exaggerated. How could this happen and she not know? Well, this had to end. The girls must concentrate in order to survive.

"Go tell the trainlings to assemble in the healer's area. I will be waiting for them, so they had best not tarry," Eldin commanded.

She grabbed Maric's arm as the woman started off. Eldin leaned over and spoke directly into her favorite guard's ear.

"Wipe that smug look off your face before they see you. Oh, and by the Goddess, do not encourage them," Eldin spoke clearly, but quietly, before releasing Maric to continue to the stable area.

Maric clasped her hands together in front of her heart and tilted her head to the side. She batted her eyelashes exaggeratedly at Eldin in a mock swoon.

"Who, me? I would never do such a thing, Captain. Those girls look to me for guidance," Maric teased her friend.

"That is what I most fear," Eldin stated under her breath as she walked away, rolling her eyes.

At the healer's area, Eldin watched in silent admiration as Kiya went about the unenviable task of caring for the battle-mangled warriors. Her fire-touched hair glowed in the sunlight, and she absently tucked an un-cooperative strand behind her ear and out of her face. Her facial features bespoke of a deep rooted compassion for those in her care. Even from this distance, Eldin could see the gentleness of her touch. By the Goddess, she was beautiful. *Ah, Demon Shamaness.* Eldin could almost feel Kiya's touch, so soft against her battle-hardened flesh. She shivered at the thought.

Maric's voice interrupted Eldin's thoughts. She turned to face the assembled youngsters. Before she could speak, Maric leaned over and whispered into her ear, "Be gentle."

Eldin walked around the girls, inspecting them for some sort of visible sign acknowledging them as warriors. She sighed. They carried swords, wore armor…and still looked like little girls. The trainlings were curious, but none dared to look at her. Finally, Eldin turned back toward them with her bloodstained hands outstretched, palms up.

"I am not a hero. Look at me; I have the blood of at least a dozen Drakknians on my hands. I also have the blood of a thousand more that stains my soul. I will *never* be able to wash that away. You will soon face the blood of your kills, because that is what we must do in order to protect Yashor and all that we love. It is not a glorious thing to take the life of another, but it is a necessity. If you want a hero, look over there," Eldin pointed to Kiya. "Kiya, as a healer, is a true hero. She preserves life. She believes in the sanctity of it. She cherishes it, nourishes it. That is the definition of a true hero. I just want to get to the end of each day without having to light any funeral pyres. Now follow Sgt. Maric out to collect the useful items from those who have fallen today, and think on what I have said. War is no place for children."

Eldin watched as Maric marched the trainlings toward their first inti-mate encounter with death. Just as the last of them was disappearing over the ridge, the air grew chill and clouds invaded overhead. By the time Eldin had walked to Seldar's wagon, rain was falling. Eldin helped erect lean-tos over the wagons to keep the rain off the wounded. It took several candlemarks before all of the wagons were covered. Once the task was completed, Eldin stopped by to check on Seldar before she fled to her own tent for some much-needed rest.

Eldin paused at the opening to her tent. Someone had been inside without her knowledge. The ground inside was beginning to get damp from the rainfall, and small rivulets of water made a pathway snaking through the tent. Eldin saw that her uninvited guest had prepared a bed for her that was elevated off the ground.

Upon a closer examination of the bed, she discovered that quite a bit of effort had gone into its construction. The base of the bed was made from large stones stacked long and about three feet high. This allowed water to travel under the bed without its occupant getting wet. Next, a frame had been constructed from a huge hollowed-out tree trunk. Inside this, a mattress of straw-stuffed cloth lay underneath a second mattress of gurgin feather–stuffed cloth. Finally, Eldin's benefactor had given her expertly tanned wolf pelts for blankets. She shook her head. Was someone trying to impress her? Well, this was a pleasant surprise.

Eldin removed her armor and then peeled off her wet under-tunic. She hung this over a tree stump along with the soaked binding cloth. Next, she worked her way out of her wet suede pants and hung them up next to the tunic. Eldin hoped they would dry out before she had to put them back on. She propped her sword against the bed so that it was easily within reach… just in case. Then Eldin snuggled down into the soft, warm bed and drifted off into a dreamless slumber. Her mind registered nothing but the pattering of raindrops hitting the outside of her tent.

Maric opened the flap of Eldin's tent. She smiled and closed the flap when she spotted Eldin deeply asleep. So, someone did appreciate her talents for furniture construction. Good, Eldin had needed restful slumber. It had been almost three full turns of the dual moons since they last slept in a bed, back at Romyl's fortress. That was the last bit of civilization before the long trek through the forbidden forest to the borderlands. Unfortunately, that was also the last time that Eldin had adequate rest, and the lack of it had begun to show.

"Make certain that no one disturbs the captain. She is asleep, and unless we are attacked, the business can wait until she is awake," Maric instructed the two guards at the entrance.

The guards answered in the affirmative and crossed their pikes in front of the entrance to dissuade visitors. Maric left to bring back the trainlings. It had been over a candlemark and a half since Delyn had returned and taken over leadership of them. Surely, she must be finished with them by now.

* * *

Kiya finished feeding her injured and decided to check on Seldar. When she arrived at his wagon, she was surprised to find him awake. Seldar looked Kiya up and down before he cast his eyes downward in the expected show of respect for the healer. Kiya smiled; he was a little bold but overall a well-mannered fellow.

"How stands the day with thee?" Kiya inquired.

"I have a great pain in my leg, but I think I shall live, therefore the day is grand. Are you the great Healer who wasted your gifts on me?" Seldar asked quietly.

Kiya smiled and nodded, forgetting that he was not looking directly at her. "I do not feel as though I wasted my gifts on you. You are part of the Yashor Sword Corps, and you risk your life to defend our way of life. You have value; otherwise Captain Eldin would not have brought you to me. Do not ever forget that. You are a male-child, yes, but you also have value."

Seldar watched as Kiya pulled herself into the wagon. Up close, he noticed lines forming around her eyes. She looked exhausted. Perhaps he could find a way to suggest some rest. Seldar quickly looked back down at his feet when Kiya stood in the wagon and turned toward him.

Kiya gently checked his bandage. It would not require changing for several more candlemarks. She caught him watching her and showed him his wound.

"This is where the sword entered your leg. You were lucky that Captain Eldin was able to get you to me quickly. The sword cut one of your bloodlines." Kiya pointed to the area that she stitched. "This is going to take some time to heal. I cannot be certain how long, but if you do not bend your leg for a few days, it will give your skin time to close. If you bend your leg a lot, it will prevent your skin from closing as quickly."

Seldar winced as he shifted slightly. His leg was throbbing with pain. *Yeah, sure, I am going to jump right up and dance the Harvest jig for her.* Who was she kidding? He was not going anywhere in the near future. Seldar bit down on his lip to keep from crying out. Kiya smiled at him and touched his shoulder softly.

"You know it is all right to cry when it hurts, Seldar. I have seen grown women who have cried when they were in pain. No matter what the Council thinks, it is a natural response to pain and is nothing to be ashamed about," Kiya told him.

Seldar fought to keep his voice even as he spoke through pursed lips. "I cannot show weakness, Honorable Healer, for I could not live with myself if I ever brought dishonor upon my mother, Dinyar, or my sib, Captain Eldin. Thank you for your kindness and understanding. I shall never forget how you have treated me, and I shall always owe you the debt of my life."

Kiya nodded. When were these people ever going to get it through their thick skulls that crying did not make you weak? Pain hurts; it was as simple as that.

"Pardon the intrusion, Honorable Healer. I have a question if it is not too much trouble," Seldar quietly inquired.

"Yes, Seldar, please ask your question," Kiya responded with a smile.

"Who decides when you are pulled off of the fighting scroll?" Seldar asked innocently, although he already knew the answer.

"Your healer does, Seldar. It is only for those who, like you, are too injured to fight or are too tired and have not eaten enough to stay strong. Do not worry; you will not be in any kind of trouble for missing battles. I have already listed you on the injured warrior scroll," Kiya explained.

"So who decides when to pull the healer off the healing scroll?" Seldar made his point with a question.

Kiya felt the lines on her overtired face. This male-child was surprising in his insight. She nodded her understanding and turned to leave. He certainly had an eloquent way with his words, almost too eloquent for a male-child. Perhaps it was his sib's influence. By the Goddess! Kiya made the realization for the first time. She was certain that Eldin had told her, but she had been too distracted to make the connection. She turned back to Seldar.

"So the captain is your sib, eh? Perhaps you could tell me what it was like growing up with Eldin, when you are feeling better," Kiya ventured.

"Anything you wish from me, it is yours. I owe you more than I could ever repay you in a thousand lifetimes," Seldar replied, bowing his head deeply.

Seldar watched as Kiya climbed down from the wagon. Was that a look of interest in her eyes? Hmm, perhaps she would be the one to heal Eldin's shattered heart. Seldar would do his best to see that happen. He loved Eldin greatly, and he owed the healer nothing less. Seldar smiled; Eldin would not know what had hit her.

* * *

Delyn finished cleaning her sword just as the rain stopped. It was getting late in the afternoon, and if she hurried, she would have enough time to see Eldin before even-feast was served. Ah, she sighed; it would be the perfect ending to a wonderful day's fighting. Delyn stroked her sword lovingly before sliding it into its sheath. The weight felt good on her hip, comforting, like the embrace of a lover.

Delyn poured fresh water into the wooden basin beside her sleeping skins. She closed her eyes and thanked the great Goddess for the blood of her enemies before she washed the day's blood and gore from her face and hands. Now it was time to visit Eldin.

A cool breeze blew over Delyn as she threw back the flap to her tent and stepped out into the early evening. Trainlings were busy running food to the wounded and preparing even-feast for the warriors. Delyn remembered her days as a trainling. They were up before the sun collecting firewood, helping to cook, and then serving the warriors whom they admired. Running food to the wounded and helping them to eat. Cleaning up the dishes after the meal, hurrying to sword practice, and then they were quickly off to strategy sessions. Afterward, more camp chores. Just how many privies did she dig anyway? *Hmm, lost count.* It seemed as if the day never had enough candlemarks in it to do all that was required, yet somehow they always managed. How wonderful was the day that she received her commission and could concentrate on the battles, letting the next wave of trainlings do the day-to-day chores!

Delyn saw the guards with their crossed pikes as she approached Eldin's tent. She was just about six paces from them when the older of the two called out a challenge.

"Stand firm! Who approaches?" The words carried the guard's intensity.

"Lt. Delyn to see the captain," Delyn replied.

Delyn started for the tent flap and was stopped again.

"Stand firm! State your business; battle or pleasure," the guard ordered.

"That is none of your concern. Stand aside!" Delyn answered, becoming irritated.

Both of the guards readied their pikes as Delyn once again made a move for the tent flap. The older guard pointed her pike at Delyn's chest, over the heart region. Delyn looked at the point of the pike, then back at the guard. She pushed it aside, only to have it brought perilously close to her throat.

"Stand firm, or we shall be forced to kill you. You may return when the captain is awake. Until such time, may I suggest that you go enjoy your even-feast," the guard stated firmly.

Delyn's hand hovered over the hilt of the sword. These two may just need a lesson in warrior etiquette. Just as she closed her hand around the hilt, she felt the sharp edge of a sword against her forearm. One quick move and Delyn would lose her sword hand.

"Is there a problem, Lt. Delyn?" Maric's inquiry came from behind, while she held her sword firmly against Delyn's forearm.

Delyn released the hilt of her sword. "Apparently, your little watchdogs have no idea what I mean to Eldin. She would want to wake for this visit."

"I know what you are. Come back later," Maric insisted.

"By whose orders?" Delyn challenged.

"Mine. Now since we are not soldiers, we do not take our orders from you. Your rank means nothing here. My authority does. Captain Eldin pays us directly; we work for her. Go eat, or die. It really makes no difference to me which you choose," Maric threatened.

Delyn turned to go. She stopped and stared hard at Maric.

"This is far from over, watchdog. Pray you never need a soldier's sword to save your hide, for you will not find it. I'll see to that," Delyn told Maric before she stalked back toward her own tent.

"I'll never understand what Eldin sees in that one. Goddess knows she could have her pick," Maric mused under her breath as she watched Delyn retreating into the shadows.

Maric turned back to her guards. "I'll be close by. If you should have any more trouble, just shout."

"As you command, so shall it be done." The guards saluted in perfect unison.

* * *

Delyn made her way to the soldiers' quarters. She knew who could help her, and at what price. She entered tent after tent in search of the one known only as a "shadow" to everyone but Delyn. Delyn had known this shadow since childhood. Finally, after an exhaustive search proved to be futile, she returned to her own tent.

Delyn threw back the flap to her tent in disgust. She stopped in her tracks as she entered, seeing the shadow sitting on her bedroll.

"You were looking for me?" Celdi remarked through the darkness.

"I have a favor to ask," Delyn replied.

"Are you willing to pay my price?" Celdi inquired.

Delyn took a bold step toward Celdi. "Yes. I know your price, and I am willing to give you what you desire."

"Then I want my payment up front. I will accept your mission," Celdi stated, never taking her eyes from the approaching Delyn.

Delyn slowly walked toward Celdi and reached underneath her arm to the clasps of her chest plate. She unhooked them and cast off the armor. Delyn knelt before Celdi. Celdi pulled Delyn's under-tunic over her head and kissed the flesh of her exposed shoulder. She allowed her hands to roam around Delyn's waist and up her back to her binding. In one deft motion, Celdi released Delyn's binding and slipped her hands underneath to the small mounds of Delyn's breasts.

Delyn ran her fingers through Celdi's shoulder-length black hair. Celdi responded by shivering with delight. Delyn could give her body to anyone. This was easy. After Eldin's tragedy, she had offered her this "no strings attached" relationship since Delyn's true love was the Sword Corps. Soul declarations were for the weak. Only, somewhere all that had changed. Delyn did not even know when exactly Eldin had stolen her heart. Now that she had, Delyn would be damned to Hades if anyone were going to come between them; especially an old has-been watchdog!

Celdi removed the remaining undergarments, and her eyes hungrily devoured Delyn. She leaned forward slowly, still not totally convinced that this was just some cruel dream she was about to wake from, and captured Delyn's mouth with her own. Delyn was sweating and her lips tasted pleasingly salty from the perspiration. Celdi pulled back and admired Delyn once again.

"By the Great Goddess, you are a magnificent woman. Perhaps one day I shall have your heart as well, but for now..." Celdi whispered to Delyn as she ran her hands along Delyn's body.

Celdi gently helped Delyn to the bedroll and removed the remainder of her own clothing. She had wanted this for so long now, since they were both schoolgirls, back what seemed lifetimes ago. Celdi knew she was the only one making love, but in this heartbeat, it did not matter.

Celdi's body melted into Delyn as her tongue danced with Delyn's. Delyn gave back to Celdi as she could. She ran her fingernails along Celdi's muscular back, causing a slight moan to escape Celdi's throat. Celdi's hands explored Delyn's fine, lithe body, pausing at her breasts to knead the soft flesh. She rolled Delyn's nipples between her fingertips until they were both hard as pebbles and Delyn was thrusting back against her. Celdi kissed her way along Delyn's jawline to her neck. Once there, she nibbled her way up and down the sensitive flesh between Delyn's earlobe and collarbone. Goddess, this was just as she had always dreamed.

The moons were just rising as Celdi moved lower, capturing Delyn's right breast with her mouth. She gently sucked on the small mound of flesh and tortured Delyn's nipple with her tongue. Celdi put all of her love for Delyn into every touch, every kiss. Celdi might never get another chance to show Delyn her love, and she was not about to waste this opportunity worrying about tomorrows.

"Please, Celdi, I cannot wait longer. You are driving me mad," Delyn's voice betrayed her need.

Delyn's hand found Celdi's, and she guided her inside. A tear made its way down Celdi's cheek as she felt Delyn's hot, wet center. In the end, Delyn had given herself freely. Celdi ran her tongue down Delyn's stomach, and then along the insides of her thighs as Delyn thrust herself against Celdi's fingers. Celdi finally settled herself down and plunged her tongue into Delyn as she withdrew her fingers. She tasted like a goddess.

Delyn moaned, and her hips betrayed her as they moved against Celdi's tongue. Faster and harder, her hips kept pace with her need. A wolf howled somewhere in the forest, rejoicing at the capture of its prey. Finally, it would have its fill and be satiated.

* * *

There were still a few candlemarks of darkness before camp would come to life, and Delyn was just finishing Celdi's travel scrolls. If she hurried, she could be long gone before first-feast began. Celdi finished sharpening her sword and slid it into its sheath. She looked up at Delyn and smiled.

"Do you regret paying my price?" Celdi asked.

"No, you were...surprising," Delyn replied, carefully choosing her words.

"Then leave Eldin and become my shield mate," Celdi boldly requested.

Delyn cocked her eyebrows and leaned her head to the side while she fixed her gaze on Celdi.

"I didn't say you were *that* good," Delyn shot back.

Celdi took the travel scrolls and tucked them into her belt pouch. She could ill afford to lose those documents. Delyn watched the young spy make her final preparations.

"The woman's name is Maric. She came from somewhere close to

Three Rivers originally. I think she may be a Drakknian sympathizer, and I want to know if there is anything out of the ordinary about her background," Delyn instructed.

"I think that you are just a little jealous of her intimate friendship with Eldin," Celdi correctly guessed out loud.

Delyn captured Celdi's mouth with her own and kissed her hard and quick. Celdi tasted the salty metallic flavor of her blood and knew that her lower lip was split and bruised from the savage intensity of Delyn's kiss. She tongued the split in her lip; Delyn's kiss would remain with her for at least a fortnight.

"I didn't pay you to think," Delyn reminded Celdi. "Now go, before all of camp is awake."

Celdi slipped out of the tent and silently crossed camp. She could have shown the travel orders to the sentries at the horse tents, but that would have taken all of the fun out of it. Instead, she traveled like the wind through the horses until she reached her own mount and led him away. The sentries never knew until the count a few candlemarks later.

2

Eldin sat bolt upright as the sunlight burst into her tent when Maric threw open the flap. Maric allowed her eyes to travel the length of Eldin's exposed torso, openly admiring her naked body's strength. Eldin pushed back the wolf pelts and rolled out of her bed. She had never been shy with Maric.

"I see you still bear my mark," Maric teased as Eldin turned her backside toward her, exposing a deep scar that ran the width of Eldin's bum.

"Come in, Maric, unless your intent is for all of camp to watch me dress," Eldin said absently, while she searched for a clean tunic. "And yes, I do still have a reminder of your lesson that day. You were not a very patient sword master."

"Ah, but then you never left that portion unguarded after that day, did you?" Maric retorted.

Eldin grinned. "No, I must say that I have been mindful of my ass ever since."

Eldin was still searching for a clean tunic when Maric tapped her lightly on the shoulder. Eldin turned to find Maric grinning at her conspiratorially.

"As much as I would enjoy watching you turn your entire tent upside down in search of something clean to wear, I must confess, I had the train-lings in here earlier to collect your clothes for washing. I was verily afraid that they would start fighting the Drakknians on their own soon. I did bring a clean tunic and riding pants, though," Maric admitted as she offered the garments in her outstretched hands.

Eldin seized the clean clothing and slipped into the soft leather riding pants. They fit like a gauntlet.

"Will you help me with my binding, Maric?" Eldin asked.

Maric's battle-scarred hands trembled ever so slightly as she wound the cloth strip around Eldin's midsection, effectively harnessing her breasts, and tied the loose ends in the back.

"Too tight?" Maric inquired.

"No, just right," Eldin replied, swinging her sword arm in a mock attack.

Maric silently watched the muscles of Eldin's back ripple with the movement. *Such a perfect Amazon, too perfect to waste herself with that bloodthirsty lieutenant,* Maric thought.

"Maric, why have you never been declared? You would have made a fine provider and mother. You also would have been an excellent partner. I know there have been offers," Eldin asked as she slipped into her under tunic.

Maric felt her face flush at the compliments. "Because the one I love… fell in love with another. I could not bring myself to love again."

"Ah ha! And you lecture me in matters of the heart?" Eldin stated smugly.

"Only because I do not wish to see you make the same lonely mistakes that I have made. I want to see you happy, dear friend, not some old, weary, has-been sword master with no one to mourn her passing," Maric shot back.

Eldin clasped Maric's shoulder. "I shall miss you until the day that we sit at the Great Feast together and await our rebirth. You have always been special to me, Maric, in ways that I cannot explain. Just be assured that you will be missed and thought of constantly."

Eldin released Maric and then put her into a headlock. "Besides, who will bind me when you are gone?" Eldin joked to ease the somber mood.

"Oh, let me think, there is just about half the population of Yashor that would fight to the death for the honor of touching *your* naked body. Give or take a few thousand," Maric teased back.

"Perhaps I should start charging you krillits for the honor, then," Eldin retorted.

Eldin released Maric as soon as Maric brushed her fingertips across a spot just below Eldin's ribcage.

"I see that you have not overcome that wiggle-spot. That is a dangerous weakness my friend," Maric commented.

"I do not fear that my enemy is going to play with my wiggle-spot in the middle of battle, Maric, unless he tries to do so with the edge of a sword. I have no problems dealing with Drakknian swords...wiggle-spot or no," Eldin replied as she slipped the clean tunic over her head, somewhat embarrassed at still having a child's weakness.

"Maric, have you seen my boot dagger? I have not been able to find it since that last battle," Eldin inquired of her friend while she continued to search through her tent.

"Did you draw it during the battle, Captain?" Maric asked, trying to understand why Eldin's backup weapon was missing.

"Not that I can remember. I hope it did not slip out of my sheath on the battlefield; my mother gave me that as a commissioning present. It has been in our family for hundreds of season marks. The general will have my hide if I do not find it!" Eldin lamented.

"By the way, Eldin, you had two visitors last night," Maric continued as she helped Eldin search for the ornamental daggar. "The healer, Kiya..."

"Kiya!" Eldin interrupted. "Is there something wrong with Seldar?! My sib, I must go see her at once!"

Maric waited to continue until Eldin had reached the tent flap. "And Delyn came to see you," she reported quietly to Eldin's back, fully aware that her words would not be heard.

Eldin's heart pounded in her chest as if it meant to leap right through her ribcage and free itself from her. A cold sweat, born of fear, beaded on her forehead as she ran across the encampment. Eldin dodged trainlings and the camp guards on her way to the healer's area. She did not even slow as she reached Kiya's tent.

Kiya spun around out of instinct to face the person who had just barged through the opening of her tent like a crazed bull calf.

"What in Hades?! Are you injured?!" Kiya dropped the clean dress to the ground, exposing her naked body as she quickly closed the distance to Eldin and began inspecting her for wounds.

Eldin's face burned bright crimson, and she snapped her eyes shut out of respect.

"Um, no Great Healer, I am not wounded. I just heard that you had come to see me last night. I feared it might be news of Seldar…bad news," Eldin admitted.

"I see. You barge in on me while I am dressing because you thought that your sib was not well. Hmm, I suppose I can forgive you that. Seldar is doing much better. I stopped by to tell you that he was awake. You may see him if you wish," Kiya reported while she quickly retrieved her dress and slipped it on.

She looked up and noticed Eldin's eyes were shut tight. Kiya smiled. Well, at least Eldin had tried to be chivalrous. She wondered if Eldin was this impulsive in combat. Surely not, for that would be reckless, and reckless warriors most often ended up dead.

"By your leave, Honorable Healer…" Eldin began.

"Kiya!" She corrected.

"By your leave, Kiya, I shall go visit my sib," Eldin finished.

Kiya shook her head; warriors were so hard to train.

"Please, Eldin, go visit Seldar," she dismissed Eldin.

Eldin placed her right fist over her heart and bowed her head in a salute to the healer as she backed out of Kiya's tent.

Morning sunlight glinted off the dew that dotted the moss-covered trees like tiny stars in a galaxy of green. The few clouds overhead were just losing the last of their lavender tinge as the sun climbed well past the peaks on the mountains of fire in the distance. Plumes of white wispy smoke rose from the crater-laden peaks, adding to the cloud coverage. A brilliant crimson, gold, and sapphire gurgin started to sing in a nearby tree, and Eldin smiled. Morning was her favorite time of day. Amazons claimed that gurgin were very tasty eating, but Eldin could not see how anyone could eat something with a voice so sweet. Perhaps Delyn was right after all; maybe she was a little "soft in the middle."

Seldar's face lit up when he saw Eldin approaching. It was going to be a beautiful day, and he could instigate his plan. Eldin was lost in thought as she approached. Seldar realized Eldin was not even aware that she was being watched, but he noticed the healer standing just inside the opening to her tent. She was absently twisting a long strand of her fire-touched hair around her finger while she admired Eldin's backside. Yes, this was a much better choice for Eldin than that Delyn. Seldar prayed that he could help his sib see the wisdom in that.

"Ho, Seldar! How stands the morning?" Eldin greeted him warmly.

"It is a fair morning, indeed. Did you hear the gurgin welcoming the day? It was very beautiful, just like back home," Seldar replied.

Eldin climbed into the wagon and sat next to Seldar. He was looking much better, she decided.

"Do you miss home much? Do you miss our mothers?" Eldin asked.

"I miss Dinyar. You know Elrik has no use for me. She never has. I am but a male-child…a disappointment. I think the only thing that mother Elrik misses about me is that I cook better than Daji," Seldar explained.

Eldin could see the sadness reflected in her sib's eyes. It really was not fair, the way that he was treated. Why? Just because he was born a male-child? How stupid. She would find a way to get the laws changed. She had to; she only had a few more seasons at the most before Seldar would have to choose his path. She hoped she would be able to save him from all that.

"Where are you, Eldin? You certainly aren't here," Seldar teased.

"I was just wondering…how does your leg feel?" Eldin lied. No sense in raising his hopes if she could not come through for him in time.

"It hurts, but it is nothing that the sib of Captain Eldin cannot handle! I shall live; besides, the injury is a long way from mine heart," Seldar commented, not fooled for one heartbeat.

Eldin reached out and scuffed Seldar's hair. "That's the spirit, little one!"

"I do not know why the healer wasted her gifts on the likes of me. However, I am verily glad that she did," Seldar started.

"That makes two of us," Eldin interrupted, flashing her sib a brilliant smile.

"She must be a special, gentle soul to do that for a lowly male-child," Seldar stated, hoping to bait Eldin into divulging her feelings for the healer.

Eldin looked at Seldar. His big brown eyes sparkled mischievously.

"Yes…I suppose that Kiya is a special soul indeed. It is a great honor to fight for women such as the healer, is it not, little one?" Eldin conceded, choosing her words carefully as she formulated her own plan.

"Indeed it is, Captain," Seldar heartily replied.

"Perhaps you are struck with her, Seldar," Eldin teased as she poked his shoulder.

Seldar's eyes grew as wide as the dual full moons with shock at the very idea.

"No, Captain, not at all. Besides, the healer is a genuine Amazon, I have witnessed," Seldar explained quickly.

Eldin smiled; Seldar had fallen right into her verbal trap.

"Oh, I see. So you *have* been watching her," Eldin exclaimed, holding back the laughter that threatened to expose her plot.

Seldar squirmed. It was suddenly very warm inside that wagon.

"No…I mean…yes. But…but…not in that manner," Seldar fought for the words to express himself.

Seldar's eyes lost a little of their sparkle. How did Eldin always manage to turn things around on him, anyway? Hades' fire! This was not going according to his plan.

"I only jest with you, little one. However, I am glad to see you doing so well. When you have healed better, we shall start drilling until you are my match," Eldin promised.

"I could never be *your* match, Captain," Seldar exclaimed, the hero-worship evident on his face.

"Then I shall drill you until you are as close to my match as your little male-child body shall allow!" Eldin retorted.

Eldin stood and stretched her aching muscles. It must be from all that sleep she got the night before. As badly as she wanted to stay and spend more time with Seldar, Eldin knew she had to get back to her job of leading the Sword Corps.

"I do need to get back to my troops. Is there anything that I can send you?" Eldin asked.

"No, Captain, I am fine. Besides, 'a male-child is not worthy of requesting anything from an Amazon'…even if she is his sib," Seldar gently reminded her of the phrase that he had been told since birth.

Eldin closed her eyes and inwardly cursed at that reminder of her country's cruelty toward male-children. It was not right. How could an otherwise fine society harbor such cruel and almost criminal attitudes toward the opposite gender? Eldin sighed.

"Have a fine day watching the healer," Eldin tried to joke, but the joy had already abandoned her voice.

Seldar watched Eldin leave the healer's area. She was really starting to look prematurely crone. Perhaps if she had love in her life again, she would recapture some of her stolen youth. Seldar could only pray.

* * *

Delyn smiled seductively as Eldin entered the command tent.

"Good morning, Captain. I came by to see you last night, but your guards would not let me pass," Delyn explained as she slowly stalked over to Eldin and wrapped her arms around her neck. "And I had such plans for us."

Eldin was in too foul a mood to really care that she had missed Delyn's visit. Delyn leaned up and tenderly kissed Eldin. As Delyn's kiss turned more passionate, Eldin reached up and pulled Delyn's arms from her neck and stepped away from her.

"I'm sorry, Delyn. I fear that I am just not in the mood. What say you? Did you find any prisoners yesterday?" Eldin asked.

"Of course. Would you care for me to fetch them for you? Perhaps you should allow me to interrogate them for you as well, since you do not seem to be 'in the mood.' Or perhaps it is just that you have not the stomach for it," Delyn replied, verbally lashing out at Eldin for her rejection.

Eldin stared at Delyn. She was really trying to get underneath Eldin's skin. Well, she had picked the wrong morning for a fight.

"When is the last time you visited any of our wounded warriors, Lieutenant? I shall tell you. Perhaps since the day you received your commission and were no longer required to bring food to them. If I seem not in the mood for your attentions, it is because I just came from the healer's area. I just came from wagon upon wagon full of warriors who are laying there almost dead, or dying. I feel responsible for them. They follow my orders. It is up to me to come up with a better battle plan than the last one, so that just maybe, tomorrow I shall not have as many funeral pyres to light as I do today! That is what is on my mind, not your beauty, nor your kiss. I am responsible for all of their deaths! Now, fetch me the prisoners and quit feeling sorry for yourself," Eldin snapped.

Delyn glared at Eldin. "I never realized you were as a goddess. How foolish of me to think you only flesh and blood. Of course, you are responsible, just as you are responsible for the rains that flood the fields and the Goddess Fire that streaks from the heavens to touch a family's keep and burn it to the ground. I shall remember next time, oh giver of life."

Before Eldin could protest, Delyn stormed out of the tent. Hades fire! First-feast had not even been served yet, and already Eldin had managed to anger two women. The day looked as though it did not hold much promise.

Outside the tent, Delyn ran into a trainling, knocking her to the ground and sending the bowls of corn mush she was carrying flying. A good portion of the mush splattered Delyn. Now she would have to change as well.

"Do you not have eyes, child?!" Delyn roared.

"I am sorry, Lieutenant. It was clumsy of me," the young girl apologized, casting her eyes down to show respect to Delyn.

The act was not lost on Delyn. She felt some of her anger dissipate.

"Well, at least you are not clumsy *and* stupid. Tell your sword master she needs to teach you how to anticipate," Delyn suggested sarcastically as she scraped handfuls of mush from her uniform and flung them to the ground in distaste before stomping off in the direction of her tent.

The trainling watched Delyn cross the busy camp in silent admiration. One day, she would be a powerful warrior like the lieutenant. However, one day was not *this* day, and she scooped up the bowls and hurried back for more food.

Delyn finally reached the holding cell after retrieving clean clothes and looked at the four pathetic excuses for warriors. She watched the Drakknian pond scum for a candledrip before deciding which one to take to

Eldin. Eldin wanted to interrogate a prisoner? Let her have the strongest.

"You there; do you speak?" Delyn taunted the prisoner.

Hatred blazed brightly in his dark chestnut eyes. He locked eyes with Delyn, and his gaze remained steady. Yes, this one would do quite nicely. Perhaps she may even be allowed to assist in his breaking. Goddess knows Eldin had no taste for such things.

Delyn drew her sword and handed it to the guard. The woman's eyes grew big as she realized Delyn meant to go into the cell unarmed and outnumbered four to one.

"Lieutenant, do you think it is wise?" the guard asked.

"Do you think it wiser to give them the chance to arm themselves? Besides, there are not enough of them to take me," Delyn replied as she unlocked the door and stepped inside.

"Come, who's first, then?" Delyn challenged.

The Amazon's code of battle was well known to the Drakknians, and the two more seriously wounded sat down and turned their backs to Delyn's challenge. They were in no mood for a beating and knew that she would not attack them from behind. The remaining two started to circle Delyn. Suddenly, the smaller Drakknian lunged at her. Delyn moved away from the attack and used a roundhouse kick to his back that sent him flying into the wooden wall. He smashed face-first and crumpled to the ground. Delyn spun quickly to face the man still standing.

The tanned man smiled. A worthy opponent. He would rather enjoy this. Before he could launch his attack, he felt the sharp edge of a blade at this throat.

"Put your hands out, dog!" the guard ordered.

The tanned man placed his hands out to be bound while he mocked Delyn with his eyes. After he was secured, the guard led him outside of the cell, where Delyn punched her square in the nose, breaking it.

"Don't you *ever* do that again! I do not need, nor do I want, your help with the prisoners. Do we understand one another now?" Delyn asked through clenched teeth.

The guard placed her fist over her heart and bowed her head as the blood from her nose spilled onto her uniform. "As you command, so shall it be done."

Delyn grabbed the man's bindings and pulled him along behind her. She dragged him across the camp to the command tent where Eldin was still waiting.

Delyn forced him to sit by sweeping his feet out from under him and then shoved his back up against the large tree stump they were using as a table. She untied his bindings, forced his arms behind him, and then secured them to the stump.

"Your prisoner, Captain," she stated flatly.

Eldin took Delyn's hand into her own and caressed it soothingly.

"I am sorry about earlier, Delyn. You were right. I am just flesh and blood. I guess I was the one feeling sorry for myself. Forgive me?" Eldin asked.

Delyn looked into Eldin's sad, pleading eyes and her anger melted away.

"Damn you to Hades, Eldin. When you look at me that way, I can never stay angry with you…even when I have good reason!" Delyn admitted and allowed herself to be pulled into Eldin's arms.

The tanned man cocked his head and watched intently as the two leaders embraced and kissed passionately. Now this would be useful information: the lieutenant and the captain were lovers. That bond could be used against them. A chink in the armor of the Yashor Sword Corps. All he had to do now was escape and make it back to his field marshall with this information.

Eldin felt Delyn's body pressing into her own in response to Eldin's hungry kiss. Goddess, it had been so long. Delyn smiled victoriously as Eldin nibbled on her neck. Just at that heartbeat, Delyn noticed Maric standing at the entrance to the tent, and their eyes met and locked. Delyn buried her hands in Eldin's thick blonde hair and helped herself to Eldin's shoulder. Mmmm, Eldin always tasted good. Delyn loved when Eldin wore sleeveless tunics. It must be washing day because that was the only time she did so.

"I want you," Delyn whispered, "*now*."

Eldin blinked. She was losing control. She needed to lose control.

"What about the prisoner?" Eldin asked as her body responded to Delyn's nips, unaware of Maric's presence behind her.

"Have Maric watch him. I am certain that you can trust her," Delyn suggested, knowing full well how upset it would make the little watchdog.

Maric's eyes narrowed, and she glared at Delyn. Eldin deserved so much better. This was turning her stomach. She could not take much more of this.

"Captain," Maric stated to alert Eldin to her presence, "Should you be 'otherwise occupied' in front of the prisoner?" Maric chose her words carefully.

Eldin closed her eyes. Maric was right. However good this felt, it was inappropriate in the command tent. Eldin reluctantly released Delyn and turned toward Maric.

"Sgt. Maric, I want you to guard this prisoner while the lieutenant and I...discuss strategies. If he gives you any problems, get help and put him back in the holding cell," Eldin ordered.

Maric bit the inside of her lip until she could taste the salty metallic flavor of her own blood to keep from verbally expressing her displeasure in Eldin's choice of partners. It would do no good to alienate Eldin now. Besides, the Goddess usually had a way of wiping away smug grins like the one that Delyn was giving her now.

Delyn ran her hand lightly up Eldin's arm and across her breast as she kissed the back of her shoulder. Watching Maric seethe was an unexpected bonus. Now it made sense. Delyn knew there were a great many warriors in camp that wanted Eldin. It was now painfully obvious that Maric was one of them. Delyn also knew that no one else realized that their relationship was a purely physical one born of convenience and not a partnership born of mutual love. While she alone possessed Eldin's body, Eldin's heart belonged to a ghost, and Delyn's own to the Sword Corps. At least, that is how it had started.

"Delyn!" Eldin nudged her back to the present.

"I'm sorry, I was lost in thought," Delyn replied.

"Let's go to my tent; we should be most comfortable there," Eldin suggested.

Maric watched them until they disappeared into the chaos of early morning camp.

"What's the matter, Amazon? Do not you approve? Or is it that you desire the captain for your own?" the dark-eyed man taunted.

"It matters little what you have to say, male-child. If I were you, I would save my strength for the beatings she will give you. Your life is already forfeit, unless of course, your tongue is loose," Maric replied, not looking at him.

Maric stopped a trainling and sent her to fetch a couple of guards to take the Drakknian back to the holding cell. She had better things to do than to watch over a smart-mouthed prisoner so Delyn could partake in pleasures of the flesh with Eldin. If there truly was a Great Goddess in the heavens above, may She find a way to prevent Eldin from wasting herself on that one.

* * *

Seldar winced as Kiya carefully removed his bandage and allowed some air to reach his wound. Goddess, she had such a gentle touch. Kiya looked up from the wound and smiled at Seldar.

"It looks as though it is healing nicely, Seldar. The flesh around the wound is not angry, and the stitches are healing quickly," Kiya commented.

"Then it is a tribute to your gifts, Great Healer, for I have done nothing," Seldar complimented her.

"Ah, but you see, nothing is exactly what you needed to do," Kiya reminded him.

Seldar watched Kiya grind dry herbs in her hands. Then she measured and mixed them into a fresh salve. She rubbed the concoction generously over the site of his wound before taking a fresh cloth strip and re-bandaging his leg.

"Did you have questions for me? The pain is not so bad today. I feel as though I could answer some for you, if you wish," Seldar remarked.

Kiya sat next to Seldar and absently wiped her hands clean on a piece of cloth she had draped over her shoulder.

"Hmm, what was Eldin like growing up? I mean, did she bully anyone in classes? Was she bullied? Just...oh I don't know...what was her childhood like?" Kiya inquired.

"Eldin was as a wild colt. Some days she would listen, others she only wanted to kick up her heels and play. Once school began, Eldin settled down...for the most part. She was brilliant in her academics, and she excelled in the sporting arena. Eldin could outrun, outswim, outthrow, and outlift anyone in her same season group. The only contest she would lose was fisticuffs. Eldin did not like to hurt anyone. Being the daughter of a military legend, it was expected of her to excel in this area as well. For several seasons, Eldin refused to compete, until the day a girl she had started to like was being picked on by a few of the bullies in school. Well, Eldin learned what fighting for honor meant that day. She was horribly outmatched and received quite a beating, but in doing so she allowed the other girl to escape." Seldar paused to build the healer's interest.

"So what happened, Seldar? Did she ever get revenge?" Kiya asked, finally tired of waiting for him to continue.

"Well, that very night Eldin asked her mother Elrik..."

"Elrik?! As in *General* Elrik?" Kiya interrupted, her eyes wide in surprise.

"The very same," Seldar replied. "Anyway, she asked Elrik to teach her the ways of the warrior. Eldin worked very hard, and by the next seasonmark, she was beating girls several seasons older."

Kiya closed her eyes and pictured a young Eldin, unwilling to hurt others. Well, that would certainly explain the conflict she had felt in Eldin's soul.

"Did she ever avenge the beating?" Kiya asked.

"Oh, in grand fashion. Eldin went to the Village Council and called her out. Most everyone in the village showed up to watch. You see, the bully was Terik, daughter of the Great Hills Councilwoman Tedur. I do suppose that they could have charged many krillits and still have had a big turnout," Seldar explained.

"Who was the girl? The one Eldin championed?" Kiya asked with great interest. Seldar smiled; Kiya was interested. Good, this was *very* good.

"Her name was J'min, and she stole Eldin's heart," Seldar began.

"J'min? That is a Drakknian name. Eldin loved a Drakknian?" Kiya blurted out in shock.

"Yes. J'min had been rescued by a Yashor scouting party. She was a slave to a Drakknian soldier serving close to the Yashor border. She was brought to our village, and a young couple with no children decided to raise her instead of sending her to the army as most orphans. Where was I? Oh yes, they never tried one another until Eldin was in War Academy. J'min was to become a teacher of first school. The day of Eldin's commissioning, they announced their intent to declare." Seldar's voice suddenly dropped off.

Kiya could sense a great sorrow in Seldar's heart, and she instinctively placed a hand on his shoulder for comfort.

"Seldar, I know Eldin is not declared. What happened?" Kiya ventured.

"It never came to be. We should just leave it at that," Seldar explained.

Kiya sensed it would be best if she dropped the subject, and Seldar was obviously uncomfortable with it. She would just have to find a way to get Eldin to open up to her, that's all. Right, "that's all." Kiya feared it would be easier to pull all of Eldin's teeth right out of her head than to get her to tell what had happened to her love. She was probably right.

* * *

Delyn moaned Eldin's name. Goddess, she loved it when Eldin impaled her on that hot, hard tongue! Delyn reached down and ran her fingers through Eldin's sweat-matted hair, gently coaxing her on. Delyn gasped as Eldin replaced her tongue with several fingers and plunged deep inside her. Eldin slowly pumped inside Delyn with firm strokes as she explored Delyn's nether lips with her tongue, eliciting more soft moans of pleasure. Eldin's tongue drew lazy patterns across Delyn's slick flesh until she suddenly changed course to lavish attention on Delyn's sensitized nub. Delyn gasped at the passionate attack, and she held Eldin firmly in place with a commanding grip of her hair. Eldin was an expert at anticipating Delyn's hip thrusts as she involuntarily tried to escape Eldin's insistent tongue to no avail.

Bright light suddenly burst across the tent, illuminating the bed. Delyn blinked. Eldin froze.

"Captain! Your moth…General Elrik is…" Maric started hastily.

"Here," a deep voice came from behind Maric.

General Elrik pushed Maric aside and entered the tent. Her face was unreadable.

"I found it odd that Sgt. Maric would tell me you two were in a strategy session, but you were not in the command tent. You know, when I was a young officer, we called this something else. Eldin, get dressed. We need to talk." Elrik turned to leave.

She paused at the tent flap and said, "Lieutenant."

Delyn paled but managed to reply, "General."

Maric looked at Eldin. "I'm sorry, I tried to warn you."

Maric stepped from the tent to allow Eldin to get dressed. It was hard not to gloat. When the Goddess intervened, She sure had a sense of humor! Maric smiled; she would love to see the look on Delyn's face now. She bet it was anything but smug!

Eldin gently withdrew from Delyn and kissed her stomach.

"I am sorry, Delyn. In all my life, my mother has never caught me like this. Worry not. I shall make certain it does not affect your career," Eldin promised.

Eldin stood and smiled down at Delyn. "Thank you. I needed that. I only wish I had been able to finish what I had started."

"Me too," Delyn replied, still too embarrassed to move.

Eldin slipped back into the clothes she had on earlier, washed her face and hands in her wooden basin, then she left Delyn to dress on her own. What was she going to tell her mother? Eldin followed Maric's outstretched finger to find Elrik waiting underneath a large tree.

After taking a deep breath to collect her courage and slipping a fresh mint leaf from her belt pouch into her mouth, Eldin walked over. Elrik was standing with her back toward Eldin and her hands clasped behind her. As Eldin approached, Elrik spoke.

"I am taking my last ride, Eldin. Your other mother has long waited on me, and I have finally paid the debts of my youth. I wanted to be the one to tell you, daughter, because I feel a great change coming. Make no mistake, Captain, there are enemies in the Council of Nine." Elrik spoke softly, without looking at her daughter.

"If you know of enemies in the Council, how can you take your last ride, General?" Eldin asked.

"My sword is not as swift or as steady as it once was, and to tell you the truth, I am too weary of the never-ending fight. I can no longer be a party to the slaughter of our youth. Please forgive me for leaving this up to you. Eldin, this madness must end! I am too old to fight it any longer; now it is your demon to master," Elrik explained.

Elrik started to walk slowly in the general direction of the healer's area. Eldin caught up to her and fell in step next to her mother.

"Who are the enemies, then?" Eldin inquired, accepting the responsibility to ferret out the traitors among them.

"I wish I knew, daughter. I have not been able to secure that information. Every 'shadow' I have sent has come back to Yashor dead. Please watch your back," Elrik warned.

"Are you headed to the keep from here?" Eldin wanted to know.

"Yes. I have some…" Elrik looked at Eldin out of the corner of her eyes, "'…strategy sessions' of my own to attend with your mother Dinyar."

Eldin felt the crimson invading her cheeks. So, her mother would not let it pass without comment.

"Does this mean that you and Delyn plan to be declared?" Elrik ventured.

"I am an adult, General. No, I do not wish to declare with Delyn, just as she does not wish to declare with me. We have our reasons. We simply enjoy each other's company every once in awhile. It helps break the tension of war," Eldin explained.

"Just as I thought, it is still J'min who holds your heart," Elrik commented.

Eldin shut her eyes and J'min was there smiling, reaching toward a younger version of herself. She took in a sharp breath, and Eldin's step faltered slightly as the pain hit her heart. Eldin pushed the pain aside and opened her eyes to the world around her, banishing the vision of her love once again to the far recesses of her mind. She quickly fell back in step with her mother.

"So, you are not going to lecture me on morals? You are not going to turn us in to the Council?" Eldin inquired.

"I told you, I was once a young officer too, long before I met the woman who now holds my heart. However, I shall not be mentioning this to your other mother," Elrik concluded.

"She would lecture me and try to force Delyn to the Council Hall at swordpoint," Eldin agreed.

Elrik simply nodded and clasped Eldin's shoulder conspiratorially.

"Come, daughter, show me your camp," Elrik suggested, changing the subject.

Eldin spoke as they arrived at the healer's area. "Seldar has been wounded. He shall live, but he took quite a serious wound to the leg."

"I shall inform your other mother. She is quite fond of him. It is as I always told her, 'Male-children belong in the kitchen with a spoon in their hands, not on a battlefield with a sword.' They haven't the strength, skill, or intelligence to be effective warriors."

"Is that why we have already beaten the Drakknians then, General?" Eldin asked sarcastically in Seldar's defense.

"I suppose your attitude is my fault, Captain. I allowed you far too much time to play with your sib," Elrik replied.

Eldin forced herself into silence. It would do no good to rile her mother now. Eldin knew one thing for certain—as long as they both should live, neither of them would ever change her mind about the capabilities of male-children. Eldin smiled; there was no denying whose stubborn streak she had inherited.

3

Councilwoman Kidak brushed her thick, graying, flame-tinged hair from her face with her fingertips and sat down in her seat. She looked around and sighed. As much as she hated being a witness to the violence, this was a necessary contest to weed out the unfit. Kidak watched as lead Councilwoman Arkon stood and addressed the crowd. It always amazed Kidak that so many Amazons would willingly choose to watch this bloodbath.

"Great Goddess above, please make obvious Thine choices for our survival. We humbly beseech Thine wisdom in our pairings. Behold the male-children who seek Your approval!" Arkon boomed to the crowd.

Several gates lifted and many male-children rushed out of them into the coliseum. Their small muscles twitched with anticipation as they watched Arkon intently. As soon as Arkon's arm fell, they sprinted toward the array of weapons strewn about the arena. Some fell quickly as they had not the speed to reach the weapons, nor the skill to evade a killing blow.

Kidak searched the arena and found the legendary breeder, Lytos. He had sidestepped a sword strike and managed to grab a hold of the unfortunate swordsman's arm. He snapped it like a twig and retrieved the sword while never releasing his prisoner. Lytos rammed the sword completely through his opponent up to the hilt. Using his foot, Lytos removed the corpse from his newfound blade. It looked as though he would survive this seasonmark's selections as well. Lytos had not been eliminated in twenty-four seasonmarks. She wondered if he would ever fall. His seed had produced some of the best young warriors in Yashor, including Captain Eldin of Three Rivers. Captain Eldin had been Lytos' first offspring. How quickly the seasonmarks passed.

Kidak could no longer stomach watching the process, so she closed her eyes. It seemed an eternity before Arkon announced a halt to the slaughter. She opened her eyes and found Lytos among the survivors. In fact, she did not see a wound on him. The male-children who had survived were taken back to their cells underneath the coliseum to be recorded. The Council would be getting the names soon after.

Kidak had a few Amazons from the Three Rivers district whom she hoped to petition for breeding. Lytos was always the most treasured breeder and the hardest to obtain, yet Kidak felt that she had the perfect Amazon to breed with him. The young Amazon warrior had just declared, so she was legal to breed, and if that union should produce a daughter, Yashor would have yet another great warrior to add to its ranks. Kidak would have to petition carefully as to avoid losing Lytos to Pirkyn's district again.

As Kidak rose to her feet, she looked at the male-children being hustled off to their cells and wondered why any of them would willingly choose this path. It meant certain death. The only prize given was that they were allowed to keep their "maleness." It also meant having to service whatever Amazon was chosen for them. Was sex for a male-child really worth chancing death each seasonmark? She sighed; they really were pathetic creatures.

* * *

Kidak walked along the back alley toward the Council Hall. She wanted to get the stench of death out of her mind, and a stroll in fresh air was her favorite way to cleanse her senses. Pausing at the backyard of a small house, she admired a well-tended flower garden. Kidak closed her eyes and inhaled deeply; such a lovely fragrance to chase away any lingering stench from the breeders' selection contest. Reluctantly, she continued her trek. All too soon, she arrived at the steps of the Council Hall.

Kidak entered the hall quickly and quietly took her seat. She looked skyward and silently thanked the Great Goddess once more for the honor of simply being a part of the Council. Kidak then looked around the room as the others were taking their seats. She loved this room and all it stood for. The Council Hall was huge, with a vaulted ceiling and many windows to let in the Yashor sunlight. The sunlight illuminated the walls that were covered in bright tapestries, which told the history of Yashor. At one end of the hall, was a long table where the councilwomen convened. At the other end, was a small cordoned-off area with a few bench seats. Commoners would sit here to witness the proceedings or use the pulpit to petition the Council.

Kidak was certain that this session was going to end soon, and perhaps she could take a ride out to visit Kiya. She had recently been transferred to the borderline fighting and was taking care of the Three Rivers district's troops. Oh yes, and that brash young Captain Eldin. Hopefully, her daughter didn't fall for her. That would only bring heartache. Captain Eldin's charms were well known in all of Yashor. Perhaps it was the fault of the bards. They were always telling tales of her beauty and daring battlefield victories. Kidak prayed that those tales were greatly exaggerated. If not, Kiya would most certainly be too busy to get romantic notions, would she not?

"Well, old woman, in a way it would be your own fault. You did commission her," Kidak chastised herself aloud, remembering the day she proudly pinned the Lieutenant clasp on Eldin's uniform cloak.

"What say you, Kidak?" Romyl asked, certain she had heard Kidak speak.

Kidak smiled and waved off Romyl's question with an apologetic look. Romyl smiled back; oh, how she regretted losing her those many, many seasonmarks ago. Her daughter Kiya was the spitting image of a young Kidak. It would have been a perfect life to have raised such a woman with Kidak at her side. Now, what was that blowhard Pirkyn complaining about today? Romyl reluctantly shifted her attention back to the Council meeting.

"We cannot allow this to continue, sisters. We must crush them! In order to save more lives, we need to send a lone warrior to Drakknia and infiltrate the army. This warrior must be capable of counting troops, noticing how the supplies are delivered, and have the nerve to allow herself to be captured, with the skill to escape without assistance. I know of only two such warriors, and one has just taken her last ride. That leaves her daughter, Captain Eldin of Three Rivers," Pirkyn was petitioning.

"Aye, this sounds logical. If she were to accomplish this, we could then poison the supplies and crush Drakknia when the army was at its weakest!" Gryfa exclaimed, sparing Pirkyn a conspirator's glance.

"What if she fails? We would lose one of our best and most promising young leaders. Would that not be a foolish risk?" Kidak protested.

Why must they always involve the youth of Three Rivers? It makes my position look weak if I cannot stand up to the Council in their defense, Kidak thought.

"The Borderlands agree with Three Rivers. We must not risk the life of our future. That would be madness. Why not choose one of our 'shadows'? Is that not what they were trained to do? Be as a shadow and infiltrate?" Romyl took Kidak's side, as usual.

"Oh, Romyl, have you not gotten Kidak out of your loins, yet?! That was a long time ago, and she has since declared and borne daughters of the Realm. You truly are pathetic in your pining. Why, you would take her side if she thought we should surrender to the Drakknian demons. Remember when you sided with Kidak concerning that landowner who was caught bedding an uncut male-child? She tried to claim that it was a natural attraction and harmed none. Yet the Great Goddess herself decreed that we only soil our temple to her in order to breed. We did not even sentence her to death by stoning as is the appropriate punishment. We sent her to the great Mind Healer to be cured of her affliction. We showed her mercy and you two stated that we were being too harsh. Your voice should not be recognized in this," Pirkyn tried to quell the opposition.

Arkon stood and slammed her fist against the heavy wooden table; "*I* am the lead councilwoman here, Pirkyn! *I* decide whose voice should be heard and whose should be silenced. Don't *you* forget your place, number *eight* of nine."

Arkon was tired of the petty bickering. Today was not the day for this foolishness. She had just received word of her declared's crossing over mere candledrips before the start of the day's session, and she would not tolerate any fighting today. Perhaps it was time to call a recess so she could clear her head and unburden her heavy heart. The old stateswoman could barely hold in her tears. They had loved richly for well over forty seasonmarks, and now suddenly she was all alone.

"I am invoking my right as lead to call this session in recess. We shall resume sessions by the next full moons," Arkon declared.

Voices murmured around the table. In all of her seasonmarks as lead, Arkon had never called a recess before a vote had been taken, let alone one that lasted a full ten days. This was very suspect.

"But what about this season's breeders? We cannot leave without assigning the breeders. We shall lose valuable time in which to utilize their seed. Surely you do not expect us to wait for your return," Pirkyn complained, worried that she might lose Lytos' services if the others were given too long to prepare their petitions.

"That is exactly what I expect you to do, Pirkyn. Do not cross me. You have had Lytos for the last seven seasons. Do you wish to place that in peril by making me angry with you? I must attend to my declared. I must say my good-byes. Now leave me in peace or suffer my wrath upon my return," Arkon warned.

Pirkyn reluctantly backed down. She bowed to Arkon, but her eyes blazed with hatred. *Just for that, you shall join your declared sooner.*

Romyl stood and held Kidak's chair for her as she offered Kidak her hand. Kidak graciously accepted the help rising out of her chair. Romyl bowed slightly, and Kidak patted her hand in thanks before allowing her hand to drop back to her side.

"Kidak, would you honor me this evening and join me for even-feast? I would like to discuss Pirkyn's plan. We must find a way to block it." Romyl hoped her invitation would be appropriately muted by work.

"Romyl, it has been an exhausting session, with no resolutions. I am tired…too tired to travel back to Yamouth this night. However, I also think it would not look good for us to be seen sharing even-feast with our… history. Perhaps if you had some others join us I might change my mind. You know where I stay. Have a messenger send for me," Kidak replied.

"As you wish." Romyl kept the disappointment from her voice.

"Thank you once again for your support in Council matters. You know, it does make a difference when you support Three Rivers' position. You are a dear friend and a wonderful ally. I am tired; please excuse me," Kidak commented.

Romyl bowed and held Kidak's chair for her. She felt foolish; of course Kidak could not accept her invitation to dine alone with her. How fast that rumor would spread through the Council! How long would it take to reach Yamouth, a day perhaps? How long before Yamouth reached the Council's doorstep, another day? Romyl sighed; she was indeed pathetic and still very much in love with Kidak.

Romyl gathered her wounded pride and held her head high as she exited the Council Chambers, unaware of the pair of eyes that followed her every move. The shadow moved quickly and never lost contact with Romyl as she moved through the market square. This would be too easy when the order was finally issued. First Kidak, then Romyl would fall to her blade. A feral grin spread across her face, but none saw, especially a heartbroken councilwoman. *Soon Romyl, soon.*

4

"It is a pleasure to meet you, General. My name is Kiya, daughter of Councilwoman Kidak and Yamouth, and healer just assigned," Kiya introduced herself to the older woman at Eldin's side.

Eldin did favor her mother, and it was easy to see from where she had obtained her good looks. Elrik's hair was just graying, and her eyes were a smoldering blue. Yes, it was certain.

General Elrik smiled at the beautiful young healer. She was impressed with her command presence, which was rare, especially in one so young. Humph, either the Realm was using younger women these days, or Elrik was just plain getting old. Somehow, she feared it was the latter.

"I was telling the general that my sib Seldar was injured and under your care. Is he well for visitors?" Eldin inquired.

Kiya smiled sweetly at the two strong women. "Yes, you will find him in much better condition than when you brought him to me, Captain. I think he would enjoy a visit from his mother as well."

"You do know that you are not required to aid a male-child, even if he was wounded in defense of Yashor, do you not?" Elrik stated.

"It did not bother me to lend aid to Seldar. My concern is for the welfare of the warriors that protect our great Realm. If that warrior happens to be a male-child, then…"

"Then you had better have a good reason for wasting your time on him! Please tell me that you did not take time away from Amazons to heal him," Elrik interrupted.

Eldin felt her jaw clench, and she held her hand up to silence Kiya's reply.

"General, the healer was acting on *my* orders. If you have a problem with the way that I lead my troops, then you take that up with *me*. Do I need to remind the former general that her rank is really nothing more than honorary at this time? Please, let us just go visit Seldar. Can we not do that without bickering?" Eldin came to Kiya's defense.

"Of course, Captain. We shall see Seldar. Then I must rest for my trip back to Three Rivers. I am long overdue to spend some time with Dinyar," Elrik conceded.

Kiya placed a hand lightly on Eldin's arm, stopping her from turning away and following her mother toward the wagons. Eldin's skin tingled from the contact. She looked up and was captured in those beautiful pools of liquid emerald.

"Thank you, Captain. You did not need to assume the responsibility for healing that I did willingly, but I appreciate it just the same," Kiya thanked her quietly.

"We should talk sometime; perhaps after my mother leaves. I would like to know more about your philosophies regarding your healing." Eldin did not believe she was saying this, even as the words were leaving her lips.

Kiya smiled. "I am always available to you, Captain."

Elrik turned to speak to Eldin and caught the intense looks the two exchanged. Well, *now* her daughter's actions made sense. However, she still did not like to be spoken to in that manner by her own daughter!

Eldin excused herself from the healer and went to join her mother. Did she really just suggest that the two of them spend time together?! What was that all about? *Demon Shamaness!*

Elrik continued toward the wagons, and Eldin was back at her side in a heartbeat. She looked at her daughter through a mother's eyes for the first time this visit. It was a luxury she rarely had allowed herself. Eldin was strong, confident, and looked well; however, she did notice a few lines forming around her eyes and across her forehead. Perhaps Eldin was not resting enough. That had always been her demon as well. Never getting enough rest. Then again, how well can one rest when the ghosts of those women killed under your command visit you in your sleep?

The silence was broken when Seldar caught sight of his sib and called out.

"How stands the day, Captain?" he called out before noticing the woman at Eldin's side was his second mother.

"The day is a fine one indeed, Seldar. I have a surprise for you. Look who decided to come for a visit," Eldin replied.

"More likely to force me back into her kitchen," Seldar stated under his breath.

"What say you, male-child?" Elrik shot out accusingly.

"What mother means is that she is happy to see you looking well. Isn't that right, Mother?" Eldin tried to broker a truce.

"Captain, I am quite capable of speaking for myself. Yes, I am happy that Seldar is alive. Your other mother is quite fond of him," Elrik explained.

Seldar tried to shut out the pain those words caused. He knew the woman did not care for him. He was an embarrassment to her. He was her great failure. Well, at least because of him, she did not have to hire as many domestic serfs. He had saved the family thousands of krillits over the seasonmarks. That meant that Eldin had been given the best of everything. Seldar smiled; Eldin deserved the best of everything.

"Something amuses you, male-child?" Elrik asked flatly.

"I was just remembering a time from my youth that was pleasant, Mother Elrik," Seldar answered truthfully.

"I wanted to show Mother Elrik your progress under the healer's care. We do need to get back to the troops, Seldar. I shall come back around even-feast while on my rounds. You rest now. You need your strength so that you may return to defending Yashor as quickly as possible," Eldin explained while interrupting the two to come to Seldar's defense.

"Have a fine day, Captain," Seldar called after her as she and Elrik turned to walk back to the warriors' side of camp.

* * *

Lieutenant Delyn paced in her tent. She was whirling at the implications to her career. If the general saw fit, she could take away her commission for "improper acts." Perhaps she should just ask Eldin if she would consider becoming her declared mate. It would lend credibility to their relationship. Hades fire, then it would be legal for them to enjoy pleasures of the flesh as much as they desired! Now, there was a thought. Delyn grinned wolfishly. It only lasted a heartbeat as reality came crashing in on her fantasy. Eldin was not looking for love, only release. That had been made clear to her from the beginning. Well, on the other hand, it had been *her* intent in the beginning as well. Had not her feelings for Eldin changed? Perhaps Eldin felt the same. It was possible, was it not? Delyn smiled; of course it was! After all, what was not to love?

* * *

Maric smiled. She bent down to inspect the condition of the fragile scarlet blooms for which she had been searching the forest carpet several candlemarks. Ah, these would be perfect! She carefully harvested three buds and secured them in her belt pouch. Only one more ingredient to find, and the general would have her favorite tea for even-feast. It was the least she could do for all the general had done for her over the seasons.

Why Elrik had to favor the rare brew known as Hades Revenge was beyond Maric, but she happily scoured the area for the woman who had taken her off the streets and made her respectable again. Maric joked that had it not been for Elrik, she would still be lost inside a tavern with a flagon of cheap mead, too drunk to find the door and too poor to pay for directions. That seemed like a lifetime ago, now.

A birdcall overhead caused Maric to look up, and it was there that she spotted the last ingredient growing on a limb up in the tall tree behind her. Good, one small climb and the general would have a great surprise! Maric enjoyed taking care of others, making them smile. It was her greatest strength, and her greatest weakness.

* * *

It was a brilliant day, and the camp was in full swing as Eldin and Elrik made their way to the command tent. Trainlings were running supplies to the cooks and getting prepared for afternoon sword drills. Word had spread quickly about the general's surprise visit, and the youngsters were riding a storm of excitement. None had ever seen the general in person, but all of them had studied her life in school. She was a living legend and the birth mother of their hero, Captain Eldin. As they approached, many stopped in their tracks just to gawk.

"Captain, do all of your trainlings catch flies on their own, or is it something that you train them to do?" Elrik teased her daughter about the gaping mouths of the youth.

"Oh, they are highly trained in the art, General. Can you not see? Have you no eyes?" Eldin teased back.

Eldin loved these rare but precious playful heartbeats that she shared with her mother. Elrik's responsibilities had prevented her from many such indulgences throughout Eldin's life.

The general laughed heartily as they entered the command tent. After the two disappeared inside, the trainlings resumed their tasks. Inside, away from prying eyes, Elrik drew her sword. She grinned at her daughter.

"Indulge me in a little sparring, Captain?" she challenged.

"Old woman, you do not stand a chance in Hades of defeating me, but if you wish a beating, I will gladly oblige," Eldin teased her mother, accepting the challenge with a flourish.

"I will show you who is an old woman when I leave my mark upon you!" Elrik retorted.

Elrik spun and swung her sword at Eldin's right knee. Eldin easily blocked the blow and reversed, tapping Elrik's shoulder with the flat of her blade.

"Oh, how the mighty have fallen! You would now be begging me for mercy," Eldin stated cockily.

While Eldin was spouting off, Elrik feigned left and spun back right to tap Eldin's right thigh. It was higher than she had wanted, but the wound would have affected Eldin's mobility just the same.

"Not so quick, pup. You have bitten off more than you can chew, I'm afraid," Elrik replied.

"A lucky blow," Eldin scoffed.

"It only takes one lucky blow to kill a cocky little captain," Elrik reminded her.

They crossed blades and went through a series of moves that started to wind the general. She was enjoying the competition. Not many could match her skill and seasons of experience swinging a sword. A thin sheen of sweat covered the two combatants as they continued to drill.

Eldin made a move for Elrik's midsection, a "death blow." Elrik seized her opportunity and struck forward to beat Eldin to the victory, when Eldin surprised her by leaping over her blade and sweeping the general's feet out from under her with a low roundhouse maneuver. Before the general knew what had happened, Eldin was standing above her with her sword at the general's throat.

"I believe you have reached the yielding point, General," Eldin quietly reminded her mother.

"Bravo, Captain. You are every bit as good as I had hoped. I not only yield, but I also salute you," Elrik stated, pride gleaming from her smoldering blue eyes.

Eldin helped Elrik to her feet. It was then that the tent flap opened, and a young soldier entered.

"Captain, the cooks wanted to remind you that even-feast will be served at sunset. The hunters have returned with a bounty, and in celebration of the general's visit, they are preparing a traditional General's Feast," The soldier relayed the information.

"If it pleases the general, that is," She quickly amended.

Elrik smiled. Ah, the perks of rank. How long did it take her to ride out here, living on dried meat and a few root vegetables? Too long.

"You tell the cook that the general would be honored by a feast and that the general's stomach is already eagerly awaiting sunset," Elrik spoke to the warrior.

The young woman placed her fist over her heart and bowed her head. "As you command, so shall it be done."

* * *

Delyn washed her face again. How quickly the sweat stained her fore-head. Her palms itched and were quite wet with sweat as well. Oh Hades! This was a lot easier in her youthful dreams than in reality. *Well, you just march up to her and say, "Eldin, I think we need to talk. I want you as my declared mate."* Delyn put her face in her hands and shook her head.

"Yeah, then she tells you to lay off of the mead and laughs you out of the tent. Who am I kidding? I can't just walk up to her and say that," Delyn chastised herself aloud.

Delyn exited her tent. She needed some fresh air. She needed to think. She needed to relax. Delyn smiled. What she needed was to find about ten young soldiers and drill; that always made things right. Delyn started off in the direction of the soldiers' tents.

Maric smiled as she carefully placed the tasty fungus into her belt pouch. She was extended as far as the limb would allow, but she was certain it would support her long enough to climb back down. Just as she was about to climb down she smelled the faint odor of a campfire. She squinted into the sunlight but was able to make out the traces of smoke in the distance. It was about thirty kligs away. Hmm. It could be Drakknian or maybe the reinforcements they were promised. Whichever it was, it was important that she tell Eldin of her discovery as soon as she made it back to camp. Perhaps they would send out a scouting party.

* * *

Delyn growled at the youngster as she back-fisted her in the face, drawing blood from the young one's nose. She recoiled in pain, but did not drop her defense. Delyn grinned. Well, at least *this* one did not go running for the comfort of her mother's teat when something hurt. Delyn spun left and was surprised to find a sword waiting for her face. She instantly hit the ground and rolled under the strike. Delyn used her catlike agility to pop back up to her feet and make a strike of her own. The blade just caught the edge of the girl's arm, drawing a thin red line of blood.

"Wear it proudly, trainling. Not many people bear my mark and live to tell about it," Delyn stated smugly.

Delyn's smile instantly faded as the pain in her thigh told her she had just been marked as well.

"Sorry, Lt. Delyn, but I only wear my uniform proudly. Perhaps you should bear my mark proudly, for I am going to be the one who commands you someday," Rikyn retorted.

Delyn lost her restraint and began swinging for real. Rikyn was not used to this level of intensity. She was losing her confidence and afraid that with one misstep she would lose her life as well.

"Hold!" the weapons master called to no avail. "I said hold!"

Delyn blinked as she felt her sword arm being held. She spun around to face her assailant, wild-eyed. Recognition caused Delyn to stop struggling.

"Do you wish to kill yourself, Lieutenant? That is Councilwoman Pirkyn's brat. As much as I would love to watch you rip her apart, I would also miss seeing your beautiful face around camp," the weapons master whispered to Delyn.

Delyn stopped and glared at Rikyn. "You should learn some respect, because you can't hide behind your mother's cloak forever."

"I respect those that earn it, Lieutenant," Rikyn shrugged.

"Rikyn! I have heard enough from you this day. Go back to camp and clean the refuse area. I think you need to dig some new privies, perhaps that shall give you time to reflect on the proper way to speak to higher-ranking Amazons. Go now," the weapons master ordered.

"As you command, so shall it be done," Rikyn replied, halfheartedly.

The two older women watched as the youngster gathered her pride and headed for the refuse area. Digging privies with only one's bare hands was punishment, but not as bad as it got. This was mild compared to some of the punishments that they could have doled out.

When Rikyn was out of sight, the weapons master turned to Delyn and said, "As for you, you look like you need some release. Might I suggest something, Lieutenant?"

Delyn looked at the woman. She allowed herself to be lead to a tent. The weapons master opened the flap and pointed inside. Delyn looked in.

She found a pair of female Drakknian slaves inside. They were perhaps thirteen to fifteen seasonmarks old. Dressed scantily, it was quite clear what their position with the woman was. They still bore the leather collars and armbands of slaves.

"Don't let their age fool you, Delyn. They are quite experienced in the art of making you feel like a goddess. I won them in a game of skull. It seems that they were rescued by a Yashor scouting party and laid claim to by the leader. Then she lost them to me. Go ahead, give them a try. You will feel much better," she explained.

Delyn looked them over from head to toe. They were quite attractive and well kept. She looked around and, seeing no one, entered the tent.

"Oh, and Lieutenant, you need not be gentle with them if it pleases you; they know how to handle battle-lust," the weapons master concluded as she dropped the flap on a leering Delyn.

* * *

Eldin was glad that the day seemed to fly by. Her mother was happily inspecting her troops, and the soldiers were a big reason for her improved mood. It seemed they could not get enough of the former general. Well, she was a legend, Eldin supposed. No, she still could not see it. It was her mother, after all. Eldin was just happy that Elrik's mood had been lifted. Perhaps they would not argue anymore while the general was here.

Eldin's arm tingled as a hand lightly touched her biceps. She turned to find the healer standing next to her. Eldin smiled; Kiya looked radiant.

"Hello, Captain. I hope that I'm not interrupting anything," Kiya started, a little uncertainty in her voice.

"No, not at all, Kiya. What may I do for you?" Eldin replied, flashing her most brilliant smile.

Kiya felt her insides turn to jelly. What a beautiful smile! Goddess, she was handsome...strong...and Goddess...those eyes!

"Kiya?" Eldin tried once more to get her attention.

"Sorry, I just had something on my mind," Kiya replied, a little embarrassed.

Eldin placed her hand over Kiya's. "What may I do for you?"

Kiya reluctantly pulled her hand away, as there were many eyes upon them. She looked around and felt very aware of the scrutiny.

"I was wondering when we might expect some more healing supplies. I am running dangerously low on some things, and if I don't get them soon, I am verily afraid I might lose some warriors unnecessarily," Kiya relayed the bad news.

Eldin stiffened. She had been afraid of this. She was aware of the shortage of camp supplies, that was the reason she had sent out hunters, but healing supplies were different. Oh sure, some could be found growing in the forest, but too many had to be cured, dried, mixed, measured, and Hades knows what else.

"How long do we have?" Eldin inquired.

"That depends on how many warriors get wounded, Captain. It also depends on the wounds. I am almost out of treated cat-gut. Without that, I cannot stitch up cuts, so no more getting cut. I am running out of fire-salve, so no more getting burned. Hmm, if I tell you that I am running out of everything, do you think we could all go home?" Kiya asked, a small barb directed at the insanity of the never-ending war with the Drakknians.

Eldin spared her a small smile. "If it were up to me, Kiya, none of us would be here. However, it is not up to me. Why not ask the Council of Nine, or try to talk the Drakknians out of invading Yashor? Without that threat, we could go home. Now, how long do you think the supplies will last?"

"Perhaps one more big battle or two to three smaller ones. It really depends on the amount of wounded that you bring me. I have already searched the surrounding woods for herbs and fungus that I can use to make salves and some potions. However, I cannot find everything that I will need. I just thought you should know," Kiya said.

Eldin thought for a moment. Continuing to fight without healing supplies was a bit like assisting in one's own death; however, if they retreated they would be giving Drakknia precious kligs of land that was paid for with the blood of hundreds of her warriors. She would have to think of some alternative if the reinforcements did not arrive today.

"Kiya, how far is the nearest healer's post?" Eldin asked quietly.

"I estimate it to be about twenty kligs, or more," Kiya responded.

Eldin closed her eyes. It would be madness to send her away now, but really what choice did she have? It was only a matter of time until Drakknia attacked again. Perhaps if she left now, she could be back by the time she was really needed. Hades fire! Nothing like making life-and-death decisions for hundreds of women. That was what being a leader was all about in the end—who lives and who dies.

"Kiya, I am going to send you back to the healer's post for supplies. Send out another healer as soon as you get there, and then rejoin us as soon as you are rested and restocked with supplies. We are too close to Drakknia, and it is too late in the day for you to leave now. You shall leave at first light. With a full day's journey, you should be able to get far enough back into Yashor territory as to avoid the Drakknian scouting parties in this area. They are most active after the sun has fled the sky." Eldin relayed her orders to the young woman.

Kiya blinked. Was Eldin drunk or just insane? What kind of leader would make that decision? She was placing her troops in grave danger. Even small wounds could be deadly with no one to heal them.

"Do not look at me as if I have three heads. I know how crazy it sounds. Kiya, if we do not get supplies soon, we are all going to die anyway. This way, we at least have a chance! I cannot spare you any guard; the walking wounded will have to protect the others. It is our only hope," Eldin explained.

"Then, Captain, please be careful. You know without a healer even a flesh wound could be fatal if the flesh gets angry and weeps," Kiya reminded her.

Eldin smiled. This woman was so nurturing. She could make you feel like you were the most important person in the world. It was nice to feel that way again. Eldin stiffened.

"I'm sorry, Kiya. I have to go. I have to prepare a battle plan for when we are attacked again," Eldin spoke hastily and then turned abruptly and left.

"Run away, Eldin. Run away from your heart. You cannot hide it forever. My krillits are on the healer," Elrik stated under her breath as she watched the exchange from across the way.

Elrik turned back to the troops as Kiya turned and headed to the healer's area. *Poor child; she is in for a long fight if her prize is Eldin's heart*, Elrik thought.

* * *

Maric stumbled into the command tent, out of breath. She had been running a great distance and was learning just how old and out of shape she really was. No matter, she had to find Eldin. She had to let her know about the smoke. That was what was important now.

Maric doubled over and put her head between her legs to try to catch her breath. It figured that Eldin was not here, either. It was going to be her dumb luck that she would be in the last place that Maric would think to look. Maric gulped in a big breath and coughed. Oh well, no rest for the wicked, or the reformed drunks. She threw back the flap and trotted out in search again. She noticed that her running was much more like a fast stumbling. *Please, Great Goddess let Eldin be at the baths!*

* * *

Eldin reached for the small woman and captured her lips in a fierce kiss. The woman fought at first, but then Eldin felt her surrender and her lips parted, allowing Eldin's tongue entry. She was so beautiful, so soft, and smelled like a rose garden after a spring rain. She was melting into Eldin's strong embrace, her long fiery hair tickling Eldin's face. Eldin's kiss was demanding, and she could feel herself getting...hungry...very hungry. Eldin's hands traveled to the woman's creamy breasts. She began kneading the flesh slowly, avoiding the nipples that were now hard as pebbles on the beach of Tolkoi. The woman moaned.

Eldin closed her eyes and deepened the kiss. It was more passionate.

"Eldin...Eldin," the voice drifted to her ears.

Eldin's eyes flew open and she grabbed the throat that was directly in front of her face. Maric winced. Eldin's eyes slowly focused and lost the wild look of an interrupted predator. She released Maric from her stranglehold and slipped her hand beneath the warm water once more.

"What do you want, Maric? Can you not see that I am bathing?" Eldin grumbled; it had been such a pleasant dream.

Maric took in a deep breath, "I'm sorry, Captain. I have to tell you that I saw…"

Eldin looked up just in time to see the healer drop her bathing wrap to step into the hot spring. Eldin's eyes traveled the expanse of leg from her heels to the small patch of reddish-blonde hair at the apex of the healer's shapely legs before she realized what she was doing and promptly snapped her eyes shut.

"Yes, yes, Maric. Do what you need to do. I need to get ready for the feast. Make certain that the guard is in place for the ceremony. I do not want anyone to be fool enough to challenge my mother for her rank. Make it widely known that if anyone challenges her, I shall be her champion. Understood?" Eldin ordered, not waiting for an answer before standing and pulling herself from the water over a slight rocky ledge.

Kiya sat across from the two and watched as Eldin exited the hot spring. Her wet muscles rippled as she reached for her bathing wrap that hung from a tree branch. Kiya's breath caught in her throat. Rivulets of water cascaded down from Eldin's wet hair and over her muscles, accentuating their appearance. Eldin's dripping backside was literally breathtaking.

Maric looked at the healer and back at Eldin, "…smoke."

* * *

Eldin combed her hair out with a chiseled shell. It was almost as good as bone but broke easier. Some fools thought that shells were prettier, but what good was pretty when the fool things break? After that, she found her dress uniform. It was still in good condition, as Eldin brushed it frequently. She slipped on the white under-tunic and slid into her berry-dyed suede riding pants. It had a stripe of white stag fur down each leg. Next, she donned her white stag coat that tapered down to her waist. It had a short berry-dyed collar with matching cuffs. Lastly, she put on her berry-dyed cloak and closed it with the silver cloak clasp that identified her as a captain.

"Well, aren't you a sight, Captain? I'd wager you won't find it hard to get attention tonight," Maric complimented Eldin.

"Yeah, and then my mother can come bursting in again. That always makes them come running back for more," Eldin responded ruefully.

"Ah, yes, the general. You really think that she will bother you again tonight? After all, she may find it necessary to go to bed early herself. What with the soldiers moony-eyed and all," Maric joked.

Eldin spun around and whacked Maric's arm.

"Shut your mouth! I do have another mother you know," Eldin feigned indignant.

"You are right. Elrik would not stray from Dinyar," Maric conceded.

"Dinyar would kill them both," Eldin and Maric said in unison.

Laughter erupted from the two old friends, and Eldin clasped Maric's shoulder.

"Maric, I am going to go get the general for her feast. If you would be so kind as to set up the perimeter watch and have all the guards in place, I would be in your debt," Eldin said as she made her way to the tent flap.

"Consider it done, Eldin," Maric replied.

Eldin exited the tent, and Maric hit herself in the forehead! Oh, the smoke!

"Eldin! Eldin wait!" Maric called after her, too late.

Maric tried to catch Eldin, but by the time she reached the tent flap, Eldin had disappeared into the sea of soldiers.

"Well, you old drunk, now you better wait until after the feast and hope that she is alone," Maric chastised herself aloud.

5

idak paid her fare to the carriage driver and stepped across the cobblestone street to the Grey Fox tavern. Kidak's great-aunt owned it, and she was one of the oldest women in all of Yashor. The old woman considered the name a small joke, since most in the area said she was "wily as a fox" in her business dealings. It was getting late in the day, and the tavern was beginning to fill for even-feast.

Kidak chose a small table by the fireplace and sat down to warm herself. In this northern city, it seemed that every night was chilled, even in the middle of summer. As soon as she found her seat, a young barmaid came by to take her order.

"Welcome back to the Grey Fox, Councilwoman. What may I bring you tonight? We have a special meal since the hunting: gurkin with mangin sauce. The mangins are fresh off the tree in the back, and I made the sauce myself," the waif proudly exclaimed.

Kidak smiled. Most women would not be so proud of accomplishments in the kitchen. That was male-children's work. However, she had to admit that nothing was normal in the Grey Fox. It was one of the reasons that Kidak loved this small place.

"Gurkin, eh? Well, if you made the sauce, then certainly I shall try that. What is it served with?" Kidak replied.

"You have a choice of breads: molasses oat, soured, or creamed wheat. Then you may have sweet or white root vegetables baked, and your choice of drink. We have the finest dark ale, wine, or water," the barmaid recited.

"I believe I shall have the molasses oat, white root, and wine. Tell that old coot that I want to see her at my table as well," Kidak placed her order.

"I shall tell Master Terdak that her favorite great-niece is here to see her," the young woman eagerly agreed before bouncing off to the kitchens.

A few heartbeats later, Terdak came out of the back wiping her hands on a dishrag that hung from her shoulder. She smiled broadly at the woman sitting by the fire. Her gait was not as swift as it once was, but she was still far from an invalid, even at her great age. Her bright green eyes danced with obvious glee as she approached.

"Ah, my favorite niece," Terdak exclaimed as she reached to embrace Kidak.

"Great-niece, Auntie Terdak," Kidak teased.

"Oh, and what makes you so certain that you are all that 'great'? I may find you a pain in the backside," Terdak gave as good as she got.

Kidak chuckled. She was indeed sharp as a lynx tooth. She melted into Terdak's embrace. The old woman smelled of kitchen spices and roses. It was a pleasing aroma.

Terdak placed a kiss on Kidak's head before she stepped back to take in the sight of her.

"You look well, Kidak. You must be on your way to see Yamouth," Terdak exclaimed.

"What makes you think that, Auntie? Have you never considered that I may have just journeyed here to see you?" Kidak asked.

"Oh, panther piss; if you are here, it is only because this old fox was clever enough to move her establishment to the most likely place that her favorite niece, who is sometimes great, would stop for the night on her travels back from the Council to her keep. Hades fire child, you really think me daft enough to believe you would travel two days just to see my old wrinkled hide?" Terdak spouted.

Kidak laughed at the cantankerous old woman. She could curse with the best of them. To look at her, you would think she would be sweet as berry pie, then she would open her mouth and the air would turn blue from the curses that poured out. Kidak truly loved her great-aunt.

"Oh, Auntie, you know I love you. Why else would I not turn and go down the main road to Forest Glen? Why would I travel up the side of this forsaken mountain? Honestly, I do not know how you live here. It is always cold," Kidak complained.

Terdak grinned. "The cold is what keeps me alive. I think it keeps me from aging as quickly. Think about it. When you hunt and kill something, what keeps the meat fresh?"

Kidak shook her head.

"Putting it into an icehouse. Hades fire, child, you really are daft sometimes. Living here is like putting *me* into an icehouse. I am properly preserved," Terdak finished with a flourish.

Terdak looked around at the room. It was starting to fill up. As much as she would have loved to stay and chat with her niece, she had customers with hungry bellies to feed.

"I must get back to the kitchen. You may have your favorite room. It is always ready for you. I will feed this mob, and perhaps later we can catch up. How does that sound?" Terdak exclaimed.

"Wonderful, Auntie. My mouth already tastes your unrivaled cooking," Kidak complimented her.

"Panther piss," Terdak exclaimed as she headed back to the kitchen.

* * *

A dark figure in the far corner bent her head to hide the feral grin. So the councilwoman has a favorite old bat. Well, it would be fun to see how well she took to watching that old piece of leather carved up. Oh, and what fun it was going to be! If only the order would be given. *Soon, Kidak, soon.*

* * *

Delyn pushed back the tent flap and felt the cool evening breeze on her sweaty face. It was refreshing, just like the afternoon with the two young slaves had been. They had taken both punishment and passion alike, and not once a complaint. The activities had settled Delyn's nerves, and now she was ready to face Elrik at the feast. Oh, Goddess! The feast. It had to be soon! She needed to wash the passion from her body before she could attend.

Delyn ran at top speed to the hot springs and removed her clothing quickly. She jumped into the warm mineral water and dunked her head under. This had to be fast.

* * *

Seldar smiled as he watched Eldin's effect on the neighboring warriors in the healer's area while she approached. They seemed mesmerized by their leader in her dress uniform. She did look splendid, he had to admit. Finally, he caught sight of Kiya as she climbed out of a nearby wagon and turned toward Eldin. Seldar had to stifle a laugh as she got weak-kneed and almost stumbled.

"Oh, sweet Goddess, they are going to be a match made at the Great Feast by Your hand," Seldar stated to himself.

Eldin made her way to Seldar, and Kiya made a hasty retreat to her tent.

"Good eve, Captain. How stands the day for you?" Seldar inquired.

"It has been a good day indeed, little one," Eldin replied as she hoisted herself into the wagon.

Eldin grinned conspiratorially at Seldar. She could see it made him a bit nervous.

"What is it, Captain?" Seldar managed to choke out.

"I have a surprise for you. Close your eyes," Eldin demanded.

Seldar obeyed without question. Well, that was no fun. Eldin signaled Maric, who had followed her at a distance. Maric came hustling over with an armload of goodies they had intercepted on their way to be served at the feast.

Eldin set a plate down in Seldar's lap. The aroma of spiced elken meat combined with molasses oat bread, sweet root, white root, green beans, and butter drifted to Seldar's senses. He dared not even dream of such foods. He must smell the warrior's fare from the next wagon. He would open his eyes and find oat gruel. Maybe Eldin had a piece of molasses oat bread for him! Oh, that would taste wonderful.

"Seldar, for the sake of the Great Goddess, would you open your eyes?!" Eldin ordered her sib for the third time.

Seldar opened one eye slowly, and then the other flew open at the sight of the overflowing plate of treasures! Never had he been allowed food like this! Seldar looked at Eldin.

"Are you certain that there is enough for all of the Amazons, Captain? I could not eat this knowing that an Amazon would not get her share. It is against nature," Seldar said quietly.

"Oh, my little one, there is plenty. Please, eat this. You should have been eating like this since you were born. I am sorry that I did not make it so before now. Forgive me, my dear sib," Eldin replied.

Seldar looked at his plate. What would he eat first? Oh, the meat was so tempting. Seldar grabbed the slab of meat and bit off a large bite. His whole mouth danced with the joyous flavors! So this was what elken tasted like. It was a symphony for the palate.

Eldin enjoyed watching her sib eating like an Amazon for the first time. He was so much like a newborn babe at times it touched her heart. Maric was enraptured at Eldin's expression. How simple it was to bring her joy. All right, maybe it was not the safest of things to do with that old-fashioned general hanging about, but it sure was worth the risk. Besides, a ship is safe in the harbor, but that is not what a ship is made for. Eldin was a ship. Eldin was destined for great things, Maric was certain of it.

"Seldar, I am sorry, but I have to get going. I do not wish for the general to start looking for me and find us here. I will come back for a longer visit after she leaves. How would that be?" Eldin inquired.

"Oh, that would be most enjoyed, Captain!" Seldar heartily agreed.

"Good, then I shall leave you in the company of dear Maric, here. She will take your plate when you are finished, and no complaints about it either. That is an order," Eldin said as she turned to go.

"As you command, so shall it be done, my Captain," Seldar replied.

Eldin smiled. Ah, it was good to be in charge...some of the time. Eldin hurried back to the feast site. She noticed the general over by her tent and doubled her speed. In a few strides, she had closed the distance between them.

"Good eve, General. I see you are ready to eat. Shall we?" Eldin greeted her mother.

"Ah, Captain. You look splendid, indeed. I am certain that your lieutenant will find it most difficult to concentrate on her food," Elrik teased her daughter.

Just then, Elrik's stomach grumbled in a loud protest to its being quite empty. Eldin smirked and turned her back to her mother.

"It is too late for that, Eldin. I saw you. Come; give an old woman her dignity now. Let's just go sit down," Elrik suggested.

"As you wish," Eldin replied, still trying to wipe the silly grin off her face.

Ever since Eldin could remember, her mother Elrik had been one for proper protocol. It was nice to see that Elrik could not control every situation simply with her iron will.

As they entered the feast area, a silence fell over the troops. Eldin could feel so many eyes upon them it made her want to squirm. She felt like an object...as if those eyes were undressing her. Keeping her own eyes forward, she held her head high and managed to make it to the head of the table. There were two place settings there. She took the place on the right, and Elrik took the one to the left. It was proper military seating. The highest-ranking woman was always on the left. As they reached for their chairs, the rest of the troops stood and bowed their heads.

"Please, sit. Enjoy the feast. It appears that the hunters were very successful. Let us thank the Great Goddess for Her bounty!" Elrik projected to the three long tables of warriors.

After they sat, the normal buzz of talking and bantering began again, and Eldin's queasy stomach settled. She reached for some elken meat as the tray passed and placed a slab on her plate. She loved elken. It was a very tender meat, and when the spices were rubbed in and allowed to penetrate, Eldin was certain it was served right off the tables of the Goddess's Great Feast itself!

"Captain, I think that your healer has arrived," Elrik pointed out.

Eldin looked up from her plate, her gaze captured by Kiya's beauty. Kiya continued toward the head of the table. A hush fell over the feast as the soldiers looked on in silent admiration. Kiya's hair was let down, and the soft curls cascaded over her shoulders. She was wearing an elegant berry-dyed dress that was bare on the shoulders. With it, she wore a white stag wrap. Somehow, Eldin doubted that anyone had ever made Yashor's colors look better.

Eldin practically stumbled over the bench in her haste and started toward Kiya. They met halfway down the long table. Eldin held out her arm, and Kiya placed her small hand on Eldin's forearm. Eldin was taking great pleasure in her duty to escort the healer to her seat.

"You look incredible this eve, Kiya," Eldin remarked.

"Well, I suppose it does help when I wash all the blood off, eh Captain? Besides, you look quite handsome yourself," Kiya returned the compliment.

All too soon, Eldin had arrived at Kiya's place at the end of the table. It was the seat next to her mother. Of all the luck! Well, Elrik had always said that rank had its privileges.

"Perhaps we could talk after the feast? I would be glad to escort you to your tent, Kiya," Eldin ventured.

"That would be most kind of the captain, thank you," Kiya replied.

Eldin returned to her seat and tried to concentrate on her food. Unfortunately, she did not taste a bite after Kiya joined them.

Eldin jumped as she felt a hand on her shoulder. It was the arrival of Delyn. Elrik nodded her acknowledgment of the lieutenant's presence and then resumed her delightful conversation with the healer.

"You look good enough to eat, Eldin," Delyn stated quietly.

"Did you have to say that in front of my mother, Delyn?" Eldin groused.

"I don't think she heard me. She is much too enraptured with the healer. Do not ask me why. Healers are a weird lot. They don't fight, generally are smallish women that look like they would break if you got too passionate with them, and I think that they secretly desire male-children," Delyn wrinkled up her nose at the last statement.

"Delyn, how crude. Have you actually ever seen a healer fawning over a male-child? Ever see one kiss a male-child? That is like saying that all wolves desire lynx, just because they are wolves." Eldin was getting angry at Delyn's verbal healer-bashing, "Besides, when you get wounded, aren't you glad that there is a healer around to take good care of you?"

"I have never been wounded enough to warrant a healer's care," Delyn spouted off.

Eldin rolled her eyes. She looked over at Kiya. She was laughing at something her mother had said to her. She was radiant...lovely...soft. *Oh, Demon Shamaness!* Eldin tore her gaze off Kiya and resumed eating. She was convinced there was no justice in life. If there were, she would be sitting next to the healer instead of her mother!

* * *

It seemed an eternity before the feast ended. The fires had burned low several candlemarks before, and Eldin was sulking. She pushed a piece of white root around her plate as she waited for her opportunity to escort the healer to her tent. Would her mother never tire?

"Did you hear me, Eldin?" Delyn asked as she gripped Eldin's hand underneath the table.

Eldin glanced up at her. "I'm sorry, what did you say?"

"I said that I want to meet you by the waterfall later. I have something to ask you," Delyn replied.

"Cannot you just ask me now? No one is listening, least of all my mother," Eldin grumbled.

"Eldin, I...I just wanted to ask you this in a place I knew you loved. I thought you might...well...enjoy it more," Delyn tried to convince Eldin without actually tipping her hand.

"I cannot meet you tonight. I have business to which I need to attend. I will meet you tomorrow, as long as we are not attacked during the night," Eldin finally conceded.

"As you wish," Delyn pouted.

Delyn sat next to Eldin in silence for a few candledrips, and then she rose and bowed slightly to the general.

"I beg your leave, General. I am weary of this day," Delyn stated.

Elrik looked up at the young woman that she knew shared her daughter's bedroll. It was scandalous, and somehow she could not look at Delyn without seeing her as the one who had corrupted her Eldin.

"Please, feel free to leave, Lieutenant. You will need your rest for the coming battles," Elrik stated, a little less than a friendly undertone in her voice.

Brrr. Eldin felt the chill from her mother's icy stare bearing down on Delyn. She chuckled inside. Oh yes, it was not acceptable for them to share pleasures of the flesh without being declared first, yet, the old warrior had so much as admitted to doing the same thing while she was young and in the field. She knew her mother understood bloodlust. It was amusing to see Delyn squirm under her scrutiny, however.

Delyn skulked away. In a heartbeat, she was lost to the shadows. Kiya looked up at the captain. Her face was bathed in light from the twin moons and the flickering of the candle on the tabletop next to her. She truly did look handsome sitting there, lost in a world of her own making. Kiya silently wondered where Eldin had traveled, her gaze a million kligs away.

Elrik watched the healer as she studied Eldin. Ah, well, perhaps she had drawn this out long enough. By the looks of it, she figured that the healer intended to make a run at Eldin's frozen heart. *The luck of the Goddess to you*, Elrik silently spurred Kiya on. She was impressed with her and approved of a match between the two.

"Captain, I am verily weary from good food and too much ale. Please excuse me. I wish to rest now for my trip back to my keep," Elrik asked permission to leave.

Eldin felt odd. It had finally come, the point when Elrik was no longer a member of the Sword Corps. She considered herself beneath Eldin's command now.

"Please, General…" Eldin started.

"Not anymore, Captain. I am simply Elrik, or Mother, however you wish to address me," Elrik reminded her.

"If it pleases you, Mother. Would you like an escort back to your tent? I am certain that I could scare up a few guards for you," Eldin asked.

Elrik's face screwed up in a conflict of indignation and laughter. "I said that I was no longer a general, not that I was now an invalid incapable of taking care of myself in a fight. However, you are in command here, and if it is your wish that I have an escort, then so be it."

Eldin looked over at the two members of her personal honor guard. They had stood stock-still for the entire feast behind the two. The poor things looked like they could use a change of position.

"Please take my mother to her tent, and take care that no harm should come of her, for I shall hold you responsible with your lives," Eldin ordered.

The two saluted Eldin and helped Elrik from her seat. Then they took up positions on either side of her for the walk back to her tent. By the Goddess, it felt good to move their legs again!

"Shall I see thee in the morn before I leave, Captain?" Elrik inquired.

"Most assuredly, treasured Mother," Eldin replied.

With that said, Elrik slowly strode away from the table, leaving Kiya and Eldin alone at last.

"Eldin, I would verily enjoy if we strolled by the waterfall. The way the moonlight dances off of the water, well, it just does my soul good," Kiya broke the silence.

"If you wish it to be so, then I shall make it so," Eldin replied, rising from the bench and offering Kiya her hand.

Eldin helped Kiya to her feet and felt a jolt of electricity flow up her arm as Kiya placed her hand on Eldin's forearm. Eldin loved the way the moonlight lit up Kiya's face; she looked like an angel. She positively glowed. Such radiant beauty, almost like...Eldin stiffened slightly.

"Is something wrong, Captain?" Kiya inquired, feeling Eldin's muscles tense under her hand.

"No, nothing is wrong. I just was thinking," Eldin started.

"Well, that explains it," Kiya baited her trap.

Eldin looked at the young woman questioningly. Kiya just grinned as a response.

"Explains what?" Eldin finally gave in and asked as her curiosity got the better of her.

"The smoke pouring out of your ears. I must say, you have positively set your brains on fire from the effort of it," Kiya sprung the trap.

Eldin laughed as the tension drained from her. *Oh, demon Shamaness, how easily you make me forget my troubles!* They continued a slow stroll toward the waterfall, unaware of the eyes that were on them.

Suddenly, the hairs on the back of Eldin's neck rose as she got the feeling of the intruder's watchful gaze. She looked around warily. Her senses were very rarely wrong about things like this.

A large figure ducked back into her tent.

"My krillits are on the healer," Elrik restated as she blew out the candle next to her sleeping skins.

Eldin gently guided them away from the direct route to the waterfall. Kiya realized the change in direction but kept her silence. She placed her trust in the handsome captain.

After walking an additional ten candledrips, the two appeared on the far side of the waterfall. This side was more secluded, and Eldin would be able to hear someone trying to sneak up on them as they walked across the carpet of deadfall to reach that position. Not having anything else to offer, Eldin removed her cloak and laid it on the ground at Kiya's feet.

"Kiya, if it pleases you," Eldin stated as she helped Kiya to sit upon the cloak.

"Oh, it pleases me very much," Kiya exclaimed enthusiastically as she looked at the waterfall and the beauty of the surrounding forest.

Eldin joined her on the cloak and stretched out. She reminded Kiya of a contented panther after a big kill. Kiya smiled; she was indeed the most handsome woman she had ever met.

"Eldin, would you tell me a little about your childhood? What was it like growing up as the daughter of General Elrik? I wager you were hard-pressed to succeed," Kiya inquired.

"Do you wager?" Eldin chuckled. "I guess I was. I never thought it was that bad, except maybe for the fisticuffs. You may find this hard to believe, but I did not want to hurt anyone. I thought it was wrong. Most thought I was weak for that."

"I would not. I do not believe in harming others," Kiya lent Eldin her support.

"Well, no offense, but there is a big difference in being a warrior and a healer. It is kind of expected that the firstborn daughter of a military legend would follow in her footsteps and take up the sword," Eldin remarked.

"Did you have no choice, then?" Kiya asked, concern evident in her voice.

"Oh, I had a choice, either follow the sword or find a new family," Eldin replied. "And since I verily like the one I have…"

"Here you are today," Kiya finished for her.

Eldin nodded. She looked out at the plunging water. How much like her life it was. Rushing out of control, finally taking a leap of faith into… what exactly? Would there be a calm pool in the end or just more rapids? Eldin flinched a little as she felt a tiny hand on her shoulder.

Kiya could not help herself. She reached out to place a consoling hand on Eldin's shoulder. She knew it could verily well cost her another whack on the nose, but she wanted so much to ease Eldin's obvious pain; she would risk it.

Eldin started to relax under Kiya's touch. It was comforting, Eldin decided. She closed her eyes and surrendered herself to the feeling of Kiya's hands as they started to knead the tension from the muscles of her neck and shoulders.

"Have you ever disagreed with Yashor laws or expectations, Kiya?" Eldin asked almost too quietly to be heard.

"Yes. I feel that we wrong a great many people. How can it be the will of the Great Goddess to enslave male-children? Why do we stone to death Amazons who love male-children instead of being a true Amazon? Why can not we accept that they were born different? How about the Amazon children we send to fight just because they are orphaned? How can that be just and right? What about the Jahru?" Kiya started her list.

Eldin's eyes opened at the last comment. The Jahru? No one spoke of them. It was as if by the simple act of speaking aloud their name, they would rise from their graves to live again. Yashor had waged a civil war with them many seasonmarks ago and had wiped them from existence… or had they?

"You would actually speak of…them? Are you not afraid?" Eldin asked.

"Humph, you act as if they were truly the demonic shamanesses the

Council declared them to be. If they were all that evil, do you not wager that they would have come back by now to avenge themselves? They are dead, and we killed them. They were our sisters, our mothers, and our lovers. They had great powers, yes; I do believe that. I also believe that they were the best healers our beloved Yashor ever knew. They were different. We feared them, and what we fear, we destroy," Kiya exclaimed before she realized that her entire tirade was high treason.

Eldin caught her momentary hesitation and regret.

"Hey, do not fear me. I shall never tell anyone of what we speak in private. It is ours alone," Eldin assured her. "Besides I too feel that Yashor deals too harshly with male-children. I wish that we would allow them their freedom. I never understood the attraction to a male-child for an Amazon, but that does not mean it could not happen simply because I do not understand it. I do not think they deserve to die for who they love in life. Who am I to judge them? I leave that to the Great Goddess. I also feel bad about the orphans. I have had to send far too many of them to the Great Feast before their time. I just had never thought much on the...others."

"Still cannot bring yourself to say 'Jahru,' Captain? Here all along I believed you to be fearless," Kiya teased her.

"Yeah, well...just do not let that get around, or my reputation will wallow with the stable muck," Eldin remarked back.

Kiya laughed at Eldin's analogy, as she could picture Eldin sitting in the middle of a stable covered with manure. Somehow, she doubted anything could ever harm the captain's reputation.

Eldin patted the spot next to her, and Kiya lay down. They looked up at the stars in companionable silence, each lost to her own thoughts.

6

The sharp blade of the dagger slid easily through the soft flesh of the rogue's throat. Warm blood exploded out of the wound, splattering the wall in a macabre tale of the woman's last few heartbeats of life. Celdi placed the body quietly to the floor. She had to make it back to Delyn before it was too late! She had to warn her!

Celdi looked out the window and quickly spotted the rest of the woman's band of brigands around her horse. Hades fire! Could they not pick a better time to wake from their drunken stupor? Celdi kicked the body at her feet out of frustration. If what she had been able to torture out of this pathetic hired sword was true, it might already be too late. Well then, what did she have to lose?

The three women looked up as pebbles rained down on them from above. Before they realized what was happening, Celdi dropped on top of the nearest one to the inn, knocking her unconscious. She quickly threw her dagger, striking another one in the throat. The woman reached up wildly, clutching at the handle as a gurgling noise was all that came of her scream. Two down, and one very enraged killer to go.

Swords were drawn in haste, and Celdi faced the last cutthroat.

"You would do well to lay down that sword and walk away from this," Celdi remarked.

"You just killed my declared; I think I would rather make a coat from your hide!" replied the tall woman.

Celdi flashed her sword in big circles at the woman. They were complex maneuvers she had learned over the seasons. Suddenly, the woman saw her other hand release the hand-dart too late. She had been distracted, and that had cost her. The dart lodged in the woman's right eye, and the venom-tipped dart worked instantly. The woman could feel her throat beginning to swell closed. In a matter of heartbeats, she would die.

"It matters little, shadow. We shall still have Yashor in the end," the woman choked out.

Celdi slid her sword back into its sheath. She had to make a decision, and fast. If she warned the Council, she would be unable to save Delyn. If she saved Delyn...well...it would be too late for the Council.

Celdi leaped upon her horse and encouraged the large mare into a gallop. She rode hard out of the small village. It was going to take her a few days of hard riding to make it back to Delyn. Her decision made, Celdi never turned back to look at the road to Yashor's capitol. The council-women, she knew, were as good as dead.

* * *

As the first rays of sunlight began to peer over the mountains of fire, Eldin snuggled into the warm body she held next to her. First one eye, then the other flew open as Eldin woke suddenly. Her arms were wrapped protectively around the small healer. She was sleeping peacefully. When exactly had they fallen asleep? Eldin smiled; the soft light of dawn made Kiya's hair glow, and she looked like a sleeping goddess in Eldin's arms. Eldin indulged herself and took in a deep breath of Kiya's scent. Her hair smelled of faint rose water and grass. Eldin knew it would only be a few more candledrips before all of camp was awake, and she knew it would be best for all concerned if they were not discovered in this manner. Reluctantly,

Eldin leaned down and was about to place a small kiss on Kiya's cheek when the healer jerked awake, bumping their heads together.

Eldin rubbed her nose. "Well, I see that you have claimed your revenge, Kiya."

Kiya blinked the sleep from her eyes.

"I am sorry. Where are we? Oh!" Kiya realized what had happened.

"I do not know when we fell asleep, only that if we do not hurry, all of camp will see us leave this place. I do not wish that reputation on you, Kiya. You are a most honorable woman," Eldin remarked.

"Thank you for your kind words, Captain," Kiya replied.

Eldin helped Kiya to her feet, and they walked swiftly back toward the healer's area. The hairs on the back of Eldin's neck rose, and she felt danger. Eldin placed a hand on Kiya's arm to stop her. Kiya looked up at Eldin, and Eldin placed her fingers over Kiya's mouth to prevent her from asking the question that was already upon her lips. Eldin sniffed the air; ah, there it was. Her senses had alerted her to the faint odor of strange campfires. It could be a raiding party of Drakknians.

"Come, Kiya. I have to get my troops ready, and we need to get you and the wounded on your way to the nearest healer's post," Eldin stated as she lengthened her stride.

Kiya felt it hard to keep up, as her legs were not nearly as long as the captain's. She was beginning to grow weary, as the pace was much faster than that to which she was accustomed. Eldin was concentrating on something, and her face showed the strain, but Kiya still found her to be the most handsome she had ever seen.

As they approached Kiya's tent, Eldin slowed. She held the tent flap open for the beautiful healer. Kiya smiled; yes, Eldin was gallant, and she was greatly enjoying the attention.

"Thank you, Captain," Kiya stated as she passed by Eldin into her tent.

"Thank you for a wonderful conversation. I would most enjoy it if we could continue it after your return," Eldin replied.

"Well then, I suggest that you do not go out and get yourself killed doing something silly and heroic in my absence, Captain," Kiya teased.

Eldin's brows knitted together as she digested this. Was she being serious?

"I only jest with you. Well, perhaps truth be told, half-jest. I would enjoy it if you were still alive when I return with the supplies," Kiya replied in earnest.

"I shall give it my greatest attention then, dear healer," Eldin stated, then turned to go.

"Will you see us before we leave, Captain?" Kiya quickly asked before Eldin got too far away to hear her.

"You may wager your krillits on it," Eldin replied. "Better hurry and get your wagons together. Perhaps my mother will accompany you to the post on her way back to her keep."

* * *

Elrik stared at her daughter in disgust. When had she gotten so soft?

"You want me to overlook a bunch of wounded, Eldin?! That is male-child's work. I cannot believe you would even ask it of me," Elrik grumbled.

"I do not see it as 'male-child's work,' Mother. You yourself claimed that they should be in the kitchen cooking and not with a sword in their hands. What my wounded need is a sword in capable hands. You will also have the walking wounded as guards. I am not asking you to take them all the way to the post; just stay with them until the road splits. Is that really asking too much from you, Mother?" Eldin replied.

Elrik chewed on her lower lip while she thought it over. This was certainly going to slow her down, perhaps a few extra candlemarks, perhaps an extra day. On the other hand, she had been a general and knew the risk of moving that many wounded this close to enemy territory. Resigned, Elrik let out a huge sigh.

"Fine, I shall take them as far as the split in the road. I must get back to Dinyar before the fall feast. She made me promise, and I have never broken a promise to your other mother in my life. I do not intend on starting now," Elrik stated.

* * *

Eldin stopped at a redberry bush on her way to see Kiya. It was almost first-feast, and the wounded always ate first. She wanted to pick a few berries for Kiya's gruel. They would at least make the warm mush taste a little better. Eldin had been using berries for her gruel since she found this bush two days after they arrived. That seemed an eternity ago. She picked a pouchful and continued her trek to the healer's side of camp.

Kiya spotted Eldin walking toward her. She was just finishing a bandage change. Kiya smiled at the injured warrior and wiped the salve from her hands on the cloth she had draped over her shoulder.

"I believe your captain is coming to see you," Kiya told her.

Eldin's face broke into a lopsided grin as she reached the wagon where Kiya was standing. One thing could be said for the healer, she was not lazy. She had already seen three wagons full of wounded in the time Eldin had been gone.

"Captain! I am honored that you would come to see me," the wounded warrior stated as she bowed her head and covered her heart with her fist in salute.

Eldin stole one quick look at Kiya before turning her attention to the warrior.

"I see that you are recovering quickly. I am most pleased. I must ask you, can you stand?" Eldin inquired.

"I am certain of it, Captain. If you ask it of me, I shall find a way," the warrior gushed, pride reflecting from her deep brown eyes.

"Good. I need capable hands in which to trust the healer and the other wounded. I need you to provide protection for the caravan to the nearest healer's post. I shall find others to help as well, and you will be escorted by my mother as far as the split in the road," Eldin explained.

"I will guard them with my life, Captain. You may count on me!" the warrior stated.

"What is your name, proud warrior?" Eldin asked.

"I am called Lyndon, though I know not who my mothers were. I have been with you as a trainling for eight seasonmarks and a warrior for three turns of the moons. I have dreamed of the day that you would ask me to carry a sword for you. I am honored to guard the wounded," Lyndon explained.

"I am the one who is honored, Lyndon. I am honored that you would show me such loyalty when I have not even learned your name in all this time. I am truly sorry for that. I am shamed that I did not learn it sooner," Eldin replied.

"Do not even think it, Captain. You have been busy leading this Sword Corps. No one expects you to learn all of our names, especially when some of us are only here for a few sunrises before we are killed," Lyndon excused.

Eldin looked at her boots. Suddenly, they seemed too large for her. Perhaps the warrior was right. Perhaps it was just as well; if she knew all of their names, it would be a slippery slope into friendship. Then it would be almost impossible to order them into peril. That was the perfect reasoning behind the Council's laws separating warriors and officers. For the sake of Yashor, Eldin must remain mostly aloof, with no real friends, except those of her honor guard, other officers, and perhaps the healer.

"I shall leave you to eat your first-feast, then I shall return and get you and the others armed," Eldin replied.

Eldin turned towards Kiya and motioned her head to the side toward Kiya's tent. Kiya nodded a response. Eldin walked alone to Kiya's tent and slipped inside. Mere heartbeats later, Kiya joined her.

"You wanted something of me, Captain?" Kiya asked.

"Not really, I wanted to give you these berries that I picked on my way over here. I use them in my gruel. It helps the flavor and makes it more palatable," Eldin explained while she emptied the berries into her hand.

Kiya smiled; she was indeed enjoying all of this attention. She walked past Eldin to a big iron kettle that was suspended over a fire-pit in the center of the tent. She lifted the lid and motioned for Eldin to dump the entire contents of her hands into the pot. Eldin walked to the pot and looked in; it was nearly filled with hot gruel. The gruel had a peculiar blue tint.

"Is this fresh?" Eldin asked, as she added the redberries.

Kiya smiled. "Yes, Eldin, it is fresh. The redberries will go well with the blueberries that I picked a few days ago. I always add berries to the wounded warriors' gruel. It helps them heal quicker. I also add nuts when they are available. Would you help me shell some?"

Eldin felt her cheeks turning crimson; of course the healer would already know about any berry bushes in the area. Eldin helped Kiya shell the small pile of walnuts. Then Kiya broke them into smaller pieces before they too were dumped into the gruel.

"It helps stretch the nuts if I break them up. The warriors have a greater chance of getting a few smaller pieces in their bowls as opposed to only a few getting the larger nuts," Kiya explained to Eldin.

Eldin turned to leave when she felt a shiver run up her spine. She looked at Kiya's small hand on her arm and turned back toward the healer.

"Captain, would you consider sharing first-feast with me? Usually, I eat last, but I know how busy you are; perhaps if we eat fast..." Kiya rationalized.

Eldin flashed her a brilliant grin.

"I would be most honored. We will eat fast, serve the wounded, and then I must get your wagons on the road," Eldin replied.

"Please, have a seat," Kiya invited Eldin to sit in one of two chairs at her small table in the corner.

"Do you often have company for meals, Kiya?" Eldin teased.

"I often have wounded that come in need of stitching small wounds. However, today this table shall serve a nicer function," Kiya replied.

Eldin sat, and Kiya placed a bowl of gruel in front of her. She handed Eldin a wooden spoon and then went back for a bowl of her own. When Kiya returned, Eldin was standing, waiting for her. Eldin pulled the chair out for Kiya and helped her to her seat. Then Eldin returned to her own chair.

"I must say, I have never seen gruel look better. I am actually looking forward to eating it," Eldin said in wonder.

Eldin shoveled a spoonful of the warm gruel into her mouth. It was fruity, nutty, and actually delicious. She rolled it around on her tongue, savoring the flavor before swallowing. Only a Demon Shamaness could make gruel taste good!

Kiya watched Eldin taste her special concoction. She was enjoying the look of utter euphoria on the captain's face. How nice it would be to wake to such a face every day. How nice to...

Eldin looked up suddenly and caught Kiya watching her. Kiya looked down at her own spoonful of gruel. She was certainly aware of those intense ice-blue eyes upon her.

"So tell me, Kiya, what is your favorite part of the day?" Eldin asked.

"I enjoy watching the sun set. It is usually quiet and peaceful. It means that another day of work is over, and I can relax a bit. I also like it just before dawn. It is cool, and the birds start their chirping. I enjoy the serenade," Kiya explained.

Suddenly, the tent flap flew open, and Maric came bursting through. Eldin, startled, jumped to her feet and almost spilled the bowls of gruel.

Maric's eyes widened as she realized what she had interrupted. "I am sorry, Captain. I have been searching for you. There are reports of riders coming hard toward camp. They will reach camp in about five more candledrips. What are your orders?" Maric relayed the message.

"Have a receiving party ride out and intercept them. If they are enemy scouts, I do not want them getting close enough to read our camp layout and then change course and outrun us back to their camp. If they are friendly, then the receiving party may welcome them to camp and give them an escort. Go quickly, and send the party," Eldin decided in a heartbeat.

Eldin turned back toward Kiya as Maric raced from the tent. "I'm sorry, Kiya. I must attend to this. Perhaps we shall be able to share a meal sometime soon."

Eldin bowed to Kiya and retreated quickly from the tent. Goddess, why was it so difficult to leave? What form of magic was drawing her to Kiya? Why was the healer so easily able to make her forget about the impending danger? *Remember the smoke you smelled, you fool?* Perhaps it was better that she left anyway. *Demon Shamaness.*

Kiya watched the tent flap close on Eldin's lovely backside. She sighed. Was it worth all of the interruptions to get to know the captain? Was it worth her stomach being tied in knots whenever the captain was close by?

"Yes, it is worth that and much more," Kiya answered herself aloud.

* * *

Maric's legs protested the pace that she was forcing them to keep. Funny, how she never felt her age more than when she had to run. *Bah, what is age but a number? Oh and kligage, do not forget the kligage that has been placed upon this old body,* Maric reminded herself. It is like a wagon. When the wagon is new, everything works so well. After many kligs, little parts begin to creak. Maric smiled; her body creaked a lot. She really was an "old battle wagon." Finding the guards that she needed, Maric relayed the captain's orders and watched as the young women broke into two groups, one forming a pike line and the others getting on their horses and taking off in the direction of the threat. *No creaky ones there,* she admired their agility and strength.

* * *

Delyn heard the horses' hooves tearing up the ground as they thundered toward camp. She grabbed her sword and emerged from her tent, ready to face any challenge. Delyn caught sight of Elrik emerging from a tent across the pathway from her. How easy it would be in all of the chaos to slip up behind her and... The gleam in Delyn's eyes flashed her vengeful soul. In the next heartbeat, Elrik turned and met her glare with a steady gaze. Delyn felt the rage subside while trapped in the legend's icy stare. Delyn broke the contact and looked at the ground, silently admitting defeat.

* * *

Eldin relaxed a little as she heard the sound of the all-clear blown on the ram horn by the receiving party. She slowed back down to a walk. She could concentrate on seeing her mother and the healer off. Eldin grabbed a nearby guard and sent her to relay a message to Delyn. Delyn could handle the receiving party and whoever had come to camp.

Eldin returned to Kiya and helped her finish feeding the wounded. It had taken half a candlemark; however, they were just about ready to leave. Kiya was inside her tent marking the remainder of the supplies, should Eldin's troops need them in her absence. Eldin opened the flap and peeked inside.

Kiya absently took a dagger from the table and used it to cut some twine. Eldin's eyes grew large as she recognized her missing backup weapon. Eldin strode inside and stood beside Kiya, watching her cut twine with the ultra-sharp blade, dulling many candlemarks of Eldin's sweat-breaking work with the whetting stone.

"May I please have my dagger back?" Eldin inquired, a little annoyed.

"It depends; are you going to use it to kill someone?" Kiya asked.

Eldin's forehead wrinkled as she scowled at the healer; what kind of question was that?

"Of course I will kill someone with it if need be. It is my backup weapon. I rely on that should I be separated from my sword," Eldin replied to the silly question.

"Then no, you may not have it back. You would use this as an instrument of death; I use it as a tool for preserving life. Which do you find more noble, Captain?" Kiya argued.

"What kind of demon-possessed thinking is that? First, you tell me not to go out and get myself killed in your absence. Then you tell me that I may not have my backup weapon because I may kill someone with it. What is it you are trying to do? Drive me absolutely mad?! You are the most infuriating woman, Kiya. I cannot believe that I was starting to…that is…I mean…oh, never mind!" Eldin stammered, searching for the words to express her confused heart.

Kiya turned away from Eldin. "Then go, you big overgrown…"

Eldin interrupted Kiya. "Oh, I see what you are trying to do, here. Now it is as obvious as the nose on my face. You figure it will be easier to leave me if you are angry with me. It will be easier for all concerned. You almost managed it."

Eldin spun Kiya around to face her and lifted her chin with her fingers. She could feel Kiya's breath coming in great gasps, near sobs. Eldin bent forward, her heart pounding in her chest. This desire, this…need, it was all consuming. She felt Kiya coursing through her veins. There had only been one other who affected her this way. Eldin blinked; maybe it was time to put J'min's ghost to rest. She watched as Kiya closed her eyes and surrendered to her. Eldin took a deep breath, closed her eyes, and prepared to lose her soul to another.

"Captain!"

Eldin's eyes flew open from the familiar voice. She turned to see an enraged Delyn staring at them. She shuddered from the intensity of Delyn's stare.

"The visitors are from the Council. You have been summoned to leave for the Council at once," Delyn stated through clenched teeth.

Eldin stepped between Kiya and Delyn. "Do you have a problem, Lieutenant?"

"Nothing that cannot be solved," Delyn stated ominously, her hand resting on the hilt of her sword.

"Delyn, you go back to the command tent. I will be there in a few candledrips," Eldin commanded.

"No. I am not leaving here without you, Eldin," Delyn defied her.

Eldin turned to Kiya. She gently caressed Kiya's face with the back of her fingers and said, "I shall return before you leave; that is a promise."

Delyn glared at Kiya. If it were possible to kill with a single look, Kiya would have been reduced to ashes on the spot.

Eldin turned, grabbed Delyn by the arm, and pulled her from Kiya's tent.

"Come. We need to talk in the command tent," Eldin told her.

Delyn grinned at Kiya through the open tent flap like a predator that has just spotted its prey. She made a threat without saying a word. Kiya stared after the lieutenant. What was wrong with her?

"I now understand why you have not come to visit me, Eldin; you have been too busy with that...that *Jahru*," Delyn slandered Kiya.

"I cannot believe that you would call our healer a..." Eldin's voice drifted off.

"Something wrong, Eldin? Can you not say the words? It is easy. Jah... ru, and if you cannot say that word, just say what she is: an abomination," Delyn spat angrily.

"That is enough, Lieutenant! You would be wise to mind your tongue," Eldin admonished.

"Ha! Mind my tongue, it is *yours* that was about to be plunged into the healer," Delyn retorted.

"Listen to me, Lieutenant. I am leaving, but if I hear that you have so much as uttered a cross word to our healer, I shall make certain you are tried before the Council and stripped of your rank. I shall further make certain that you rot in a dungeon so deep underneath Yashor that even the worms won't find your stinking corpse!" Eldin threatened Delyn.

"My, my, how the mighty have fallen. Are you so certain of your feelings for the little whore? Have you indeed given her your heart? You never offered me such a prize. To think, I was going to ask you to declare with me, and all the while you were playing 'keep' with our disgusting healer! Be careful that you do not break her, Eldin. She is such a tiny, frail thing; much like my grandmother!" Delyn seethed.

Eldin grabbed Delyn by the collar of her tunic. She picked the woman up off the ground with one arm and drew back her fist. Delyn smirked at Eldin. Slowly, Eldin returned to her senses and released her second-in-command.

"Just go. Go to whatever soldier is giving you pleasure this day. Oh, do not think I have not known about the others. You see, they never bothered me. It was as our arrangement. When did you become my keeper? I never offered you my heart, because I never loved you. We were partners of release; that was all. You agreed to that. Now, I am no longer in need of that arrangement. Mark my words, Delyn, you have never shown me anything of yourself that I would value in a mate. You are a wonderful soldier, but you have no understanding of compassion. I could never love someone who was as cold in killing as you," Eldin explained.

Delyn stared at Eldin. She knew it was over. It was over; however, Eldin would be away for a long time to Council. In all of that time, there were things that could happen to a small, frail healer out on the front lines. Delyn's lips curled in a feral grin. *Just you wait, healer.*

"So go then, Eldin. Go back to your Jahru. I will have my fill of all these soldiers. Then maybe I will educate the trainlings. Oh, they are hot for you, but I am sure that I can turn their heads as well. I know they find powerful Amazons a turn-on, and none is as powerful as I am. Not even you, Eldin. You have become *soft.* Go on and get back to your little whore before she changes her mind," Delyn stated.

Delyn turned and left alone. Eldin watched her leave, and sighed. She had never meant to hurt the lieutenant. It had been Delyn's idea in the first place. When had Delyn changed?

7

Kidak opened her eyes slowly. It was morning, and that old fox had already been in her room and had started a fire in the small fireplace. The small banked fire had chased away the early morning chill. Kidak pushed back the heavy quilts and slowly swung her legs over the edge of the bed. She quickly found her soft fur-lined chamber shoes and slipped them on. Ah, now that felt good. Before the cold could set into her bones, she found her chamber coat and slipped it over her sleeping shift.

Kidak rose and stretched the kinks out of her body. Great Goddess, growing older was a pain in more ways than one! After a quick visit with the chamber pot, she padded softly over to the small desk in the corner of her room and retrieved her medicinal pouch. Kidak opened the small leather pouch and pinched off a small piece of "well" tree bark. Her ancestors had been nothing if practical in their naming all of the Goddess' creations. Kidak placed the bark in her mouth and began to chew it slowly. It was a spicy bark, but it did give one a sense of wellness and much energy.

Kidak jumped as she heard a quiet rapping on her bedroom door.

"Come in; it is unlocked," Kidak called out.

Kidak was startled when the young woman that her aunt employed entered the room, looking wildly about.

"Have you seen Master Terdak? I cannot seem to find her anywhere," the small girl managed to ask.

Kidak's chest seemed to tighten and squeeze the breath from her. What had happened to her auntie? *Great Goddess, let her still live…*

Kidak took the stairs two at a time as she bolted down the stairwell. She only slowed enough to keep from losing her balance as she reached the bottom. Kidak searched the great room for any sign of Terdak. The room looked undisturbed. She then headed for the kitchen. The wood stove was lit, but the fire was almost out, and the morning's firewood was not in yet. Perhaps she was just running late and was out at the woodpile gathering the morning's supply.

Kidak exited the inn and ran to the back of the barn. There was an enormous woodpile, but no Terdak. Now panic was setting in on Kidak. She could only think of one other place. *Goddess, let Terdak be in the privy!*

* * *

Terdak could not see; her attacker had blindfolded her, but she could hear their footsteps as they paced back and forth before her.

"Hades fire, would you stop? You are going to wear a hole in the floor with all of that pacing! Besides, you are not going to get out of the trouble you are in just by pacing yourself silly." Terdak exclaimed.

"Shut up! Just shut up, you old bat!" The assassin yelled.

Terdak heard more footsteps outside the room.

"You would do well to be silent. I have no use for you…I would just as soon cut you where you sit; however, I must wait for your great-niece. I think she should enjoy watching you scream as I skin you from head to toe," the assassin proclaimed.

Well, they must obviously be outside of the village, for the attacker was not afraid to raise her voice. And that voice *was* obviously female.

"What has Kidak done to you? What could possibly be so grievous as to make you act in this uncivilized manner?" Terdak inquired.

"Don't try to get into my head, old woman. You wouldn't like it there. We are going to cleanse Yashor and raise a nation founded on strong leadership. Kidak is weak. She does not value the strength of our Amazon sisters any longer. She will pay for that with her life. First, she will watch me as I carve a new suit from your hide," the assassin promised.

Please Goddess, no. I was so close. I do not wish to live forever. Terdak worked on her bonds. They were tight. If only she could get them to just loosen a little, maybe she could work them off and stop this madness before it was too late.

* * *

Kidak was almost at the privy when she felt a slight sting in her neck. She reached up toward it. Before she could pull the dart from her neck, her world went black. Kidak fell to the ground. No one heard the thump except the shadow that moved toward her unconscious form. Quickly, the rogue ripped the dart from the councilwoman's neck and picked her up. She was whisked away before anyone noticed she was gone.

* * *

Kidak slowly opened one eye and then the other as her head felt like she had consumed too many flagons of wine. Kidak tried to raise her hand to stop the pounding in her temples but found to her horror that her hands were bound behind her back. Pushing the fuzziness from her mind proved difficult, yet Kidak knew she must.

"Don't fight the ties, Kidak. They will only hear you and come running," Terdak whispered.

Kidak tried to focus. Slowly, her favorite aunt's face started to appear before her.

"Where are we, Auntie?" Kidak asked.

"I do not know, precious. I only know that they left me blindfolded until they brought you in. Then they removed the blindfold and told me to enjoy my view. I was wondering if you were dead, but then they tied your hands and I knew that you were not," Terdak quietly explained.

All too soon, two rough-looking women entered the room. Kidak worried for Terdak's safety as she noticed they both carried swords. Sharp-looking swords.

"I demand to know what your intentions are toward my aunt," Kidak boomed in her very most authoritative voice.

"You are not in a position to demand anything, Councilwoman. If I were you, I would be telling this old waste of breath that I loved her, for she is soon to pass on to the Great Feast. Do not fret; you shall join her soon after," the smaller woman with the dark hair sneered.

"If you dare to touch..." Kidak started.

Suddenly, Kidak felt the sharp edge of a blade at her throat.

"What? Just what shall you do about it? You are about to die, Councilwoman, and the new Yashor is about to be born," the tall blonde woman interrupted.

Terdak tried desperately to untie her hands. Her wrists were raw from the constant rubbing friction. She bit back the pain and continued to work at loosening them.

"Listen to me; I do not know who you are or what you want, but I beg you to hear me out. Please, do not try to harm me. I am *Jahru*. I cannot be killed. If you try, every wound you inflict on me shall only make me younger and stronger while robbing you of your own strength until you die," Terdak admitted.

The assassins looked at each other. Laughter erupted inside the small room. Jovial tears born from the outburst streamed down the two cut-throats' cheeks.

"I must admit; that is the best excuse we have heard yet as to why we should not kill an ordered death-mark. I have to tell my declared that one," the dark assassin giggled.

"Enough talk! Everyone knows that the Jahru are dead and gone, and we have a job to do. It is nothing personal, old woman. However, I intend to make you scream. Please try to stay awake. It shall only take longer if I have to keep stopping to wake you," the blonde stated as she approached Terdak.

Kidak tried to stand. She was fighting with all of her might against her bonds, but she could not break free.

"No! You leave her alone. Your quarrel is with me! Do what you want with me, but you leave my aunt out of this!" Kidak screamed.

The dark assassin grabbed a hold of the struggling Kidak to force her to watch. Kidak could not stop them, no matter how hard she tried.

"Please, do not do this. I have warned you. Please, I am so close to dying this time. Only by nature will I pass, not by violence. It is irreversible. Please!" Terdak pleaded.

Terdak felt the blade slicing through her cheek. It hurt, but only for a heartbeat. She felt the burst of energy within her. *Damn them to Hades!* She felt the blade slicing along her arm, neatly removing a long section of skin. Again the energy flowed through her veins. *Stupid, stupid girl! They never listen.*

Terdak tried to keep from screaming as the blonde continued to cut. Suddenly, the blonde dropped the sword from her hand as she doubled over in pain.

"Deras, what is wrong?" the dark one asked, almost in a panic.

"Goddess, it hurts! I feel so weak. What form of magic is this?!" Deras cried.

Kidak could not believe her eyes as Deras' skin began to darken and wrinkle. It was as if she were aging centuries a candledrip. Deras held her hand up in front of her face and screamed. Dark liver-colored age spots covered the wrinkled flesh. Deras felt a pain in her chest. It was as if someone were sitting on her, preventing her from breathing.

"You demon! You die now!" the dark assassin yelled as she stepped to Deras' aid.

The dark one took up Deras' sword and sliced Terdak's throat. Immediately, she grabbed her own throat and looked at the old woman through panic-stricken eyes. The old woman's throat wound was closing and healing itself at an incredible rate. It was not possible! Suddenly the pain hit the dark one and she could not breathe. Kidak watched as blood flowed down the dark assassin's neck. It was as if she had cut her own throat. She too fell at Terdak's feet. Deras looked at her dead friend and clutched at her chest. It felt as if some unseen hand were squeezing the life from her barely beating heart. It took less than five candledrips for her heart to stop beating altogether. Deras now lay dead at Terdak's feet as well.

Kidak watched in disbelief as her ancient aunt's wounds healed on their own and the wrinkles faded from her face. She lost all trace of age and looked to be the age of her own daughter, Kiya.

"You were not lying?" Kidak managed, barely able to keep her fear from the surface.

"No, Kidak. I was not lying. I am Jahru. I come from a long line of Jahru. In fact, I believe you and Kiya are probably gifted with Jahru blood; you just never knew about it to use it," Terdak quietly responded.

"How? How can this be? All of the Jahru were killed hundreds of seasonmarks ago," Kidak asked in disbelief.

"No, not all. Several of us formed a pact. We went to the great Jahru leader, Rydak. We asked to be blessed with an irreversible spell. We could never be killed with violence. Only natural aging could kill us. It would give us the chance to reproduce and protect the Jahru line. If we had not done this, we most certainly would have been wiped out by our own people," Terdak explained.

"Rydak. Why, that would make me a descendant of the Jahru leader?" Kidak questioned.

"Yes, Kidak. That is your heritage. I am actually approaching 257 seasonmarks of age. I was so looking forward to dying. I have seen too much. I am tired. I wished to pass on to the Great Feast. Rydak was my mother. I am also your great, great, great, great, grandmother. I have had to change my name every time some fool tried to take my life. Now, Terdak will be 'dead,' and I will have to create a new name for myself, a new life, and start over. I really do not wish it, but what else can I do?" Terdak admitted.

"You really are that old? Why not become a councilwoman and try to change the laws so that you may live in peace without fear of retribution?" Kidak inquired.

Terdak gave Kidak the "look." Kidak realized she had just asked an obvious question.

"Kidak, my precious, do you think I have not already tried that, more than once? It only made me a target, and after several assassination attempts made me live much longer than I ever wanted to suffer. I have buried more declared life-mates than I ever wanted to love in the first place. I have had to watch other life-mates suffer as they have thought me dead. I have been to four of my own funeral pyres. Never did they have a body, but with all of the blood, and with me never returning, it is always assumed that I was killed and my body consumed by scavengers," Terdak reflected. "As it will be assumed here."

Terdak was able to finally loosen her bindings and slip free. She untied Kidak, who examined their two attackers. Both of them looked as though they were over a hundred seasonmarks old. Their skin was as wrinkled as dried-out rotten fruit, and they smelled of age and death.

"Are we to just leave them here?" Kidak inquired.

"I would think it only fair," Terdak replied.

"As you wish, Auntie," Kidak relented.

Kidak could not bring herself to turn away from the attackers. It was beginning to sink in, and reality was far stranger than all of the tall tales she had ever heard, combined. It was also sinking in that she was now an outlaw, albeit one that no one knew existed but a small select group.

"What have we done?" Kidak whispered.

8

Eldin stood in front of her district's army and addressed the warriors. "It is true. I have been summoned to the Council of Nine. I have no idea how long I shall be gone, but until I return, or until another superior ranking officer arrives, Lieutenant Delyn is in command. I trust that none shall give her a difficult time, as this shall result in severe punishments. I shall miss you all. It has been an honor serving with each one of you," Eldin concluded.

Eldin walked over to where her mother stood and grasped her forearm in a warrior's handshake. Elrik pulled her daughter to her and embraced her in a fierce hug. It was the kind that she had rarely allowed herself to indulge in as a military leader, the kind that said, "I am your mother, and I love you beyond reason." Eldin allowed herself to feel all of her mother's love, for she knew it could be a long time until she was able to see her again. Finally, Eldin reluctantly pulled back from the tight embrace.

"I shall miss you, Mother. I shall try to stop by the keep on my way to the Council Hall and on the way back here. I hope that I am able to stay for a few candlemarks each way. Thank you for taking care of my wounded," Eldin quietly spoke.

"And the healer? You did not thank me for taking care of your healer, Eldin. I should think *that* was what you had really wanted to thank me for," Elrik replied.

Eldin shifted, visibly uncomfortable. *Demon Shamaness, even Mother sees what you have done to me.*

"Oh, do not fret. I am not going to spook her away. I shall not even mention you. I know how shy your heart has become," Elrik reassured her.

"My heart is bold enough in battle, which is what counts to a soldier. Love...now that is the fool's folly. I shall leave that for the poets and politicians," Eldin spouted.

"As you wish, Captain," Elrik responded. *I still have my krillits on the healer.*

Eldin walked back to the healer's area. The wagons were loaded, and the walking wounded were getting prepared for the trip. They were checking swords, bows, arrows, crossbows, bolts, and their armor for any damage that needed mending. Eldin smiled; they would do anything for Yashor. It was heartening to see the devotion of these soldiers.

"Were you looking for someone in particular, or could any old healer do?" Kiya asked as she walked up behind Eldin.

"Well, that depends on the healer. I have a wound that needs tending," Eldin answered.

"Then you better get inside my tent. I only have a few supplies left. I should take a look at that wound," Kiya ordered softly.

Eldin chuckled at the soft command. She walked to the tent, feeling Kiya's eyes devouring her with each step. It was a little disconcerting. Eldin suddenly felt like...prey. She grinned at a memory that feeling triggered. The last woman who had so openly stalked her backside had been a lot like the healer. *J'min...I wonder where you are now? Are you in pain? Are you saving me a place at the Great Feast?*

Kiya watched Eldin's perfect backside as she walked toward Kiya's tent. It was such a lovely sight. Kiya continued stealing glances at Eldin's body until they reached the tent.

Once inside, Kiya watched as Eldin shuffled her feet nervously. It was almost as if she were changing her mind about being there.

"Why was your lieutenant so upset with finding us here together? Are you indeed spoken for?" Kiya asked the question that had been on her mind since the early morning.

"Goddess, no. I...we...I...I cannot speak of this! Trust me when I say that I am not spoken for in any way." Eldin tried to get Kiya to drop the shameful subject.

"You better speak of it, for I am still not understanding why your lieutenant was so upset. Who owns your heart? Why is she upset?" Kiya demanded.

"I cannot tell you that. It...it just would not be...I...you would...just please trust me." Eldin pleaded.

"Why cannot you trust me enough to tell me? What is going on, Eldin? You say trust you, yet you do not extend the same courtesy to me," Kiya replied, her voice raising a little in frustration. "If you cannot speak truth to me, then why should I believe that you have honorable intentions toward me? Either tell me what is going on, or leave, Eldin."

Eldin closed her eyes. She felt trapped. If she told Kiya the truth, would Kiya just turn her away in disgust? If she said nothing, then Kiya would send her away because she could not trust her. Damn it to Hades! Eldin took a deep breath. Well, if she confessed to the illegal pleasures of the flesh and explained it, perhaps Kiya would understand, and she would still have a chance to win her heart.

"The lieutenant and I share pleasures of the flesh because it...well, it helps to relieve the battlefield lust. It is not about holding her heart, but about holding her...flesh. Through mutual release we are able to... that is...surely you must understand. I do not wish anything with her but release. That is all. I mean...I could never...not with you...I cannot speak of this. It is best if you just trust me. I can make it so good for you." Eldin fought for the words to explain how little Delyn meant to her and how much Kiya was like J'min.

Kiya felt Eldin's words hit her like a physical slap. How dare Eldin try to seduce her for only release! Kiya felt foolish. Eldin was probably sharing her bedroll with half of this army! Why did she think that she would be special?

"Get out! Get out now! I do not wish to see you again," Kiya ordered.

"Kiya, what have I done? I thought you would understand…" Eldin tried to explain herself again.

Kiya leveled the captain with a look that burned into Eldin's flesh. The fire inside those green eyes would have reduced Eldin to ashes. Eldin shuddered.

"I have no intention of 'understanding' the way you play with a gift from the Goddess. You make me sick, Captain. Now get out of my tent." Kiya spat the words out of her mouth as though she were physically making herself dirty through the mere act of saying them.

Eldin took a step toward Kiya. Kiya grabbed a bowl off the table and threw it at Eldin. It flew perilously close to her head. Eldin felt the air disturbed by her ear as the dish sailed past.

"Don't…don't you come near me! I shall never allow you to take me, so do not even try it. I would die before I suffered your foul lips upon me!" Kiya promised.

Eldin felt her heart breaking. What had she said? What had she done that was so foul? She only felt love for this woman. Eldin gasped. Love? Could it really be?

Kiya picked up a heavy metal skillet that one of the smithies had forged for her. She turned toward Eldin, holding the object as a weapon.

"I said, get out!" Kiya screamed.

Eldin felt the words. They washed over her body like a flood…drowning her. She lowered her head, and her shoulders slumped in defeat as she started for the tent flap.

"I shall not be returning to your army, Captain. I shall be writing the Council for a transfer," Kiya told the retreating captain.

"As you wish, Honorable Healer," Eldin responded in defeat.

* * *

Maric held Thunder's reins for Eldin. She noticed that Eldin did not look well as she approached. Were Eldin's proud shoulders…slumping?

"Maric, do not concern yourself. I see the look in your eyes, dear friend. It is better this way. I am leaving you in charge of the honor guard.

Please continue to provide the camp with guards. It allows the soldiers to get much-deserved rest; rest that they will need when the Drakknians attack again. I will send word if your orders are to change." Eldin quietly gave her orders as she took the reins and mounted Thunder. "Please look after the healer. I fear that Lieutenant Delyn is going to try to harm her in some way. Please ensure that she is not successful."

"As you command, so shall it be done." Maric saluted Eldin, the timbre of her voice making her confusion evident.

Eldin spurred Thunder lightly. She rode quickly out of the camp, never looking back. Maric could only watch as Eldin's heart broke.

Kiya watched Eldin ride out of sight. She sighed. If she did not love Eldin, then why did it hurt so much to send her away? It did not matter anymore. The captain was only interested in pleasures of the flesh, not a life-mate. That was something that Kiya would never do. When she finally gave her body away, it would be to the woman that she was to spend all eternity with. It would be to the woman who also held and protected her heart.

Eldin rode Thunder as silent tears streaked down her face. The passing landscape began to blur. Her eyes were beginning to get red and puffy. *Demon Shamaness! How dare you? How dare you do this to my heart? I do not understand what I did to make you so angry. What does it matter now anyway? I shall never see you again…*

Eldin began to replace the bricks that had come down off the wall she had placed around her heart so many seasonmarks ago. It would be a cold day in Hades before she ever let anyone hurt her this way again! Love was indeed the fool's folly.

Thunder's hooves beat a soothing rhythm against the trail headed to Romyl's fortress. Eldin's misery was echoed in the song of a gurgin in the trees nearby.

9

Delyn wasted no time in hunting down Kiya. She found her gathering her belongings for the journey to the nearest healer's post. Delyn entered the tent.

"Healer, what were your last orders?" Delyn inquired, eager to find out what Eldin had been up to.

Kiya closed her eyes at the sound of Delyn's voice. She decided that it was the most evil sound she had ever heard. She could not help but to envision Eldin kissing Delyn. The image flashed before her eyes and burned into her memory. Kiya's eyes flew open and narrowed.

"My orders are to take the wounded to the nearest healer's post and resupply. I am to send out a replacement as soon as I arrive," Kiya relayed the information.

"I am curious. Why would the captain want you to leave? That would be madness. We would have no one to tend to the freshly wounded. You will stay. That is *my* order. *I* am now in command here," Delyn stated, her voice dripping with barely concealed contempt.

"As you wish. However, as I told the captain, we are almost completely out of supplies. Soon, I will have nothing with which to heal your wounded," Kiya answered.

"So be it, Jahru. Heal them with your words or suffer the consequences of allowing the warriors to die," Delyn threatened.

"I believe you have outstayed your welcome, Lieutenant. You may show yourself out. I need to check on my wounded and have the others stand down," Kiya replied, showing no concern for Delyn's threat.

Delyn glared at Kiya, and their eyes locked. The war of wills had begun in earnest. Delyn felt Kiya's gaze as almost a physical grip. She was strong. How fun it was going to be to beat her down, to break her and leave her a crumpled mess for the captain's return! *Just you wait, Jahru.*

Delyn stepped from Kiya's tent and stalked toward the command tent unaware of the eyes that followed her every move.

Maric "shadowed" Delyn until she was safely away from Kiya. How long was this going to last? How long before the inevitable happened? Maric gripped the hilt of her sword; would she be strong enough to stop the lieutenant? Goddess, she would die happy trying! *Please, Delyn, give me a reason to draw on you!*

* * *

Kiya reached the wagon train of wounded. She found Elrik and relayed the change in orders to her. Elrik's face scrunched in a scowl. Obviously, she also did not agree with the lieutenant's decision.

"Dear Healer, if you need my sword it is yours for the asking. I know not of the treachery that is surely to follow, only that my old nose smells a rat. I have learned that if you smell the stench, be careful how you step. I would be honored to take up your defense," Elrik offered, fearing that Delyn would try to harm the young woman that Eldin so openly admired… yet denied.

Kiya placed a gentle hand on Elrik's forearm. "General Elrik, I could never ask such a thing. I…I just would not feel worthy of your sword. Please, continue your journey. I believe the captain mentioned you were returning to your keep."

Elrik could do no more than offer. She had to obey the wishes of the healer. Her rank was nothing more than honorary anymore. Elrik bent her head in a silent salute to the remarkable young healer.

Kiya spread the word to the walking wounded so that they may relax and return to her care. Elrik watched her care for the wounded. It was an inspiring sight. She had no doubt as to why this woman had caught Eldin's attention. Kiya had a quiet strength that was undeniable to someone if they only took the time to look. She was also quite a beauty. Elrik silently wished Kiya well in her conquest of Eldin's heart. Then she turned to leave.

Kiya watched as Elrik mounted her horse and rode in the direction of Romyl's fortress. It had been so hard to keep her emotions from the general. Why had she even bothered? It was not like she cared if Eldin were to get into trouble over her lack of morals…right? Kiya sighed. Her head was clear, but her heart still longed for Eldin.

Kiya continued her day's work. It was the only thing that was able to keep her mind occupied and off one very attractive captain. She was grateful for the distraction.

* * *

Delyn continued to plan her revenge. It would be sweet as a river of Drakknian blood. If the Jahru was that good, perhaps she herself should sample. Delyn licked her lips in anticipation. Why yes, that would be the ultimate form of revenge. She would simply take what the captain valued, use it, and leave it broken and bloodied. When Delyn finished with the healer, she would be of no use to anyone…

* * *

Time was of no concern to Eldin. Her heart ached in ways she could not explain. It had never been this hurt. What had she done? She, Captain Eldin of Three Rivers, was considered one of the most eligible warriors in all of Yashor! Her heart was a highly sought prize, or so Maric had informed her. Maric had said the local bards tell of her life. These bards created interest in her from far and wide. Eldin scoffed at the idea. What a pile of horse dung that was! She was nobody special, just a tired warrior; just a soldier who hated having blood and gore on her hands. Eldin shook her head; she was merely a woman who was living in the shadow of her mother. More tears streamed down her cheek. How Yashor would laugh at her if anyone saw her now. She would bring dishonor upon Elrik for the tears that she shed. She was weak. Elrik had chosen wrong; Yashor was doomed.

Days had blended into one another. The sun rose; Eldin's heart ached. The sun was overhead, and she stopped and allowed Thunder to feed and rest before continuing. The sun set, and she stopped to make camp for the night. Since her heart ached so badly, she always had a cold camp. What difference was a fire? She wasn't cooking anyway. Eldin curled into a ball and allowed herself to sleep.

* * *

"Eldin, I thought you would never ask me. It would be my pleasure to accompany you to your commissioning feast. I cannot wait to see the look on my schoolmaster's face when I tell her that *my* Eldin is going to be an officer in the great Yashor Sword Corps!" J'min exclaimed, pride gleaming in her bright eyes.

Eldin grinned. She had been working so hard lately. She had just returned from her final training in the field, where she had been responsible for running food, making fires, collecting firewood, digging privies, and still having lessons in sword mastery and strategies. She could not wait to see her J'min and ask her. All Eldin had dreamed of lately involved a small woman with long hair the color of chestnuts and eyes of gold that sparkled with green flecks. Eldin's heart raced every time she saw J'min. Perhaps it was time to ask her. Perhaps it was time to lay claim to J'min's heart.

Eldin reminded J'min when she would be stopping by to escort her to the commissioning feast before she headed toward the village's market.

She walked through a maze of small shops and wagons full of goods for sale. She was looking for the perfect gift...a gift that would leave J'min speechless.

Eldin felt the small pouch that she had tucked away inside her belt. It contained her entire stipend from the War Academy. She had exactly fifteen krillits and one ruby stone that her mother Dinyar had given to her for luck. Eldin found the smithy and inquired about the horses for sale in her yard. Forty-five candledrips later, Eldin emerged from the smithy one horse wealthier and headed for the flower crone. She entered the old woman's shop and began to spin her magic with the shop's owner. Thirty candledrips passed and Eldin once again left victorious. Down to ten krillits, she went to see the jeweler. After a candlemark, Eldin shut the door to the shop behind her and placed the slip of leather that marked her purchase into her dwindling belt pouch. She would be back later to collect her most prized bobble.

It was time to see the district's council regent about a keep. Eldin felt as though she were walking on air; she had three days left to create a home that was worthy of J'min. Only three days' time until her final commissioning ceremony, where she would be commissioned by her councilwoman and assigned a post. If she did not act quickly, J'min might be spoken for the next time Eldin would be home.

* * *

Eldin's eyes flew open at the screech of an owl overhead. She looked around confused and then closed her eyes as sleep beckoned once more.

* * *

J'min leaned back into Eldin's strong chest while they rode. It was like riding in the Goddess' own garden to have Eldin's arms around her and to feel the strength of the woman that she loved surrounding her. That was the reason that J'min always insisted upon riding in front of Eldin when they shared a horse. Of course, it did not seem as though Eldin had any objections either.

It had been almost a full candlemark since they left the village of Three Rivers. J'min was curious, but Eldin would not tell her where they were going. It really did not matter, J'min would gladly go anywhere with the handsome young soldier.

Suddenly, Eldin turned her horse off the road and onto a small path. It was barely wide enough for the single horse to traverse through the thick trees, but Eldin thought it would be better if she left it this way instead of trimming the branches back. It would hide the way to their home. Then only wanted guests would know of its existence. J'min gasped as they broke through to a clearing after fifteen candledrips on the small trail. In the center of the clearing was a small keep. Its stone walls were not really very tall, and the "moat" was more of a small stream with a little arched wooden bridge over it, but it was beautiful. The bridge was adorned with ropes of flowers, and flowers cascaded over the archway into the yard. Inside the yard, a beautiful paint horse was grazing on wild grass and swatting flies with its long tail.

Eldin slowly encouraged her horse over the bridge, through the archway, and they stopped in front of the house. Unlike many houses of Yashor keeps, this one was not made of cold stone. It was an unusual wooden structure. Not as good in a defensive sense, but much prettier to the eye.

Eldin dismounted and helped J'min to the ground. She brought J'min to the doorstep of the home and stopped. Eldin got down upon one knee and held onto J'min's hand for dear life. A wreath of flowers hung on the door that spelled "Eldin and J'min." In her wildest dreams, J'min never thought she would find someone as strong and romantic as Eldin.

"J'min, I lost my heart to you long ago. I now ask that you share yours with me or return mine to me. I know that as a soldier I will not be home as often as other declared life-mates might be. I cannot offer you the peace of mind that I shall not fall in battle to leave you a premature loner. I can only offer you that while I am home and while my heart still beats, I shall love you like none other. I promise you that I shall hold your love in my soul while on the battlefield, and I shall always remain true to you. Please, will you declare yourself with me, forsaking all others?" Eldin quietly petitioned her love.

Tears of joy welled in J'min's eyes. She could find no fault in her Eldin's request. J'min nodded, as Eldin had been successful...she was utterly speechless.

Eldin placed a ring upon J'min's finger. It was a simple gold band with a single ruby cut into the shape of a heart set in its center. Eldin stood and bent forward to kiss J'min. Their lips joined in a sweet dance. Eldin burned with love. She could feel the kiss all the way through her body. She was losing her breath to the kiss. Finally, she had to come up for air. Eldin opened her eyes and gazed at Kiya.

* * *

Eldin sat bolt upright. It was still candlemarks from daylight, but she was wide awake now. She opened her belt pouch, reached inside, and felt the small gold ring with the heart of ruby. A small sigh escaped her throat. It was still there.

Eldin brushed her fingertips through her hair and collected her sleeping gear. She woke a tired and protesting Thunder to pack the rest of the supplies and then slipped the tack onto him. He nickered his protest as she climbed onto the saddle.

"Oh, I know it is early, Thunder, but who wants to sleep their life away? I promise that if we leave now, you shall have a nice stall filled with hay to sleep in and grain to feast upon tonight. We should make Romyl's fortress by nightfall. Otherwise, we shall camp another night out in the cold forest," Eldin tried to reason with the beast.

Thunder fairly grumbled as best a horse can do under the circumstances, but he picked up the pace soon after. Eldin was too disturbed to notice. What did her dream mean? Eldin looked up at the twin moons and felt a twinge in her heart.

* * *

Kiya watched the moons disappearing behind the mountains of fire. It would soon be daybreak, and she would have a full day's chores ahead of her. Was this going to be her life...day after day of wounded to attend? Would she ever again have a day to herself? Was she just being selfish? She allowed the tent flap to fall from her grasp, and she moved back to her small fire-ring.

Kiya stirred the mush in the big cauldron that hung over the fire-ring. Soon she would have plenty of mouths to feed. She reached for the kettle of water warming on the stones from the far side of the fire and poured some into her cup. She placed some leaves in it to make her morning tea.

As Kiya brought the mixture to her lips, she felt hands upon her. Her relaxing drink was knocked to the ground, and she was forced to the ground as well. Kiya felt the scream leave her lips just as a hand clamped down upon them. A fist pummeled her face over and over until all she saw was stars. When her eyes opened, she was staring into the wild eyes of a vicious predator: Delyn.

Kiya tried to fight back, but Delyn was strong and had the advantage of surprise. Delyn pinned Kiya to the ground with her body and started choking her. Kiya could not get any breath past those strong fingers that threatened to crush the life from her.

"Thought you could take what was mine, did you?! Thought I would just let a Jahru like you have *my* Eldin? You are going to pay now! Stupid little Jahru," Delyn mocked the healer.

Kiya's head was beginning to get light. Delyn was beginning to look fuzzy. Kiya felt Delyn's hand ripping her dress. A cold hand grabbed her left breast and twisted her nipple cruelly. Kiya's scream of pain was choked off by Delyn's hand on her throat. Delyn's thigh was forcing her legs apart. Kiya knew she could not hold out much longer. Without air she would pass out soon, and Goddess only knew what sort of evil treachery Delyn was capable of. *Eldin, where are you?*

* * *

Eldin pulled up on the reins suddenly as the hairs on the back of her neck stood out, warning her of danger. She scanned the area quickly, every fiber of her body screaming that something was amiss. She could find no evidence of anything out of place. Eldin gently nudged Thunder into a cautious canter; still she could not shake the ominous feeling.

* * *

Delyn released Kiya's nipple and instead sucked it into her mouth. She bit down on the sensitive nub with a vengeance. The sweet taste of blood trickled from Kiya's puncture wounds and across Delyn's taste buds. Kiya tried to scream, but once again the hand on her throat choked it back.

Delyn's hand worked its way under Kiya's dress to her mound. She felt Delyn's fingers roughly exploring her dry center, frantically searching for her opening. Kiya managed to get one arm free and clawed the right side of Delyn's face with her fingernails. She gouged the flesh, wanting to leave a lasting mark on her attacker.

Delyn howled in pain and anger, knowing full well that her beauty was forever marred by the healer. Delyn glared into Kiya's eyes as she savagely plunged three fingers into Kiya, ripping away the thin membrane of her hymen. Delyn grinned viciously, as Kiya would never again be able to offer her Goddess gift along with her heart. She would always be used... dirty...foul. Again and again, Delyn rammed herself into Kiya, tearing the lining of Kiya's walls. Warm sticky blood flowed over Delyn's fingers as she worked to get as much of herself inside of Kiya as possible...to inflict as much pain as possible. Kiya struggled with one free hand against Delyn, but it was of no use. Delyn was much too strong for her.

"You thought you could take what was mine? Mmmm, I can see now why Eldin favored you. You are so tight. Or is that just a Jahru trick? You are mine now and will always be mine. I have taken your gift. No one will want you. You are a whore, *my* whore!" Delyn sneered as she repeatedly savaged Kiya.

Pain exploded from her nether regions, and Kiya tried to make sense of it. She saw a face above Delyn's head. *Oh sweet Goddess, have you come to claim me so quickly? Thank you.*

Suddenly, the hand around her throat was gone, and Kiya filled her lungs with breath. Her demanding lungs still burned from lack of air, and she quickly gulped in another breath.

Delyn felt the blow to her head as it knocked her off of Kiya. She looked up to see Eldin's sib standing above her with her own sword in his hands. He was pointing it at her throat, and he looked like he meant to kill her.

"What do you think you are doing, male-child?! Do you not know your actions have made your life forfeit to me?" Delyn spat out as she tried to stand.

Seldar quickly brought the sword point to the soft flesh of Delyn's throat. He applied enough pressure to cause the tip to pierce the flesh and draw blood but not enough to plunge it through and kill her.

"I understand that I have drawn Amazon blood. I understand that the law allows you to take my life. However, I will not allow you to savage the healer. If you make one more move, I shall take your head. I am dead either way. Just know that I will not allow you to harm her," Seldar replied, standing firm.

"You are too late, male-child! I already had my way with that *whore!*" Delyn exclaimed proudly, holding her bloody hand before him.

Kiya could not believe her eyes. Seldar must have heard her muffled cries and come to help. He was standing there, blood flowing from his torn stitches, willing to sacrifice himself for her. How odd that Delyn could have learned something of honor from a lowly male-child.

Maric burst through the tent flap with her sword drawn. Hades fire, of all the times for nature to call. She was too late! She saw Kiya's torn dress, blood flowing down her legs, and Seldar standing between Delyn and Kiya. Had Seldar gone mad? Was he the one who attacked the healer?

"Maric, I want you to arrest this male-child. He has broken the sacred vow not to spill Amazon blood. Take him to the holding room," Delyn ordered, glaring at the male-child.

Maric misunderstood and believed Seldar to be the cause of Kiya's injuries. He would die for that! Maric turned and glared at Seldar as she advanced on him, ready to take his head off his body. She raised her sword to strike a death blow, but oddly, he did not move his sword from the lieutenant to block her strike. Kiya finally found her voice.

"Hold, Maric! Seldar saved me from the lieutenant. She...she...savaged me. If he had not come to my aid when he did..." Kiya's voice trailed off as realization hit. *...she would have killed me.*

"Maric, the law is very clear here. His life is forfeit to me. Take him to the holding cell until I am ready to claim it," Delyn repeated her order.

"If you want to arrest him, you will have to disarm him yourself. I only see a savage in front of me; I see not an Amazon," Maric replied in disgust.

Delyn started to lunge for Seldar. Kiya realized that Delyn was going to attack him.

"No!" Kiya screamed, more of a command than anything else.

Delyn found her muscles to be frozen. She could not move. Delyn looked at Kiya with horror; could she truly be a Jahru?!

Maric quickly covered the distance between the two and knocked Delyn to the ground. She hastily bound Delyn with the leather straps all of the elite guards carried. They were useful in subduing drunken warriors.

Maric noticed the fear in Delyn's eyes but chose not to inquire. She looked at Seldar. He was losing blood to his now reopened wound.

"Seldar, you must put down that sword. It is the law. You are not allowed to draw upon any Amazon," Maric reminded him.

Seldar nodded. He handed Maric the weapon, hilt first.

"I only wished to preserve the healer's honor. I did not wish to spill her blood. The lieutenant would not stand down," Seldar explained himself.

"It is true. He only used enough force to keep her from hurting me. He could teach the lieutenant something about honor." Kiya rose to Seldar's defense.

"Look, I do not wish to arrest Seldar. However, the law *is* clear on this. I have to take the lieutenant to the holding cell. When I return, *if* Seldar is still in this camp, I must arrest him," Maric stated, hoping he would take the hint and run away.

"Do what you must. My only thoughts were of the healer," Seldar exclaimed.

Maric forced Delyn to her feet and pushed her out of the tent. Kiya looked at Seldar, her eyes brimming with tears.

"Please, Seldar, run away! Do not allow yourself to die for that woman. She is hardly worth it," Kiya exclaimed.

"But you are," Seldar replied evenly.

Kiya winced in pain as she tried to stand. Seldar reached down and placed his arms around her waist, helping her to her feet. She stood, a little shaky at first. Seldar quickly grabbed a blanket from a stack near Kiya's bedroll and wrapped it around her shoulders to offer her a measure of dignity.

Nausea threatened to cause her morning's gruel revisit her, but Kiya managed to keep it down. There were more important things that needed to be done; she did not have time to be weak now! She would be strong, for Seldar's sake. He deserved to live.

"Seldar, what if I take you to the healer's post? You know, like Captain Eldin had wanted. Would you travel with me, protect me until we get there?" Kiya asked as she tried to come up with reasoning that would sway Seldar's position.

"Of course! I swore an oath to the captain to see you to the post safely," Seldar replied.

Kiya smiled sadly. Oh how these soldiers loved their "orders."

"Good, then get into the wagon; we are leaving right this heartbeat!" Kiya ordered.

Maric saw the male-child getting into the wagon. She smiled. *Good for them. I cannot protect them forever. Goddess be with you both!* Maric informed her camp guards to allow them to leave. She would deal with the consequences later.

Kiya quickly slipped into a fresh dress, then hitched the team to the wagon and climbed in. She had to hurry if she wanted to be gone by the time Maric came for Seldar. Kiya gently slapped the reins down on the team, and they started to pull. She took the back way to the road from camp. This way, if the soldiers wanted to catch them, they at least had a little head start. Kiya looked down at Seldar's leg. At the first chance they got, she would have to stitch that wound again.

10

Kidak found the district's council regent and reported the attack of the two assassins. She also reported her aunt's death at their hands. It was as Terdak had wished. This time, there was no one left behind to mourn, or so she thought.

When she had finished giving her report and taking the condolences of the Regent, Kidak headed back to the Gray Fox. Inside, she found the fire in the great fireplace burning and a wonderful smell coming from the kitchen. Kidak made her way slowly to the kitchen. Inside she saw a tiny woman stirring the great cauldron. Sweat creased her brow, and she had a smudge of soot on her face where she must have cleaned the previous day's ashes from the wood stove. The young woman looked up, and she read the expression on Kidak's face. Tears welled in the youngster's eyes, but she refused to allow them to fall.

"Is my master Terdak dead, then?" she inquired quietly.

"I am afraid so. I shall be staying here for another day, and then I shall head back to the Council. We are having an emergency session. I'm sorry I never bothered to ask before, but what is your name, wee one?" Kidak asked gently.

"I do not remember my given name. It was too long ago. When I was three seasonmarks old, my mothers were killed. I was found and brought to this village. Master Terdak did not want me to be sent to the Sword Corps so she paid the Regent for my services. She sent me to live with a couple whose own daughter had died of the fever. When I turned fourteen seasonmarks, they brought me back to repay my debt. I was her indentured. The Regent had named me Rynar, and my other mothers kept this name as well," Rynar explained.

"So you have no idea who your mothers were? That must have been hard on you." Kidak tried to imagine a life such as Rynar's.

"I remember the local girls teasing me about being a slave. They said I was worthless. When I saw Terdak later, she told me to eat my dinner, but I told her that I did not deserve the respect of eating an Amazon dinner. She said…" Rynar started.

"She said, 'Panther piss. You deserve all the respect due any Amazon,'" Kidak interrupted and finished Rynar's sentence for her.

Rynar's eyes widened, and she nodded, "How…how did you know?"

"Terdak was my favorite aunt. I believe I memorized every word she ever uttered to me, and those two were among her favorite expressions. 'Panther piss' had to have been her all-time favorite, though," Kidak explained.

"Do you know if Master Terdak had any written wishes?" Rynar asked, uncertainty evident in her tiny voice.

"As a matter of fact, she did. I took them to the Regent this morning to be recorded. It seems that you are to be given your freedom and this place. All but twenty-five krillits she has saved and hidden in the dry well underneath the stable is yours to keep the Gray Fox up and running. She only asks that if someone comes along who needs a place to work, you give it as well as saving them a special place in your heart," Kidak informed Rynar of her aunt's wishes.

Rynar could no longer keep the tears from falling. They trickled down her face and into the flames of the stove, causing small hisses that sounded like tiny serpents. She looked up at Kidak and tried to wipe away the evidence, but Kidak reached out and took her hands into her own.

"Do not concern yourself. I am not ashamed that you weep for my aunt. I consider it a compliment," Kidak assured her. "I am going to my room. I need to be alone for awhile. Please forgive me, but I must collect my thoughts."

Kidak went to her room and started packing her things. She was going to miss this place and her aunt. She wondered where Terdak was going to go now that she had another full life ahead of her. Kidak grinned mischievously; perhaps she should send Terdak to the Drakknians. Then she could mouth off, and when they tried to kill her...but that wouldn't be fair to Terdak. It was evident that she wished to grow old and die.

After Kidak had finished packing, she left her room and took the staircase down to the great room. She paused at the landing and watched as Rynar served a very familiar-looking young redheaded woman who was sitting at the bar. The woman was talking with Rynar and must have said something particularly witty, as Rynar giggled. Kidak shook her head; her auntie had always had a way with the ladies.

Rynar looked up and saw Kidak. She smiled and waved her over.

"Look who is here, Councilwoman! It is your cousin, Dedak," Rynar called out.

Kidak smiled at Rynar and spared "Dedak" a glance. Dedak smiled and ever so slightly shrugged her shoulders as if to say, "Well, what did you want me to say my name was?"

"I should leave you two alone to get reacquainted. I shall make certain that you both have a *wonderful* meal," Rynar gushed, obviously taken with the handsome young redhead.

"That would be most welcomed, dear lady," Dedak stated.

Kidak waited until Rynar had bounced back into the kitchen to speak.

"All right, 'Dedak,' what are you doing here? I thought you were going to travel on, away from here. I thought you were going to 'start over.' How is flirting with your former indentured 'starting over'? Hmm?" Kidak asked sarcastically.

The newly renamed woman looked at Kidak. She shook her head.

"I honestly do not know what I am doing here, Kidak. I know I should move on, but...I always did favor that young girl. As you know, I never declared with anyone in this past lifetime. I was just not ready to go through that torture again. However, I was too old for the one woman who turned my head..." Dedak explained.

"So, you have always been attracted to Rynar?" Kidak inquired.

"No, of course not in the beginning, she was verily young when she came to live with me. I believe she was thirteen or fourteen seasonmarks, just a child. I think I grew fond of her over the eight seasonmarks since. She started to turn my head because of the woman she grew to be." Dedak paused as she reflected on the emotions swirling inside her. "It is so confusing when you are old one day and young the next, over and over. My head and heart start to feel things I would not have felt if I had but one lifetime under my belt. Instead, I am never-ending, it seems. I love her, and if that is wrong, then I shall hold no hope for Yashor. How can love be wrong? Love from one woman to another who share no blood ties? I know it will be best if I move on. I just wanted to see her one last time. I think I shall move to the far side of the Mountains of Fire and live out the rest of my days in peace," Dedak replied.

"The far side of the Mountains of Fire?! That would be madness! No one knows what lies beyond those peaks. For all we know, the world may drop off," Kidak remarked.

Dedak patted Kidak's hand. "I know, Precious. However, if no one is there, I will actually grow old, for there will be no one to do violence against me," Dedak shared her logic with Kidak.

"What of wild beasts? What happens if you are attacked and mauled? Does this spell cause them to die as well?" Kidak was trying to understand.

Dedak rubbed her chin in contemplation. "You know, that is a good question. I have never been attacked by an animal yet, so I do not know the answer."

"Well, it sounds like a foolish plan to me. 'Go to the other side of the mountains of fire.' How many seasonmarks do you think you shall live? Perhaps another fifty? Do you not think that you will go mad from aloneness?" Kidak worried.

"I think I have learned how to be easy in my own company over the last two hundred or so seasonmarks, Precious," Dedak answered, a slight sarcastic undertone coming through.

"Then I shall miss you and think on you often. When are you planning on leaving?" Kidak asked, afraid that if Dedak stayed too long, Rynar would fall for her.

"I was thinking perhaps a day or two," Dedak replied.

"Good. I think it is unfair to woo someone that you have no intentions of being with," Kidak spoke her mind, as always.

Dedak let out a small breath. It was true, however painful to hear. She was being selfish lavishing her Rynar with attention, knowing full well that Rynar was unaware of her true identity. Even if she knew, she would simply be repulsed or frightened. Just as all of her other lives had come to an end, so too this one was now history. Time to move on...

* * *

A chill wind howled through the trees and Eldin placed the hood of her cloak over her head. She leaned closer to Thunder to borrow the beast's warmth. This bit of unseasonably cold weather had taken her by surprise. Thankfully, Romyl's fortress was not far now. She would continue to ride through the day and by nightfall be sitting in a nice warm tavern. Eldin smiled; a warm bath sounded like heaven right now. At least the weather had given her something other than Kiya to focus on.

* * *

Kiya finally stopped the wagon, convinced that she was not going to be pursued. She looked at Seldar's leg. It was still bleeding. Kiya rummaged through her bag and found a small amount of treated cat-gut thread. It was all that she had left. She prayed that it would be enough.

"Seldar, I need to fix the stitches in your wound. It is going to hurt, but I know that being the brave warrior you are, you will be able to handle the pain," Kiya tried to prepare him.

"I am ready, Great Healer. I shall not give away our position by screaming from the pain. Do not worry, I will not dishonor you, nor endanger you further," Seldar replied.

Kiya smiled; she truly liked this male-child. He showed a nature to his character that she had been taught was impossible for a male-child to possess. If the Council could see Seldar, they would have to agree that they were making a mistake by perpetuating the myth that male-children were soulless shells of flesh not worthy of full citizenship.

Seldar looked at the dried blood on the inside of Kiya's legs. How did she put that out of her mind? Why was she tending to his injuries while ignoring her own? It was not right.

"Honorable healer…" he started.

"I have no honor, Seldar. She took that from me. I am no more than her dirty whore. You need not address me as anything other than what I am," Kiya interjected, not willing to face him as she spoke the brutal truth.

Seldar sighed; well, he had already committed the ultimate sin, so why not add another one for his trouble? Seldar tentatively reached forward and gently touched the healer, turning her face to him.

"I think that you will *always* be honorable. Honor is not something that can be taken. I think that the only way you can lose it, is if you throw it away through actions of your own making. You did not give your gift; it was *stolen*. Those were not actions of your own making. Do not confuse the two; it shall only cause you further pain and allow *her* the victory," Seldar reasoned.

Tears welled up in Kiya's eyes and then spilled. Once they started, it was as if a dam had given way, for she could not control the sobs as they poured from her soul. With each tear that fell, her soul cleansed itself a little of the guilt she felt. Kiya involuntarily flinched as Seldar put his arms around her as she wept. *Where did he learn such compassion and wisdom?*

* * *

Delyn prowled around the small cage of a room she had been locked into several candlemarks earlier. She was not in the mood for this! How dare that watchdog lock her up like a common criminal! When she was free, she would make her pay for this. Oh, how she was going to enjoy making her pay for this.

Delyn gripped the strong wooden bars that had been placed into the window slot to allow the guards to view the prisoner's activities at all times. She saw the same camp guard standing several body lengths away that had been there since she was brought in by Maric.

"Ho, you there!" Delyn called out to the guard.

The guard ignored her, as usual. She even turned her back on the prisoner. Delyn fumed at this obvious lack of respect. She searched the ground until she spotted a small pebble in the corner. Delyn retrieved the small stone and returned to the window. She took careful aim at the guard's head.

"Ho, I want to talk to your sergeant," Delyn tried again.

The guard continued to ignore Delyn. Delyn's face broke out into a familiar feral grin. *Ignore me, will you!* Delyn threw the pebble with all of her strength. It found its mark and hit the woman at the base of her skull. The guard spun around to face Delyn and reached up to rub the sting away. She glared at Delyn; a small knot was growing where the missile had hit.

"I said I want to speak to your sergeant. Perhaps now I have your attention," Delyn spoke sarcastically to the guardswoman.

"You will speak to Sgt. Maric when *she* is ready. Until then, might I suggest that you practice your *lies* for the Regent," the guard spat at Delyn.

"I want to face my accuser! If she cannot face me, you have no choice but to release me; that is the law!" Delyn demanded.

"If you had tried to have your way with a member of my family, I would have gutted you there in the tent. There would have been no need for a trial. Be lucky your victim has no relatives this far away. However, she *is* the daughter of Councilwoman Kidak. You remember her, the one that commissioned you?" the guard taunted Delyn.

Suddenly, a cold burst of air blew through the holding cell. Delyn shivered. It was too early in the season for winds like this. Another cold blast found its way inside. This was not a good omen. The healer was the councilwoman's daughter? She hadn't known. Hades fire...

* * *

Maric knew that she was not going to be able to hold Delyn much longer. If Kiya did not step forward soon to formally accuse Delyn in a public forum, Delyn would not be judged for her crimes. In essence, Maric and Kiya had traded Seldar's life for Delyn's freedom. Maric hated the thought that Delyn would be free to pursue her career while Seldar would have to live his life as a fugitive. Best that he go somewhere and change his name. Then he could gain a contract with some landowner. Eldin had said Seldar was an accomplished cook. It was a pity when a person got persecuted for doing the honorable thing.

Maric's thoughts were interrupted by one of her guards. Maric looked up as the young woman entered her tent.

"I'm sorry to disturb you, Sergeant. The reinforcements have arrived. There is a captain among them. She should be given control over all these troops. Her name is Berdyk. She is from the Twin Peaks district. She would like to meet with you in the command tent as soon as possible," the youngster reported.

"Thank you, Lydra. I shall meet her at once. Tell the guard at the holding cell to be prepared to release the lieutenant. Kiya has fled and will not be here to accuse her attacker. We must follow the law concerning this," Maric ordered, hating the words even as they came from her own lips; they still felt like a betrayal.

"But, Sergeant, the law is wrong! Lieutenant Delyn attacked and savaged our healer! Why should she be allowed to go free?" Lydra exclaimed.

Maric spared a small smile for her favorite young guard. She rose from her seat and gestured to all of the surroundings.

"Because if we ignore the law, we make all of this mean nothing as well. We make the sacrifices of our sisters meaningless. If we ignore the law, we turn our backs on everything that Yashor stands for. If we do not agree with a law, we should petition for its change or removal. That is the only way we continue to live as a civilized society. Does that make any kind of sense to you?" Maric asked.

"Yes, Sergeant. You always have a way of making me understand things. I guess that is why I am just a guard and you are a sergeant," Lydra complimented her mentor.

"Come; let us go welcome our new captain. Berdyk, I believe you said is her name," Maric stated as she ushered Lydra outside the tent.

* * *

The chill wind brought gooseflesh to Kiya's arms as she finished stitching Seldar's wound. She looked at him through new eyes. How could a lowly male-child save her if he was of inferior character? How could he show more honor than that of an officer in the great Yashor Sword Corps? If Yashor dealt with male-children the way the Goddess had wanted, why did he seem above reproach? Perhaps the Council was wrong. Perhaps male-children were indeed capable of being contributing members of society. Perhaps the laws should be changed. Kiya blinked away a tear; for the first time in her life she felt shame for the way she had treated male-children.

Seldar noticed a great sadness come over the healer. He was worried that she regretted her decision to leave the troops. It was his fault, after all. He was the one who had raised a sword against the lieutenant. He knew it was forbidden, yet he had done it anyway. He had expected to forfeit his life to the lieutenant, not to make the healer a fugitive as well. *Eldin, what would you have done?*

"The same thing, Seldar. She would have done exactly the same thing," Kiya whispered, unaware that she had just answered an unspoken question.

Seldar cocked his head at Kiya. This was odd and a bit frightening. Kiya began rummaging through her bag for any warm clothing to offer Seldar. She was not even aware that she had defended Eldin. Kiya found a couple of hooded cloaks stuffed in among her other dresses and pulled them out. She offered one to Seldar, and he gratefully accepted. Then she wrapped the other around herself and pulled the hood up. This would cut the wind and help keep in her body heat.

Kiya soon had the wagon moving again. Seldar watched her for any other strange signs or omens. There were legends that spoke of women who could read your mind. Only…those women were long dead.

"Kiya, why are you so sad? I am sorry to have caused you so much trouble," Seldar apologized.

"Nonsense, Seldar. I am sad because I found out something. I found out something about Eldin, about you, about me, about all of Yashor. I found out that I do not like who I allowed myself to become. I should be the one apologizing to you," Kiya replied.

Seldar scowled. What the Hades was she talking about? Were they having the same discussion?

"What did you discover?" Seldar gently probed.

"That male-children are capable of honor, and that all officers of the Yashor Sword Corps are not honorable. That we talk about the Drakknians being demons, yet we victimize the smallest among us. I have not treated you as an equal, and that is what I do not like about myself," Kiya confided.

Seldar's eyes grew wide; the healer was going stark raving mad!

"Great Healer, you have not treated me as an equal because I am *not* an equal. I am merely a male-child. I do not even possess a soul. I was not born in Her divine image! I am the lowest of the low. Please, do not affect yourself so on my account. I am hardly worth the effort of it," Seldar exclaimed.

Kiya tried to smile. It was beginning to become so clear to her now. Yashor had put mind control over all of its male-children to think that they were somehow less than deserving of equal treatment. Some religious nonsense had dictated that they were to be treated as second-class citizens. What kind of Goddess would allow such a thing?

"It is all right, Seldar. I know you only speak as you were taught. I just wonder if the lesson was correct," Kiya ventured.

They continued their journey in silence, each lost in their own thoughts.

11

Kiya finally saw the stone walls of the healer's post rising up in the distance. Perhaps ten more candledrips and they should be at the front gate. She was afraid that she was still bleeding inside. She was dizzy and getting very sleepy. Her belly hurt. Her breast hurt. Her heart hurt. She just wanted to close her eyes.

Seldar took the reins out of Kiya's hands. She was asleep or trapped inside her own mind; he could not tell which. He guided the horses to the gate of the healer's post.

"Ho, who goes there?" the sentry called down to him.

"It is Seldar, swordsman basic of Three Rivers. I have the healer Kiya with me. She is in need of healing gifts. She was attacked," Seldar replied in the most soldierly manner that he knew.

Slowly, the gate to the fortress was raised, and Seldar encouraged the horses to pull the wagon through. Instantly, he was surrounded by armed Amazon warriors. They would take no chances being this close to Drakknian territory.

"Get down from that wagon, but do it slowly. There are archers with itchy fingers watching you, male-child," a sentry close to Seldar commanded.

Seldar complied with the order and climbed down. As soon as he was off of the wagon, he was tackled and brought to the ground. Several Amazons used small leather bits to tie his arms behind him and tether his legs together so that he would be unable to run very fast. Seldar tried not to struggle. He knew that if he allowed his body to act on its natural fight response, he would die.

"Hey, this woman has been violated!" a sentry from the wagon exclaimed.

Instantly, Seldar felt a boot connect solidly with his face. Someone grabbed his crotch none too gently.

"Yeah, he is uncut!" a voice next to him called out.

"It was not me! It was the lieuten…" Seldar's explanation was cut off in mid-sentence when a boot connected with his stomach, knocking the wind out of him.

Pain exploded in Seldar as a barrage of kicks and punches landed on his head and body. Seldar tried to curl into a fetal position to protect his vital organs, but it was too late. He could only pray that they would stop before he died. Already his vision was getting blurry. *Please, Great Goddess…*

One of the sentries reached down and grabbed Seldar by his blood-matted hair. She dragged his unconscious body through the post and into a holding cell. Once there, she stomped on his groin once more for good measure. Then she left the badly beaten male-child on the floor and took away the small thin blanket. Oh, this male-child would suffer before his death!

The sentry that had taken Seldar to the holding cell went to the infirmary to check on the poor abused woman that had been brought in. There was a large gathering of soldiers around the entrance to the building. A slight buzz could be heard as she got closer, for most of them were talking about the attack. One of the soldiers looked up and saw the sentry coming closer. She straightened up and elbowed the other soldier close to her.

"Sgt. Vanik is coming! Make way for the sergeant!" the soldier called out.

As Vanik approached, a small pathway formed through the center of the mob. She continued into the infirmary and stopped just inside the doorway. In a bed not far away was a very beautiful young woman who had obviously met with violence. Vanik cursed under her breath. Well, she could only offer her a measure of privacy now. Vanik closed the door to the outside, despite the protests from the soldiers who had gathered.

"Do you think that she shall live?" Vanik asked the healer.

"I do not know, Sergeant. She has lost a lot of blood. Most of it from wounds inflicted from the inside. I have done the best that I can. Now I can only pray that the Goddess heals her. Even if she lives, she may never be the same person, for her gift was stolen," the healer confirmed the violation.

Vanik moved closer to the woman who lay in the bed. She felt for this woman. Her mother had been attacked by Drakknian scum. She had not been able to live with the stigma and so had taken her own life when Vanik was a mere twelve seasonmarks. Vanik had found her hanging from a tree just outside of their house on her way home from school. She sighed and then turned to go. The healer placed a hand on Vanik to stop her before she could leave.

"Vanik, I know this woman. She is also a healer. She is Kiya, daughter of Councilwoman Kidak. Her other mother is Yamouth of Three Rivers. I grew up in Three Rivers with Yamouth. I should hope that you take care of the one responsible for this atrocity," the elder healer stated as she stroked Kiya's brow.

"I will deal with that male-child. Worry not, he shall regret the day he could not control himself!" Vanik assured her.

"Good. I think it would be best if we let Kiya rest now. Even if she is trapped inside her mind, I believe her to still hear us, poor child," the healer explained.

* * *

Eldin finally finished brushing Thunder down and pitched a fresh bale of hay over into his stall. Thunder snorted and butted Eldin's shoulder with his muzzle.

"Hey! It is not my fault that you eat like a pig and are already out of oats. Perhaps I shall purchase more tomorrow, if you behave yourself," Eldin exclaimed as she started to leave.

Eldin turned up the collar of her cloak against the insistent wind. She made her way to the tavern and paid for a room and a hot bath. Oh, that water was going to feel good! Eldin hurried to the bathing chamber and quickly removed her clothing. Stepping over the side of the tub, she allowed herself to sink into the warmth. The water embraced her body like a lover, and she closed her eyes in contentment. Eldin had needed to wash the road dust off her for several days now, but the streams had been way too chill, and truth be told, she had not been all that concerned.

* * *

Delyn seethed as Maric turned the key ever so slowly to open the lock. She nearly pushed the door into Maric's face, but Maric caught the door and held it closed for a heartbeat as she glared at the lieutenant.

"Your accuser has not come forward; you are free to go. However, you have been relieved of duty. Captain Berdyk from Twin Peaks is here. She is now in command. Her orders are for you to remain in your tent for the next fortnight. After that, if your accuser has not stepped forward, all charges will be dropped. Is that understood?" Maric relayed the orders of the new captain.

"I am perfectly aware of the law, watchdog. Now get out of my way!" Delyn snarled as she once again pushed against the door.

Maric stepped back and allowed Delyn to pass. She gripped Delyn's arm tightly.

"You are right about one thing, Delyn; this is far from over. I know what you did, and if it takes me a lifetime, I shall make certain that you pay for your crimes against the healer," Maric threatened.

Delyn pulled her arm out of Maric's grip. She leaned toward the sergeant so that Maric was the only one who could hear her.

"You should try an untouched woman sometime," Delyn sneered.

Maric drew back her fist to strike the lieutenant. Delyn cocked her head to the side and wagged her right index finger at Maric.

"Temper, temper. I still outrank you, and since there is no accuser, I have committed no crime," Delyn mocked Maric.

"Get out of my sight. Guards! Take the lieutenant to her tent. She is to remain there until a fortnight has passed. Please post three guards," Maric commanded.

Maric's guards removed Delyn from the holding cell. Maric's eyes narrowed as she watched the lieutenant walk carefree toward her tent. *You will pay.*

* * *

Eldin took in a deep breath of fresh spring air. Ah, the mountain blooms were fragrant, and the sunlight danced off of J'min's hair. Eldin reached over to her love and touched her face lightly. J'min leaned into the contact. It would take another fortnight to reach the capitol city of Valley Glen. That seemed like an eternity. Unless…Eldin shook her head. Everyone said that the forest was filled with brigands and the like. Not many people dared to take the shortcut through there. But then again, not many people were as strong as Eldin or had as much skill with a blade. It would cut off a week's travel time.

"J'min, I want to take the pathway through the forest. You know what is said of these woods. However, I promise you that I will keep you safe. What say you?" Eldin asked.

"I trust you, Eldin. If you say that I am safe by your side, then I am safe. I shall go wherever you go. You are my hero, Lieutenant, and I think that I shall enjoy the extra week of being your declared," J'min answered.

Eldin grinned. She leaned over in her saddle and placed a burning kiss on J'min's lips. She would keep her safe. It would be worth it. She would have an extra week to show J'min exactly how much she loved her.

Eldin turned onto the pathway and J'min followed. They spent an uneventful three days riding through the forest. On the fourth day, Eldin woke early to go to the river and wash up. She looked at J'min sleeping peacefully and placed a tender kiss on her forehead. Eldin's body responded to the curves of J'min's firm breasts as they rose and fell with her breathing. It would only be a few more days' ride, and then they would be joined. Eldin sighed; she had been saving herself for her love since she had been seven seasonmarks old. She realized the first time that she had met J'min that they belonged together. Eldin rose and made her way to the river.

The peaceful river was a tad chilly, and Eldin submerged quickly before she lost her nerve. The cold made her want to take in a breath, but Eldin resisted the urge to breathe until she broke the surface of the water. She splashed around for a few minutes until she heard a noise coming from camp. The hair on Eldin's neck stood on end. Something was wrong!

Eldin quickly fled the river to find her clothes. She slipped them on in a hurry and made her way back to camp. At the edge of her camp, she saw a sight that made her blood run cold; two male-children that looked about twenty seasonmarks old were holding down J'min and binding her hands. Eldin charged. She could handle two male-children with ease. No one was going to hurt her J'min. Just as she reached J'min's side, she felt the blow to the back of her head. Eldin crumpled, unconscious.

Eldin woke with her arms pulled painfully behind her and her hands tied together around the trunk of a large tree. As her eyesight cleared, she saw four male-children laughing at J'min.

"Come on, you whore! You know you really want this!" a rough-looking male-child sneered as he grabbed his crotch.

"Look, M'albo, I think she wants it. Oh yes, she wants it bad," another one chimed in.

Eldin struggled against the rope. If she could only manage to get free, she would dispatch them all! Eldin watched helplessly as they tore at J'min's dress.

"No! Do not lay a hand on her! If you so much as make one tear fall from her eyes, I shall gouge out yours before I run you through. Mark my words!" Eldin howled in rage.

"You dare raise your voice to us, little Amazon warrior?! What is she to you, your pet?" M'albo taunted.

"Eldin...please. Please do something. I love you, only you. My gift I saved for you," J'min cried.

M'albo's evil grin spread slowly across his face. So, that was what they meant to each other. It was obvious that the one tied to the tree was in the Yashor army. She was the threat, but M'albo knew many ways to break the spirit of courageous fighters.

"Take off her clothes, T'eln. We are going to have some fun with the Amazon warrior's little pet," M'albo promised.

Eldin watched in horror as J'min was gagged with a remnant of her own dress. Eldin could not turn away as she struggled to free herself and save her love from this violation. J'min did not cry out even as the searing pain hit her from M'albo thrusting himself deep within her unprepared flesh. J'min felt her insides ripping as the Drakknian scouting party took turns at her. The more viciously they pumped inside her, the more she withdrew from reality. J'min only saw Eldin in her mind. She tried to make herself believe that it was just she and Eldin making passionate love. Perhaps that would make the pain stop. J'min turned her head toward Eldin.

"I love you," J'min quietly spoke to Eldin.

"No! No, this is not happening! This is just a night terror. Please, Great Goddess, let this just be a night terror!" Eldin screamed as she fought against the rope that kept her a helpless prisoner.

After what seemed an eternity, the Drakknians were spent. The last one removed himself after he shot his seed into J'min, and he backhanded her for good measure. Not once had she cried out. Not once had she screamed in terror. She had remained strong throughout the entire attack.

"Shall we let her go, Commander?" T'eln inquired.

"Why not? She proved herself to me. I grant her one wish," M'albo replied.

They looked at J'min. She stared at them slightly dazed. Were they just teasing her?

"I wish to go to Eldin," J'min quietly stated.

M'albo flicked his wrist at her, indicating that the others should release her. The other scouts untied her and stepped away from her.

J'min stood, her head held high, and started to walk toward Eldin. Blood was flowing from her internal injuries. Just walking felt like someone had used her insides for sword practice.

M'albo narrowed his eyes. How dare that Amazon whore put on airs after they had just used her! She was not leaving with dignity!

Eldin saw the commander rise to his feet behind J'min. He stood about thirty paces behind her. Eldin tried to get to her feet. Time slowed to a crawl. A light breeze danced through J'min's sweat-matted hair. She was only several steps from Eldin. M'albo reached down and unhooked his ax. Eldin's eyes widened. She had seen the damage that Drakknian throwing axes could inflict. Eldin screamed. M'albo released the ax. J'min's eyes blinked as the ax found its mark deep in her back. J'min's footsteps faltered. She stumbled two more steps forward and fell. J'min struggled to her feet once more. She opened her mouth to speak, but instead pink frothy blood spewed from the corner of her mouth, staining her beautiful white teeth red. Eldin still screamed. J'min held herself upright, swaying slightly from her weakened state, and took one last step. She looked into Eldin's eyes and smiled peacefully. Eldin's scream caught in her throat as J'min cocked her head. She reached toward Eldin as her legs crumpled, finally unable to bear her weight any longer. J'min died before she landed, her face turned to the side, in Eldin's lap, her unseeing eyes staring up at her.

* * *

Eldin sloshed water out of the cold tub as she sat bolt upright. *Goddess! How dare you make me live her death again! Why do you punish me so?!* Slowly the night terror faded as Eldin cried. Love was a cruel master.

12

Dedak placed her fork on her empty plate as she finished eating. It was a wonderful meal. Rynar's cooking was getting to be almost as good as her own. Dedak felt her skin tingle as Rynar's hand brushed against her forearm. The sensation was a pleasant one, to say the least. It had been so long since she had known a woman's touch. Why, it had been nearly seventy seasonmarks! Since she had no choice but to live her life over again from her twentieth seasonmark, perhaps she would allow herself to have the company of another woman this time around.

Dedak smiled; it was a good thing that Kidak had left days ago. She would be all in a twit over this obvious flirting. She watched as Rynar tucked a strand of her golden hair behind her ear while she poured Dedak another ale. *Oh to Hades with Kidak, and to Hades with the lot of them! I will know love this lifetime! It is not natural to be a loner in the world.*

Dedak realized that they were alone in the tavern. All the other patrons had either gone home or already turned in for the night. The fire was burning low in the fireplace, and a banked fire was beginning to burn inside Dedak.

Dedak used her foot to push Rynar's small footstool away from the side of the bar and into Rynar's path. When Rynar walked around the other side of the bar, she tripped over the stool, landing conveniently in Dedak's lap. Rynar watched in fascination as Dedak leaned down and claimed her lips in a gentle kiss. Rynar's eyes closed as she surrendered her heart to this mysterious and charming woman. The kiss turned more passionate, and Rynar wrapped her arms around Dedak's neck. Rynar's lips were as soft as the petal of a rose, and Dedak whimpered in pleasure. Finally, the need for oxygen caused them to break from the kiss and come up for air.

Rynar's whole face lit up with an ear-to-ear smile. She was totally enamored of this stranger, who felt so familiar.

"Have you ever believed in love at first sight, Dedak?" Rynar shyly inquired.

"Oh, I have no doubt about its existence. I have loved you since I first lay eyes on your lovely face upon my arrival," Dedak replied.

"And I you, my handsome Dedak," Rynar confessed.

Dedak's arms felt so good wrapped around her small waist. They made her feel safe and secure. She had never known a feeling such as this. Rynar had secretly felt love for Terdak and had often dreamed that had they born under the same seasonmark she would have made a run at Terdak's heart, but Terdak had made her feel loved none the less. This was a different feeling; it was exciting and comforting at the same time.

"Would you do me a small favor?" Rynar asked.

"Name it, and if it is in my power, I shall grant it to you," Dedak responded, kissing Rynar lightly on the shoulder.

Rynar shivered. Oh that felt good…too good! She lay her head down on Dedak's shoulder to give herself a chance to gain control of her raging hormones.

"If I promised to behave myself, would you consider holding me tonight? I just want to feel your arms around me, and I want to hear your heart beating as I sleep. I have had such a hard time sleeping since Master Terdak's death. If it is too much trouble, I shall understand," Rynar explained.

"No trouble at all. I would be honored to hold you," Dedak replied.

Dedak scooped up Rynar and carried her down the hall to her room.

She paused at the doorway, trying to juggle Rynar and turn the doorknob at the same time. Rynar giggled and ran her fingers through Dedak's thick fiery hair. Dedak finally managed to get the door open without dropping Rynar, and she carried her into the room. Dedak closed the door with her foot and then placed her precious bundle on the bed.

Time stood still as Dedak paused to consider what she was doing. Was this fair to Rynar? She gazed lovingly down at Rynar and watched her take off her soft leather shoes. Rynar placed them carefully under the bed. She looked up at Dedak and waited several heartbeats before she tilted her head to the side and raised her eyebrows.

"Oh! Oh, Rynar, I am sorry. I shall go to my room to give you privacy while you get prepared for bed," Dedak exclaimed as she finally caught the hint.

"Thank you. If you could return in five candledrips' time, I shall be finished," Rynar instructed.

Dedak fled to her room and frantically pulled her clothing off. She reached up and untied her binding, then she rummaged through the clothing she had recently purchased and selected a fine dark-green silk sleeping shift. As Dedak slipped the fine garment on and let it cascade over her once-again-youthful body, she marveled at the complete lack of aches and pains. This was indeed unnatural, but now she had no choice. Her heart was pounding in her chest, and her breathing had increased. Dedak was surprised to find her palms were a tad sweaty as well.

"Good grief, old woman, you would think that you had never spent the night with another woman in all 257 seasonmarks of your life! Get a hold of yourself! Be calm. Be gentle...women like gentle. Be charming. Be...ah, panther piss, be yourself!" Dedak gave herself a pep talk to try and calm her nerves.

Dedak once again ran down the narrow staircase, taking the steps two at a time, and nearly fell at the bottom. She turned and ran down the bottom hallway and slid to a stop in front of Rynar's door. Taking a deep breath, Dedak lifted her fist to knock. Stopping her fist in midair, Dedak hit her head with the heel of her hand and took off down the hall at a full sprint. She nearly knocked over a table in the great room of the tavern before she managed to turn the corner into the kitchen.

Dedak sprinted out the back door and into the small yard of the tavern. She practically flew to the back side of the barn, where the most beautiful purple flowers grew. Dedak carefully selected one that was barely starting to open and picked it. *Just like our love, it is beginning to bloom.*

Dedak raced back through the kitchen but this time was not as successful at navigating the turn and stumbled over a chair and into a table, bringing both crashing to the floor with her.

"Who is there?!" Rynar called out a challenge.

"Um, it's just me, Rynar. I sort of…well in my haste… that is to say… oh, panther piss, I'll be right there," Dedak called back as she untangled herself and got back on her feet.

Dedak sighed; the flower had not been damaged in her fall. She limped down the hallway on a sore ankle and paused at Rynar's door. Just before she knocked, Rynar opened the door. She was wearing the wine-colored sleeping shift that Terdak had given her for her last birthing-day celebration. Dedak's face broke into a toothy grin; she was a beautiful young lady. *I was right. She looks great in that color.*

"This bloom blushes because it knows your beauty far surpasses its own," Dedak exclaimed as she held out the blossoming treasure.

"You are such a romantic soul. Come and hold me, please," Rynar said as she stepped aside to allow Dedak to enter her room. "Please place that in the vase on my table. I think there is still some water in it."

Dedak placed the single scarlet bud into the vase that sat on Rynar's small table by the window and checked the fire. She put a few pieces of wood on it and stirred the coals. In a few candlemarks, she would need to get up and bank the coals to keep the heat going for morning.

Rynar yawned and stretched. She patted the bed next to her and silently requested Dedak to join her. Dedak smiled and padded over to the bed. She lay down under the covers that Rynar held open for her. Dedak opened her arms and Rynar laid her head upon Dedak's chest. Rynar blinked away a tear and closed her eyes. She inhaled deeply of Dedak's pleasing aroma. Rynar opened her eyes and looked up at Dedak. Dedak's eyes were closed. She inhaled deeply again…kitchen spices and rose water.

"Goodnight, Terdak." Rynar whispered as she kissed Dedak's lips softly. *Thank you great Goddess for answering my prayers!*

"Mm, goodnight, my precious," Dedak answered, oblivious to Rynar's words.

A few heartbeats later, Dedak's eyes flew open as realization hit. She gazed down at the precious gift in her arms and cleared her throat.

"Rynar, are you sleeping?" Dedak quietly inquired.

"Yes, and so are you," Rynar whispered back, keeping her eyes closed.

"What did you call me earlier?" Dedak persisted.

"Your name, silly. I do not know how it is possible, but you are not Dedak. You are Terdak. I would know your smell anywhere," Rynar replied matter-of-factly.

"Ah, so, I have been foiled by my own body. Do you not wonder how this is possible? Do you not fear me?" Dedak wondered aloud.

"What is there to fear? I know your heart is a good one, no matter what has happened to change your appearance. Perhaps it is a blessing from the Great Goddess; who am I to judge Her will?" Rynar explained as she suppressed a slight yawn.

Dedak shifted slightly and propped herself up on one elbow so she could see Rynar's face better.

"I am Jahru, Rynar. I am over two hundred seasonmarks old. Does that not frighten you?" Dedak confessed, her need to be truthful with Rynar overpowering her fear of rejection.

Rynar pulled Dedak's arms tighter around her waist, causing the woman to lie back down, and brushed her fingertips up and down Dedak's forearms in a soothing manner.

"I already told you. I know your heart. You say you are Jahru, I believe you. What I do not believe is that you would ever harm me. Now, go to sleep; we have many days ahead of us to discuss this gift of the Goddess," Rynar put an end to the late-night discussion.

Dedak smiled as she snuggled closer to Rynar. She was a lucky woman indeed. The Goddess had blessed her with an incredible Amazon to love.

* * *

Celdi fought the exhaustion that threatened to overcome her and knock her from the saddle. She had to get back to Delyn. She needed to warn her. Finally, Celdi could fight no more, and she gently pulled up on the reins.

"Easy…easy does it, girl," Celdi soothed her horse.

The mare slowed her pace to a walk. Celdi guided the horse off the road and into the thicket. She dismounted and tethered the horse so it could eat and rest. Celdi pulled her sleeping skins from the horse's back and laid them out. She fell into them. Perhaps two or three more days of hard riding and she would reach her Delyn. *Goddess let it not be too late…*

* * *

Vanik opened the cell door and stepped inside. Sometime during the night the male-child had vomited. The stench permeated the cell. She dragged him up by his hair until he was eye level with her. Seldar's body was wracked with pain. He slowly opened his swollen and blackened eyes and stared into the eyes of pure hatred.

"You piece of Drakknian scum! I am going to make you wish you were never born. You are going to beg me to kill you before I oblige. Perhaps it will take a fortnight, perhaps a full turn of the moons. What say you? Are you prepared to face your punishment like a woman, or are you still a cowardice male-child?" Vanik taunted in a voice so low, even Seldar had trouble hearing her.

"I accept whatever you judge of me, but know this, I am no Drakknian!" Seldar replied, barely able to move his mouth to form the words.

"Liar!" Vanik screamed as she punched him in the mouth, her past demons not allowing her to see him as anything but the enemy.

Blood flowed from his mouth, and Seldar swallowed a piece of a tooth. Vanik dragged the prisoner from the cell and into the center of the fortress square. She tied his arms to the wooden post, and he hung limply. Seldar was too tired to fight this. He did feel responsible in a way; if only he had been faster, Kiya would never have been harmed. It was through his failure that she was injured. He deserved this.

Vanik uncoiled the whip attached to her belt. She was going to make him scream for mercy, just as she believed he had done to the poor healer. Vanik ripped the tunic from Seldar's back, baring his flesh to her vengeance. The sun was just rising over the tops of the mountains in the distance, and Seldar looked up at them as the whip bit deep into his back for the first time.

Seldar smiled at Vanik, blood dripping from his abused mouth. Vanik glared at his insolence. She brought the whip back around and hit him again. Over and over the whip landed on Seldar, each blow leaving a deep gash in his flesh. Each blow he weathered without making a sound. Sweat beaded on Vanik's forehead from the effort of her blows. Vanik's arm was growing weak, and still the male-child had not broken. Finally, Vanik was forced to switch hands. She wielded the whip in her weaker left hand and continued to beat the male-child. When Seldar could take no more punishment, he silently slipped into his mind.

Vanik wiped the sweat from her face and recoiled her whip. As she approached the limp male-child, she shook her head slightly in wonder. Throughout the entire beating, the male-child had not once uttered a cry. By Yashor standards, that was quite an honorable performance, and an impossibility for a lowly male-child. *How did he do it?*

Vanik unhooked the male-child from the post and he fell to the ground. She reached down and grabbed his hair to drag him once more. Vanik took Seldar to a nearby tree. She tied his wrists together tightly with a thin piece of strong rope. Vanik knew this next torture always made the male-children beg for mercy. It was designed to put pressure on the shoulders and wrists, and often resulted in dislocations. Rarely, one of the hands might give and totally rip away from the body as well.

Vanik grabbed the hook that was attached at the end of a rope that was wrapped several times around the lowest-hanging thick branch. She measured the length against the height of the male-child. It would work, but Vanik wrapped the rope around the branch once more to be certain that the male-child would not be able to touch the ground with his feet.

"Good morning, Sgt. Vanik. Have you had your first-feast yet?" a soldier called out as she passed by the tree.

"I have no stomach for first-feast this morning, Dakyn. I have this Drakknian savage to deal with," Vanik answered.

"Would you allow me the honor of helping you hang him?" Dakyn inquired, fairly certain that the Sergeant would just send her on her way.

Vanik hesitated. What harm would it do to allow the youngster a chance to help serve justice?

"Come. You may indeed be of some help," Vanik replied.

As Vanik turned, she was startled by the sight of Seldar standing behind her with his arms outstretched toward the hook. It was as if he were trying to hook himself. *He could have attacked me from behind, yet he did not. He did the honorable thing. How is this possible?*

"Do not move, male-child. If you as much as twitch a muscle, I shall rip you apart limb from limb," Vanik threatened, somewhat embarrassed at her loss of concentration, which allowed her to become vulnerable to an attack from him.

"Is that not what you intend on doing with me already?" Seldar asked innocently as he pointed to the crude torture device above his head.

Vanik punched Seldar in the stomach. Seldar doubled over from the force of the blow. It was meant to knock the wind out of him, to silence him. It was certainly effective.

Vanik hoisted Seldar, and Dakyn secured his bound wrists into the large hook. When she had him secured, Dakyn signaled Vanik. Vanik stepped away from Seldar and left him to dangle by his wrists.

Seldar closed his eyes against the pain. It was intense. His shoulders burned from the burden of his body weight. His wrists felt the rope as it bit deeply into his flesh. Seldar was not going to scream. He refused to give in to that urge. It would only bring dishonor upon Eldin and Dinyar. Seldar allowed his mind to travel to his childhood. He and Eldin were brigands searching for the buried treasure of Twin Peaks. Each armed with a stick-sword, they were invincible! Nothing was going to take away the pain in his shoulders, but at least he could think of something more pleasant while he endured it. A peaceful smile curled his lips.

Vanik could not believe her eyes. The male-child was actually smiling at his torture! *What power does he possess to handle this like an Amazon?*

"Dakyn, stand watch here. I shall return in a candlemark. I am going to visit the healer," Vanik ordered.

Vanik pushed Seldar as she walked toward the healer's building; it would place more stress on his shoulders as he swung back and forth. Seldar bit down on his lower lip to keep from crying out as his shoulders screamed with the increased agony. Vanik wondered if he was really a demon incapable of feeling pain as she hurried to check on the progress of the young savaged victim.

* * *

Eldin smiled as she encouraged Thunder into the cool water of the small stream that ran along the border of her mothers' land. It would only be a matter of a quarter-candlemark until she saw her mother Dinyar again. It would be a blessing to speak with her mother. It had been almost three full seasonmarks since she last saw Dinyar.

Three long seasonmarks at the mercy and whim of the Council of Nine. She had been commissioned and sent to the Drakknian border. With the death of Captain Ishva, the Council had promoted her to take Ishva's rank and position. They had then sent her a second-in-command to fill her slot. It had been the first she had seen of Delyn.

Eldin pushed thoughts of Delyn away as she crested a hill and caught sight of her mothers' keep. Soon she would be able to give her other mother a hug and let her know that Elrik would arrive soon after.

* * *

Malfi's eyes widened as he spotted the rider along the western path. He strained to make out the features of the rider, then his weathered face broke into a wide grin.

"Master Dinyar! Eldin approaches from the west!" Malfi yelled as he started down the staircase from his position in the western-facing turret.

Dinyar looked up from her garden. She placed a hand over her eyes to shade them from the sun overhead. What was her eunuch trying to tell her? She could barely hear his voice over the constant clanging of the traveling smithy's hammer coming from the open barn. Her favorite mount had thrown a shoe a few days before, and as chance would have it, a young smithy traveling through had stopped to ask for water and directions.

Dinyar smiled; the stranger had been most eager to help out and insisted on taking only half the normal fee to make and shoe a horse.

"Master Dinyar, open the gates! Eldin approaches!" Malfi yelled as loud as he could.

Dinyar's face brightened. Her daughter was returning home to her. What a glorious day! Dinyar dropped her trowel and started for the gate.

She turned to one of the other eunuchs in her employ and gave him a message for the kitchen. "Tell Daji to set out some food and ale. I am certain that my daughter has missed more than one feast on her way home. She is verily much like her mother, and they both hate trail rations."

Dinyar stopped at the well to draw a bucket of water. As she hoisted the bucket up and onto the ledge, she could hear the horse's hooves beating against the trail just outside the gate. She quickly dipped some water and turned to see her daughter entering the compound.

Eldin's bright blue eyes sparkled as she noticed Dinyar standing by the well with a dipper of water. She had always been thoughtful that way. Eldin could remember Dinyar greeting Elrik in the same manner. "It is important to chase away the trail dust," she had always said. Now with the trail dust in her own throat, Eldin could not agree more. She dismounted and took the dipper from her mother. After downing the cool, crisp water, Eldin tossed the dipper back inside the bucket and picked her mother up off the ground in a bear hug.

"Oh, Eldin, I have missed you. You are looking well. You look like your mother used to when she returned from the field," Dinyar complimented her daughter.

"Mother, you give me far too much credit. My uniform is dusty, and I must smell like that cantankerous horse," Eldin replied.

"Well, you are a bit dusty, and yes you do smell like that beast. However, it is nothing that a little water and herbs cannot fix. I shall have a bath drawn for you. Would you like that?" Dinyar teased.

"Verily much so," Eldin answered as she gently placed her mother back on her feet.

"Let me look at you," Dinyar fussed as she lovingly gazed at her daughter from head to toe. "You look thin. Do they feed you out there?"

"Yes, Mother. They feed me quite well." Eldin was interrupted by a long low grumbling in her stomach.

"Oh, they feed you so well that your stomach is complaining. I have the kitchen preparing a plate for you. It will be ready within the half candlemark," Dinyar explained.

"I won't argue with that," Eldin joyously agreed.

Eldin handed Thunder's reins to Malfi and started toward the living quarters inside the small compound. Eldin looked up at the sound of a hammer striking metal. Dinyar caught her daughter's concern as it etched across her brow.

"Now, Eldin, I am a grown woman and quite capable of taking care of myself. You remember my old mare, Folly? She threw a shoe a couple of days ago. It wasn't maybe a day later that Kornat stopped in for some water on her journey," Dinyar started to explain.

"Water?! There is plenty of water *outside* the gates in that stream!" Eldin protested loudly.

"Eldin! Mind your tongue! I am still your mother," Dinyar chastised. "As I was saying, she was also a bit lost. She wanted directions. We were having a pleasant chat when I found out that she was a smithy. She is moving to a new town, and she offered to repay my kindness by shoeing Folly for me at *half the price*."

Eldin looked at Dinyar. She was practically glowing with pride at having saved so much on a service that she would have normally had to go into town to receive.

"Well, I would like to meet this 'Kornat,'" Eldin grumbled; she had always feared for her mother's safety while Elrik was away.

* * *

Kornat looked up from her work as Malfi brought Thunder into the barn. She smiled warmly at the eunuch.

"That looks like a military horse. Is the master of the keep home?" Kornat innocently inquired.

"No, Smithy Kornat. It is the daughter, Captain Eldin," Malfi explained as he led the stallion to a stall and found a brush.

Kornat's eyes widened for a fraction of a second before she turned her attention to the open doorway. *Think! Think you fool! Will she recognize you?* Kornat grimaced. Oh Hades, Eldin was making a beeline for the barn. Kornat absently rubbed the small dagger she had hidden inside her belt as she thought.

* * *

Eldin quickly covered the ground between the well and the barn. She stopped dead in her tracks as she saw Kornat, and her eyes narrowed with recognition. Eldin grabbed Kornat by the collar and violently shoved her up against the wall.

"What are you doing in my mothers' keep?!" Eldin yelled at the woman.

"Please...please, Eldin, listen to me. I...I could not be a warrior. I...I was too...too..." Kornat stuttered.

"You were too what? Too much of a liar? Too much of a coward?" Eldin spat out.

Kornat tried to step forward only to have Eldin shove her back against the wall.

"Eldin, I...I ran away and wrote the Council. I explained," Kornat tried to diffuse Eldin's anger.

"Did they pardon you, or are you wanted for desertion?" Eldin tried to instigate a fight.

Kornat simply hung her head.

"I see, so you come here and place my mothers in danger of harboring a deserter. You are worse than a filthy Drakknian. At least with the Drakknian, you know that they are an enemy. You better get finished here and leave. I know that my mother wants to have Folly shoed. That is the only reason that I am not throwing you out now. Mark my words: you *will* be gone by even-feast...one way or another," Eldin threatened.

"You are not going to turn me into the Council?" Kornat asked in disbelief.

"Why should I waste my time with you? You are the one who shall have to live with what you have done. That is more of a punishment than anything the Council could think of," Eldin explained.

Eldin released Kornat's collar. "You have until even-feast. You had better hurry."

Eldin left the barn in disgust. She did not want to ruin her mother's good mood, so she forced her features to soften. By the time she reached the living quarters, Eldin was practically smiling.

13

Kidak paced inside her room at the Council Hall. Had the attack on her been an isolated incident, or was there something else going on? She checked to make certain that the door to her chamber was still bolted. It was the third time she had checked it in a half-candlemark.

Kidak moved from the door to the window and gazed out at the city around her. People were milling around the market square, looking at goods and haggling prices. She stepped away from the window. It was almost time to go to the Council Chamber.

A knock on the door caused Kidak to jump. She started for the door, then stopped. What if it was an assassin? Another knock, more insistent. *Oh Hades, you old fool, assassins don't knock!*

"Councilwoman Kidak, I am here to escort you to Council Chambers. Councilwoman Arkon has called for an immediate session," a familiar voice called out.

Kidak smiled. It was the Council of Nine's honor guard captain. She rushed to the door and slid open the bolt. Kidak opened the door and her smile widened. She felt safe for the first time since the attack.

"Captain Ragart, how pleasant to see you. It is an honor to have your sword at my side," Kidak greeted the young soldier.

"The honor is mine, Councilwoman Kidak. Shall we go? I have orders to see you to the Chambers personally," Ragart stated as she motioned toward the hallway.

"Really? I wonder what that is about?" Kidak mused.

"Have you not heard? Oh, there is a danger lurking about, Councilwoman. You had best keep your wits about you. I am certain that Arkon shall inform you all of the events that have taken place. Until then, let me assure you that you shall always be accompanied by one of the guardswomen for your protection," Ragart explained as they walked the great hallway.

Kidak and Ragart passed by a long line of prisoners awaiting trial by the Council. Kidak shivered; any of them could be assassins. She felt so vulnerable. It was better with Captain Ragart at her side, yet she still felt like a target.

Soon they arrived at the back doorway to the Council Chambers. Ragart opened the door and looked around inside. Satisfied that there was no danger present, she left Kidak to enter and take her place at the Council table.

As Kidak took her place, she noticed two chairs were empty. She also noticed that their occupants had been against Councilwoman Pirkyn's plan. That was odd. Arkon stood.

Motioning for the guards to surround the table and its occupants, Arkon closed the Council Hall to all outsiders. She turned to the rest of the councilwomen and finally brought up the subject that so many of them had on their minds.

"I know that many of you were shocked to have an escort to Council Chambers. It was a shock to me when I heard what had happened to members of my own family. Last moon-cycle, I was informed of my Welka's passing. She held my heart for so many seasonmarks, I am still at a loss of how to continue living. Ah, but that is not the reason I bring up this tragedy. I also discovered it was by an assassin that she passed, not by nature. This assassin was meant for me. How they made the mistake, I shall never know. I have been made aware that others have been killed while away from Council. Narik of the Mountain Divide and Jerya of the Mid Lands Districts have also fallen to assassins. No one is safe. I am sorry I did not find out about this plot sooner. I have made arrangements for all councilwomen to have honor-guard escorts for your own protection. We shall adjourn now for mid-meal. Please keep your wits about you. I do not wish to have any more empty seats at this table," Arkon explained.

Pirkyn stood and addressed the Council. "Arkon, I wish to put forward my suggestion to an immediate vote. I think that there can only be one explanation for the assassinations: the Drakknians are closer than we think. We need to crush them! We need to send Captain Eldin to infiltrate them and to discover their weaknesses. She is the only one who can deliver us from this evil."

Arkon looked annoyed with Pirkyn, but she was within her rights to call for a vote, however insensitive the timing.

"Fine, a vote is called. All those in favor of sending Captain Eldin on this mission, vote now with a show of hands," Arkon stated.

Just as Pirkyn had anticipated, her four votes remained. Now her plan won four to three instead of losing four to five. Pirkyn smirked at Kidak; it really was a pity that *all* of the assassinations hadn't been successful.

Arkon looked around the table. Surely the councilwomen were aware of the consequences of failure in this mission. However foolish this vote was, Arkon had to abide by it.

"The will of the Council is registered. Captain Eldin shall be contacted and brought before the Council. We shall send her to Drakknia. Goddess, help us in our darkest days," Arkon stated before releasing the Council.

14

Kiya opened her eyes slowly. Her vision was still fuzzy, and she did not recognize her surroundings. Where was the familiar odor of blood, horses, and warriors mixed with the fragrant tree blooms that she had come to accept as the smell of her "home"? Where were the sounds of the army?

"Eldin?" Kiya whispered before she slipped back into unconsciousness.

Vanik looked over at Kiya. Had she said something? Vanik sighed; the healer looked like she was still asleep.

"How fares the healer, Siden?" Vanik inquired after Kiya.

"Kiya is not healing as fast as I would like. I have packed her wounds with healing herbs and moss, but I think that she still has angry flesh. She started to fever this morning. Poor child was savaged inside. As far as her mind is concerned, I fear for her. It is hard to recover from an attack like this. She may be forever changed," Siden stated quietly.

Vanik leaned over Kiya and startled when Kiya's eyes fluttered open. Kiya grabbed Vanik's arm and clung onto it as a scared child would.

"Eldin, where are you? Please Eldin, come save me..." Kiya called out in a haunted voice.

* * *

Eldin looked around the great room as the hairs on the back of her neck stood out. Was this some ghost that kept touching her, making her feel haunted? No...not haunted...more like...disturbed. The feeling passed quickly, and Eldin resumed her meal.

* * *

Kiya brought Vanik's callused hand to her mouth and placed a gentle kiss on the palm, "I've missed you, Eldin. I am so sorry. I do love you."

Vanik froze. Eldin? That could only be Captain Eldin of Three Rivers. Did this woman hold Eldin's heart? Vanik shook her head; if it were true, Eldin would create a river of blood in her search for vengeance. *What should I do?*

Siden noticed the exchange. She looked into Vanik's terrified eyes and smiled.

"Be calm, Sergeant. It is the fever talking. I believe she thinks you are Captain Eldin. Soothe her. It may be of some benefit to her healing," Siden prompted Vanik to play along.

"I...I'm right here, Kiya," Vanik tried Siden's idea.

Kiya's face was flushed with fever, and her hair was wet with sweat. She looked deeply into Eldin's pools of blue. Something was wrong; was Eldin sick? Her eyes were not the right shade of blue.

"I need to look after you. I think you are hurt. I should never have sent you into battle without me there to heal you," Kiya babbled.

Kiya pulled on Vanik's arm. Vanik lay down next to Kiya on the small pallet and allowed the sick woman to cuddle into her. She tenderly stroked her hair, and Kiya responded with a contented sigh.

"Do you love me, Eldin? Truly, do you wish to hold my heart for all of eternity?" Kiya inquired.

"You know the answer to that by now, do you not?" Vanik tried to deflect the question since she had no clue as to the answer.

"Mmm. I would say you do. That is what frightens me. I do not know if I am ready for that. What if you were to get killed in a battle? Would you not give up that sword for me?" Kiya continued to think aloud.

"Rest now. I am here with you. You are safe in my arms, and I shall not allow any harm to come to you. You need to sleep," Vanik convinced Kiya to close her eyes.

Sleep claimed Kiya very quickly. Vanik smiled. Kiya was a beautiful woman. Vanik's smile vanished; she was a beautiful woman whose heart was already claimed.

* * *

Captain Berdyk paced in front of the holding cell. Inside were three Drakknian prisoners. Another had already died while being interrogated. Of the three, there was only one that looked as though he still had any fight left in him. The one with the dark hair had a blazing stare.

"You there, the dark one, do you wish to talk or die?" Berdyk inquired.

"Your threats mean little to me. Drakknia will defeat you in the end, and you will all have to bow down to your male masters!" the dark man replied.

Berdyk motioned for the man to be brought to her interrogation tent. The guards separated him from the others and bound his wrists. He resisted a little, which earned him a quick beating, before he allowed himself to be led away.

Berdyk looked up as the tent flap opened and the guards shoved the prisoner through. She smiled at them and motioned for them to tie him to a whipping post set in the center of the tent. As the guards tied his arms to the post, the man kicked out at the nearest one, his foot landing square on her knee with a resounding crack. She crumpled to the ground. The other guard finished tying him before she pummeled the man with her fists. The prisoner kneed her in the groin. Berdyk rolled her eyes; she had seen more competent trainlings then these two guards. Did Captain Eldin really allow such ineptitude to go unpunished?

Berdyk grabbed the standing guard by the back of the head and pulled her to the tent flap. She threw her out of the tent and then turned toward the guard that was still on the ground holding her broken knee. The guard looked up at Berdyk with a mixture of awe and fear. Berdyk grabbed a handful of the guard's hair, picked her up and placed the guard over her shoulder. Berdyk carried her over to the tent flap and unceremoniously dumped her out as well.

"Do not come back until you have learned how to deal with a small male-child," Berdyk growled.

Berdyk turned her attention back to her prisoner. "Now, where were we?"

"You were going to attempt to beat me into submission and force me to tell you what knowledge I possess about the strength and movement of my troops," the male-child replied evenly.

"What makes you think that?" Berdyk inquired.

"It is what I would do to you if the situation were reversed. Only I would beat you *after* I had used you to pleasure myself," the prisoner rationalized.

Berdyk walked toward the man. Suddenly she reached out and grabbed his crotch. She stared into his intense dark eyes.

"What makes you think I won't?" Berdyk stated as she began to stroke his hardening flesh.

The prisoner shivered with a mixture of fear and delight as he felt Berdyk slip her hand inside his leathers. She was not acting verily much like any Amazon he had known. Perhaps he *could* strike a deal with this one.

"What is it that you wish to know?" the dark man inquired.

"First, if I allow you to escape, will you give me four days before you attack again?" Berdyk responded as she intensified her strokes.

"What makes you think that I can even make that guarantee?" the prisoner asked, his face flush with pleasure.

"Oh, you are high-ranking, I can tell. It is the way you think, the way that you act. So, will you give me four days if I will guarantee you that when you return, this valley will be empty of all troops?" Berdyk responded while she secretly thrilled to the feeling of his hardness.

"Fine. You will have four days," the man agreed.

"Here is the second part of the deal. You must tell me what weaknesses you have observed in these troops," Berdyk brokered for his information.

"How do I know that I can trust that you will not use the information to simply correct any defect in your army?" the prisoner remembered her remarks about sexually using him before she would beat him.

Berdyk took a dagger from her belt and held it in front of his face. She slowly reached down, and the prisoner's eyes widened as he felt the tip of it against the crotch of his leathers. Before he could utter a protest, Berdyk punched a small hole into them. She worked carefully to cut an opening in them without causing the prisoner any harm. A small sigh of relief sneaked past the prisoner's lips, and he blinked.

"The first thing I overheard is that you are low on healing supplies. I also heard that you were low on food, although I think you sent out hunters and they were successful. That is all that you get until you release me." The man now demanded his freedom.

Berdyk already knew these things, but perhaps the male-child was holding out on her. Oh well, any excuse to indulge in her secret passions was a good excuse. Berdyk reached up and cut his bindings, effectively freeing him.

"Do you wish me inside you, Amazon? Do you wish me to be deep inside of you?" the man asked, his voice husky with desire.

Berdyk could not bring herself to verbally admit it, so she nodded.

"No, from your lips. I want to hear you beg me for my maleness," the man stated as he turned the table on the captain; now *he* was in control.

"Ye...ye...yes. I want to feel you inside me, please," Berdyk barely whispered.

The man pulled her down, and they rolled on the ground for a few seconds, each fighting for the dominant position of being on top. Finally, the man grinned at her. He rolled on his side and motioned for her to do the same. He would give her equality if she would give him the same respect.

Berdyk smiled and rolled over next to the man. He was attractive. Shoulder-length dark hair, and those eyes. Berdyk allowed the man to pull down her riding pants, and she held her breath as she felt him explore her. Finally, she felt him enter her, and she caught her whimper before it left her lips. It was painful at first, but then his slow pumping began to feel good. As he pleasured Berdyk, he whispered his findings into her ear.

"The last thing that I noticed was that the captain and the lieutenant are lovers," the man told her after he emptied his seed into her.

Berdyk hurried to stand and get dressed again. She did not want to get caught in this position. If she were, she would surely be stoned to death.

Berdyk unsheathed her sword, cut a slit into the back of the tent, and motioned for the dark man to use this as his means of escape. He motioned for her to return to him. Berdyk moved quickly to his side, and she gazed into his fiery eyes once more. Understanding passed between them without a word being uttered, and Berdyk turned her back to him. She placed her trust in this man. She silently prayed that the blow would not be fatal.

The man took Berdyk's sword and hit her at the base of her skull with the ball of the hilt, knocking her unconscious. He could have betrayed her and killed her. However, if she were telling the truth then Drakknia had more to gain by allowing her to live. Quietly the man ducked through the slit and out into the back of the Amazon camp. He stealthily made his way to the edge of the forest and quickly disappeared into the trees and underbrush.

* * *

Kiya slowly opened her eyes. She cringed. There was great pain inside her nether region. She looked around at the unfamiliar surroundings and then noticed the older woman in the room. Her mind felt fuzzy recognition for this woman, but Kiya could not remember her name. Siden turned and startled to find Kiya awake and staring at her.

"How do you feel, child?" Siden gently probed.

"I am in great pain. Are you a healer?" Kiya asked.

"I am. Do you not recognize me?" Siden inquired as she moved over to the pallet that Kiya was sleeping on.

"You seem familiar, yet I cannot recall your name," Kiya replied.

"Ah, I see. I am Siden, and friend of your other mother Yamouth," Siden introduced herself.

Kiya's eyes filled with unspilled tears at the mention of her mother. How would her mothers react to her now? She was a common whore. Kiya cast her eyes downward, unable to bring herself to face a woman of such honor as the healer.

"Child, what are you thinking? Why have you averted your eyes from me?" Siden wondered aloud.

A whip cracking pierced the air, and Kiya shied from the noise. She looked at Siden and silently questioned the reason.

"It is the sergeant. She is punishing your attacker," Siden explained, hoping to soothe Kiya.

"My attacker is here?! Lieutenant Delyn is *here*?" Kiya exclaimed, fear trembling in her voice.

Siden's brows knitted in confusion, "No, not Lieutenant Delyn; some Drakknian male-child that had captured you."

Kiya swung her legs over the edge of the pallet and searched for the ground with unsteady legs. "Seldar!"

"No, Siden," Siden corrected Kiya as she tried to keep her from leaving the bed.

"Not you, the male-child who was with me. His name is Seldar, and he is the one who saved me from being killed by that savage Delyn. Now let me go so I can save him from the punishment that should be Delyn's!" Kiya explained as she struggled against Siden's grip.

Siden's grip loosened as she realized the mistake that the entire healer's post had committed. Kiya took advantage of the heartbeat and seized her opportunity for escape. She burst out of the healer's hut with Siden on her heels and stormed over to the tree where Seldar hung limply. Vanik could not stop her forward momentum with the whip in time to prevent it from lashing the young victim who had stepped in front of the male-child. The flesh of Kiya's right shoulder burned with an angry red mark where the whip had bit.

"Stop this madness! This male-child saved me from the true savage. Not that you should care. Not that you even bothered to look for the truth before you beat him. What kind of monsters are you?" Kiya cried out as she held onto Seldar's badly beaten and bruised body.

"We did not know. He came to this post with you in his wagon. We saw that you had been…well, violated. He was uncut. Anyone with eyes could see that he had been the source of your injuries," Vanik reasoned.

Kiya snapped her head in Vanik's direction. Her eyes were red and puffy, and her face streaked with tears and Seldar's blood drops. "Yes, that is what you would see. You would not see the honor of a male-child coming to the defense of his healer when I was attacked by a ruthless Amazon. You would not see the selfless courage of a male-child who prevented this Amazon from killing me, even though it most likely would mean his own death. You would not see the compassion in a male-child risking his life to drive me into a healer's post. You only see him as a servant, an expendable shell of life. You probably see me as weak for shedding tears. Have you no heart?" Kiya railed against Vanik.

Vanik could not believe her ears. This male-child actually saved Kiya? Vanik's hand released the whip, and it fell to the ground. She slowly approached Kiya.

"Please, forgive me. My only thought was to punish the one who had hurt you. Surely you cannot fault me for that," Vanik started.

"Release him now! I want you to release him and bring me my wagon. We are leaving this place," Kiya ordered.

"But, you have no travel scrolls," Vanik stated incredulously.

Kiya's eyes narrowed to slits. She was quickly losing her patience.

"I am so sorry that Captain Eldin did not have time to quill her orders that her sib Seldar accompany me to a healer's post and send out supplies and reinforcements to her troops. I am leaving regardless. I need to see my mother, Councilwoman Kidak. If you have a problem with that, I suggest that you take it up with her. Now give me my wagon and get out of my way!" Kiya barked.

The stunned guards looked to Vanik. She motioned for them to obey. They hastily took Seldar down from the tree and retrieved her wagon as Kiya had demanded.

Kiya cradled Seldar's broken body inside the wagon. She feared he would die. Kiya silently prayed to the Goddess that She would allow his unjust injuries to heal.

Before Vanik could further protest, Kiya turned the wagon team toward the gate and left. She was miserable as the wagon creaked out of the small post.

15

Eldin stood by the barn doors and listened to the rhythmic clanging of Kornat's hammer shaping Folly's shoe. Malfi was to bring Kornat a plate of food at Dinyar's insistence; however, Eldin had "persuaded" Malfi to allow her to take the plate in his stead. Kornat seemed to work at a tireless pace, and Eldin was beginning to think that perhaps this woman had been telling the truth after all. She had known some Amazons that became too frightened to lift their swords in a battle, and it had cost them. It cost not only their lives, but those around them who had relied on a coward's sword to protect their backs. Perhaps her running away had been better for all involved. Eldin sighed and prepared to enter the barn.

"Ho, Kornat. The lady of the keep insists on you eating now. She sent Malfi after a plate; however, I decided that I wanted to bring it to you myself. You see, I have been doing some thinking, and I wish to know more about your reason for fleeing my troops. Were you overcome with fear?" Eldin inquired as she held the plate of food out to the stunned smithy.

Kornat eyed Eldin suspiciously. Was she just trying to insult her, or was she truly trying to understand?

"Why would you care? You already know that I ran, that I changed my name, and that I am trying to start my life over. What more is there to understand?" Kornat reasoned.

"Perhaps I wish to know if I could have prevented it somehow. Perhaps if I had seen your fear, I could have helped you to deal with it before you deserted," Eldin tried to explain her own cloudy motives.

Kornat could see no malicious intent veiled in Eldin's eyes. Could she trust Eldin? The Fates must surely be getting a big chuckle out of this day.

"I ran because I do not believe in the war we fight against our neighbors. What right have we to say that male-children are no good? What right have we to impose our ideals on another nation? I ran because I did not want to spill anyone's blood, not even a male-child. When my mothers died, I was sent to you. I had no choice! Do you not believe that I would rather swing a hammer than a sword? Does that make me less of an Amazon than you? My mother Melika was a smithy. She taught me. Then the Council gave me to you, and all you had to teach me was how to kill. I do not wish to use that knowledge, Captain. So go ahead and turn me into your Council because I am a traitor. At least my conscience is clean," Kornat confessed.

Eldin set the plate of meat, cheese, and fruits down on top of a barrel of oats. She looked into the deeply hurt eyes of Kornat and knew the truth of her words. In all honesty, she felt as if Kornat was actually the braver of the two of them; at least she lived her ideals.

"It may shock you to know that I too do not like swinging a sword, nor did I have a choice about it. If I gave up the sword, I would also have to give up my family, and I am not willing to do that. I do understand how you feel. I wish you well, and may you find your happiness," Eldin remarked before she turned to leave.

* * *

Berdyk grimaced as she woke and felt the full force of her throbbing head wound. She looked around the tent and realized that she had been moved.

"Guards!" Berdyk called out groggily.

Maric heard the slightly slurred command coming from inside the tent. She sighed and started for the tent flap; might as well get it over with. How the captain could have been attacked had only one answer: Maric's guards had failed the captain. Maric would shoulder the responsibility for their failure.

Berdyk tried to focus on the figure coming through the flap. It was the sergeant of the honor guard. What was her name again?

"You called, Captain?" Maric gently inquired.

"Yes. Where am I? Where is the prisoner that I was interrogating?" Berdyk played it up.

"I am verily ashamed to report that our prisoner has escaped. He somehow got free and attacked you. I know not the circumstances since my guards were not inside the tent. You had ordered them out. My guards have failed you, and I take full responsibility for them. What is your desire for restitution? Shall I prepare myself for your whip?" Maric ventured.

Berdyk hesitated. If she whipped the sergeant, would she seem like too harsh of a leader? If she did not, would she be seen as weak? What would Captain Eldin have done? Someone had to be accountable for the prisoner escaping.

"Nonsense, Sergeant. The failure was that of your guards. I hold no one responsible for the actions of others. I want you to whip them. I want them each to receive ten lashes," Berdyk decided.

"But, Captain, I must protest. I am willing to take the punishment, as I am responsible for them," Maric reiterated.

"Oh, but you are. Do you think it is so easy to wield a whip against your fellow Amazons? It would be far easier to have the whip biting your own flesh. Physical pain goes away relatively quickly; emotional pain fades much slower. In this way, your guards get a taste of their failure, and you are punished as well. Ten lashes each, Sergeant," Berdyk held firm.

Maric resigned herself to the whippings. It was true. It would not be easy, especially since one of the guards had a broken knee and could not stand on her own. It would be a test of Maric's inner strength.

"Oh, and Sergeant, please send the trainling Rikyn. I have a message from her mother, Councilwoman Pirkyn," Berdyk ordered.

"As you command, so shall it be done." Maric saluted the captain before striding out through the tent flap.

Berdyk smiled. This was going to be easy. No one would even see it coming...

* * *

Celdi pulled up on the reins of her mount and wearily slipped off the mare. She stumbled slightly as she took a few steps toward a small stream. She needed to fill her water skin before she could continue. *Goddess, let it not be too late!* Celdi took several long draws from the stream before she filled her water skin. The stream was cool and refreshing. Celdi splashed a few handfuls of the cool water on her face. Perhaps she could ride several more kligs before nightfall...

* * *

Rikyn opened the tent flap and strode confidently through. She faced Captain Berdyk, and slowly a vicious grin spread over her face, like a stain.

"I have received word that you have our next orders. I need them now," Berdyk informed the youth.

"Oh, I have the orders all right. I just don't know, by looking at you, if you are up to the challenge," Rikyn taunted Berdyk.

"I see that you have taken far less time to prove the words of the Council were true than even I had wagered," Berdyk retorted.

"Oh? And just what words were those?" Rikyn felt the electricity of a challenge charge the air.

"That you are an insolent, incompetent, spoiled brat," Berdyk replied with a bored tone as she pretended to clean dirt from underneath her fingernails.

"You will die for that!" Rikyn screamed as she rushed the captain.

Berdyk waited until Rikyn was a half step away before she swiftly reached out like a cobra strike and grabbed Rikyn by the throat. Rikyn struggled against Berdyk's hand, but the older woman was much too strong. The grip choked off her breath, and Rikyn knew that Berdyk held her life in her hands. If Berdyk would not release her, she would slowly die.

"As I was saying, an insolent, incompetent, spoiled brat. Now, when I release you, you will tell me the rest of the plan. Do we understand one another?" Berdyk increased the stranglehold to drive home her point.

Rikyn nodded as best she could. Berdyk released Rikyn. Rikyn rubbed her throat and glared at the older woman.

"You are to slaughter Eldin's troops in their sleep. My mother can then claim that she is a traitor," Rikyn explained.

"This sounds like it is going to be a fun night. Why don't you show me around camp and point out all of the places that the honor guard hangs about? That should prove to be most helpful," Berdyk directed.

Rikyn was all too eager to help in the demise of Eldin's troops. She had always felt superior to them anyway. These women were nothing more than "common folk." Rikyn led the way out of the tent.

Once outside, Berdyk dismissed her honor-guard escort. As they were walking past the main interrogation tent, Berdyk heard a whip landing on bare flesh. She turned to see Maric administering the lashes. Maric raised the whip again. She closed her eyes as she arched her arm forward, and the whip uncoiled its fury once again. A resounding crack pierced the air, along with the faint whimpering of the young guard whose back bore the angry bleeding marks of the whip.

Maric looked up and found Berdyk. Their eyes locked onto each other. Maric threw the whip to the ground in disgust and purposefully strode over to the young guard. She tenderly untied the guard's hands and helped her toward the healer's area. At least Berdyk's reinforcements had included a healer who had a few supplies with her. Perhaps she had some salve that would ease this guard's pain.

Rikyn eagerly showed Berdyk the entire camp and where the night guards usually stationed themselves. Berdyk made mental notes on the best way to slaughter Eldin's troops without raising the alarm.

"Rikyn, would you please show me the waterfall that is rumored to be near here?" Berdyk innocently inquired.

"It would be my honor. Actually, I had thought that it would be a great place for me to hide until you have finished your 'job,'" Rikyn commented.

Berdyk followed Rikyn into the forest. It was almost a ten-candledrip walk before they emerged by the bottom of a lovely waterfall. Berdyk smiled. This was going to be most enjoyable.

"Rikyn, I have one other directive for you," Berdyk stated as she drew her sword. "Die."

Rikyn turned back toward Berdyk and saw the blade in her hands.

"What are you doing?!" Rikyn panicked.

Berdyk calmly impaled Rikyn up to the hilt on her sword. Rikyn grabbed Berdyk's forearm, and her eyes were wide with shock and pain. She looked down at the sword hilt protruding from her belly and then back at Berdyk.

"Why?" Rikyn managed to ask. "Do you not know what my mother will do to you?"

"Who do you think ordered me to do this? Foolish child. If you do not die, it places suspicion squarely on Pirkyn. Besides which, if your birth mother Ritel had not whored around on Pirkyn, perhaps she would have had more mercy for you," Berdyk explained as she pulled the sword from Rikyn.

Rykin's knees felt weak, but she struggled to remain standing. If she could just make it to the water, perhaps she could float downstream to the healer's area. Maybe someone would see her and rescue her. Rikyn lunged for the water.

"Oh, no, you don't. We do not want you raising the alarm by floating by the camp dead," Berdyk stated as she intercepted Rikyn.

"Damn you to Hades!" Rikyn cursed Berdyk.

Berdyk threw Rikyn to the ground and stabbed her repeatedly. Rikyn was having trouble breathing, and she felt cold. She looked into Berdyk's eyes as the woman towered over her. Berdyk was poised to plunge her sword into Rykin's chest. As Berdyk struck the blow, she crouched very near Rykin's face. Rikyn summoned all of her remaining strength and spit a mouthful of blood at Berdyk. Rikyn died before the blood splattered Berdyk's face.

Berdyk angrily wiped the sticky blood with the back of her hand

and flicked the residue at Rykin's body. She kicked Rykin's corpse and beheaded her. Before Berdyk could return, she would have to wash all of the evidence of slaughter from her.

* * *

Eldin gazed at her mother across the table from her. She had her long, soft blonde curls pulled back from her face and tied with a ribbon of silk that matched the emerald dress she wore. The dress had been a gift from Elrik. She had been away on a mission for several seasons, and when she returned, she had brought several dresses and other gifts for her beloved. Eldin smiled; Dinyar was still a stunning woman. She had a quiet strength tempered with compassion that Eldin adored. Perhaps if she were lucky enough, someday she would possess those same qualities.

Eldin watched as Dinyar moved with a confident grace. She was every bit the lady that Eldin remembered from her childhood. Eldin silently wished for a mate who would be able to rival Dinyar's natural charm and grace. She also wished for a mate who would have her intelligence and independent nature. Reluctantly, Eldin knew she must continue her journey. She was not going to have time to wait for Elrik to return.

"Mother, I regret that I have to return to the road. I must continue my journey, as the Council has summoned me," Eldin broke the companionable silence.

"Already? You have not even rested the night. Is it that you prefer the company of that war beast over your mother?" Dinyar protested Eldin's short stay.

"But that my time were my own. I would love nothing more than to stay in your company, Mother. However, I am due to appear before the Council, and I must not tarry. I promise to stop again on my way back through. I shall try to stay longer next time," Eldin promised.

"I sometimes wonder what my life would have been like had I declared with a farmer instead of a soldier. Would I have had my four greatest loves around me all the time? Would I have become weary of them?" Dinyar wondered aloud.

Eldin clasped her mother's petite hands. "I would think you would not cherish our time together if we were not separated. You see, a blooming rose in the spring is not nearly as beautiful as the one that blooms in the dead of winter."

"My child, you have the body of a soldier but the heart of a poet. I am truly proud to be called your mother. May the Goddess never extinguish that light in your soul," Dinyar prayed.

Eldin reluctantly had to get herself ready for the road once more. Perhaps on her return trip she would be able to spend more time with her family. It had been such a long time. As she walked through the castle, Eldin's thoughts drifted back to Seldar and Kiya. She hoped that Seldar was still healing, but she worried about Kiya. Delyn was capable of almost anything. *Goddess, please keep Kiya safe. Please let her know that I love her.*

Eldin's lips curled up in a haunted smile as she remembered the exquisite feeling of Kiya's small hands working the tension out of her shoulders, followed by the pain of Kiya's rejection. It was sweet and bitter all in the span of a heartbeat. *Goddess, please...*

* * *

Kiya looked up from the road as she felt Eldin's words. She cocked her head, as she could almost hear the faint whispering on the wind. *Goddess, please keep Kiya safe. Please let her know that I...* Kiya strained, but it was of no use. The words were gone as quickly as they had come. Kiya looked around for the source of the voice but realized that no one was near. She felt unsure of herself. Was this some trick her mind was playing on her? She tapped the horse with its reins to urge it into a faster pace, and the wagon slowly picked up speed. She wanted to be far away from this place by the time she had to set up camp for the night.

16

Maric could not sleep. Something did not feel right about this night. There was a tension in the air that was hard to miss, yet harder still to identify. Perhaps it was because she was the only one who had missed the celebration and feast for Captain Berdyk earlier in the evening. The captain had announced her intent to declare with the scribe who had accompanied her reinforcement troops. Naturally, there had been much good food, much music, and too much ale.

Maric decided to go for a walk to clear her head. She opened the flap to her tent and slipped out into the night. It was darker than usual around the camp. Had no one stoked the fires? Maric was going to check up on her guards and make certain that they were not too drunk for duty. She sighed; it seemed as if her workday never ended.

Maric heard a muffled cry come from one of the long troop tents. The hair on the back of her neck rose. Instinct told her to hide in the shadows, and she never disobeyed her instincts. Maric ducked behind the back of the tent as ten of Berdyk's troops exited the tent. They were all carrying their swords. Maric caught her breath as she saw their swords dripping with gore.

As soon as the ten warriors left the area, she cut a small slit into the back of the tent. Maric entered the tent and instantly smelled the evidence of a slaughter. Her stomach threatened to betray her, and Maric had to leave quickly. She ducked back out the slit in the back and took in several deep breaths of fresh air.

Why? Why would they do such a thing? Maric had no time to ponder the questions in her mind, for she realized that Berdyk's troops were on the hunt, and she was part of their prey. How could she raise the alarm without being found?

Maric thought about the ways to escape. It would be madness to make an attempt to ride away from camp. Too many horses to choose from, and how would she be able to tell which one was the fastest? Maric looked around and spotted Eldin's tent. Ah, yes, Eldin's bed! It was verily much like a canoe already. Now, how could she get it to the river?

Maric stalked around the outside of the camp, being careful to avoid the groups of Berdyk's troops. She wanted to wake Eldin's troops, to give them a chance to defend themselves, but how drunk were they? Even if she could sound the horn, would they be able to hold a sword?

Maric's thoughts were interrupted by a loud blast on the horn. Good! Someone had made it to the horn. In seconds, the horn was silenced. Maric could only hope now.

* * *

Delyn woke to the sound of the horn just as three women entered her tent. She grabbed her sword and leapt to her feet. She barely recognized that they had come to attack in time to defend herself. Delyn deflected the first strike. The woman who had swung the sword was strong. As soon as the first strike had been deflected, a second attacker was swinging her sword at Delyn's back. Delyn reached her hands over her head and blocked the stroke with her own sword. While she blocked the attack from the back, the third assailant tried to thrust her sword into Delyn's midsection. Delyn used her right foot to kick the flat of that blade and knock the sword from the assailant's hands.

Sweat streamed down Delyn's face as her efforts were slowly gaining her the upper hand. The first attacker charged Delyn and she ducked and rolled at the last moment, causing the two attackers to fatally plunge their swords into each other. The remaining assassin tried to flee through the tent flap, but Delyn grabbed her dagger from the top of a tree-stump table and threw it at the woman. It found its mark deep in the woman's neck. She was dead before she hit the ground.

Delyn looked around the camp from her tent flap. It was chaos. It appeared as though Berdyk's troops were attacking Eldin's troops. It also appeared that Eldin's troops were still drunk from the celebration feast. Many of the women that Delyn had fought beside were like lambs to the slaughter, and Delyn cringed. What sort of madness was this? It made no difference now; she just had to find a way to escape and warn the Council of this band of brigands.

Delyn removed her dagger from the corpse of the woman at her feet and used it to slice through the fabric of her tent. What she needed was a "back door." Delyn lunged out of the slit and rolled into the thick underbrush at the back of her tent. She lay still for a moment and watched the groups of attackers to be certain that none had heard her before she slowly made her way along the back of the camp. She had to make it to the weapons tent. She wanted a few of the crossbows and a large supply of bolts to be able to defend herself from a distance. That way, she would be able to escape…she hoped.

Delyn moved through the shadows until she was just opposite the weapons tent. She paused to gauge how best to cross the open ground between her position and the tent. As Delyn contemplated her next move, two of Berdyk's warriors emerged from within. Delyn smiled; they each carried a crossbow with a quiver of bolts. *Goddess, let them come to this side of camp*, Delyn prayed.

As Delyn watched, the two warriors headed for the troop tent just beyond her own position. Delyn unsheathed her dagger and prepared to strike quickly. She would have the advantage of surprise. When the two turned to enter the tent, Delyn slipped out of her hiding spot and closed the distance behind them. She slit the closest warrior's throat from behind and tossed her to the side. The second warrior turned back toward Delyn as Delyn reached out to slice her. This warrior proved to be much quicker than Delyn had anticipated and side-stepped the attack.

Delyn dropped her dagger instantly, because she needed both hands to deflect the warrior's sword. Delyn grabbed the warrior's sword arm and used her leverage to break the elbow. The warrior howled in pain. Delyn immediately released the warrior's arm. She then stepped forward while using the heel of her hand to break her opponent's nose. Delyn knew she had to finish this quickly, as she had spent far too much time out in the open as it was. When she felt the bones of the nose cracking, Delyn shifted the angle of her hand and drove the bone fragments into the doomed warrior's brain. The second warrior's lifeless body crumpled to the ground at her feet.

Delyn quickly retrieved her dagger from the ground along with the two crossbows and quivers of bolts from the dead warriors. Delyn looked up and saw a squad of Berdyk's warriors headed in her direction. It didn't appear as if they had seen her yet. She slung the crossbows over her shoulders then grabbed a leg of each dead warrior. Quickly, Delyn dragged the bodies of the dead back into the underbrush. The squad arrived just as they were hidden, and Delyn held her breath. Once the "death squad" entered the tent, Delyn started making her way to the horses.

* * *

Maric felt the hand close over her mouth, and she brought her foot back to try a knee strike. Her foot did not connect with anything, and Maric was certain that she was about to die.

"Shh. Stop fighting, watchdog. It would appear that we are once more on the same side of things," Delyn whispered into Maric's ear.

Maric nodded. She recognized that voice, and as much as she was repulsed by Delyn, she understood how verily much they needed each other in this heartbeat. Delyn slowly removed her hand.

"How many of our troops live?" Maric asked.

"I do not know. I only know of the two of us," Delyn replied, all hint of arrogance in her voice gone.

"Have you a plan?" Maric wondered aloud.

"I was trying to make it to the horses. I figure that I can keep dwindling the number of my pursuers with these," Delyn replied as she showed Maric the two crossbows in her possession.

"I had thought about the horses, but do you know which is the fastest? I do not. Then I thought, *I made Eldin a bed from a hollow tree trunk. It is just like a canoe.* I was thinking that the river runs verily fast near here for several kligs. If we could get the bed to the river, I think it would be impossible for them to follow us," Maric explained her plan of escape.

"That sounds better than trying to pick off dozens of riders. How will we get the bed from Eldin's tent to the river?" Delyn asked.

"I think that Berdyk's troops are going to be fairly occupied for the next several candlemarks. Perhaps I could sneak into Eldin's tent and work for a few candlemarks, unnoticed. I could insert two pegs into the head of the bed. You could bring rope and a horse. When you arrive outside, throw me the rope, and I shall tie the rope to the pegs. We can then use the horse to pull the bed to the river. Once we are there, we can cut the rope and launch the bed. Then all we have to do is allow the current to take us out of danger," Maric reasoned.

"I can see now why Eldin tried to keep you back at the camp; you are a lunatic. However, your plan is just crazy enough to work. Either that or get us killed. I just have one little thing to add to this plan of yours," Delyn commented. "I will not be able to know if you have been discovered and killed, so I shall only wait for the count of ten. If you do not grab the rope by then, I shall continue to ride out of the camp and use my first plan of escape."

"That is reasonable. We shall have to trust each other for this to work," Maric replied.

"You had better get started. I am giving you a candlemark and a half. By then, the sun should be coming up. We cannot afford to be here much after daybreak. It is with the light that we lose our ability to hide in the shadows," Delyn reminded Maric.

"May the Goddess help you in your selection," Maric stated as she parted ways with Delyn.

Delyn smirked at the retreating Maric. *Oh, the Goddess has already been a great help...*

Once Maric reached Eldin's tent, she worked feverishly. Someone had to warn Eldin! There could only be one explanation for this slaughter. They were trying to somehow discredit Eldin in the eyes of the Council, but why?

Maric used one of Eldin's sharp camp knives to bore holes for the wooden pegs. It was slow but steady pacing. Having to work in the dark to avoid detection, it was hard to tell how much progress had been made. She only knew that her time was growing short. Maric felt the holes and decided that they were big enough. Now she would have to insert the wooden pegs.

Maric felt around the tent for a tool that she could use. After finding a small hand ax, Maric made her way back to the bed. She placed a peg to the hole and used a wolf pelt to muffle the sound of the ax head hitting the peg head. Even with the pelt, each strike sounded like thunder to Maric. Surely they would hear her.

Maric dropped the ax. She realized that she was not going to be able to drive the pegs in without alerting Berdyk's troops to her presence. Maric grabbed the slightly dulled knife she had abandoned earlier, and went back to work on the holes. She would just have to make the holes all the way through so that she could thread the rope through and tie it off on itself.

* * *

Delyn waited until the first purple rays of sunrise were visible over the mountains of fire, and then she calmly took one of her pilfered crossbows and loaded a bolt into it. Throughout the night, there had only been one guard at the horse corral. Delyn leveled her weapon at the guard and squeezed the trigger. The guard fell backward as the bolt found its mark deep in her chest.

Delyn worked quickly. First she found a bridle and picked out a mount. She gained the horse's trust and worked the bridle on. After that, she put a saddle on the selected mount. She found some rope coiled and hanging inside the horse tent. Once she had a good length of rope, Delyn opened the gate. She then leapt upon her horse and scared the other horses to stampede. There was no going back into hiding now.

Delyn felt the thrill of the stampede as the horses spilled out into the camp. Berdyk's troops were not prepared for this. Many were caught without a means of escape and were trampled to death. The stampede threw the camp into chaos. Delyn used her crossbows to shoot the soldiers who posed the most direct threat to her as she rode like a demon through the camp. An arrow flew passed Delyn's right ear and she ducked closer to her mount's neck. She turned back and spotted the archer. Delyn leveled her crossbow and sent a bolt that killed her attacker.

Delyn whooped. As she rounded a bend in the camp, Delyn noticed Berdyk emerging from the command tent. She shot her crossbow once more. Berdyk took the bolt to her left shoulder and fell backward. She had not even seen Delyn before the shot hit her. Delyn looked behind her. It appeared as if most of Berdyk's troops were going to give pursuit. Delyn fumbled and dropped a bolt trying to reload. She reached for another one, and this time was successful at reloading. *That watchdog better have that canoe ready!*

* * *

Maric heard the commotion and struggled to get the last hole completed. She picked up the ax and used it as a hammer once more. With the added weight of the ax strike, the final chunk of wood gave way. She now had two holes that a rope would fit into. Maric heard Delyn yell for her. She saw the rope lying at the tent flap.

Maric raced over and grabbed the rope. She hustled back to the bed and worked the rope through the rough holes and tied it off. Sweat glistened on her forehead. Maric could not think of a time when she had felt this much pressure.

Maric finished her knot and then raced to the tent flap. She signaled Delyn, who offered Maric her arm to pull herself up behind Delyn on the horse. Maric grabbed Delyn's forearm, and she pulled the sergeant up. Once Maric was behind her on the horse's back, Delyn touched the horse's flanks with her heels to urge it into action.

Maric noticed that Delyn had the other end of the rope tied around the saddle horn. Maric was glad that Delyn had thought of that, for even if they had both held onto the rope, when the weight of the bed hit, it would have most certainly knocked them from the saddle. Maric felt the sting of an arrow as it tore through the flesh on the outside of her right shoulder in the same instant that the horse jumped forward.

"Keep low! They have some archers out," Delyn stated as she shot one of the crossbows again.

"I noticed," Maric replied as she inspected her shoulder.

Luckily, it was just a flesh wound. When they got on the river and away from their enemies, she would wash the wound.

Delyn shot again at the group of women chasing them. She did not know if she was hitting any of them or not. At least they knew she had lethal weaponry at her disposal. Delyn chose her path through the trees carefully. She did not want the bed to get hung up on something short of the river. It might prove to be fatal if it did.

It seemed like an eternity passed before they broke through the tree line and saw the river ahead. As Delyn pulled back on the reins, Maric slipped off the side and took out her boot knife. She ran back to the bed and started slicing through the thick rope. Delyn came back to help, and together they managed to get the rope out of the bed. The two of them strained to push the bed into the water.

Once they were knee deep, they both entered the bed. The only way for them to fit comfortably was to sit facing each other with one set of legs outside the bed. Delyn felt the cold water on her bum and looked over her shoulder to the front of the bed. Their combined weight had the bed riding low in the water. The holes that had been used to tow the bed now were filling the bed with water.

"Out! We have to get out. The holes are going to swamp us if we don't get out," Delyn commanded.

Because of their body position, Delyn had to roll out first. Maric did not hesitate to follow. They stood looking at each other and the bed. Only one would be able to use it as an escape. Delyn looked at the tree line. Berdyk's troops were breaking through. One would have no chance at escape. It was a death sentence.

Maric unsheathed her sword and put it hilt up in between the two of them. She placed her hand on the hilt, and nodded at Delyn to follow suit.

"Top of the hilt is the victor," Maric stated.

Delyn placed her hand above Maric's. Maric bent over slightly to see how much room was left on the hilt. Suddenly, Delyn forced the sword upward. The ball of the hilt hit Maric full in the jaw. Maric fell backward, unconscious.

"I don't have time for games, watchdog," Delyn growled as she pushed the bed out into the current.

Maric opened her eyes. Everything was a little fuzzy. She felt a hand on her leg shoving it over the side of the bed. Maric looked up at Delyn.

"What are you doing?" Maric exclaimed.

"Tell Eldin that I finally showed her something. She will know what it means," Delyn stated as she pushed a final time.

"But why?" Maric could not understand.

"Because I love her, and because she would miss you more than she will me. Besides, you aren't good enough with the sword to keep them back long enough for me to escape, watchdog." Delyn tried to hide her good deed with an insult so she would not be seen as weak.

Maric watched as Delyn turned back toward the bank of the river to meet her fate. She could not turn away as the current carried the bed farther downstream. Delyn shot her crossbows until the bolts ran out. Maric watched as Delyn took them on with the sword. Before long, Delyn was swarmed with soldiers. Maric tried to see the end, but a bend in the river caused her to lose sight of the massacre.

Maric was numb. Delyn had committed such evil acts, how could she now atone for them? Why now? Why did Maric feel guilty at her death? Maric sighed.

"It is because I wished for her to die," Maric reasoned away her guilt.

She looked up at the cloudless sky. She had better come up with a good way to cover her head, or she might well get sun sickness. Maric was glad that a single wolf pelt remained in the bottom of the bed. She used her short sword as a pole and stretched the pelt across and fastened it to the edges of the bed with her boot knife on one side and a clasp she tore off her armor on the other. It made a small tentlike structure at the end of the bed. Maric lay down with her head inside the shade. Now all she had to do was wait for the bed to land along the river bank.

Sleep would prove elusive as Maric thought of all the young soldiers and trainlings who were undoubtedly dead now. Everyone that she had fought beside in the last three seasonmarks with the exception of Eldin, Kiya, and Seldar were gone. At least there were a few survivors. What sort of evil would justify this type of slaughter?

17

Pirkyn paced inside her bed chamber. It was going to be a long session if that brat captain did not hurry and show herself. *How long does it take one to ride from the Drakknian border to the capitol anyway?* Pirkyn was frustrated. She was more than ready to assume control over Yashor. Pirkyn smirked. Soon she would be able to see the slaughter of these soft councilwomen. That would be a glorious day for Yashor!

A small knock at the door interrupted Pyrkin's thoughts. She padded over to the door and slid the bolt back. Once the heavy wooden door was unlocked, Pirkyn opened it to find a young messenger outside. She appeared to be around Rikyn's age. Pirkyn felt a pang of guilt, but she quickly remembered how she had come home from Council once to find her declared Ritel in bed with the town smithy. Not only had Ritel cheated, but she had given herself to a smelly, lowly smithy; a peasant! She did not even have the decency to cheat with someone of the same upper class as Pirkyn. The guilty feelings subsided, replaced by a simmering hatred. It was this fire that Pirkyn used to commit her heinous acts and not feel affected by them.

"Well, are you going to stand there all day, or are you going to tell me why you have interrupted my nap?" Pirkyn snapped at the youth.

"I...I am sorry. I have been sent by lead Councilwoman Arkon to assemble the Council. Captain Eldin has arrived," The young messenger relayed her information.

"Excellent news." Pirkyn's face broke into a wide smile, and she absently reached into her belt pouch and tossed the girl a few coins.

Pirkyn closed the door on the girl as she dove on the ground after the carelessly tossed coins. Obviously the girl had been raised by peasants, Pirkyn noted with disdain.

* * *

Eldin closed the clasp that designated her rank, securing her cape around her neck. She sighed as she adjusted her sword belt to the perfect position. Funny how quickly the sword becomes a part of you. She never really felt the weight on her hip any longer. It was as if the sword were just an extension of her body, a deadly extension.

Gathering her courage, Eldin opened the door to her room and exited into the hallway of the small tavern. She had chosen to distance herself from the Council Chambers because she was uncertain if they had received Kiya's request for a transfer yet. Eldin worried that Kiya had divulged the fact that she and Delyn had participated in pleasures of the flesh. That could verily well ruin her career.

As she moved into the great room of the tavern, Eldin could feel the admiring eyes upon her. It was a little unnerving.

"Hello there, soldier. Are you thirsty?" a voice purred from a nearby table.

Eldin looked over to see an attractive young dark-haired woman indicating that Eldin could join her. Eldin gave the woman a polite smile.

"I am afraid that my time is otherwise spoken for. I appreciate your kind offer, but I must leave, as the Council is awaiting my arrival." Eldin tried to be as kind in her refusal as possible.

"Well, I shall be here all night if you should change your mind.

Besides, when the Council is finished with you, you might need a good flagon of wine and even better company," the woman responded, not the least bit dissuaded.

Eldin politely excused herself and exited the small tavern. The evening breeze still carried the smells from the day's market. The streets were still bustling with activity. Many Amazons were headed for the theatre to see the latest play. Others were headed for a tavern for good ale and a story or two from a traveling bard. Occasionally Eldin would see a woman who obviously did not have a place to live. This always touched her heart. She knew that work was hard to come by unless you were fit enough to swing a sword for Yashor.

The sound of a struggle caused Eldin to draw her sword. Her head snapped to the left and she saw a woman trying to ward off three attackers. Eldin raced down the small alleyway toward the group. When she was only paces away, she noticed that the attackers were a patrol of soldiers. They had already shackled the woman, yet they were continuing to strike her about the face with their fists.

"Hold! What is the meaning of this?" Eldin boomed a challenge.

The soldiers looked up and, recognizing Eldin's rank clasp, snapped to attention.

"This is business of the Council. This woman is a wanted rogue. Now allow us to finish our job and arrest this woman, Captain," the senior ranking soldier explained with a tone of superiority in her voice.

"Please, Captain, I beg of you to place me under your authority. Take me to the Council. I shall not live if you leave me with..." the woman begged before being silenced with a kick to the mouth.

"Enough, soldiers! Have you no decency? We do not beat our prisoners before they have had a trial, been convicted, and been sentenced. We are not the judges. That is why we have the Council of Nine," Eldin admonished.

"With all due respect, Captain. You know not our orders. Our orders came from Councilwoman Pirkyn directly. This is a dangerous rogue and one that you cannot possibly believe, as her tongue is forked from all of the lies she has uttered," the ranking soldier explained. "Now allow us to finish our mission, Captain."

Eldin was about to turn away when she noticed the captive's eyes. No, there was a measure of truth in them. This was no lie.

Eldin turned toward the prisoner and said, "Stick out your tongue."

The prisoner looked up at Eldin as if she were a Hades Hound.

"I said, stick out your tongue," Eldin repeated herself.

The prisoner poked her tongue out of her mouth at Eldin. Eldin grasped the tongue and bent forward to inspect it. She turned to the three soldiers.

"Do any of you see a fork in this woman's tongue?" Eldin asked sarcastically.

"Captain, you know well that is just a measure of speech," the senior soldier spoke up.

"I asked if you saw a fork in this woman's tongue, Sergeant," Eldin called the senior soldier by her rank.

"No, Captain, her tongue does not fork," the sergeant conceded.

Eldin released the woman's tongue. She glared at the three soldiers.

"Then I insist that we take the prisoner to the Council together. Now get her up and let's get moving. I have but ten candledrips before I am to be in Chambers," Eldin ordered.

The soldiers pulled the badly beaten woman to her feet and shoved her toward the street. The group moved in silence toward the Council Hall. It was an impressive building made from the large green stones that were found abundantly in the river bed.

The sergeant pulled one of the other soldiers aside. "Run back to the Council and inform Councilwoman Pirkyn what has happened here. Tell her that we were intercepted by Captain Eldin of Three Rivers. Hurry."

The other soldier broke away from the group and ran down the alley in the other direction. She hoped to cut across the market square and beat the group to the Council Hall. Eldin noticed the soldier leave but felt it was more important to stay with the prisoner until she was recorded into the dungeon scrolls. There was definitely something wrong here, and the hair on the back of her neck was standing on end again. Which councilwoman had they said gave them their orders? Hades Fire, she could not remember!

* * *

Pirkyn looked up, startled by the appearance of a young soldier sprinting through the hallway toward her. Pirkyn was at the doorway to the back entrance of the Council Chambers. She hesitated.

"Councilwoman Pirkyn, wait! I have important news for you!" the soldier called out to her as she continued her sprint.

Pirkyn decided to wait and hear the news. Perhaps it was some pleasant news, such as the capture of one of her enemies. That would make her day even more joyous. Imagine, sending Eldin off to die and take the blame for the coup, as well as the capture of another who could damage her bid for control of Yashor! A glorious day indeed!

"Councilwoman, Sergeant Dansyl captured the farmer Rinter as you ordered. Before we could dispatch her, she was saved by Captain Eldin of Three Rivers. She is personally escorting her to the Council Hall dungeon to be recorded," the soldier reported.

"Go back to the holding cell and offer anyone who kills Rinter freedom and ten krillits. I care not by whose hand she dies; she must not be allowed to speak in front of the Council! She knows too much," Pirkyn ordered.

"As you command, so shall it be done." The soldier bowed her head and placed her right fist over her heart in salute to Pirkyn.

* * *

Eldin watched as the soldiers recorded the prisoner's name into the scrolls. The prisoner, named Rinter, was hauled off to a cell in the dungeon. Eldin wondered what crime a poor farmer could be guilty of. Oh well, it was out of her hands now. She had made certain that the woman had made it safely to the dungeon to await her trial. It was all she could do for her.

Eldin turned her attention to her own meeting with the Council. She assumed that since she was not under any type of arrest, that the meeting was to do with strategy and not punishment. Eldin sighed as she walked along the corridor to the Council Chambers. She was uncomfortable in formal settings such as these. Eldin was a common soldier. True, she was an officer, but she was no politician, and Eldin hated politics as a matter of personal ideology. Perhaps she could think of a way to bring up the treatment of male-children while she was here.

Before she was prepared, the doors to the Great Chamber loomed in front of her. Eldin turned to the crier and said, "Captain Eldin of Three Rivers here to see the Council as ordered."

The old woman looked the soldier up and down appreciatively before nodding. She started to swing one of the doors open and motioned for Eldin to follow. Eldin took in a deep breath and allowed the crier to lead her to the pulpit. Once there, the crier turned to the assembly of councilwomen.

"Captain Eldin of Three Rivers," The crier called out to the council women.

It seemed to Eldin as if her name echoed through the chamber. She felt very small next to these women of great power. She felt even smaller as the crier left her alone at the pulpit to stand her post at the doors again.

Arkon stood and addressed Eldin. "Captain Eldin, it is good to have you here so quickly. Have you been informed of the nature of this meeting?"

"No, your Grace, I have not been informed," Eldin replied.

"I see. Well, it is the decision of this Council that you are to go on a mission into Drakknian territory. We want you to allow yourself to be captured. When they take you to their camp, we need you to discover how they are resupplied. Also, we need to know where their main grain supply is kept. It is our plan to have you poison either the grain or the water supply and attack them with your troops while they are at their weakest. We hope to crush them once and for all in this manner," Arkon revealed the Council's plan.

Eldin stood at attention. She heard the words yet could not believe them. How foolish was the Council? She had been raised to think that they were infallible. She could not possibly live through such a capture. Even if she were to sacrifice her life in this mission, how would she be able to poison the Drakknian supplies and get word back to Yashor that they could launch the attack? This plan was complete madness.

"Captain Eldin, we believe you are the only one who is capable of success in this mission. We will not force you to go, but we would like for you to volunteer," Arkon finished.

"You honestly think I am capable of surviving that mission?" Eldin asked incredulously.

"We have faith in you, the daughter of General Elrik. You, Captain Eldin, and no one else," Arkon explained. "Do you have self-doubts?"

Eldin paused. Did she believe in her own abilities enough to accept this mission?

"Have you heard from my healer, Kiya?" Eldin inquired.

Arkon looked at Kidak. She motioned for Kidak to respond. Kidak stood and faced Eldin.

"I have received only a few scrolls from her. The last scroll I received, she was still at your camp taking care of your soldiers. Why? Have you reason to fear that she is not well?" Kidak gave voice to her own fears.

"I do fear for Kiya's safety, Councilwoman Kidak. She and my lieutenant were at odds with each other. I can only say that from experience, I do not trust Lieutenant Delyn to let this matter pass without her taking some form of revenge. I left standing orders with my personal honor guard to watch over Kiya in my absence," Eldin explained.

"Why would your lieutenant and my daughter be at odds, Captain? Did my daughter spurn the lieutenant's advances?" Kidak tried to understand the situation.

Eldin wanted to squirm, but she forced herself to stand at attention. She would not lose her military bearing now.

"There was a big misunderstanding. It is all I can tell you without breaking confidence. I shall strike a deal with the Council." Eldin finally thought of a way out of this mess.

Arkon stood, and Kidak took her seat. This would be Arkon's place.

"What deal is it that you wish to make, Captain? Providing that the Council is in the mood to 'deal?'" Arkon inquired, curious at the captain's audacity.

"I shall accept your mission into Drakknia if you will transfer Kiya away from the front lines. Transfer her to a healer's post inside a well-protected city. That is the place she deserves. Kiya has more than proven herself to me, and she is in great danger. I shall pay for my honor guard to accompany her there. I only wish to know she shall be safe," Eldin laid out the terms of her deal.

Pirkyn smirked. It was quite obvious to anyone in the Chamber that the captain was smitten with this healer. Pirkyn now had another name to add to the list of rogues to be arrested and executed…if she were not already slaughtered by Captain Berdyk's troops. Pity that Kidak would already be dead. It would have been fun to force her to watch the execution.

Eldin watched as Arkon conferred with the others. She wondered if she had overestimated her value. Had she just brought more pain Kiya's way? *Goddess, please let her be safe.*

Arkon turned back toward Eldin. "We shall accept your offer. You will be packed and ready to leave by morning. We shall give you a scroll to take to the merchants in the city. Anything that you believe you shall need, they shall supply you with free of charge."

Eldin allowed a small sigh to escape her lips, certain that none in the Council had heard. She watched each face of the councilwomen and tried to find the ones that her mother had warned her about. This was more difficult than she had imagined. One of the women smirked, but it could just be her normal posturing since she was sitting in the eighth chair. Number eight of nine. Eldin committed her face to memory.

Kidak studied Eldin. There was only one reason why the captain would make an offer like that—Eldin was worried. That meant that she cared for, or loved, Kiya. *Great Goddess, have I just sent Kiya's heart to her death?* Kidak would need to speak privately with Eldin.

"You are dismissed, Captain Eldin. Please get your list together," Arkon stated, waving her hand toward the doors.

Eldin was all too happy to leave that Chamber. She bowed her head and placed her right fist over her heart in salute to the councilwomen. Eldin forced herself to remain calm and dignified as she walked toward the great doors. Inside she felt like running. Eldin had much to do to prepare for her mission. She needed to get started.

* * *

Dedak looked out the window over her kitchen sink one more time. She had an uneasy feeling that she could not shake. Something was terribly wrong. Outside, the evening breeze blew gentle the fragrance of the mountain blooms. By all outward appearances, everything was as it should be in town. Dedak shuddered. There it was again, that awful foreboding feeling.

Dedak nearly jumped out of her skin as Rynar came up behind her and slipped her small arms around her waist. Rynar recoiled in alarm.

"What have I done, love? Do you wish me not to touch you?" Rynar asked, dreading the answer.

"Nothing, my pet. It is not you. I was startled, that is all. I feel something is amiss, yet I can see no wrong. I have learned to trust my feelings over the many seasons," Dedak explained as she stared out the window.

"You have always worried. How many seasons have I heard you proclaim that there would not be enough honey for mead to last throughout the winter?" Rynar tried to soothe Dedak.

Dedak turned toward Rynar just as several shadowy figures slipped past the barn into the house across the way. She smiled lovingly at Rynar.

"You are right. I am always worried about something. Yes, we always managed to make the honey last," Dedak replied as she wrapped her arms around Rynar's tiny waist.

Dedak bent and lovingly caressed Rynar's lips in a sweet, gentle kiss. Rynar returned the kiss and wrapped her arms around Dedak's neck. Rynar buried her fingers into her fiery mane. Reluctantly, Rynar pulled away, breathless.

"You always manage to take my breath away. I love you, Terdak," Rynar whispered.

Dedak placed a fingertip on Rynar's lips.

"Shh. Remember, you *must* call me Dedak. If anyone were to hear you, I might be found out. Then they would hunt me," Dedak reminded her young love.

"Dedak, my love, I want to spend all of your days by your side. You once told me that it was possible for Jahru to link souls with Amazons who lack Jahru blood. Was that simply a night story to make me travel to the land of dreams?" Rynar asked.

"It was a true story, and yes, I was trying to get you to sleep. At sixteen seasonmarks you had more energy than I could keep up with," Dedak admitted. "Why do you ask?"

"I wish to be linked with you more than anything," Rynar confided.

Dedak gazed into Rynar's eyes and knew the truth of her words. It still left an uneasy feeling in her stomach. The girl did not know what she asked.

"Remember when I told you how verily much I wished for my mortality? How much I wanted to go to the Great Feast? How could I link our souls and not worry that you would change your mind and grow to despise me?" Dedak replied.

"I could never despise you. You are my life, my joy and pain. I only wish to share whatever days remain for you. I do not wish to outlive you or die before you. I only wish to hold your hand as we both enter the Great Feast together. I want to sit by your side as we await our rebirth," Rynar poured out her heart.

"Rebirth. Now there is a scary thought. It is my sincere hope that my rebirth does not happen for many, many seasonmarks after I die. I wish to have some rest," Dedak commented.

Just as Dedak bent forward to kiss Rynar again, the back door was thrown open and a group of five armed women stormed through. Rynar screamed as Dedak placed herself between Rynar and the armed women.

"Is this the tavern known as 'the Grey Fox'?" the tallest woman asked.

"Yes. This is the Grey Fox. Are you always in the habit of storming through people's back doors? There is a sign out front that states the name of this tavern, had you bothered to enter from the public entrance," Dedak fumed.

The women were dressed in soldier's uniforms. They looked as though they had seen many battlefields, for their faces were road-mapped with scars. The tall woman with hair as dark as night stepped toward Dedak. She stood inches away from her and barely concealed her contempt for the tavern worker.

"Are you the woman called 'Rynar'?" the soldier demanded.

"Rynar is on holiday. I am watching this tavern for her until she returns," Dedak replied, sensing the underlying threat. "What may I do for you?"

"What is your name?" the soldier snapped.

"Mandyl, and this is my declared mate Shandyk," Dedak lied as she squeezed Rynar reassuringly.

"Well, Mandyl, we need all of your rooms. We will be here for at least the next fortnight. By order of the Council of Nine, you must give us these rooms free of charge," the soldier spouted.

"Certainly, ah, I do understand that you are a soldier, but I am verily poor at guessing rank and names," Dedak replied, hinting that the soldier should introduce herself.

"You may call me Sergeant Moukri. The rest of these troops you will never address. You will have our first-feast made and on the table by the candlemark before sunrise. You will have our mid-meal packed and ready to go by sunrise. You will have our rooms cleaned and our even-feast on the table by half a candlemark to sunset. We shall be in and out of our rooms throughout the days. It is verily important that you understand that if our hospitality here suffers, so shall you. You shall find yourselves arrested and tried for crimes against Yashor's soldiers. Do you understand, Mandyl?" Moukri laid out the terms for the soldiers' occupation of the tavern.

Dedak could feel Rynar shivering from fright against her back. She needed to soothe the woman that she loved. Dedak would never allow any harm to come to her.

"I understand, Sgt. Moukri. I shall have Shandyk prepare your rooms. Have you need of even-feast this eve, or have you already feasted?" Dedak tried to placate the soldiers.

"I believe that all we require is some free-flowing ale, tavern keep," Moukri replied as the other soldiers filed past her into the great room and found themselves seats at the long table closest to the fireplace.

"I shall bring the ale straight away," Dedak responded as she moved toward the back of the bar and gently nudged Rynar toward the rooms.

As soon as every soldier in the room had a half mug of ale in hand and another full mug beside them, Dedak fled for the rooms. She was desperate to check on Rynar. Dedak slowly walked down the row of rooms until she heard a soft whimpering from within. It was the unmistakable sound of Rynar trying to hold back her tears. Dedak slowly opened the door and entered.

Rynar looked up at the sound of the door opening. She held her breath, hoping that it would not be a soldier. For some reason, these soldiers did not put her at ease. They oozed deceit from their pores. Rynar watched Dedak close the door behind her and then turn to her with her arms open in invitation. She closed the distance in a heartbeat. Rynar felt Dedak's arms wrap around her and she felt safe for the first time since the soldiers had arrived.

"Why are they looking for me? What do they want?" Rynar whispered against Dedak's chest.

"I do not know, my love. I only know that I am going to get you away from here. They are not going to get you, I promise you that," Dedak replied, then kissed Rynar's forehead gently.

"I am scared, Dedak…really frightened. I have never seen these soldiers before. I mean, it may sound silly because they are wearing Yashor uniforms, but I do not think that they are Yashor soldiers. Am I completely mad?" Rynar confided.

"Not at all. I have had those same feelings, my love. Let's finish these rooms, and then I am going to lock you in our room. Do not argue with me. If they get drunk and try to harm me, well, they shall simply not live to see the dawn. I will not have you in harm's way. Perhaps I can persuade them to help themselves to the ale barrels, then I can come be with you," Dedak shared her plan.

Dedak helped Rynar finish lighting small fires in all of the rooms and turning down the covers on the beds and sleeping pallets. She then escorted Rynar to the room that they recently shared. It was the master suite. Dedak kissed Rynar gently, then closed the door and locked it with her key.

* * *

Kiya rejoiced in seeing the torches of Romyl's fortress shining in the distance. She had restitched Seldar's leg, but the poor lad could do with a good night's rest in a comfortable place. Kiya encouraged the horses to pick up speed. They would reach the fortress in a few candlemarks. Hopefully, one of the taverns would still have a room available.

"Kiya, do you think that I will be labeled a traitor?" Seldar inquired quietly.

"Not if I have anything to say about the matter. I know that you have acted only with the utmost honor. If you had not saved me, Lieutenant Delyn would have killed me for certain," Kiya replied, trying to ease the male-child's fear.

Seldar winced as he shifted positions in the wagon. Goddess, would it never stop hurting? His leg throbbed with every creak of the wagon as it slowly made its way along the rutted dirt road.

"Kiya, do you believe in the powers of the Jahru?" Seldar blurted out suddenly.

Kiya cocked her head at the question.

"I do not know, Seldar. I suppose it is possible. I mean, we killed them all, so we shall never be certain that they were magical women at all. I don't know if it was magic or just something that they were born with. It is like having better eyesight than most. Who can say why that happens? Is it magic or just the way you were born?" Kiya reasoned.

Kiya noticed the way that the young male-child gazed at her. What was he thinking?

"Why do you ask me such questions, Seldar?" Kiya puzzled.

"I do not mean you any dishonor. I was curious. I am deeply sorry if I have offended you," Seldar tried to reason away his question.

"Perhaps it would be best if we rode in silence," Kiya suggested, still puzzled by Seldar's question.

* * *

Maric shivered. She felt cold from having been out in the sun all day at the mercy of the river. As the sun set behind the mountains, the cold was seeping into her bones. Maric tried to sleep. The sight of Delyn being overrun by Captain Berdyk's troops haunted her. She felt sickened by the loss of her friends and the rest of her honor guard. There were some trainlings that were only eight seasonmarks old. By the Goddess, what treachery had befallen Eldin's troops! Maric had a hard time believing that Amazons were capable of such cruelty.

Maric sat up. She felt as though the sun had drained her strength. She dipped her hand into the river and took a cool sip of water. She had to try again. Maric sat on her knees and tried to use her hands as a paddle. She paddled with all of her might to break free of the current and get to shore. She strained against the current. Finally, Maric doubled over inside the makeshift canoe, her energy spent. The current was still too strong.

Maric looked at the bank of the river illuminated by the light of the twin moons. It was perhaps ten boatlengths away. If only she had learned to swim when her sib had offered to teach her! Even though her sib had been younger, she had mastered many physical skills ahead of Maric. A great sigh escaped her lips. Maric knew she was a prisoner of the river.

Without any food to eat the entire day, Maric's head was beginning to pound in protest. She felt a little nauseous as well. She wanted nothing more than to escape her feelings of guilt and horror. Combined with her physical ailments, Maric was quite miserable. She decided to lie back down, and hopefully sleep would claim her. At least when she slept, she could dream of days that were not so dark. Maric was also convinced that if she had a flagon of mead close by, she would have drained it dry in one long draught.

"You can take the drink out of the soldier, but the drunk forever remains," Maric berated herself.

* * *

Kiya pulled up on the reins and the horses slowed to a stop. She looked up at the sign hanging from the front of the small stone building. A picture of a hawk was painted in berry red. Beneath the hawk were the words "Travelers Welcome." She hoped that this inn would have a room available. Kiya was desperately tired and in need of a hot bath. She turned toward Seldar.

"Stay here with the wagon. I shall return shortly," Kiya instructed.

Kiya wrapped the reins around the hand brake before she climbed down from the wagon. Seldar watched as she opened the door to the tavern and entered. Inside the tavern's great room were many Amazons drinking ale, feasting, and conversing with one another. Kiya searched through the chaos for the innkeeper.

18

Dedak waited until all of the soldiers had left the tavern for the morning. She searched for Rynar and found her making up the sleeping pallets in the cheaper section of the tavern. The night had been a long one for Rynar, and sleep had been elusive. Dedak knocked quietly on the door to alert Rynar of her presence. She jumped anyway.

"Good morning, my sweet," Dedak greeted her.

"Good morning yourself," Rynar answered as she tucked the corners of the small pallets.

"You can relax, as they have left for the morning. They are searching the countryside or Goddess knows what else. I wish to speak with you. We should pack a few changes of clothes and put the packs out in the barn by the trap door. I shall pack clothes while you pack some road rations. Nothing fancy, just some staples to get us through for several days. We need to leave while they believe our story. Sooner or later, I am afraid that the townsfolk shall return to the tavern and expose us," Dedak explained her worries.

"I keep expecting the very same. It is like the whole town is under arrest...no one leaves their house. I feel the soldiers are evil, my love. It scares me to think what they want of me," Rynar admitted.

"We shall soon rid ourselves of the lot of them. Do not worry, I am not letting any harm come to you," Dedak pledged.

Rynar turned, and Dedak could see the fear in her eyes.

"You cannot make that guarantee! If they should try to harm you, you shall live. I am not charmed as you. I shall die. I shall die and have to sit at the Great Feast all alone," Rynar accused, tears streaming down her cheeks.

"Rynar, I will not..." Dedak started to explain, but Rynar shoved past her and left the room.

Dedak watched her young love run down the hallway and out the back door. She did not know what she was asking! Dedak's heart felt heavy. If she gave in and linked their souls, she may verily well be dooming Rynar to live forever. It was madness! Had Dedak a chance to do it all over, she would not have chosen this "immortality." Dedak wanted nothing more than to ease her love's fears, but she could not bring herself to doom the naïve woman to a never-ending Hades existence. Dedak prayed that it would not cost her Rynar's love.

Dedak returned to the room she shared with Rynar. She began to pack clothing for their journey. Dedak was careful to pack clothing for every type of weather that they could encounter, be it wet, cold, or hot and sunny. As she folded the last of the clothing and set it into the small pack, she sighed. She looked around the room and knew by the shadows of the tall shade tree that chased up the west wall that it was almost mid-meal. She was going to miss this place that she had grown to love. Dedak had wanted to grow old here and die.

No time for tears, old woman. Dedak padded across the room to her dresser. She opened the top right drawer. She reached out her index finger and lovingly traced the carvings of a small wooden box in the back of the drawer. Gingerly, Dedak picked up the box and carefully placed it inside her pack. It was now time to see if Rynar had packed the road rations. She would need to hide it all in the barn before the soldiers returned for mid-meal. They were leaving this night.

* * *

A light rapping at the door startled Eldin as she was packing the last of her newly acquired weapons. She dropped the new boot dagger on the sleeping pallet and made her way to the door. Eldin slid the bolt back and opened the heavy dark wooden door to reveal Councilwoman Kidak standing on the other side.

"Councilwoman, what an honor. Please come in," Eldin invited as she opened the door wider and gestured inside.

Kidak entered the small room and looked around. She caught sight of Eldin's muscles rippling as she closed the heavy door and slid the bolt back into place. The captain was quite attractive, Kidak had to concede.

"You are a hard woman to find, Captain. I had thought that you would be staying at the Council Hall. It took me quite some time to find this place," Kidak commented.

"This must be something important, then," Eldin reasoned aloud.

"Well, you could consider it important and personal," Kidak replied.

Eldin cringed. Oh no, here it comes. The Council must have received Kiya's scrolls and sent Kidak here to punish me. Eldin pulled the rickety chair, fashioned from lashed oak branches, away from the small table in the center of the room. She held the chair for the councilwoman, and Kidak graciously accepted the offer. *At least she has nice manners. I must give her credit for that,* Kidak thought as she sank into the chair.

Kidak studied Eldin's face for a heartbeat. She had a decidedly distinguished angle to her jawline. As her gaze came to rest on Eldin's eyes, Kidak decided that they were indeed "ice on fire" as in the legends that the bards told. It was easy to see that Eldin favored Elrik in physical appearance.

"I need to know why the lieutenant and your healer were at odds with each other. Did they try each other and have a falling out? Did Kiya reject the lieutenant? But first and foremost, I need to know why you made your deal with the Council," Kidak peppered Eldin with the questions that had been plaguing her mind since the Council meeting.

"I cannot tell you why I did it. I guess in truth…I just wanted to see her safe. I know that she is in danger from my lieutenant," Eldin admitted.

"Why is she in danger, Captain?" Kidak tried a different approach.

Eldin was visibly uncomfortable at the line of questioning. Kidak noticed that she shifted her body weight back and forth between her feet and had averted her eyes.

"I need to know, Captain. It is important." Kidak softened her voice a little.

Eldin watched a bug slowly crawling along the top of the wall. How she wished in that heartbeat she could switch places! A bug's life must be simpler. Hunt for food and avoid being squashed, but then, perhaps it would be a boring existence. She closed her eyes and brought thoughts back to the councilwoman's questions.

Eldin took a deep breath; there would be no going back now. "Lieutenant Delyn and I had an 'arrangement.' We were not in love, yet we would indulge in pleasures of the flesh for mutual release. It is quite a common practice among soldiers. She approached me and offered me this 'no strings attached' arrangement because Delyn's true love is the Sword Corps."

Kidak's eyes widened. She had never heard of such actions. Why, that was scandalous! Eldin noticed Kidak's reaction and hurriedly continued her story.

"It helps to deal with the fear and burden of combat. Sometimes you need to feel close to someone when all around you is death and gore," Eldin justified. "Not long after Kiya came to camp, I started to notice her. I was not worthy of her, however, because Kiya is pure in heart, mind, and deed."

Kidak inwardly sighed. So her daughter had not indulged in moral crimes. That was a relief. Kidak tried not to judge the captain through a mother's eyes but as an impartial councilwoman. It was all but impossible.

"I had stopped seeing Delyn because I had decided I wanted to try Kiya. I could not get her out of my mind. She was like a light that suddenly burned bright in the dark cavern of my soul. I felt like I could accomplish anything if she simply smiled at me. She had a way about her that made you feel as if you were the only Amazon in the world."

"I can understand your attraction, Captain, but please get back to my questions," Kidak spoke up to keep Eldin on track.

"Yes, well, I had been summoned here, so I went to Kiya's tent to tell her good-bye, and I was leaning forward to kiss her when Delyn walked in on us. She just went mad! She was crazy jealous of Kiya. You see, she told me later that she had planned on asking me to declare with her, but I had not been around lately. She blames Kiya for that. Delyn was enraged with Kiya, but it is me that she should be angry with. When I went back to Kiya's tent, she wanted to know why Delyn was so upset. I told her the truth, for I could never lie to Kiya, and then she assumed that I was just trying to seduce her for the same arrangement. She believed that I only wanted physical release and did not want to offer her my heart."

Kidak could hear the pain in Eldin's voice as she spoke about Kiya's interpretation of the events.

"I guess it is better this way. As I said before, I am not worthy of Kiya. Now she may find someone honorable with whom she can share the gift of her love," Eldin concluded.

"I have to know, Captain, do you love my daughter?" Kidak knew that her answer would make all of the difference.

Eldin paled. She had not known! But how could she not? She had known Councilwoman Kidak and her mate, Yamouth, before she had been assigned to the Drakknian border. Kidak had commissioned her. All Amazons born in Yashor are named after their mothers. *Kidak...Yamouth... Kiya. All the pieces had been there all along. I had been so distracted that I didn't get the connection. What was it she said to my mother? "I am Kiya, daughter of Councilwoman Kidak and Yamouth, and healer just assigned." She was so beautiful that I did not even register her words. She is indeed a Demon Shamaness.*

"So Kiya is your firstborn daughter, then?" Eldin asked weakly.

"She is the first and only daughter that grew inside me. When the Council next blessed us with the news that we were to give birth, they had selected Yamouth to carry the child. Yamouth's baby only lived a few days after birth. Kiya's sib died of a sickness that stole her breath in the night," Kidak explained. "Now I need to know, do you love my daughter?"

"I know that I do not deserve Kiya. If I should make it back from this mission alive, I shall not pursue her affections." Eldin paused as she reflected.

"Please answer the question, Captain," Kidak prompted.

"I...I...Goddess, yes, I love Kiya," Eldin haltingly admitted in a voice so soft it could barely be heard.

"Why is it so hard for you to declare your heart, Captain?" Kidak inquired gently, trying to understand Eldin.

Eldin closed her eyes. She saw the first time J'min smiled at her. She saw the ax lodge deep in J'min's back. She saw J'min fall dead into her lap. She gazed one more time into those unseeing eyes. Eldin opened her eyes. She sighed and watched the bug crawling on the wall once more. Eldin accepted that she was going to Drakknia to die for her country, so would it really matter if she told this councilwoman the truth? Would it matter if someone heard how J'min had died? She had never told anyone before. Would it ease her heavy heart to release the burden?

Eldin decided to trust Kidak with the long-buried information. As Eldin described her early life, falling in love with J'min, and J'min's death, Kidak could see another picture of Eldin's character emerge. The obvious pain that Eldin had buried for so long had torn her heart apart. The wounds were still raw and the pain unmistakable in her voice.

Eldin felt tears threatening to form in her eyes, so she turned away from Kidak. She could not risk dishonoring Elrik further by crying in front of the councilwoman. As Kidak listened to all of the events that led up to Delyn threatening Kiya, she came to some realizations. The guilt of J'min's death had driven the young captain to be more careful with the lives of her soldiers. It had made her a better leader. The emptiness she felt at losing her love had also made her vulnerable to Delyn.

Kidak could see why she had been so reluctant to share her feelings with Kiya. She had also come to the conclusion that Delyn had preyed upon Eldin's vulnerability and seized the opportunity to lure her into illegal trysts. She would make certain that Delyn was punished for that. Kidak was proud of Eldin for her candor, even when to lie would have been her best interests. Eldin was a woman of honor; she had just gotten a little lost along the way.

"Eldin, I am sorry for the pain that I have caused you to relive, but sharing the truth is worth the pain," Kidak apologized to Eldin's back.

Eldin felt the tears subside, and she wiped her eyes with her thumb and forefinger. She felt as though she had regained control of her emotions, so she turned to face Kidak. Eldin noticed for the first time how much Kiya resembled Kidak. The corners of her mouth turned slightly upward in a sad smile. Kiya would be a beauty far into her advancing years by the looks of Kidak.

"Eldin, does my daughter love you?" Kidak inquired gently.

"I think she had begun to love me until the day that Delyn walked in on us. It does not matter now, anyway. I do not think that I shall survive this mission into Drakknia. Do not worry; I shall keep my word. I will go to Drakknia and allow myself to be taken prisoner. From there I shall make every effort to succeed in my mission. I just do not believe that I shall live through the escape attempt," Eldin responded truthfully.

"Eldin, I have just one more question, and then I shall leave you to your packing. If Kiya offered you her heart, would you still go?" Kidak asked, as she needed to be certain before she would interfere in her daughter's life.

"If Kiya gave me the gift of her heart, then no, I would not go. I would stay here with her. I would make a life with Kiya if she would have me. But it matters not because she has not offered, and I am a dead woman already. I shall leave for Drakknia within the next candlemark," Eldin reasoned.

"Thank you for your honesty, Captain. I feel as though you are an honorable Amazon. You have made some mistakes and committed crimes against the Goddess, but the Goddess is like a mother. She is forgiving of our trespasses against Her. If you seek Her forgiveness, She will cleanse the sin from your soul," Kidak shared her faith with Eldin.

Eldin grabbed a bundle of five scrolls off of the table and held them out for Kidak. "Would you please see to it that these scrolls are sent to the proper people? They are my last thoughts that I wished to share with the ones closest to me. One of the scrolls also details how to distribute my worldly possessions in the event that I am killed."

Kidak took the scrolls from Eldin. She gazed into the determined eyes of the captain and found the truth in them. Kidak was humbled by what she saw there; Eldin expected to die for her country yet was resolute in her attempt for a successful mission.

"Eldin, please come back to us if it is at all possible. I know that things will work out as the Goddess intends. I also know that my daughter can fly off the handle at times, but through reflection, she is able to admit when she is wrong. Be careful, dear honorable Captain," Kidak blessed Eldin before she fled the room.

Did the councilwoman just restore her honor? A small smile slowly spread across Eldin's face. Did Kidak just allude that Kiya's heart may someday belong to her? Eldin felt the seed of hope plant itself in her heart. *Oh Kiya, if only you knew how much my heart yearns for you.*

19

Seldar watched as an indignant Kiya stormed out of the Red Hawk Tavern and stomped toward the wagon. As she was climbing back into the wagon, he noticed a tall, muscular Amazon running out the door after her. Hades fire! By the look on Kiya's face, that woman had better know what she is doing!

"Kiya, wait! Please reconsider staying here. My sib is a fool. She had no right to question your desires. You see, she walked in on her declared laying with a male-child only a few moons ago. The wound has not healed. I know that you do not possess a mind-sickness like her mate," The woman pleaded.

"I would say it is better that we leave. I would not allow this wounded male-child to sleep in such filthy conditions as were suggested by your sib. He is the sib of Captain Eldin of Three Rivers and was wounded in defense of Yashor, and myself. He has more honor in his toes than your sib has in her entire body! Good day, Kendyk," Kiya boomed as she slapped the reins across the backs of the team.

Seldar watched the woman Kiya had called Kendyk as the wagon lurched forward. She remained in the middle of the cobblestone road watching Kiya leave. There was definite interest in her eyes, but she failed to understand Kiya's anger.

Kiya suddenly looked at Seldar. "Did you hear that?"

"Yes, Kiya. I heard what was said. I was sitting right here," Seldar reminded her.

"Not the words of that merchant fool. I thought I heard something else," Kiya tried to explain the words that had tickled her ear heartbeats before.

It was something about "my heart yearns." Kiya shook her head. She must be going mad. Why else would she be hearing voices? She silently vowed to never bring up the subject again. She did not need to be carted off to some mind healer! *You did this to me, Delyn. May the Goddess punish you for your crimes.*

* * *

Kiya watched as Romyl's Fortress became smaller in the distance behind them. She did not understand why her thoughts kept traveling back to Eldin. Why had she been so upset by the captain's words? Did it matter now? She was nothing but a filthy whore. She did not deserve anyone's love now.

Seldar watched as Kiya fought her demons in silence, seeing the tears well up in her eyes and spill onto her cheeks. He reached out to lay a comforting hand on Kiya's shoulder but withdrew it when she recoiled from his touch.

It would take perhaps less than a fortnight to reach the Council Hall. Kiya wanted to feel her mother's arms wrapped around her. She wanted to feel safe again. She wanted to feel anything but this deep hollowness and pain in her soul. Perhaps she could get an assignment at a temple. She would pledge herself to the Goddess and forsake the love of another woman. Kiya hung her head. If she were not worthy of another woman's love, how in Hades would she be worthy of the Goddess? There seemed to be no answers for her future.

Seldar worried about Kiya. His wounds were easy to see, they were easy to fix. His wounds were healing nicely. Kiya's wounds were deep in her soul. No one could see how bad they were. If you cannot see something, then how can you fix it? How can you heal the wounds of the soul? Seldar figured only the Goddess could do something that hard. *Please forgive me, Great Goddess, I know I am not worthy to pray to you, but it is not for me that I petition Thee. If you could just heal Kiya, it is all that I ask. I would gladly give You my life in exchange for her soul to heal. Please think on it.*

* * *

Dedak mixed the sleeping powders she had crushed from the herbs she had harvested that day with the ale from the keg underneath the bar. If all went well, the potion would be strong enough to force the soldiers to sleep through their escape. A noise in the hallway made Dedak jump. She was on edge and would be that way until the powder was all poured. Just as Dedak hooked the mixture back up to the spigot, the soldiers returned to the small tavern. Dedak looked up from her task and placed a big, fake smile on her face. She only hoped that they bought her acting.

"Ho, Sgt. Moukri. How stands the day? If all of you would have a seat, I shall bring out your even-feast and mugs of ale," Dedak called out pleasantly to Moukri.

"That will be fine, Mandyl," Moukri grumbled.

Dedak served plates piled with slabs of tender mountain goat meat from the icehouse. She had slowly cooked it in its own juices. Around the meat she added white root, yellow squash, green stalks, onion, and crushed garlic cloves. Dedak served fresh baked brown bread in loaves at each end of the long table. She brought a large bowl of brown gravy and set it near Moukri at the head of the long table. She finished the spread with a bowl of her latest creation—creamed honey and butter whipped together, which she set in the center.

Dedak retrieved two mugs of ale apiece for the soldiers. She smiled sweetly at each one of them as she set the mugs down. She felt some satisfaction as she watched the soldiers digging into the meal. Little did they know that in the kitchen she had spit into each plate before she had served them. *Eat up, you Hades Hounds!*

ELDIN OF YASHOR

Dedak stood with her ear to the door and listened. All was quiet in the tavern. Good. Perhaps all of the soldiers were asleep. It had been several candlemarks since they had eaten even-feast and had started drinking the tainted ale.

"Stay here while I make certain that they are all firmly in the realm of dreams. I shall come back and get you if it is safe for us to leave," Dedak told Rynar.

Rynar nodded. She was nervous, and her body was tensed as if she were preparing to fight in the fisticuffs arena. Dedak smiled at Rynar and then quietly made her way down to the great room. There were soldiers asleep with their heads on the table and some with their heads on each other. Oh, but they were going to have pounding heads in the morning! Dedak was satisfied so she padded back up the hallway to get Rynar.

When she opened the door to their room, she stopped dead in her tracks. Moukri had one hand over Rynar's mouth, and the other held a dagger to her throat.

"Now, I wonder where you two would be going in the middle of the night? Why, you even have traveling clothes on. So tell me, which one of you is really Rynar?" Moukri sneered.

Dedak felt her anger boiling in her veins. She had not felt this angry in nearly two hundred seasons. Dedak could feel herself losing control over the power that dwelled within her. It was the source of her magic; it was the darkest and lightest parts of her soul. Dedak felt helpless to stop the changes taking place, and perhaps a part of her did not want to stop the fury she knew was coming.

Rynar could not take her eyes off of Dedak. Her eyes were starting to glow with an unnatural eerie reddish tinge where the whites of Dedak's eyes had been heartbeats before. Moukri's dagger dropped to the ground, forgotten. She did not even feel the warm wetness spreading down her legs. All she could see was the face of fury itself!

"Let her go!" the words came as a deep beastly growl from Dedak's throat.

Moukri's arms suddenly had a mind of their own. They fell limply to her sides. Rynar did not hesitate; she ran over to Dedak. Dedak took Rynar into her arms while never breaking eye contact with Moukri. She

— 206 —

could feel all of Rynar's pain and fear coming from her in great waves of intensity. Dedak would not allow these vermin to hunt them down. She knew there was only one way to assure that Rynar was safe.

"Burn," Dedak commanded as she covered Rynar's eyes and turned to walk out of the inn she had built so many seasonmarks ago.

Moukri could not move. She opened her mouth to scream, but no sound came out. Her body felt hot. It felt heat like she had stuffed herself into a woodstove burning at full capacity. As Dedak and Rynar walked out of the Grey Fox, Moukri's body burst into flame. The flames burned hotter and higher, catching the curtains and spreading to the thatched roof. By the time that Dedak and Rynar had gathered their packs, the whole tavern was engulfed in flame.

Dedak released the animals in the barn, coming to her horse's stall last. She slipped the bridle over the sweet animal's head and spoke soothingly to it. The horse seemed to sense that it was in no danger from the beast next to it, for it allowed her to lead it from the barn. Dedak placed a blanket over the horse's back and pulled herself up. She rode over to Rynar and held her hand out to the young woman that she loved.

Rynar grasped her hand, and Dedak pulled her up behind her. Rynar slipped her arms around Dedak's waist, and Dedak urged the horse away from the burning structure as many of the Amazons from town arrived with buckets to form a fire brigade. They never looked back as they rode out of town heading toward the mountains of fire in the distance.

They rode less than a candlemark when Dedak collapsed and fell from the horse's back, taking Rynar with her.

"Terdak! Please, speak to me. I…I do not know what to do. Please do not leave me," Rynar choked out as she cradled Dedak's head in her lap.

As Rynar held Dedak, she noticed the subtle changes in her appearance that had overtaken Dedak in the tavern were now returning to normal. Dedak trembled slightly, but she seemed to calm after a few candledrips. Rynar rocked her and kissed her head. She did not know what was happening, but she knew that Dedak still breathed, and that was all that mattered.

Rynar knew that they needed to keep traveling. Dedak seemed stable enough to be moved, so she wrapped her arms around Dedak's waist and dragged her through the road to the underbrush. She hid Dedak from view and set off to collect the spooked horse.

Dedak slowly opened her eyes. She could smell a small fire and food cooking. Had it all been a night terror after all? Dedak tried to sit up and moaned from the exertion. She felt too drained to even sit upright and fell back onto the sleeping skins. She had only felt this way one other time in her entire life. Dedak knew that she had lost control then, and it was not a night terror but reality.

Rynar heard Dedak moan, and she bounced from the campfire to check on her.

"Terdak!" She exclaimed.

Dedak did not even have the strength to utter a sound, so she slowly moved her index finger in a slow wag. Rynar understood the gesture.

"Dedak!" Rynar corrected herself with the same enthusiasm as the first outburst.

Dedak smiled and blinked. Rynar was by her side and knelt down to wrap her arms around her. She almost broke down into tears of joy. She was so afraid that Dedak would pass on and leave her behind, to see her awake was overwhelming. Rynar gently caressed Dedak's lips with her own, and Dedak felt the rush of Rynar's love envelope her. Rynar lay down next to Dedak and slowly massaged Dedak's neck, shoulder, and arm.

After a half candlemark, Dedak tried to speak again. "Ry, I need some food in me. I also need water."

Rynar heard the weak requests and tore herself away from Dedak to prepare her meal. She scooped a ladle full of the fish stew that she had boiling over the campfire into a bowl for Dedak. She broke off a hunk of bread and placed it inside the bowl. Rynar grabbed the canteen and brought it over as well.

Dedak ate in silence and felt her energy replenish slowly. It took an entire candlemark to finish her meal, but by the end, Dedak was completely reenergized. She reached for Rynar and pulled her into her arms. She nuzzled Rynar and placed a kiss on her temple.

"How did we get here? I do not remember leaving the road," Dedak asked, looking around at the campsite next to the fast-flowing river.

"Something happened to you, and you were not in your mind. We both fell from the horse. The horse got spooked and ran off. I stayed with you in the road for a long time. It scared me because I thought you were dying. When I realized you were going to live, I went and caught the horse and then put you on it. I led the horse until I heard the water from this river. I knew that I needed to make something to eat in case you woke up, and I am really only good at fishing. I cannot shoot a bow to save my life, so I made camp here. That is about it." Rynar gave her the short version of the past several candlemarks.

"You are a clever woman. I suppose you have already had a bath, eh? Did I miss all of the good parts too?" Dedak teased.

Rynar pushed her back down onto the sleeping skins. She straddled Dedak and held her arms down.

"You know good and well that you don't get to see the 'good parts' until *after* you declare with me. You might be some all-powerful Jahru, but I still control the 'good parts,' and do not you forget it!" Rynar feigned indignant.

Dedak rolled over on top of Rynar and kissed her passionately. Rynar was swept up into the kiss and returned Dedak's ardor with a whimper. Dedak ran her tongue along Rynar's pulse points in the hollow of her throat, and stopped occasionally to place strategic nips on the petal-soft flesh. Rynar moaned. It was suddenly hot on those sleeping skins. Dedak ran her hands along Rynar's side, barely touching the sides of her breasts. Rynar's body reacted to the feather-light touches, and she was covered with gooseflesh as the tiny hairs stood on end, her nipples hardening underneath her travel tunic. Dedak allowed her tongue to explore all of Rynar's exposed flesh, down to the cleavage at the bottom of the tunic's neckline. Rynar writhed beneath Dedak. It was such sweet torture. Suddenly Dedak rolled off of Rynar, and she stood up.

"While you may control the 'good parts,' I on the other hand control the very skilled naughty parts. Stay here, love. I need a quick dip in a verily cold river," Dedak exacted her "revenge" as she turned and ran to the riverbank.

Rynar lay on the skins with her heart pounding and her body screaming for release, listening to Dedak laugh all the way to the river. *Just you wait, smarty Jahru. Two can play at that game!* While Dedak quickly undressed, Rynar lay and planned her revenge.

"Ry! Ry, come quickly, and bring a rope!" Dedak yelled as loud as she could.

Rynar sprang to her feet and hustled to the saddlebag. She rummaged quickly through the contents until her hand closed on their rope. She brought it out and sprinted for the river. When Rynar got to the riverbank, she saw Dedak holding a woman's head above the water. Dedak was in a fast-moving current and trying to keep them both from being dragged under the volatile water. Rynar had to run along the riverbank, for they were quickly moving beyond her reach.

"Throw me the rope! Hurry!" Dedak yelled between sputters of water.

Goddess, please guide my hands! Rynar closed her eyes and threw the end of the rope as hard as she could in the direction of Dedak. She opened her eyes. The rope had missed, short. Rynar's heart sank.

Dedak pushed her legs and free arm hard against the current. She needed to get into the smaller current that was pushing things towards the riverbank. Dedak was a strong swimmer, and it was taking all of her strength to battle this current. Slowly she made progress. Suddenly she felt a tug against the woman she was carrying. Dedak pulled against it with all of her might. The river was trying one last desperate attempt to pull the woman back into its deadly abyss. She was quickly losing her strength.

Dedak was afraid she was going to lose the battle with the deadly current, when she suddenly felt a hand close tightly around her arm. She looked over her shoulder and into the eyes of love. Rynar had made it to them, and she had the rope tied around her waist and tied off on a tree. Rynar was using her free arm to pull against the rope. Dedak wrapped one hand into Rynar's wet clothing while she held the drowning woman with the other. Once she had her other hand free, Rynar grabbed the rope with both hands. Slowly, handful of rope by handful of rope, the three women escaped the current and got back into calm water.

When they reached the shallows, Rynar helped Dedak pull the unconscious woman from the water and onto the shore. Dedak bent over and placed her ear by the woman's mouth.

"Is she breathing?" Rynar asked, a little out of breath from exertion herself.

"I think she may have breathed in the water," Dedak replied as she rolled the woman over and started to push on the back of the woman's chest.

While Dedak tried to push the water from the woman, Rynar untied herself and ran a hand through her wet hair so it was out of her face. She went into the camp and rummaged through the saddlebags for one of the stink roots. It was known to wake people when they were trapped inside their own minds. She returned with the root in hand to see water coming in great waves from the woman's mouth.

Dedak continued until nothing more came from the woman's mouth. She rolled her back and placed her ear to the woman's mouth again. Faint whisperings of air movement tickled Dedak's sensitive ear. There was hope.

"I brought you stink root. Maybe it will help her regain her senses," Rynar said as she knelt down near Dedak.

"It might help, at that. Break some, please," Dedak instructed.

Rynar broke a piece of the pungent root, and the smell was nearly overpowering. Dedak took the offensive root from Rynar and held it under the woman's nose. A few heartbeats later, the woman gagged and took in a deep breath of air. There was more hope. Soon, the woman was taking regular breaths, but she had not opened her eyes. Dedak threw away the root and called to Rynar who had gone to change clothes and prepare a warm, dry place for the woman and Dedak beside the campfire.

Together they moved the woman to the sleeping skins and made certain that she would be comfortable if she woke. Dedak sat next to the fire and allowed the warmth to seep into her bones. Rynar came over and sat next to Dedak. Dedak opened her arms, and Rynar snuggled in.

"Some lover you are," Rynar teased.

"What are you talking about, Ry?" Dedak asked, confused.

"The river," Rynar replied cryptically.

Dedak looked down into Rynar's playful eyes. Then it dawned on her.

"You mean the 'good parts' were showing through your wet clothes, and I did not notice?" Dedak guessed.

"Yes, indeed. Now you shall have to wait until after the declaration, 'Oh mighty lover of Amazons.'" Rynar exacted her revenge for earlier.

"Hey, you have to admit, I was a little busy at the time," Dedak playfully groused in defense of her reputation.

Rynar yawned and stretched. "Whatever makes you feel better, dear."
Dedak pulled Rynar closer and kissed the top of her head. "You do."

Rynar snuggled in and closed her eyes. Dedak watched the flames of
the campfire and meditated. She noticed when Rynar's breathing became
regular and slow. Rynar had fallen asleep in her arms. Dedak thought
about the events of the last several days. Rynar had shown her the depths
of her love and trust. *She had trusted me not to harm her even through my
unnatural face of fury and had run into my open arms. Ry was correct. It is
easy to jump into a raging river when you are charmed, but Ry is not. She
jumped in because of the depth of her love for me. Am I being a stubborn
fool? If she loves me this much, perhaps I should grant her that one wish.
I just hope she realizes that we shall be bound to one another tighter than
any declaration. She will become a physical part of me, and I her.*

Her mind made up and Rynar's fate sealed, Dedak started the ancient
chant quietly while she held the still-sleeping Rynar. She said the incantation over and over until she felt the powers deep within her stir to life.
Dedak felt the powers surge into her blood and pump throughout her body.
She was fully charged with the magic of her ancestors, and she thrilled to
the feeling of that power. Dedak had suppressed the power for so many
seasonmarks that to call on it was like a baby taking its first breath of air.
She was being reborn to that which was her true essence.

Dedak reached for the cooking knife that was sitting on a piece of
firewood. She held the blade into the flames while she continued the incantation. When the knife was purified from the flames, Dedak pushed the tip
into her chest and slid the blade in until it was inside halfway to the hilt,
just above her heart. She gasped in pain as she twisted the hot blade and
was rewarded with a blade full of fresh blood "nearest her heart." Dedak
pressed on the wound with her finger, and it healed over in a heartbeat. She
ran her tongue over the blade and then kissed Ry, transferring the blood to
her young love's body, tongue-to-tongue.

Rynar started to stir. Dedak calmed her and allowed her to sleep. Her
body was going through changes, and it would need some rest. When she
woke, she would feel the bond. Dedak smiled; they were now and forever
as one.

20

The slow pace of the wagon frustrated Kiya. If they could find a way to trade the wagon for riding horses, they would be able to get to the Council Hall more than a week earlier. Kiya turned to Seldar. She noticed that he had moved to the back of the wagon. When had he done that?

"Seldar, do you think that your wound is healed enough that you can ride a horse?" Kiya inquired.

Seldar glared at Kiya. Was she ever going to stop?

"Certainly. Might I inquire as to when we are going to be stopping at a stream, lake, river, or any form of water?" Seldar fumed.

"I think that if I can talk to a horse trader in the next village, we may be able to trade for some. Then we can get to the Council Hall quicker," Kiya continued.

Seldar tapped his index fingers against the biceps of his folded arms. She did not even hear him anymore!

"What will be the use of us stopping at a village when none would dare to come within twenty paces of us, and that is if they are standing upwind?!" Seldar groused.

A quarter-candlemark passed, with Kiya continuing to detail her plan. Then Seldar heard it. It was the glorious swoosh of a waterfall close by. Seldar climbed back into the front seat.

"You do realize that you are not going to get the same reception that you received by that merchant in Romyl's Fortress, do you not?" Seldar commented.

Kiya looked at him, puzzled by his comment. Seldar could stand the road grime and stench no longer. He grabbed the reins from Kiya and pulled the horses to a stop amid her protests.

"What are you doing? Have you gone completely mad?!" Kiya complained.

Seldar stood and picked up the diminutive healer and placed her over his shoulder. He carefully climbed down out of the wagon and followed the sounds of running water to a clear stream while she squirmed in protest. He waded out into the water until it was hip deep.

"Seldar, what are you doing? Put me down this heartbeat!" Kiya demanded.

"As you command, so shall it be done," Seldar replied as he dumped her unceremoniously into the stream.

Kiya resurfaced sputtering water. She leveled Seldar with a look that would cause your heart to cease beating. Water ran in rivulets, cascading from her wet hair down her face and dripping off her chin. She looked like a drowned rat…an angry drowned rat.

"I could not stand the dirt and smell any longer. It is unhealthy to drive yourself so hard. We need to take care of our bodies. Kiya, I cannot pretend to know what it is that you are going through, but for the love of the Goddess, can we at least keep our bodies clean, please?" Seldar pleaded as he thoroughly enjoyed the feeling of cool, clean water surrounding his body for the first time since they had left the healer's post.

Kiya's eyes lost their fire. It started at the corners of her mouth. A slight twitching, a small upward tugging; soon it turned into a full smile. Laughter erupted from Kiya for the first time since the night of her brutal attack. She felt some of her burden lift. Laughter was proving to be strong medicine for her damaged soul. Kiya suddenly pushed a wall of water at Seldar, completely soaking his dry head.

When Kiya saw the water dripping off Seldar's surprised face, she burst out into a full belly laugh. Seldar soon joined her. The two enjoyed the water for several luxurious candledrips before reluctantly returning to the wagon. Thankfully, it was still there. It had only moved to the side of the road where the team of horses was happily munching away on the deep green grass and tasty patches of clover.

Seldar got out a large bowl from Kiya's pack and filled it with water from the stream. He allowed each horse to drink its fill before he climbed back into the wagon. He sat triumphantly next to Kiya. She glanced over at the smug look on his face.

"You are not going to tell anyone about that," Kiya threatened.

"No, I'm not telling anyone. I'm telling *everyone*," Seldar corrected; very pleased with himself.

Kiya playfully punched him in the arm. "You are just like the sib I never had, Seldar."

"That is a verily kind thing to say, Kiya," Seldar replied seriously.

"Good, then behave so I do not have to take you out and tie you to a tree," Kiya shot back as the wagon resumed its plodding course.

"When did Eldin tell you about that?" Seldar asked.

"When we talked one night by the waterfall. We ended up falling asleep out there," Kiya explained.

"Oh, I am certain you did," Seldar drawled out the words to inflect innuendo.

"I see a tree with your name on it," Kiya teased.

"Ok, ok. If you must, but I am giving you fair warning. I am fairly certain that Eldin did not tell you about the only thing I could do to avenge myself," Seldar replied.

"What was that?" Kiya asked, since Seldar was correct, Eldin had never mentioned the rest of the story.

"I am a male-child, so I peed on her," Seldar stated matter-of-factly.

"Eww, Seldar!" Kiya replied, wrinkling her nose.

The day had gotten much brighter as they rode along in companionable banter. Kiya was making great strides in her recovery.

* * *

Rynar stirred and slowly opened her eyes. She started to stand but felt a strange dull ache in her legs and lower back. She nudged Dedak. Perhaps she had strained something when they had saved that woman. Dedak opened her eyes and smiled at the bewildered Rynar.

"Good morning, my pet. How stands the morning?" Dedak inquired, eager to see how strong the bond was.

"I hurt this morning. I think I must have strained myself with the swimming," Rynar reported.

"Aw, you poor dear. Do you want me to get up and make you some tea?" Dedak offered.

"No, I can get it. Ohhh ouch," Rynar complained as she stood up and stretched the kinks out.

Dedak felt her lower back. The muscles were tight. So that was the source of Rynar's discomfort. She smiled; the bond was strong.

Rynar made two mugs of hot tea and brought one over to Dedak. She sat up and reached for the tea. Rynar was blowing on hers when Dedak took a large sip.

"Ow!" Rynar cried as her tongue felt the burn.

Rynar looked at Dedak as she swallowed the hot brew. Dedak looked deeply into Rynar's eyes, and they widened with realization.

"You mean we…" Rynar started.

Yes, we are bonded, Dedak silently replied.

Rynar dropped her forgotten tea and lunged at Dedak, wrapping her arms around the woman. Tears of joy fell down her cheeks. Rynar showered Dedak with kisses over her eyes, cheeks, and finally she landed a searing, passionate kiss on Dedak's lips. Rynar felt the kiss like a mirror. There was the passion she felt, but then she felt Dedak's passion echoing in her soul. It was the most incredible feeling that the youngster had ever known. Rynar now knew that she would never again be abandoned, and the security thrilled her.

Me too, Dedak responded to Rynar's thoughts about the feeling.

Wait. My lips are not moving. You can hear my thoughts? Rynar wondered.

When I want, as you can hear the thoughts that I wish for you to hear, Dedak explained.

This is so…so… Rynar could not form a word to fit the overwhelming feeling of awe.

Welcome to the world of the Jahru, my sweet. We are forever bonded one to the other. We are now two halves of a whole, Dedak commented.

Rynar felt truly blessed for the first time in her life. She lay with Dedak, learning all about the abilities of the Jahru. She would fire questions at Dedak so quickly that they would almost run continuously.

"I guess I should go check on that woman. Is that the remains of a uniform she is wearing?" Rynar asked as she reluctantly left Dedak's side.

"I think it is an honor guard uniform. You know, she is paid by a private family, not by the Council of Nine," Dedak guessed correctly. "But I have no idea how she got herself into that river. No one in their right mind would attempt to go over the falls upstream."

"I suppose we shall have to wait until she wakes to find out the answer," Rynar reasoned as she carefully placed a few drops of clean water on the woman's tongue to help keep her from getting sun sickness.

It took Dedak several candlemarks to hunt down a rabbit, but she was proud as she brought the creature into camp. Rynar smiled at her mighty huntress and set about preparing the beast to add to the already brewing stew of roots and wild vegetables she had scavenged earlier.

"Something smells mighty good," Maric commented before a coughing fit made speech impossible.

Rynar turned to see the woman they had saved from the clutches of the river sitting up. She walked over to her and knelt down beside the woman, whose coughing fit finally subsided.

"How stands the day with you?" Rynar asked, concern evident in her voice.

Be careful.

Rynar turned and glanced at Dedak, *She is weak, and I know what I am doing.*

"I think I shall live. I take it you two fished me out of the river?" Maric inquired.

Dedak joined her stubborn young love and knelt down beside the woman as well.

"Yes. I went to the river to wash, and I just happened to see you floating in the fast current. I know it is easy to die out in that type of current, so I went in after you. I would not have been able to pull you out if my committed here had not joined us. We worked together to get us all out." Dedak's voice reflected the pride she had in Rynar.

Maric looked at the two, and it was obvious, even without being told, that they were committed and waiting to be declared. What mushy looks they gave each other. Young love.

"I am Maric of Three Rivers," Maric introduced herself.

"I am Dedak, and this is Rynar," Dedak replied, gripping Maric's forearm.

"I do not suppose that you would have a tunic that might fit me? Mine seems to have snagged on branches in the river and ripped beyond repair," Maric said.

"I shall see what we have to offer you. You might want to consider having Rynar sew closed the holes in your riding pants as well," Dedak commented as she went to the saddlebags in search of something that Maric could wear.

Crimson invaded Maric's face as she realized that her pants were full of revealing holes. She covered herself with the sleeping skins next to her.

"Please remove your clothing, and I shall mend it," Rynar said sweetly.

"Sure, I get no attention whatsoever in the last nine seasonmarks, now suddenly *everyone* wants me to strip," Maric deadpanned as she worked at removing her tattered clothing.

Maric watched as Rynar took her clothing and rummaged through her small belt pouch. She pushed back a stray lock of hair. Rynar finally found the small sewing bag and triumphantly pulled it from the pouch. She sat down on a log and held up the needle to see through the eye. With steady hands, Rynar poked the end of the thread through the needle eye and started the task of mending Maric's clothes. Not many Amazons could wield a needle. Most that could were healers or their apprentices.

"Where are we?" Maric wondered aloud.

"I believe we are near Three Rivers district. Perhaps five or ten kligs to the north, northeast," Dedak replied as she returned with a tunic and riding pants that might fit Maric. "How did you get into the river, Maric?"

"It is a long story. Suffice to say that had I not gotten to the river, I would be dead along with the rest of the troops. I do not know how to swim, but I had a hollowed-out log as a canoe. I am trying to make it to Three Rivers, possibly the Council Hall itself," Maric explained, not wanting to give out too much information in case these women were part of the evil that seemed to be spreading throughout Yashor.

Dedak became very interested in this spreading evil. She turned so that Maric could try the clothing on with a measure of privacy.

"Who attacked your troops? Did they look like Yashor uniforms? Were they Amazons?" Dedak inquired.

"Why do you ask?" Maric wanted to be sure she could trust these women before she would divulge any information.

"We owned a tavern. One night several soldiers stormed in through our private entrance in the back. They demanded to know where the woman known as Rynar was. I lied to them and told them that she was traveling. They were very specific about what would happen to us if we did not allow their occupation of the tavern. Then they took up all of our rooms that we rent out. They wore Yashor uniforms, but it was more of a feeling that I could not trust them. I do not believe that they were truly Yashor soldiers. They seemed verily 'evil' to us," Dedak explained. "We escaped. That is why we are here. We are going to try to find a new place to live."

"It is worse than I feared. I must warn the Council of Nine. I think there is a new enemy. An enemy from within," Maric decided her next course of action.

"What say you? You believe it is a conspiracy? What happened to your troops, Maric?" Dedak wanted to know.

"My troops were attacked and killed in their sleep by the soldiers that had come to 'reinforce' us. I lived because I could not sleep that night. I was out for a walk when I noticed the new soldiers going through the camp. They killed everyone that I fought beside for the last five seasonmarks. I may have only been a sergeant in Eldin's honor guard, but we took our turns out on the battlefield as well. I only know of four survivors. Captain Eldin, her sib Seldar, the healer Kiya, and me," Maric reported grimly.

Dedak sat down next to Maric. It was obvious that she was traumatized by the loss of so many close friends. Maric looked at Dedak. She was so young, but there had been trainlings at camp that were only seven seasonmarks old. They had all been slaughtered like spring calves. Maric felt her stomach twist at the thought.

"Do you believe that the councilwomen are in danger?" Dedak asked Maric.

"Yes. I believe that we are all in danger," Maric replied, still trying to erase the memory of her young charges dying.

"Then we shall go with you. My nie…my cousin is Councilwoman Kidak," Dedak explained.

"We should eat first. Then break camp. The stew is ready," Rynar piped in. "Those fit you rather well Maric."

Maric nodded at the compliment. She felt a little odd in someone else's pants. The ocean-blue tunic felt comfortable, however.

* * *

Kidak pounded on the door once more. She looked behind her and saw the rogues turning the corner. It was but a heartbeat before they spotted her again. Kidak pounded even harder. *Please open the door. Please open the door.*

"It is of the utmost urgency! Open the door!" Kidak yelled.

She looked over her shoulder. The closest rogue was grinning at her now. She was only twenty paces away and closing in fast. *Oh, Goddess, they are going to kill me!*

Kidak screamed as a hand touched her arm. Romyl looked past Kidak and saw the danger. She pulled Kidak inside and slammed the door shut, sliding the bolt into place.

"Shh. It's just me. You are safe now. It's just me," Romyl soothed Kidak.

Romyl slid the long drapes to the side and came face to face with one of the rogues as she was peering in the window. What was going on? The rogue brought her sword up, and Romyl jumped away from the window just as the sword came crashing through.

"Run, Kidak! Hurry, to the kitchen," Romyl yelled as she turned to retreat as well.

Romyl looked behind her as she caught up to Kidak. The rogue was climbing in through the smashed window. It was obvious that they were assassins. They were not going to stop unless they were stopped... permanently.

Kidak reached the hallway that led to the kitchen. Before they could reach the kitchen, the sound of more windows breaking from the other rooms stopped Kidak. They were now coming through the kitchen and dining hall windows as well. Romyl grabbed Kidak by the hand and pulled her toward the staircase. No one could be coming through those windows unless they were birds.

Romyl paused at the bottom of the stairs to allow Kidak to go first. That way, she would be between the assassins and Kidak. If it came down to it, she knew in her heart that she would sacrifice herself for the woman that she had loved for more than thirty seasonmarks.

"Where are you going? Come out and play, Councilwomen. We are going to play a game with you. It is called 'hide the sword in the weakling.' I think we shall have great fun," one of the rogues taunted as she dragged the tip of her sword along the stone floor, making an eerie scraping noise.

"Do not listen to them. Keep going!" Romyl stated firmly.

At the top of the stairs, Romyl pointed Kidak to the back bed chamber. As they ran through the hallway, Romyl grabbed a heavy vase. She motioned for Kidak to keep running as she turned and headed back to the top of the stairs.

Romyl heaved the vase at the assassin who was already halfway up the staircase. It hit her square in the chest and sent her toppling down the stairs. Romyl wasted no time before she turned and retreated to the back bedroom as well. Once she was inside, the heavy door was shut and the bolt slid into place.

Romyl and Kidak worked feverishly to move other furniture to barricade the door. They could hear their attackers pacing up and down the hallway outside, occasionally taunting them with threats of death.

"Do you think that they shall give up and leave?" Kidak hoped aloud.

"No. I think that they are highly trained assassins, Kidak. I think that we need to figure out a plan," Romyl replied.

Romyl went to her clothing chamber. Inside was an old chest. She pulled it out and opened it. Inside was an assortment of weapons. She looked up at Kidak.

"Do you know how to swing a sword or use a crossbow?" Romyl asked.

"I do not. Romyl, I am verily afraid that we are going to die, and I am no help in defending us against those butchers out there," Kidak exclaimed, feeling helpless.

"Nonsense, Kidak. I wager you and Arkon are the only councilwomen who remember that I was a general before I was selected to join the Nine. I am also willing to wager that those assassins out there do not know my military background and will therefore underestimate me. I shall defend us, and I will teach you how to use a weapon," Romyl reminded Kidak as she pulled her old sword from its sheath.

The sword gleamed from constant attention. Even though she had retired from the Sword Corps, Romyl had still used the sword every day to drill. It was great exercise and made her feel young. Romyl took the sword and knelt down in front of Kidak, gripping the sword in her left hand, with the tip down. She bowed her head and placed her right fist over her heart.

"My life and my sword for you! I shall not allow you to die," Romyl vowed, repeating the ancient soldiers' pledge of fealty.

Kidak's eyes brimmed with tears and she placed a hand over her mouth. She gazed deeply into Romyl's eyes.

"Oh, Romyl, do not do this to my heart now. I need to live, to see Yamouth once more. She has been good to me. You say that pledge, and it just reminds me of…" Kidak could not finish.

"I gave up the sword for you; I have never stopped loving you," Romyl defended herself.

"You gave up the sword for me? You gave it up five seasonmarks too late. I waited and waited on you to ask me for a commitment. I dreamed of declaring with you. All I asked was that you give up the sword so I knew that you would be coming home to me at the end of each day. I just wanted to know that you would not leave me a young loner." Kidak allowed the long-buried words to flow out of her like a dam breaking.

Romyl stood and gripped the sword intimately in her right hand. "Well, I for one am glad right this heartbeat that I did not give it up too soon."

Romyl walked past Kidak to the window. She looked down and saw only one assassin guarding the back alley. Romyl squinted to try to get a better view. She gasped. The assassin was wearing a Yashor Sword Corps soldier's uniform. Romyl turned toward Kidak.

"It is worse than we thought. I believe, my dear Kidak, that we are in the midst of a coup," Romyl stated matter-of-factly.

21

Dinyar screamed as the arrows landed all around. Elrik grabbed Dinyar's hand and started to run for the protection of the stone house. Three paces from the door, an arrow found its mark deep inside Elrik's flesh. Elrik stumbled backward into Dinyar. Blood seeped from her chest and stained her tan tunic a deep crimson.

Elrik's knees buckled and she fell to ground, her breath coming in painful gasps. Elrik fought the pain. She looked up at Dinyar.

"Get into the house. Go through the tunnels and find help. I am sorry that you wasted your life to wait for me, as it appears that I shall not see tomorrow. Always know that I love you," Elrik stated as she felt her strength weakening.

"You are my life, Elrik. I shall not leave you now. If this is what the Fates have in store for us, then I shall walk hand-in-hand with you to the Great Feast," Dinyar pledged as she opened the door to their small castle.

Dinyar bent down and wrapped her arms under Elrik's arms and around her chest. She started walking backward up the three stairs and into the castle. She continued to drag Elrik through the hallway and into the great room. She propped Elrik up against the side of the fireplace and ran to get weapons. Dinyar returned with a crossbow and Elrik's sword. The sword was so heavy that Dinyar could not lift the tip up off of the floor.

"Get a short sword. You will never be able to wield that one, love," Elrik choked out, pink frothy blood coming from her pierced lung. "And I, for once, am too weak to fight...damned arrows."

Dinyar did as Elrik suggested. She returned with a short sword only candledrips later. Dinyar could hear their attackers' battering ram hitting against the metal gate. With each massive strike, the gate was weakening. It would only be a matter of time before their keep was breached. Dinyar prepared herself to protect the woman that she had spent a lifetime loving. With each strike of the battering ram, it became more and more clear that they were hopelessly outnumbered.

"You should go. Get yourself to the tunnel and leave. I cannot travel. I am verily afraid that I am dead already. You should live. I want you to live. I am mightily sorry that I cannot offer my sword for you, but I can still distract them long enough for you to escape, my beautiful Dinyar," Elrik tried to persuade Dinyar to leave her.

"Never! My place is at your side, brave gentle Elrik. I lost my heart to you the first time you smiled at me. You have always been my home. I shall not give that up for anyone. Do you honestly think I would send you to see the Goddess alone? I love you, Elrik, beyond reason. Even if my heart still beats, if you die...I die too. You are my life," Dinyar replied, firm in her love.

Dinyar looked at Elrik. She could see the truth in Elrik's eyes. She too understood the hopelessness of their situation. Dinyar made up her mind. She lowered the sword and sat down next to Elrik. Elrik cuddled Dinyar into the crook of her good arm, and they sat in loving silence. As the gate was breached, Elrik kissed Dinyar with all the passion of a lifetime. A tear made its way down Dinyar's face, and she smiled sadly at Elrik, each accepting their fate.

By the time the first of the troops made it into the great room, Dinyar and Elrik had said everything they had needed in that one kiss. Footsteps echoed closer and closer. Dinyar closed her eyes. She did not want to see it coming. She inhaled deeply of Elrik's scent, a pleasing combination of leather, musk, patchouli, and the lavender blooms she had used in her bathwater that morning. It always had a calming and reassuring affect on her before. Elrik pulled Dinyar close. She kissed the top of Dinyar's head and noticed the soldier's boots beside her.

Elrik looked up and saw Captain Berdyk. She had always thought there was something off about the woman. Now she understood where the enemy was. It was in the Council of Nine. It was a coup. Death to the old and loyal.

"General Elrik, I want you to know that this is nothing personal. I am a soldier. I follow my orders," Berdyk stated.

"I trained you, Captain," Elrik started.

"It is General now," Berdyk interrupted.

"I see why you have sold your soul. I taught you how to lead. I taught you strategy, movement, troop strength, and how to win battles. I also tried to instill honor, loyalty, and a sense of duty. I see that I failed," Elrik commented.

"My orders are to execute you. That does not have to include your declared. If you so desire, and she proves that she is not a threat to me or my troops, I shall allow her to live. Call it my 'favor' to you as a repayment for your valuable lessons," Berdyk offered out of respect for Elrik.

"Please, Dinyar, think on it hard. Think about Eldin. She needs you," Elrik labored.

"I told you before…I am not going to allow you to travel to the Great Feast without me. Eldin is an adult. She can take care of herself, and she can care for Seldar. When I declared with you, I made your path…my path. Fear not, even when Death comes for you, I will still be holding your hand. We shall walk hand-in-hand to sit at the feet of the Great Goddess and listen as she schools us on our lives. It is what I desire, Elrik," Dinyar replied softly.

Elrik lifted Dinyar's chin. Dinyar gazed lovingly into her eyes and they spoke without a word. Dinyar closed her eyes and Elrik gently kissed both of her eyelids. Dinyar grasped Elrik's hand and pulled her arm tighter around Dinyar's body.

"She wishes to travel with me to the Great Feast. I would ask that your 'favor' be a quick death and respect for our corpses," Elrik replied solemnly.

"As you wish," Berdyk remarked.

Berdyk grabbed a crossbow from the soldier standing to her left. She loaded the bolt and readied the mechanism. Berdyk placed the crossbow inches from Elrik's chest, directly over the heart region. She looked into Elrik's smoldering blue eyes and pulled the trigger while they stared at one another as equals. Elrik slumped against the fireplace.

Dinyar tried to control her breathing. She was afraid. *Oh Eldin, Seldar, please be safe! I love you both.* Dinyar felt the end of the crossbow against her chest, and she squeezed her eyes closed even tighter. Dinyar turned her head and pressed her face into Elrik's chest as Berdyk loaded the bolt and readied the mechanism for another shot. Berdyk admired the beautiful woman at Elrik's side for the strength of her love and pulled the trigger. Dinyar slumped against Elrik's shoulder. In death as they had in life, Dinyar and Elrik were hand-in-hand.

"Spread out and search the keep. Any riches you find are yours; however, any and all scrolls are to be handed over to me. No one is to touch these bodies; to do so would be an offense punishable by death. Go reward yourselves for a victorious day and the birth of a new Yashor!" General Berdyk called out, keeping her pledge to Elrik.

* * *

Dedak doubled over in obvious pain. In a heartbeat, Rynar felt the sickness in her stomach. *What is happening?!* Rynar tried in vain to keep her mid-meal down. She felt as though everything that she had eaten in the last seasonmark was about to come back to visit her. Rynar looked over at Dedak, who was trying to come to terms with her own pain.

Easy, love. It is a great disturbance. Many lives cut too short. Much pain. Nature is being violated again. Dedak silently started her chants. She had to protect them both from wave after wave of negative energy. They were being assaulted by the screams of nature. Something very evil was taking place.

Maric noticed her two traveling companions were not feeling well. It could not have been her cooking, could it? Eldin had never complained before. Yet here they were in obvious stomach distress. From now on, they could do the cooking. They seemed better at it anyway.

"How stands the candlemark? Do you need to rest?" Maric inquired.

"I think a rest would do us well, Maric. We apologize for delaying you," Rynar managed to reply before her stomach heaved again.

"I shall take care of your horse, then. You two should perhaps roll out your sleeping skins and rest," Maric suggested.

Maric sighed. They were getting fairly close to Elrik and Dinyar's keep. Only a few more candlemarks of travel and she would be able to tell Elrik about her suspicions. Maric thought about seeing Dinyar again. She had always been nice to her, and Maric would enjoy talking with her once more. She looked back at Dedak and Rynar. They were cuddled together on sleeping skins and looked like they were drifting off to slumber. Maric kicked a small stone across the road. She looked toward the northeast and smiled. It would not be long and she would be enjoying their company again.

* * *

Kiya felt her stomach lurch. It was as if someone had grabbed her entire stomach and twisted it into a knot. Something was not right. The hairs on the back of her neck stood out. Kiya looked around. Just the peaceful trees of the forest, and the trail was empty for kligs in either direction. *Strange. I must have eaten something bad.*

"We are not far from my home now, Kiya. I cannot wait to see my mother again! She is going to be surprised. She will feed you a feast, and perhaps I will even get a piece of fresh bread to go with my gruel!" Seldar babbled, excitedly.

"I shall settle for a fresh mint leaf and a comfortable sleeping pallet," Kiya replied, her stomach still giving her fits. "How much further do you think it is?"

"I think we shall be there in a few candlemarks. It cannot take much longer than that. Not since you traded for these fine riding horses," Seldar complimented Kiya.

"Good, I can use the rest," Kiya absently commented.

* * *

Romyl took Kidak by the hand and led her to the window. She pointed to the soldier behind her house. Romyl placed her crossbow in Kidak's hands. Kidak looked like she had just been handed a skunk in a cranky mood.

"First, you place a bolt into the channel like this," Romyl instructed as she loaded a bolt. "Then you pull back the mechanism here, until it locks into place. Did you hear the *click*?"

Kidak nodded. She really did not want to learn how to spill blood, but she did wish to live. Somehow, she knew that in order to keep living, she was going to have to sacrifice her blood innocence.

"Now you point the end of the crossbow at your target. Good, just like that," Romyl encouraged Kidak as she lined up the crosshairs over Kidak's shoulder. "Lastly, you need to hold your breath and squeeze the trigger gently."

Kidak closed her eyes and did as Romyl stated. She heard the *twang* of the crossbow as the bolt left the channel. It was less than a heartbeat later when she watched the soldier fall. Kidak felt ill. She had just committed murder.

"You had to do it. Do not trouble your soul over protecting your life. Come, we must hurry before the others find a way into this room," Romyl gently prompted Kidak to action.

Kidak could not take her eyes off of the crumpled soldier. She looked almost as if she were asleep. Kidak wondered if she had felt any pain.

"I am going to drop out of the window and push the hay cart over here. That way, you will have a softer place to land. When I get the cart here, you need to drop out of the window in the same way I did. Do you understand?" Romyl asked.

Kidak finally looked away from her first kill and nodded. She was beginning to feel numb. Romyl could tell that Kidak was going into shock. She had seen this happen every once in a while to young trainlings the first time that they had killed. Romyl did not have the heart to slap Kidak, so she leaned down and placed a passionate kiss on her lips instead. Kidak melted into the kiss. She returned it with a vengeance. She closed her eyes.

Kidak opened her eyes and pushed Romyl away. "What do you think you are doing?!"

"I needed to shock your mind. You were about to be lost to your first kill. I only sought to bring you back. I...I could not bring myself to strike you, so I did the only thing that I thought would work. I apologize if it caused you distress," Romyl explained.

Romyl sat on the window ledge and swung her legs out one at a time. She rolled over onto her stomach. She inched herself outside and hung by her hands from the windowsill. She allowed herself to fall and landed hard. Romyl rolled to prevent twisting an ankle. Once she was safely on the ground, Romyl stood and ran to get the hay cart for Kidak.

Kidak watched Romyl move, and her finger traced over her burning lips. *Why now, Romyl? Oh, Goddess, forgive me, Yamouth, for what I felt. I will make it back to you. I have a duty to you.* Kidak watched as Romyl pushed the hay cart underneath the window. Even at their advancing age, her muscles still stood out in well-defined bulges as she strained against the weight of the cart. *Goddess, she still makes my heart flip.* Romyl motioned for Kidak to throw the weapons into the cart. As soon as Romyl secured the sword and crossbow, she motioned for Kidak to jump.

Kidak trusted Romyl and made her way out the window, mimicking Romyl's earlier descent. She fell into the softness of the hay. Romyl held out her hand, and Kidak took it. Romyl helped her to her feet and out of the wagon. They ran to the barn, and Romyl grabbed a blanket and saddle while Kidak set about putting the bridle on the beast.

Once they had managed to secure the saddle and bridle, Romyl hoisted Kidak up into the saddle. She gripped the reins and saddle horn and pulled herself up behind Kidak. Romyl touched her heels to the beast, and they were off, Romyl's arms wrapped protectively around Kidak's waist. She kept urging the beast on until it was in a full gallop while she shielded Kidak with her body.

Romyl was not going to trust anyone. She did not slow down for anyone as they galloped through the city. At times people were forced to jump out of the way of powerful hooves as they tore through crowds. Romyl was not about to allow anyone to harm Kidak! They were going to hide out in the forest until they could sort out who was who.

* * *

Arkon ran for her life through the Council Hall. Why had she not seen this coming? Surely there had been signs? Arkon could hear the clattering of the soldiers' boots against the green stone in the hallway. She knew her only chance was to make it to the private chambers and lock them out. Perhaps then she could hide out until the real army was able to dispatch these traitors.

"Arkon! Over here! Quickly, before they catch you," Pirkyn called out as she held the door to her private chamber open.

Arkon sprinted with the last of her energy into Pirkyn's chamber. She could not see the feral grin spread across Pirkyn's face as she shut the door and slid the heavy metal bolt into place. *This is perfect. Thank you, Great Goddess, for delivering my most hated enemy into my own hands!*

"Who are these vermin?!" Arkon boomed.

"Who can say? They seem intent on destroying us all. Perhaps you might recognize one of them if you look through my spy hole," Pirkyn suggested.

Pirkyn gladly moved aside for Arkon to place her face against the door, thus turning her back on the great deceiver. Pirkyn pulled a venom-dipped dagger from its sheath, hidden under her robes. She stalked up behind Arkon, dagger poised and ready. Before Arkon moved, Pirkyn plunged the blade deep into Arkon's back and punctured a lung.

Arkon's eyes widened in pain and shock. She spun to face Pirkyn, suddenly all too aware of whom the vermin were. The more she breathed in, the harder it seemed to be to catch her breath. She leveled Pirkyn with a disdainful glare.

"What say you? You coward! Attack me from the back like a common Drakknian male-child. Why not attack me now, when I am facing you? Come then, let us see who is full of courage and who is full of manure!" Arkon challenged, even as she could feel the venom spreading in her system.

"Oh no…I prefer to stay pretty. You are much larger than I am, Arkon. I would have to be a fool to attack you when you are ready for it. Is that what you take me for, a fool?" Pirkyn asked.

Pirkyn's chuckle deepened into evil laughter. She could see that Arkon was weakening. With each heartbeat, Pirkyn grew more confident. Soon, she sheathed her dagger.

"If I am the fool, then why are you the one who is dying at my hands, Arkon?" Pirkyn gloated.

"What shall it gain you in the end? Amazons will not follow you; they shall call for another Council to be selected," Arkon reasoned.

"Oh...but there shall be no selection. You see, I will make them understand that I rule from 'Divine Right.' Since I was the only councilwoman that the Great Goddess saw fit to spare," Pirkyn revealed her plan.

"They...they will...want...justice for our...deaths," Arkon argued, even though it was increasingly difficult to breathe and speak.

"Pity that you will all be dead and I can make up any story I like. That evil, nasty Captain Eldin and her troops tried to take over Yashor. Fortunately, we were able to stop them, but not before they had decimated the Council, leaving only me," Pirkyn stated gleefully.

"So...that is...why...you...wanted Eldin..." Arkon started.

"Yes. Thank you so much for putting my plan into action. It would not have worked if Eldin had not gone on that impossible mission. Eldin had a fatal flaw you see...she was loyal to the Council. She will now be bound by her sense of 'duty' to attempt that ridiculous mission. I publicly blame her for the attacks on the Council; she and her marauders are dead. Justice has been served. Convenient, do you not agree?" Pirkyn asked sarcastically.

Arkon could feel her life force draining. She had mere heartbeats left before Death would claim her. With the last of her strength, Arkon doubled her fist. She punched Pirkyn square in the nose, breaking it. Pirkyn howled in pain.

"Now...you...not so...pretty," Arkon managed to get out as she crumpled to the ground, "Nose...crooked."

Arkon chuckled at Pirkyn's destroyed vanity. Pirkyn turned on Arkon in rage.

"Stop laughing at me! I am your ruler!! I took your life! I am as your Goddess!! Stop laughing," Pirkyn shouted.

Pirkyn snapped. She started kicking Arkon. Much to Pirkyn's chagrin,

Arkon had the last laugh...she gave into the great sleep just before Pirkyn started kicking, so she did not feel a single rage-fueled blow.

Pirkyn unlocked the door and swung it open, still seething. She looked outside at her troops in the hallway.

"What news have you for me? Is the deed complete?" Pirkyn demanded of the closest ranking soldier.

"Everyone here is dispatched, Your Grace. The only group left to check in is Darnat's group. They were after Kidak and Romyl. I would have thought they should have been finished by now, Your Grace," the soldier reported.

"Go see what is taking them so long. Tell them I only care if they are dead; I do not wish to make a new suit from their hides, so they need not take the time to skin the corpses," Pirkyn ordered, barely concealing the contempt from her voice.

Pirkyn went back into her chambers and slammed the door shut.

"Stupid soldiers," she muttered.

22

"Wait until you meet General Elrik and her mate Dinyar. They are the finest people in Yashor. I can already taste the feast this evening will bring!" Maric stated for the twentieth time that candlemark.

Perhaps I should figure out a mute incantation, Dedak thought conspiratorially. Rynar giggled. Stop that. She is a nice woman. I think the water may have made her mind stick a little. Perhaps that is why she says the same thing over...and over...and over.

It was Dedak's turn to chuckle. Maric had been hearing the two of them alternately suppressing little fits of giggles all mid-day. She was beginning to think that they might be a few bags shy of a wagon load. They seemed harmless enough, and they did rescue her, so she had no complaints. Perhaps if she mentioned what nice people Elrik and Dinyar were again, she could get them into a conversation.

Maric looked up and saw the stone walls of Elrik and Dinyar's keep rising in the not-too-far distance. A broad smile lit up her face. Soon! *Ah, I have missed you, my friends.*

"That's it up ahead! Look there, see? We shall be having a wonderful feast in no time." Maric stated excitedly.

Thank the Goddess! Perhaps these people can get her mind unstuck.

"Ouch!" Dedak exclaimed as Rynar playfully smacked her for her last thoughts.

"You said that this is the keep of General Elrik?" Rynar asked to keep Maric from repeating herself yet again.

"Yes. General Elrik just took her last ride, so I am certain that she will be back to her keep by now," Maric gladly replied. *Finally a conversation!*

Maric led the small group over the footbridge and to the outer gates. They stopped at the outer gates. Maric looked around in disbelief at the damage to the stone wall surrounding the gates. Inside the gatehouse tunnel, the heavy metal gate lay on the ground after having been ripped from its housing deep inside the stone wall. Pieces of stone were strewn around as well.

Dedak saw the evidence of carnage. She stepped in front of Maric and put her hand on Maric's shoulder.

"Stay here. I can look around and see what happened. There is no reason for you to see…" Dedak tried to save the woman from what she feared would be found inside.

Maric pushed past Dedak and strode purposefully into the courtyard. Off to the left was the abandoned battering ram. Arrows stuck out of the ground haphazardly from the garden to the stairs leading into the house. There were pools of blood in front of the stairs, with blood drops and smears on them going into the house. Maric slowly ascended the steps, and then she spotted the bodies of Malfi and the other eunuchs who served Elrik and Dinyar just inside the doorway. They had obviously given their lives trying to prevent the attackers from entering.

As Maric gingerly stepped over the bodies, she noticed that the killers had rummaged through their pockets, turning them inside-out. Looters, nothing but vermin! She searched through room after room. The killers had taken everything of value from the small keep. Maric first saw their feet sticking out from the other side of the fireplace as she entered the great room. Her stomach threatened to revisit her with each step.

Maric closed her eyes, and her hands clenched into tight fists as soon as she saw Dinyar's body huddled into the body of Elrik; both murdered.

Goddess! Maric opened her eyes and saw that the bodies at least looked undisturbed, unlike the eunuchs earlier.

"Goddess, why would You allow such treachery to befall such good people? They deserved better than this!" Maric screamed in agony. "They deserved better!"

"Maric, there are riders coming toward the keep. It looks like a female and a male-child," Dedak reported as she ducked back outside.

Maric grabbed Elrik's sword that lay at her feet and followed Dedak outside. She held Elrik's sword at the ready, hers being at the bottom of the river back at the waterfall where her canoe had capsized. She would be certain that Eldin was given her mother's sword. It was the only thing that she could do for the captain. Now, she was going to protect her friends' bodies. No one was going to make it past her into that keep!

Dedak and Rynar both had armed themselves with what remained of the weapons, which was nothing much—a pitchfork for Rynar and a short sword in Dedak's hands. They felt compelled to help Maric defend the ravaged keep.

Dedak noticed the shape of the small female rider from a quarter-klig away. It was certainly familiar. *Could it really be?* Dedak strained her eyes, although they were much sharper since her transformation a few moons back. That was one of the best parts of gaining seasonmarks back; her body felt so young again, and it worked better too.

"Who is it, dear?" Rynar inquired.

"By the Goddess, I think that is Kiya…Kidak's daughter. Do you remember her, Ry?" Dedak asked.

"I certainly do. She used to steal my toys when they would visit the Grey Fox," Rynar replied.

"I do not know who the male-child is beside her, however," Dedak explained.

Maric looked up when she heard Dedak talking about Kiya. It was true! Kiya and Seldar were approaching the keep. Her heart sank. She realized that she was going to have to be the one to do it. Maric prepared to tell Seldar the awful truth. She was not going to allow the boy to see his mothers. He did not need that night terror for the rest of his life.

Seldar saw Maric standing in front of the small footbridge blocking the way. As he neared, he recognized the sword she held in her hand. Why would she have his other mother's sword? Realization hit him like a fist in the gut, stealing his breath. Was it just Elrik? Where was his true mother? Where was Dinyar?

Seldar dismounted and felt weak-kneed. He looked at Maric's grim face.

"Where is my mother?" Seldar barely squeaked out.

"Seldar, I cannot let you pass. It is not something that you should see. By the looks of it, it was marauders." Maric tried to be forthright with the lad.

Seldar stood there with his world spinning out of control. He suddenly broke for the keep. Maric dropped the sword and grabbed the boy, wrapping strong arms around him.

"Let me go! I have to see my mother. I need her!" Seldar cried, fighting against Maric's grip.

"No! No, Seldar. Shh. Everything will be all right. Stop now. Easy," Maric tried to soothe Seldar.

Seldar's body went limp as realization hit his soul. Tears streamed unchecked down his face. The Council be damned! He would mourn his mothers' passing. Maric supported Seldar and eased him to the ground. She had always liked the male-child. He had an easy charm about him. Maric smiled sadly; Seldar had inherited that from his mother Dinyar.

Dedak meanwhile walked over to the horse that Kiya was sitting on. *My, she has grown into a lovely young lady.* Rynar followed Dedak as she recognized Kiya from her many trips to the Grey Fox with Kidak and Yamouth.

"Ho, Kiya. How stands the day with you?" Dedak asked.

"Do I know you?" Kiya remarked.

"I am your aun...er..." Dedak almost slipped up.

"She is your cousin, Kiya. She is descended from Terdak," Rynar rescued Dedak. "She finds lineage to be somewhat confusing."

Dedak smiled at Kiya. *You are going to pay for that remark, my sweet.*

Promises, promises, that is all I get from you, big bad Jahru, Rynar mentally quipped back.

Dedak could feel the power emanating from Kiya. Even unbidden, the power surged through her veins. Dedak knew that Kiya was going to have to be told the truth, and that she would need lessons on how to harness that power. If not, it would be dangerous for everyone around the young healer. *I have not known that much power since my own mother.*

"Kiya, I am Dedak. I would submit to you that perhaps the three of us should prepare those bodies for funeral pyres. It would be most kind to take the burden from Maric," Dedak suggested as she introduced herself.

Kiya dismounted from her horse and looked up at Dedak. She certainly looked like Terdak might have in younger seasonmarks. She was even roughly the same height.

"It would also be a kindness to Seldar. Dinyar was his true mother, after all," Kiya flatly remarked, irritated at his being left out by Dedak.

"Certainly, it would be nice for the male-child as well," Dedak allowed. "We should get started."

"Aye," Kiya replied, steeling herself for the all-too-familiar grisly task.

Rynar went to where Maric held Seldar. She squatted down and looked at Seldar. He had tears streaming down his face, and his eyes were red and puffy. He looked as though someone had ripped his heart right from his chest, poor boy.

"Seldar, is that right?" Rynar started.

Seldar nodded.

"Good. First, I am sorry about your mothers. I wish that I had gotten to meet them. I had heard great things about them. They must have been verily special, and I know that you will miss them terribly. Now, um, did your mothers have funeral cloaks?" Rynar asked gently.

"I...I believe they are in my mothers' sleeping chamber. They are folded in a special carved wooden funeral box that is inside their clothing chamber off to the right."

Rynar touched Seldar on the shoulder. "Thank you. You rest, and we shall prepare everything for you."

"That is far too kind. You should not do anything for me. I am but a male-child," Seldar started to protest, but his heavy heart got the better of him and he broke down into tears again thinking about his dead mother.

Maric tried to soothe him once more. She looked up at Rynar and smiled sadly at the young woman.

"Thank you for your kindness. I think neither of us would be able to prepare the bodies. I shall never forget this," Maric thanked Rynar before she turned and went into the castle behind Kiya and Dedak.

Kiya stopped at the bodies of the eunuchs. She looked at Dedak and Rynar. Kiya bent down and closed their unseeing eyes.

She cares for them almost as if they were Amazons. Rynar noticed the way Kiya administered her mercy. Dedak nodded. She bent down and started helping Kiya.

Together, they lifted the first body and brought it outside. They placed the body into a small garden cart they found nearby. While Kiya rummaged around for a couple of sheets to use as funeral cloaks, Dedak and Rynar carried out the second eunuch and placed him inside the cart as well. By the time they had the second body into the cart, Kiya returned with two sheets off of Elrik and Dinyar's bed.

"It isn't a real funeral cloak, but somehow I do not think that they would have minded," Kiya said as she tucked the sheets into the cart with the bodies.

"Kiya, do you intend on giving these two an Amazon funeral pyre?" Dedak inquired.

"Yes, I do. If you have a problem with that, then I suggest that you go wash the bodies of the general and Dinyar. I do not expect you to understand the kindness that I am showing, but I do expect you to respect my wish to do so. If you do not wish to be a party to it, I understand, and I am willing to do all of the work myself," Kiya stated passionately, defending herself.

Dedak, she must have a good reason for doing this. We should not force her to do it alone, Rynar interrupted Dedak's thoughts.

Yes, but wash a male-child? How disgusting. Dedak saw the disapproval on Rynar's face. *However, if it pleases you that I do so...* Dedak silently conceded.

Kiya was startled when Rynar suddenly sprang forward and wrapped her arms around Dedak in a fierce hug. She noticed how they seemed to communicate without words. Kiya sighed; so few couples could do that. *If only I could find that for myself. The one person I was fated to love.*

"I knew you had a soft underbelly beneath that gruff exterior," Rynar giggled.

"Oh, panther piss! Help Kiya, and I will go get a horse to pull this cart to the stream. If the horse does not wish to pull male-children then you are out of luck," Dedak grumbled, half-heartedly trying to save her tough reputation.

"I see that Auntie Terdak has rubbed off on you, cousin," Kiya laughed. "It has been many seasonmarks since I heard 'panther piss' cross anyone's lips."

Dedak grinned at Kiya while mentally smacking herself for the slip of the tongue.

"She always did have an eloquent way with words, did she not?" Rynar added coyly.

"Fine, you two discuss words; I am going to find a horse," Dedak stated as she walked away.

"Thank you for helping me with the male-children. I know that it is not normal to have a funeral for them, but I verily much think that we should honor their sacrifices in defense of Elrik and Dinyar," Kiya quickly explained herself to Rynar.

"You need never explain your reasoning to me, Kiya. I shall never tell you how to feel or what to think. Who am I to make such decisions for you? I can only be responsible for my own life," Rynar replied as she followed Kiya into the keep in search of the funeral washing oils.

After rummaging around Elrik and Dinyar's bedchambers for a half-candlemark, Rynar discovered the sacred funeral washing oils. She found Kiya in the eunuchs' cramped quarters searching through their bare essentials for ingredients to make some funeral oils for them. Rynar quietly knocked.

Kiya looked up, startled.

"Sorry about that. I found the oils that have been kept for Elrik and Dinyar. I also wanted to show you this," Rynar explained as she held out a small bottle with a handwritten label.

On the bottle's label, it read, "For Seldar, Malfi, and Daji" in General Elrik's handwriting. Kiya recognized the handwriting from years of studying the general's military strategies in school. Kiya took the bottle from Rynar and pulled out the stopper. She held the bottle to her nose and took a cautious sniff. Kiya smiled. It was funeral washing oils! Kiya suddenly realized that what she held in her hand was proof of Elrik's affection for her son.

"We need to find Seldar. He needs to know about this," Kiya stated as she placed the stopper back into the bottle and stood.

Rynar and Kiya left the keep in search of Seldar. They searched for a candlemark with no luck. Kiya looked up at the sky. They would have to abandon the search for now if they wanted to have enough time to properly prepare the bodies for the pyres before the sun set. Somewhat disappointed, Rynar agreed.

As they were walking back to the keep, they spotted Dedak guiding the horse and cart toward the stream. Rynar smiled; Dedak was going to wash the bodies by herself. She was indeed a sweet woman, no matter what she tried to get everyone else to believe!

"Let's go help my cousin. She should not bear the burden alone," Kiya suggested.

"Aye, especially since she has an aversion to washing male-children!" Rynar replied as the two of them raced to catch up with Dedak and the cart.

The three made their way down to the shallow stream that ran past the keep. Kiya and Dedak carefully unloaded the bodies and set them next to the stream. Rynar started peeling bloody clothing off of Malfi's body while Dedak grabbed a shovel from the cart and dug a hole to dispose of the clothing. Kiya waded ankle-deep into the stream. She closed her eyes and raised her arms out above her head.

"From the Great Feast we were called. We left our heavenly home to inhabit our earthly bodies. Our precious nectar of life has been spilled, and now we return to You, the Creator of all that is. These waters shall wash the evidence of violence from our bodies so that we may once again be perfect in Your sight. Bless us, Great Goddess," Kiya gave voice to the dead.

Kiya opened her eyes and motioned for the first body. Dedak helped Rynar to place Elrik's body into the stream. Kiya scrubbed the stubborn dried blood loose with her hands. She carefully washed all traces of blood from the muscular body. When Kiya had finished with Elrik, she nodded to Dedak and Rynar. They reverently picked up Elrik's body and carried it over to the wagon. Once they had Elrik in the wagon, Dedak and Rynar picked up Dinyar's body and took it out into the stream for Kiya to wash. Once again Kiya was careful to wash all of the offending blood away. Dinyar's long hair played in the stream's current, swirling in the red water. Once they were finished with the Amazons, the male-children would be next.

* * *

Seldar sat in the sands by the small stream. He had loved coming to this place with Eldin. It was where she had taught him everything. He could read, write, and do figures. What good would that do him? He was forbidden to use the skills that Eldin had taught him, and now with his mothers dead, he had no one to take care of him. Seldar sighed; he would need to make his choice sooner than he had planned.

Seldar watched the water flow over the large stones in the stream. Suddenly, a large amount of red water flowed past the stones. *They must be washing the bodies upstream.* Seldar felt his stomach start to protest at the sight. He could not stand to watch the water carrying away the last remnants of life from the bodies of his mothers. Seldar grabbed a small pebble from the sand and threw it angrily into the water before he turned and fled the ghastly scene. Besides, Maric had sent him to find the horses that were missing from his mothers' stable.

"I am not that daft, Maric. I know you sent me away so that I would not see the violence that has been done to my mother. Goddess, even without seeing it, I still feel it," Seldar grieved out loud.

* * *

Kiya sent Rynar and Dedak to collect firewood for the funeral pyres while she finished preparing the bodies of the dead. First, Kiya took the bottle of funeral oils labeled for Elrik, Dinyar, and Eldin and removed the stopper. She poured two-thirds of the contents into a wooden basin and placed the stopper back into the bottle. The oils had a very pleasing aroma; they had been mixed well. Kiya once again closed her eyes and raised her hands skyward.

"Great Goddess, hear me. We have now had our bodies washed clean of the violence from this life. We seek Your ultimate forgiveness. So that we may receive the soul-cleansing Spirit of the Fire, we beseech You to purify the oils which will invite the Fire-Spirit into our bodies and release our souls to journey home to You. We pray that You find us fit to sit at the Great Feast beside You," Kiya intoned before she dipped her hands into the thick oils.

Kiya massaged Elrik's body with the thick perfumed oils. She took care to reverently cover Elrik's entire body with the mixture. Elrik's muscular body was covered in scars from her lifetime of soldiering. The scars had been a living scroll of the sacrifices that Elrik had made for the citizens of Yashor. A deep scar ran along her left side as well as one that would have gutted her vitals; evidently, Elrik had cheated Death more than once.

"Thank you, Elrik. You shall indeed be missed," She whispered to the corpse. Next, Kiya massaged the oils into Elrik's hair. Once the entire body was massaged with the funeral oils, Kiya wrapped Elrik's body tightly in her funeral cloak. Then Kiya finished preparing the body by sealing the cloak with a thin covering of funeral oil.

Kiya repeated the process with Dinyar's body before she switched the oils and finished with the two eunuchs.

Dedak and Rynar collected deadfall from the surrounding woods and filled the garden cart. Once they had several cartloads unloaded in the courtyard of the keep, Dedak and Rynar started building the pyres. Rynar started with small twigs and hay. They made a pile in the center. Around this they built a hollowed structure made of thicker branches that were criss-crossed at the top, making a V-notch. A bed was constructed by placing smaller branches across the structure resting on the tops of the V-notches. Rynar piled hay on the top. The bodies would rest in the hay. While Dedak started to build the next pyre, Rynar carefully placed hay all around the sides of the pyre.

* * *

By the time that the last pyre was built, both Seldar and Maric had returned from hunting down the horses. The only horse they were able to track down was Folly. Seldar had found the mare munching happily on a large patch of clover a klig away.

"I see you found Folly. Good job, Seldar. You should put her into the stable. It will be time for the funeral pyres soon," Maric suggested.

"As you command, so shall it be done." Seldar saluted Maric out of habit.

"You are a good male-child, Seldar. Spend some time with Folly, and I will come get you when it is time," Maric promised.

* * *

Maric and Dedak carried the bodies to the pyres one by one. They placed Elrik beside Dinyar on the northernmost pyres. Malfi and Daji were placed on the southern pyres. Maric looked toward the west. The sun was creeping behind the Mountains of Fire in the distance. Soon, it would be dark. Maric quietly walked to the stables to get Seldar for the ceremony.

* * *

Seldar felt a great sadness wash over his soul when he first saw the pyres. He could tell which body was which, even if he could not see them. His mother Dinyar was smaller in stature than Elrik. They were both larger than Malfi, who was in turn larger than Daji. Seldar had been dreading this day ever since he had been little.

"I think that Seldar should light the pyres," Kiya suddenly spoke out.

"That is forbidden!" Dedak exclaimed.

"I do not wish to light the fires, Kiya. I could not stand it if I were the one responsible for Elrik and Dinyar being judged unworthy to sit at the Great Feast. If the fires were lit by my hand, the Great Goddess would shun them," Seldar politely refused.

Maric grabbed the torch and rubbed funeral oil from the remainder in the bowls on the end. She then took out her flint stones and started striking them together. Sparks from the stones striking each other ignited the ceremonial torch. Maric walked over to Seldar with the blazing torch.

"Wait! Seldar, your mother did not care about Yashor laws when it came to you and her eunuchs. I have the proof here," Kiya stated, extending the bottle of funeral oils that Kidak had made for them.

Seldar took the bottle from her hands and looked at the label. He read his name in Kidak's handwriting. Seldar ran his hand over her neat script and then realized that he was not supposed to know how to read. He reluctantly thrust the bottle back into Kiya's hands.

"What does it say?" Seldar asked, a lump already forming in his throat.

"It says, 'Seldar, Malfi, and Daji.' Seldar, it is a bottle of funeral oils. You see, Kidak loved you. I think that she would have wanted you to light the fire for her," Kiya explained.

Maric suddenly grabbed Seldar's hand and placed it over hers on the torch. Seldar looked into Maric's determined eyes.

"The Goddess cannot be angry if it is my hand on the torch. Come, let us say good-bye," Maric reasoned.

Maric and Seldar walked over to the first pyre.

"May my hand be as Eldin's on this day. May Eldin, the heir of Elrik and Dinyar, through me touch the fire that releases her mothers' souls," Maric called to the heavens.

Maric and Seldar thrust the torch into the hay together. The dry hay caught fire quickly, and soon the pyres burned brightly, chasing away the darkness of the night. As the fires consumed the bodies of the dead, the flames reached toward the heavens.

"See, Seldar, their souls have been released. See how they travel through the flames to the Great Feast," Maric reassured him.

As they watched in silence, Kiya felt the hairs on the back of her neck rise. Something, or someone, was watching them. Something...evil.

"Dedak, do you see anyone in the tree line?" Kiya asked suddenly, unable to take the creepy feeling in silence any longer.

"You feel something, Kiya?" Dedak asked, alarmed.

"Something is not...well...right. I do not know how to describe it," Kiya replied.

That was enough for Dedak. She looked around. Perhaps Kiya was getting the gift of sight. If that were true, they may only have candledrips to escape capture...or worse.

"I think we need to get to the horses and be away. Something is not right with this night, and we need to leave now!" Dedak called to the others.

Maric and Dedak ran for the horses. Rynar and Kiya led Seldar inside. He pointed out some hidden food stores. They took as much food as they could carry and ran out into the courtyard. Maric rode Folly, pulling the horses that Seldar and Kiya had ridden on behind her. It seemed that whoever had ransacked the keep had also stolen the military mount that had been given to the retiring general.

Kiya and Seldar each mounted a horse, and Dedak reached down for Rynar. Rynar took her place behind Dedak, and the group left quickly. The horses thundered to the top of the rise in only a few candledrips. Rynar looked back and saw, by the light of the funeral pyres, a patrol of soldiers entering the area.

Looks like we have company back at the keep...bad company. Rynar silently alerted Dedak.

I knew we should pay attention to Kiya's feelings. She does have the gift of sight. She also has great power, Dedak thought back.

I thought as much. Even I could feel it, or was it just I felt what you felt? You know, I'm not even certain what my own feelings are anymore. Do I make any sense to you? Rynar mused.

Yes. I have much left to teach you. Some of that is how to separate your feelings. How to know which are yours alone and which are mine that you are experiencing through our bond. When we have a chance, we will work on it. I promise you, Dedak vowed.

Kiya rode hard to catch up with Maric. She looked over at the older sword master.

"I know of a place where we can hide out for a while. Follow me!" Kiya called out.

Maric pulled up on her reins slightly to allow Kiya to take the lead. Through the darkness the tiny group rode like they had Hades Hounds on their heels. Kiya took them into the tree line, and then they had to slow. Everyone had their own thoughts and demons to conquer as they rode in silence. Each heartbeat was spent wondering about the soldiers that had come to investigate the funeral pyres. Each was hoping that it would not be long before they reached the safe haven that Kiya promised.

* * *

Romyl gently pulled back on the reins. They had been riding for days. The light from the moons had lit their escape. Romyl had chosen to ride at night and hide by day. She figured that they were less likely to encounter the patrols that were out looking for them. She surveyed the area for any signs of movement. Seeing no one on the road in either direction, Romyl encouraged her roan mare out of the thicket that had concealed them.

"We should be able to make it to your keep tonight. Just make certain to stay alert. There could be night patrols like there were outside of Fern Glen," Romyl reminded Kidak, trying to keep the sadness from her voice.

Romyl was going to enjoy each heartbeat that Kidak rode snuggled safely in her arms. She could feel Kidak pleasantly pressed against her chest. If only it could last forever.

Kidak soon saw the glow of a major fire in the not-so-distant east. She tried to guess how far away it was. It might certainly be in Three Rivers, or very close to it. Of course, it might be a funeral pyre.

"Do you see that?" Kidak asked as she fixed her eyes on the glow.

"The fire? Yes, I had noticed that. I do not think it is large enough for a soldiers' camp. It could always be a patrol or a funeral pyre," Romyl replied.

"That is what I had thought. Still, it is awfully close, do you not think?" Kidak inquired, still shy about seeing anyone.

"If you wish, we can go back into the woods. I am just not verily certain that I will be able to find your keep if we stray from the road," Romyl admitted, although the prospect of wandering lost with Kidak was not an altogether unpleasant one.

"No. I think that we should give the road a chance. I just hope that Yamouth is well. I have a strange twist in my stomach. A…a…feeling that things are not right," Kidak put voice to her fear.

Romyl placed her free hand over Kidak's to lend support and comfort. Kidak allowed the contact without pulling her hand away. Secretly, she enjoyed the contact as much as she imagined that Romyl did. She loved Romyl still. If only she could turn back the hands of time and undo the day she sent Romyl away. If only she could undo the day she met Yamouth and allowed the respectful horse trainer to woo her. Kidak sighed; she felt a love for Yamouth, and a duty. However, her passion had always remained for Romyl.

As the kligs went by, Kidak became more agitated. Romyl saw the signs of violence all around the peaceful valley. She pulled up hard on the reins as Clover Valley came into sight just below the rise. Romyl's horse felt the tension and sidestepped in agitation. She stroked its neck underneath the mane to calm the beast. It was then that Romyl spotted them.

"Great Goddess!" Romyl exclaimed at the crosses that lined the road between Three Rivers and Clover Valley.

Crosses that were filled with residents of Clover Valley left to die. It was a message to the populace. To speak out was to die. To question the soldiers was to die. To disobey the soldiers was to die. Romyl understood the implications. Yashor was becoming a dictatorship. But who was the dictator?

"Do…do you suppose that Yamouth is…is on one of…those things?" Kidak asked, fearing the answer.

"Wait here. I shall go see," Romyl suggested and offered Kidak her arm to help her dismount.

"No, dear Romyl, I cannot ask you to do that for me. I shall go with you. Yamouth is my declared, and if she is here, I owe her that much," Kidak politely refused Romyl's offer.

"Of course…as you wish," Romyl replied, and tapped her horse into a slow canter.

Kidak was appalled at the sight of so many innocent people crucified. There was the smithy and her declared. Next to them, their three-seasonmarks-old girl was nailed to a smaller cross. There was the regent and the regent's entire honor guard. Next were some of the local farmers and merchants. It seemed as if half of the population of Clover Valley was hanging dead on those crosses.

Kidak's breath caught in her throat. It could not be true! Yamouth hung limply from the cruel wooden cross in front of them, her once proud features twisted in agony. Kidak placed her hand over her mouth as her stomach wretched.

Romyl looked up as a few soldiers who were guarding the bodies started toward them.

"You there, hold! You are in violation of the curfew," a soldier called out.

Romyl urgently drove her heels into her horse's flanks, and the beast bolted off the road and into the woods. Behind them, she heard the soldier raising the alarm. In heartbeats, the area would be crawling with a patrol desperate to find them. Romyl urged her horse to the fastest speed they dared travel in the dark forest.

Kidak desperately clung to Romyl's strong right arm that was wrapped protectively around her waist as they plunged recklessly through the dark abyss. She felt like she was partly to blame for Yamouth's death. *If only I had warned her when they tried to kill me the first time, perhaps Yamouth could have gone into hiding. Why did I not tell her? Because you found out that you are descended from Jahru and that you have Jahru blood pumping in your veins. Because you did not know how to deal with that and did not want to worry Yamouth. Face it, you were afraid that Yamouth would find out somehow and that she would be repulsed by you.* Kidak's conscience replied to her own questions. Kidak buried her face into Romyl's muscular neck; she was such a coward!

"Do you have any idea where we are, Kidak? I fear I am not as familiar with this region as I was in my youth," Romyl inquired.

"Keep heading north. There is a place that I used to go to contemplate life. It is well secluded, and there is only one other person who knows of it. We could hide out there until the patrols stop searching for us," Kidak suggested.

"That sounds fine. Are there food and water sources close by this place?" Romyl asked, always the strategist.

"It sits next to a lake. The water is drinkable, and there are fish as well as game that use the lake as a watering hole. Will that do?" Kidak replied in a tiny, unsure voice.

"That will be just grand. I want you to know that I am deeply sorry for your loss. I know just hearing that is cold comfort, though," Romyl tried to find the words to ease Kidak's burdened heart.

Romyl felt Kidak squeeze her arm a little tighter in response. Kidak was beginning to get numb from the horror of seeing Yamouth hanging on the cross. There had been so many of her friends hanging with Yamouth. It was pure evil. Nothing could erase those images burned into her mind!

It took nearly a candlemark to find the area that Kidak remembered. Thick reeds grew in spots around the lake, and the lake itself was deep and colored like a starless night. On the far side was a rocky outcropping. Kidak pointed them in that direction. Romyl liked the peaceful area.

Once they approached the outcropping, Romyl pulled back gently on the reins and helped Kidak to dismount. She swung her leg over the back of the horse and nimbly landed on her feet beside the beast. She led the horse and followed Kidak. As they walked near the outcropping, Romyl could just make out a cave hidden from view by thick overgrown underbrush that covered the entrance and blended in with the surroundings.

Romyl removed the saddle, then tethered the horse not too far away. It was quite happy to munch on the patches of sweet yellow flowers and green fertile grass that grew close to the water. They took their possessions into the mouth of the cave. Romyl made a torch from a piece of thick branch wrapped tightly with binding cloth. Kidak located the bottle of torch oil that she had secreted behind a large stone just inside the mouth of the cave and sprinkled some on the cloth. Romyl took her flint stones out of her belt pouch and struck them against each other until a spark caught and lit the torch.

Romyl followed Kidak into the cavern. They slowly made their way through the narrow, twisting gap. A few candledrips later, the narrow passageway gave way to a fair-sized inner chamber. It had the smallest hole in the top, and Romyl noticed that it would be a perfect natural flue for a fire.

Romyl grinned at Kidak. This was absolutely perfect for their needs!

They would be dry, warm, and hidden. Now all they needed was a cozy fire. Romyl set about starting one with the old dry fall that was stacked in the back from Kidak's previous visits, while Kidak laid out their sleeping skins. Romyl noticed that Kidak had laid them next to each other. She figured that Kidak wanted some comfort. *Poor Kidak. I know her heart must be hurting. I will do what I can, but how do you take away the pain of a shattered heart? I never figured that out.*

Kidak looked at Romyl as she stoked the now blazing fire. She had missed out on so much of this woman's life. Now she felt guilty for Yamouth's death, and she felt guilty for giving up on Romyl. Kidak shook her head sadly. She had made such a mess out of her life. Kidak decided to rest. She lay down in her sleeping skins and closed her eyes. *Please come hold me. Please, Romyl. I could never ask it of you; please feel my thoughts.* Kidak tried to hold back the tears, but eventually the tears won the war.

Romyl banked the fledgling coals and walked over to her sleeping skins. She gazed down at Kidak. She could tell that Kidak was crying. Soft sobs wracked her body. Romyl could not fight the urge any longer. She lay down beside Kidak and wrapped her arms around the woman that she still loved with all of her heart. Kidak melted into the embrace and allowed Romyl's strong arms to make her feel safe. If only...

23

Blood flew from Eldin's mouth as the booted foot landed square on her jaw. She glared at her attacker with smoldering disgust. If she had not promised the Council to allow herself to be captured, this little male-child would already be dead.

"Did you hear me, Amazon? I told you to kneel!" the man repeated.

Eldin decided that it would be better to kneel than risk that he might actually know the knee strike. If he used it, it might break her kneecap and make escape impossible later. *Just wait until I get back to Yashor. The Council is going to owe me more krillits than they have in the Council's treasure chest! I cannot believe that I have to put up with this!*

The Drakknian started to unfurl his whip. He was going to make this Amazon know what male dominance was all about! He pulled the whip tight in front of her face and it made a resounding crack.

Eldin suddenly lunged at the doomed man. She struck his testes with her head, causing him to crumple to the ground. While he writhed in pain, Eldin rolled onto her back. In a heartbeat she had worked her bound hands around her feet so that they were now in front of her. Eldin rolled onto her side and pushed herself up onto her feet. She grabbed his sword from its sheath that hung unguarded from the saddle horn of his mount.

"Why is it you demons cannot keep from attempting to beat your prisoners? I agreed to be captured, but it will be a cold day in Hades before I allow you to mar my temple to the Great Goddess!" Eldin growled as she planted the sword deep into his chest, through his heart, and into his lung.

The man tried to scream but choked on his own pink, frothy blood. While he died, Eldin used the sharp blade of the sword to cut through the rope that bound her wrists together. She sighed, that had been the third male-child she had attempted to "surrender" to and later had to kill for her own personal safety. Her captors had such contempt for Amazons, that they had each thought of a different way to punish her. At this rate, it would take several seasonmarks to be captured. Eldin sighed. It was time to hunt for another captor.

Eldin found her sword belt and wrapped it around her waist, securing the buckle without conscious thought. She felt whole once more. As she prepared to search out another male-child, a sudden overwhelming feeling of loss came over her. It was as if someone had plunged a sword through her heart. Eldin sunk to her knees in emotional agony. What manner of magic was this? Eldin felt tears welling up in her eyes. Something was horribly wrong, but what?

Knowing that she was in danger out in the open beside a murdered male-child, Eldin forced herself to her feet. She pushed the feeling deep down inside and ran into the bush candlemarks ahead of a patrol on their way to the border with Yashor.

* * *

"Mother! What are you doing?!" Kiya exclaimed as she stopped at the entrance to the small cavern.

Kidak's eyes flew open at the sound of Kiya's voice. She blinked back the sleep and felt Romyl's body still wrapped with hers. Romyl woke and lifted herself up onto her elbow.

"Get away from my mother, or I shall run you through!" Kiya threatened Romyl as she reached for the sword hanging on Maric's hip.

"Kiya, it is not as it appears," Kidak tried to defuse Kiya's anger.

"Get your filthy hands off of my mother! Have you no ears, woman?!" Kiya threatened again while trying to wrestle the sword hilt from a disagreeable Maric.

Romyl stood and strode over to Kiya. She towered over Kiya by a full two hands. Kiya's hands fell from the hilt of Maric's sword. Seldar and Maric both jumped in between them to defend Kiya. Romyl shook her head at the irony of the action. She had done nothing for Kidak besides what these two were doing for Kiya.

"Listen, child, I would never dishonor your mother. I was simply comforting Kidak for her loss. If you would but give her a heartbeat to explain, you would see that. I am sorry for your loss as well. Now I am going to get some fresh air and give you two the opportunity to talk. If by chance any of your friends care to join me, I would think it most appropriate to give you privacy," Romyl explained before she pushed past a stunned Seldar to walk out of the cavern.

Seldar and Maric looked at Kiya.

"Go ahead. I need to speak to my mother. Take my cousin and Rynar with you. Something tells me that I am not going to like this conversation verily much," Kiya commented.

All four of Kiya's traveling companions followed Romyl out of the hidden cavern. Kidak motioned for Kiya to sit next to her on the sleeping skins. Kiya stood for a few heartbeats, then walked over and sat down next to Kidak. She wanted her mother's comfort, after all.

"Kiya, have you seen the crosses on the east side of Clover Valley?" Kidak inquired.

"No. We saw no crosses. Seldar and I had stopped at General Elrik's keep in Three Rivers on our way home. I was going to see Yamouth and then come straight to the Council to see you. Mother, General Elrik and her mate Dinyar were murdered. Wait a heartbeat, did you say there were crosses?!" Kiya repeated, trying to wrap her mind around the implications.

"Yes. I think that half of Clover Valley is hanging dead outside the east town gates. Romyl saved me from an assassination attempt at the Council

Hall. I believe that we are the only councilwomen to have survived. When we rode here, we saw Yamouth on one of those crosses. My heart is hurting. It hurts beyond just the passing of my declared," Kidak started to explain.

"You mean…my…Yamie is…is…" Kiya started.

"Yes, honey. Your Yamie is gone. She is at the Great Feast saving us both a place at the table," Kidak confirmed.

Kiya collapsed into Kidak's embrace, and Kidak ran her fingers through Kiya's long fiery hair in comfort. She remembered the first word that Kiya had ever uttered.

It had been "Yamie." She could not say "Yamouth" for several seasonmarks. Truth be told, the horse trainer had liked it when her young daughter called her Yamie.

Kiya buried her face into her mother's chest. It had been a long journey, and her emotions were spinning out of control. She felt as if her world were crumbling around her.

"I know, my lil sweet one. I know. We shall make it somehow, you and me. I promise that we shall. Goddess only knows what sort of evil has taken over Yashor, but we shall survive!" Kidak promised.

"My Yamie is dead. The Council of Nine is destroyed. Eldin betrayed my heart, and Delyn stole my gift. Tell me, Mother, what does it really matter if we survive?" Kiya spat out bitterly into her mother's bosom.

"What say you? You wish to cross over too? Kiya, do not give up the gift your Goddess bestowed upon you that easily! Yes, Yamie is dead. We shall miss her, but our hearts beat still. In time, the ache will not seem as bad. We will learn to live and smile without her. The Council is destroyed, then so be it. We will find a way to restore that which is lost, or we shall make a new covenant with the Goddess. Eldin did not betray your heart. She and I spoke at great length about you. In fact, the only reason she accepted the mission from the Council was in exchange for you to be transferred away from danger. She has told me her heart. If only you could have seen…" Kidak started.

"Have you no eyes, Mother? Eldin speaks with a forked tongue. She lies like a serpent," Kiya interjected venomously.

"You think I have no eyes, child? I have eyes enough to see the love that you both share yet deny. I saw the love in her eyes when she spoke your name. I saw the conflict in her when she was sent into Drakknia. I saw the pain when she spoke of your misunderstanding and how she did not deserve your heart, just as I see the love in your eyes when you speak Eldin's name. The love...the fear...the pain in your eyes speaks volumes. She told me that if you but promised her your heart, she would have defied the Council for you. She would have stayed in Yashor," Kidak defended Eldin.

"What say you? Eldin would have defied the Council for...me?" Kiya repeated, trying to grasp the words her mother spoke.

"Yes, Kiya, she would; however, Eldin feels unworthy of your love. I have determined that it was the lieutenant who seduced her when she was mourning the death of her Committed. You were hurt and did not listen to the entire story. Eldin was after your heart, not another situation like the lieutenant. Kiya, you have much to learn of Eldin's heart. I would suggest that you start by listening to your heart instead of your head. Your head tends to be much too hard," Kidak gently chastised her daughter.

"You truly believe she wishes to pursue my heart?" Kiya asked, unsure of herself.

"I do," Kidak replied.

Kiya buried her face into her mother's bosom, "I have been such a fool, Mother!"

"Everything will work out. You shall see, doubting daughter of mine," Kidak soothed Kiya as she ran her fingers through her daughter's hair and wondered what exactly Kiya had meant when she said Delyn had stolen her gift.

"Mother, what mission did Eldin accept?" Kiya finally spoke after several candledrips.

"She was sent into Drakknia to be captured. She is to find the manner in which the army feeds itself. Then when she finds the main grain stores and water supply, she is to poison them. After most of the soldiers are sick and dying, she will attempt to escape and, with the help of her troops, crush the Drakknians. Then she may return home to Yashor." Kidak relayed the basic plan to her daughter.

"That is madness, Mother! No one can escape by themselves against so many. Eldin will be killed!" Kiya exclaimed, horrified.

"Verily likely, yes, Eldin shall die for Yashor," Kidak agreed.

"Why did she not stay? What fool would go up against that many enemies without so much as another sword at her side?" Kiya lamented.

"The honorable kind, Kiya." Kidak drove her point home.

* * *

Romyl sat down in the tall grass near the edge of the lake and watched the dark water ripple and curl in the moonlight. *Where are we going to go from here? We cannot possibly stay here until this coup is over. Goddess knows how long the traitors will be in control of Yashor. How long before a patrol finds this place? What of Kidak? How is she going to feel about me now that Yamouth has crossed over? Perhaps she shall become bitter and grow cold toward me. Goddess, I could handle anything but that.*

Romyl's thoughts were interrupted by the young male-child. He sat down next to the elder stateswoman. His face was contorted in barely contained emotional pain. Suddenly, he turned to Romyl and spoke.

"Councilwoman, I know that I am not allowed to speak to you, but since we are not in the Council Hall, I was hoping that you would overlook that law just this once," Seldar petitioned.

"You may speak." Romyl decided to be charitable with her time, under the circumstances.

"Do you know what has happened to my sib, Captain Eldin of Three Rivers? She was summoned to the Council Hall, and I have not seen her since. I am verily worried about her. Since my mothers were murdered, she is all the family that I have." Seldar gave voice to his fears.

"You are Captain Eldin's sib? Ah, well, yes, you should know the truth. Your sib has accepted a mission into Drakknia. It is verily unlikely that she shall survive." Romyl did not sweeten the words, choosing, as always, the direct approach.

Seldar's eyes widened. Why would Eldin accept such a mission? *Oh Goddess, I am utterly alone now.* Seldar's head hung and he felt worse than he had after all of the beatings he took at the healer's post. Seldar stood. He fled into the woods so no one would see the tears that streamed from his eyes. *Goddess, how could you be so cruel?*

Maric watched the exchange between Romyl and Seldar. It had not been her intent to listen, but she had heard the words just the same. Maric would give him ten candledrips to come back, and then she would go after him. She did not want him to run into any patrols. It seemed far less than ten candledrips when Seldar returned, his eyes red and puffy. Maric watched as he made his way to the lake and washed his face with the cool water. He finished washing his face and sat beside the lake. His shoulders slumped in defeat. Maric felt bad for the male-child. He had always been protected by his sib. Now he was alone in the world, and the world was not kind to male-children.

* * *

Kidak emerged from the cavern and collected everyone. As the group entered the small cavern they noticed Kiya. She had long since run out of tears and lay on a sleeping skin with her arms wrapped tightly around her body. Though she lay still, sleep had not claimed Kiya.

"Did you tell them?" Kidak asked Romyl.

"I felt it was not my place. If you wish me to be the one to tell them, I would gladly spare you the pain," Romyl replied.

"That would be most appreciated, dear Romyl. I am going back to my sleeping skins. Please join me when you have finished informing everyone. I still need the comfort of your strong arms around me," Kidak admitted as she moved toward the warmth of her abandoned bedding.

Romyl checked on Kiya. The poor child was still awake, so Romyl decided to lead everyone out of Kiya's earshot. Once they had obtained a safe distance, Romyl turned to the small group.

"Kidak and I found crosses that lined the eastern road into Clover Valley for at least a klig. Kidak's declared, Yamouth, was hanging dead on one of those crosses. We barely escaped a patrol of soldiers that were guarding the bodies. It would appear as though Yashor is under attack from within. I believe Yashor is under siege from a coup," Romyl explained, as she was never one to pull punches, though the Council had mellowed her a bit.

"Poor Kiya. I knew that she was close to Yamouth. Yamouth raised her while Kidak was away at Council. They had a special bond," Dedak commented.

"We found General Elrik and Dinyar murdered inside their keep. The gate had been breeched with a battering ram, and as far as I know, I am one of only four to survive the slaughter of Eldin's troops stationed in your district along the border. The murderers were a regiment of Yashor soldiers under Captain Berdyk. I would tend to agree with you about a coup," Maric relayed her personal horror to Romyl.

"Perhaps we should all turn in and get a fresh start in the morning. We need to make a plan of survival. It would seem as though we are now wanted fugitives in our own country." Romyl suggested.

* * *

Kiya opened her eyes. The fire had burned low, and the banked coals glowed an eerie red with their concealed heat. Sweat dripped down her face, and she wiped it with the back of her hand, only to feel the sting when she spread it to her eyes. *The dream had been so real. Goddess Eldin, what have you done to my heart? I cannot allow you to die without knowing. Eldin of Yashor, I am going to find you and rescue you...somehow.*

Quietly, Kiya stood and rolled her sleeping skin. She tied it with a small leather strap that held it together quite nicely. Next, Kiya rummaged through the dried food.

"What are you doing, Kiya?" Romyl's voice pierced the silence of the cavern.

Kiya froze. *Think, Kiya!*

"I...have a headache. I was looking for the well bark. Sometimes it helps me with my headaches. I am going to get some fresh air now. Thank you for your concern, but all is well," Kiya lied.

"Perhaps I should go with you, in case you should be surprised by a roving patrol," Romyl reasoned.

Great Goddess, the last thing I need now is a chivalrous gesture!

"Um, no, that shall not be necessary. I need to relieve myself, and I won't venture too far," Kiya lied again.

"My sincere apologies, dear child. I shall give it no further thought. Take care to stay quiet," Romyl reminded as she once again closed her eyes.

Kiya waited for a few heartbeats until she heard Romyl's breathing become long and even as sleep claimed the councilwoman once more before she gathered a few provisions for herself and took one of the water skins. She made certain to take the smallest one since she would only have to contend with her own thirst. Silently, Kiya bade farewell to her mother and the small group of women. She looked down at Seldar. Hopefully Maric would see to it that he was well cared for in her absence. Kiya took in a deep breath and left her security behind.

* * *

Seldar jerked awake. He sat bolt upright. Something was not right. Seldar looked around the small cavern and noticed Kiya was missing. Her sleeping skins were missing as well. Seldar stood and listened intently. He heard the unmistakable sounds of a horse leaving the area in front of the cave.

Quickly, Seldar packed up his sleeping skin and grabbed a small bag of food on his way out of the cavern. There was no time to find a water skin if he hoped to track her. Seldar knew it was his duty to follow Kiya and make certain that nothing bad happened to her. Hopefully, the rest of the group would understand. Seldar prayed that he would not be stopped by anyone and asked for his traveling papers. He knew that without them, he would be considered a fugitive or a spy for Drakknia. Either way, it would not bode well for him.

Light from the dual moons lit up the trail and Seldar tracked Kiya easily. From the looks of her tracks, she was doubling back toward the Drakknian border. What was she thinking? Did she even have a weapon to fight off wandering Drakknian raiding parties? *I will not let you down, Eldin. I will keep her safe for you. I shall protect her with my life!*

* * *

Kiya's heart felt heavy as her thoughts turned to Eldin. Had she judged the captain wrong? Eldin's gorgeous blue eyes haunted Kiya as the landscape became a blur. Traveling alone it was easy to ignore the passing kligs of land. Kiya vowed to ride all night and well past dawn.

* * *

Sunlight trickled in through the hole in the top of the cavern. Maric sat up and stretched the kinks out of her back. She looked over at her companions. Maric jumped to her feet as realization suddenly hit her.

"Wake up! Wake up, everyone! Kiya and Seldar are missing!" Maric raised the alarm.

Romyl opened her eyes and hastily stood. She was on her feet before she had fully pushed the sleep from her mind. Dedak was close on her heels as she woke with a start and stood protectively over Rynar. Kidak looked up at Romyl through sleep's haze.

"What is going on, Romyl?" Kidak inquired.

"Kiya and Seldar are missing. Hades fire! I felt as though something was wrong last night when I woke and Kiya was rummaging through the saddlebags. I accepted her story about a headache. Then she told me that she had to go relieve herself. Why did I not listen to my feelings? Do you have any idea why she would have run away or where she may be going?" Romyl asked Kidak gently.

"I told her about Yamouth; she became quite upset as I knew she would. She was lost, bitter, and searching for meaning in life. I told her about a conversation that I had with Captain Eldin. I do not know, perhaps she went to see her Yamie, or worse, to try to rescue the captain," Kidak reasoned.

"Would she have taken the male-child?" Romyl further probed.

"I do not know. If she had promised to look after him, I am certain that she would not break that promise. Other than that, I can see no reason why Kiya would prefer the company of a male-child over that of Amazons," Kidak defended Kiya.

"She may have taken Seldar with her because he is the one who saved her from Lieutenant Delyn," Maric piped up.

"What say you?" Kidak demanded knowledge of the incident.

Maric shuffled her feet nervously. It was not every day that you had to explain to someone's mother that they had been savaged, especially when that mother was a councilwoman.

"Lieutenant Delyn of the Three Rivers District attacked Kiya. She forced brutal sharing of the flesh upon Kiya, savaging her, and physically beat her. Delyn stole Kiya's gift. I believe this was due to Captain Eldin's affections for the healer. Eldin's sib Seldar heard Kiya's screams and attacked Delyn. Seldar managed to overpower the lieutenant and was holding her at swordpoint when I arrived. The lieutenant was placed under arrest and thrown into the holding cell. When the healer failed to formally accuse her attacker, we had no choice but to follow Yashor law and release the prisoner." Maric used formal accusatory language as a way to distance herself from the task at hand.

A multitude of emotions contorted Kidak's face as she heard the tale. Maric shivered as the emotion that won out was one of pure fury.

"I want Lieutenant Delyn's head on a spike!" Kidak spat out through her clenched jaws.

"The penalty for savaging another is not death but rather a lifetime of hard labor at the mines," Romyl gently reminded Kidak.

"I care not what the penalty is! I shall have her head on a spike!" Kidak flashed her rage at Romyl.

"Please, Councilwoman. I have to inform you that the lieutenant is already dead. She gave her life so that I might escape the clutches of the death squads. They are the ones who killed all of Eldin's troops," Maric explained quickly.

"Goddess, why do you take pleasure in torturing me?!" Kidak challenged toward the heavens.

"Kidak, we must not invite the Goddess to show us Her wrath. It is a most inopportune time. I wish to hear the voices of all on this matter. I believe that we should go after your daughter. If we do, it will be dangerous; however, I do not believe that we are entirely safe here. Besides which, how long can we reasonably expect to remain undetected by the patrols of this area? I say we should take our chances and leave immediately before Kiya has much more of a head start. Anyone else?" Romyl suggested a vote.

What do you think? Should we go? Rynar silently asked Dedak.

I have no doubt that it will be dangerous, but I also believe that we cannot allow the girl to come to harm through our inaction, Dedak replied.

"I say we go get her," Maric seconded the opinion.

"It seems that we are all in agreement, as Ry and I would like to get her as well," Dedak spoke for them both.

Kidak smiled at each of them. They were all willing to risk their lives to find her daughter. The act was humbling to her.

"It is agreed, then. Let us pack our things quickly and leave this place," Romyl stated as she moved toward the saddlebags.

* * *

Celdi rode through the ravaged camp of the Three Rivers District, and her heart grew heavier with each stride her horse took. It had been a massacre. The sandy earth ran red with blood. Fallen soldiers and trainlings were scattered throughout the camp, but

Celdi had not found Delyn, so she still held out hope that Delyn had escaped somehow. As she neared the edge of camp, Celdi spotted a crude stretching rack.

"No! Goddess, no!" Celdi screamed as she squeezed her eyes shut from the sight of Delyn's broken and naked body lying limply on the wooden executioner.

"Are you…going to get…me off of this…or just sit there…crying like a male-child?" Delyn managed to rasp.

Celdi's eyes flew open at the sound of Delyn's voice. She could not believe that Delyn still lived. Celdi threw her leg over the back of her horse and jumped to the ground. She covered the distance between her horse and the rack in heartbeats.

Celdi unsheathed her dagger. She used it to cut the ropes binding Delyn's wrists to the crude torture device. Gently, Celdi tried to move

Delyn's severely dislocated arms. Delyn screamed in agony.

"Celdi…kill me, please," Delyn begged.

"How can you ask that of me? Do you not know how much I love you?" Celdi replied in horror to Delyn's request.

"I am…counting on it," Delyn answered.

"I will get you to a healer. You will see; they will fix you good as new," Celdi tried to persuade Delyn.

"No. I am going to…die. Please." Delyn knew she would not be able to survive her wounds, but she was ready for the pain to end.

Celdi lifted Delyn off the rack and carried her to the river. Delyn bit her lip against the pain each footstep brought with it. She looked up into Celdi's eyes and her heart broke a little. How could this woman still love her so much after all she had done? The thought then struck her, *She has been gone. She knows not of my actions.*

Celdi laid Delyn on a soft patch of cool green grass. Delyn moaned as the pain shot through her body again. Celdi noticed her arms were covered with Delyn's blood. She tore a bit of cloth from her tunic and wet it in the cold water of the river. She then tried to clean all of the blood from Delyn's wounds.

There was too much blood. It covered Delyn's legs, and a pool was starting to form underneath her. Celdi hung her head. She knew that no one survived when they lost this much blood. Something had torn Delyn's insides to shreds.

"By the Goddess, what did they do to you?" Celdi exclaimed as she worked to clean the evidence of violence from Delyn.

"They beat me…savaged me repeatedly…broke me…and left me to die," Delyn answered Celdi's rhetorical question.

With great effort and pain, Delyn moved her hand to Celdi's. She wanted Celdi to stop fussing over her.

"It was nothing…I did not…deserve. Thank you, Celdi. I did not wish… to die…alone," Delyn managed as her breathing got more difficult.

"Is there nothing I can do for you?" Celdi inquired, tears welling up in her eyes.

"Forgive me," Delyn replied.

Celdi leaned down and placed a kiss on Delyn's cool lips. She ran her fingers through Delyn's blood-matted hair.

"There is nothing to forgive. You have always held my heart, Delyn of Fern Glen. I only wish that I had been able to make you happy," Celdi lamented as she plunged her dagger into Delyn's heart.

"You…just…did." Delyn died as the last word escaped her upturned lips.

24

Kiya opened her eyes. It had been seven days since she had left her mother and friends behind in the cave, and she felt no closer to finding Eldin. Frustration mixed with fear had been her only companion. She stretched and went to the stream she had camped beside to wash up.

Kiya peeled off her clothing and waded into the stream knee-deep. She sat down and lay back in the water. Kiya tried to wash away the feeling that she was being watched. She had felt this nagging feeling since the day after she had left the cave. Was she paranoid, or could there really be someone out there? Kiya dunked her head and then sat upright. As the cool water cascaded down her face and off her chin, she realized that if a Drakknian had been watching her, they would have already attacked her.

* * *

Seldar woke to the sound of splashing in the stream nearby. He sat up and looked around. Seldar rubbed the sleep from his eyes and stood. He quietly walked toward the stream to check the trap he had set the night before. Seldar was looking forward to eating a spicy rabbit stew or perhaps even a chilak. Did chilak live this far south? They did have a pretty heavy coat of fur. Oh well, he would soon find out.

As he got closer to the stream, he noticed Kiya bathing. Seldar immediately dove on his belly and closed his eyes. He hoped that she did not see him or she might order him away. While Seldar waited for Kiya to finish bathing, he noticed that he could do with a little clean water as well. He would definitely have to remain downwind of her until he could bathe.

* * *

"Looky what we got here, T'vic," G'nay commented as his eyes devoured Kiya's naked body.

Kiya jumped, startled by the voice slicing through the silence. She saw the male-children standing on the bank of the stream a few body lengths away from her. *Oh Goddess, what am I going to do now?*

"Looks like another runaway. Guess we can add her to our collection for reeducation," T'vic answered.

"You demons better stay away from me!" Kiya threatened.

"Or what are you going to do about it?" T'vic sneered.

Kiya felt her heart racing with fear. What could she do? Nothing, she did not even have a scrap of clothing on, much less a weapon.

"Come here, woman. Save yourself a worse beating by cooperating," G'nay ordered.

"Are you a runaway?" T'vic demanded.

Kiya felt the best thing to do would be to remain silent. This way, she could not possibly slip up and alert them to the fact that she was an Amazon. Kiya looked toward the far side of the stream and then back at the two male-children. Did she stand a chance of outrunning them? It was not likely; she had no boots on her feet, and her feet would be tender. *Goddess, help me!*

Kiya made up her mind and slowly walked toward the two male-children. She would wait until her first opportunity to escape. T'vic grabbed her arm and dragged her the rest of the way out of the stream. He nuzzled her breast and flicked his tongue across her nipple. Kiya froze. She started to scream. Delyn's mouth was on her. She pushed at the offending mouth and received a resounding slap across the face.

"She is indeed tasty if not a bit feisty as well," T'vic announced.

G'nay agreed. T'vic shoved Kiya to the ground. She looked up at the two male-children in horror as she realized what they meant by "reeducation." Kiya did not see them as male-children. In her mind, she saw them both as Delyn standing over her, ready to violate her once more. Tears of pain started to spill onto her cheeks.

"Hold! What are you two doing with my wife?" a rich, deep baritone voice boomed from beyond the bushes.

"Show yourself. If she be your wife, why was she bathing alone?" G'nay challenged.

A small man burst through the bushes carrying a freshly killed rabbit. He held up the rabbit as if in answer to their question.

"Seldar!" Kiya exclaimed, relieved.

"Quiet, woman! We know not these two ruffians," Seldar admonished, hoping that Kiya would understand what he was attempting.

Seldar turned his attention back to the two male-children. "As you can see, I was hunting our first-feast."

T'vic squinted his eyes in scrutiny of the young man who stood before him. It could be a trick. The man was verily young. Still, in all, he did have what appeared to be a first beard growing.

"Come here, stranger," T'vic called.

"I think I would rather not. I want my wife to come to me," Seldar politely refused.

G'nay rushed Seldar. Seldar ducked his attack and sent G'nay flying past him.

"Are you always in the habit of attacking other Drakknian men?" Seldar hoped he had gotten the words right.

"Enough, G'nay. This stranger is correct. We should not be attacking him. What did you say your name was?" T'vic asked innocently.

"I did not say. My name is S'eldar," Seldar tried to make his name sound more Drakknian-like.

"S'eldar. Odd, that would make you a descendent of the elders. Are you descended from royalty, S'eldar?" G'nay sneered, not trusting this man at all.

"I am not certain. No one is. If there was indeed a single nation, then the answer is yes. If it be a mere myth, then the answer is no," Seldar tried to defuse the situation by applying the ancient history theories that Eldin had taught him many seasonmarks ago.

Kiya cocked her head. *How can he know all of this? He must have been schooled, but by whom?* Kiya's eyes widened; the answer was crystal clear: *Eldin.*

Suddenly, the two male-children seemed to accept them. They laughed at Seldar's answer.

"We are sorry to have doubted you, Brother S'eldar. However, we are verily close to the Yashor border. One never knows," T'vic apologized as he held his hand out.

Seldar gripped the hand and they shook. It was a custom known only to Drakknians. In Yashor, the Amazons gripped each other's forearms. Seldar had passed yet another test.

Thank the Goddess that Eldin taught me about Drakknian customs. I wonder if she thought I might one day try to live here?

"Wife, come to me," Seldar boomed.

Kiya had no choice but to follow Seldar's commands. She got to her feet and walked over to Seldar. She noticed he used his head to motion ever-so-slightly that she should kneel before him. Kiya went to her knees in front of him. The Drakknian male-children approved.

"Yes, S'eldar?" Kiya used the unfamiliar sounding name.

"First put your clothing on. It displeases me to have others look on your flesh. You are mine alone. Then take this rabbit downstream and clean it for first-feast," Seldar gently commanded.

Kiya accepted the beast from Seldar's hands but looked at him with panic in her eyes. She had never cooked anything other than gruel before in her life! How would she be able to fake it now under the scrutiny of these male-children?

"Yes, my lord," Kiya stated as she rose to walk away from the intruders.

Seldar turned his attention back to the two Drakknian male-children.

They seemed to have accepted him. He would have to stay on his guard if he and Kiya were to make it out of this situation alive.

Kiya walked back to her clothing and slipped the light green dress over her head. She instantly felt more at ease. *What in Hades is Seldar thinking? How am I going to be able to cook a meal that the Drakknian male-children will enjoy without raising their suspicions? Great Goddess, please guide me!*

Before Kiya had realized, she had wandered upstream and stumbled upon Seldar's camp. He had a pot with some vegetables already cut inside. Kiya looked around and spotted a knife and cutting stone. She took the rabbit to the cutting stone and laid it across.

Gingerly, Kiya picked up the knife and held it at different angles trying to figure out how to best cut the small beast. Sweat beaded on her forehead. Kiya felt unsure of herself. Why could Seldar not have already made the meal before this had happened? Of all the foul luck!

Kiya held the small beast with her left hand and made an incision. She attempted to peel back the skin as she sliced along the underbelly. She tried to envision the rabbit as an Amazon she was healing. It helped...some.

Kiya jumped at the feel of hands on her shoulders. Delyn was grabbing her!

"I am sorry, Kiya. I did not mean to frighten you. Here, allow me to help you. I will show you how it is done. In that way, should we ever have to do this again, you shall be more at ease with the ruse," Seldar commented as he took the knife from Kiya's hand.

It took a few heartbeats for Kiya's mind to return to the present. When his words sunk in, she moved out of Seldar's way and watched intently as he sliced through the throat and removed the head. Then he finished slicing the underbelly and retracted the skin. Where the skin held, Seldar used small incisions with the knife to free the skin from the underlying muscle tissue.

Once the beast was skinned properly, Seldar took the rabbit to the stream and gutted it with Kiya observing his every movement. He washed the carcass thoroughly and brought it back to the cutting stone. Kiya made mental notes of the process as Seldar methodically cut the rabbit into sections along the joints. Then Seldar dumped the meat into the pot and turned to Kiya.

"Just add some water, start a fire, and heat up the pot. I have already seasoned the stew. Once this boils for a candlemark, it should be finished. When it is complete, come to fetch us. I shall keep the Drakknians occupied; that is, if my plan is acceptable to you," Seldar commented, not wanting to overstep his authority.

Kiya smiled at Seldar. She understood that for this to work, it had to appear as if Seldar were in charge.

"I will follow your lead, Seldar. I am verily glad that the Great Goddess sent you to save me from this living night terror. I only ask one thing," Kiya admitted.

"Name it, and I shall make it so," Seldar replied.

"If it should come to pass that the Drakknians do not believe us, I want you to kill me. Do not allow them to use me, please. I could not... go through...that again," Kiya asked haltingly, pushing down the sobs of her soul.

"I shall never allow any harm to come to you, dear Healer. My life and my sword for you, this I pledge," Seldar replied in earnest.

Kiya turned back toward the pot of food.

"Kiya, I have to know one thing. Why are you here?" Seldar inquired.

"I came to rescue Eldin. My mother told me of the mission that they sent her on, and I do not think it is right for her to die a useless death. Why are you here?" Kiya returned the question.

"I made a pledge to watch over you to my captain. I never break my oaths. I must get back there now before they become suspicious and start looking for us," Seldar admitted freely before he returned to the Drakknians downstream.

Kiya felt more at ease after Seldar's pledge of fealty. She knew that she could trust him. As Kiya worked to start a fire, her thoughts turned to Eldin. How had Seldar learned to be so honorable if not for Eldin's example? Certainly she had misjudged the captain. Goddess, please protect Eldin until I can rescue her. She deserves an honorable death, not a meaningless gesture to a Council that no longer exists.

* * *

Eldin held her hands in front of her face and silently curled her fingers inward, moving the foliage that concealed her from her line of sight. She counted the number of male-children in the scouting party. There were six of them. She relaxed her fingers slowly, and the hole in the foliage disappeared. Eldin cupped her face in her right hand and wiped the sweat from it in frustration. Six male-children! Should she allow them to capture her? *Great Goddess, Creator of all life, if I allow them to capture me I will be at their mercy. They number enough to overpower me; if they should choose to abuse me I shall be as a child against them. What is your will?*

Eldin closed her eyes. She became still and allowed her mind to accept the message she was certain that the Goddess would send to her. There was only one face she saw. Long, flowing, flame-tinged hair that cascaded past rose-petal-soft shoulders. Pools of the deepest green beckoned Eldin to lose herself in their endless depths. *Hades Fire! Kiya you are the Demon Shamaness that haunts my very soul. Should I do this? I have never felt this alone.*

Eldin's eyes flew open. She looked around nervously. Eldin felt the sensation again. It was as if Kiya had wrapped her arms around Eldin in a comforting embrace.

"You are a Demon Shamaness, but I no longer feel alone." The admission tumbled from Eldin's lips.

Emboldened, Eldin drew her sword and held it loosely at the ready should her attempt to surrender be met with potentially fatal indifference. Eldin controlled her breathing as she stepped from the cover of the bush directly in front of the six male-children.

"Ho there! I wish to surrender and claim the protection of the House of Elders," Eldin quickly called out her rehearsed speech.

Eldin watched as the male-children hastily drew their swords. They formed a protective semicircular human shield around their leader. *He must be high ranking to elicit such a response,* Eldin noted.

"You invoke a protection from a long-broken treaty, Amazon. What makes you think that we would honor such a request?" a voice from behind the wall of soldiers questioned.

Eldin used her forefinger and thumb to thoughtfully pinch her protruding lower lip in a show of exaggerated thought. "I had heard that the House of Elders was honorable. Is this not true?" Eldin quipped back.

"Aye, it is true." The voice was quick to defend the honor of the Elders.

Eldin threw her hand up and shrugged her shoulder in another act, this time of exaggerated indifference.

"I had also heard that the soldiers of Drakknia were honorable. Are you saying that they are actually corrupt dogs?" Eldin once again put them on the defensive.

"No, Amazon! The soldiers of Drakknia are not morally corrupt. They are honorable," the deep voice conceded.

"Then you have answered your own question. I believe what you say is true. I believe that you shall take me safely to the House of Elders to petition for a life inside Drakknia," Eldin stated simply as she lay down her sword and kicked it out of her reach, trusting the voice she heard from within that guaranteed her safety.

The soldiers rushed her. This was it! Eldin held her breath as she stared straight ahead at the male-children's armed advance. Suddenly she was surrounded and she felt hands on her. Eldin stumbled forward as one of the soldiers became a little overzealous.

"No! No harm shall befall this Amazon while she is in our custody. Take care in securing her," the familiar voice commanded.

"But Lord A'toha, she is a lowly woman!" the young soldier complained.

Eldin's blue eyes smoldered with disgust. She knew his type well; young and full of contempt. Not one drop of discipline in his entire body. His hatred fueled his fight, not his intellect. Eldin regained her feet. It mattered little; hatred would only get him killed.

A small but powerfully built male-child stepped forward. His square face was framed with golden hair. His bright blue eyes held a deep understanding and sorrow. His eyes had seen the horrors of combat.

"I am Lord A'toha, as you probably had already learned from my outspoken guard. I apologize for your rough treatment and guarantee it will not happen again. I pledge that you shall have safe passage to the House of Elders," A'toha promised.

"I am Eldin of Three Rivers; firstborn daughter of Elrik and Dinyar. I pledge that I shall not give you reason to mistreat me," Eldin introduced herself and tried to put the male-children at ease.

"Why do you wish to live in Drakknia, Eldin of Three Rivers?" A'toha asked, genuine curiosity getting the better of him.

"I have a younger sib, a male-child." Eldin looked around as the male-children grumbled at her description.

"In Drakknia, we refer to ourselves as men or man if you speak of only one, Amazon. You would do well to remember that, for it will go hard on you otherwise," A'toha interrupted, in an attempt to help the woman.

"Yes, my Lord. I am not entirely certain of all the Drakknian customs, but be assured, I do not wish to insult," Eldin offered an apology before she continued with her contrived story. "It is my sincere dream for my sib to live a life of freedom here in Drakknia. I wish him to live a life free from the yolk of oppression. He is a good male...man."

A'toha studied the woman before him. She was quite large and well muscled. Her hands were calloused with multiple scars that told him she was not a stranger to life with a sword in her hands. She was beautiful and had only one slight scar from her right ear down through her jawline that ended under her chin. It was quite faded. She had probably received it early in her training. It had been many seasonmarks since a blade had touched her face. That meant she was good with the sword. Why would she surrender if her story were not true?

"You do realize that the House of Elders may not grant you your wish. They may execute you instead. Are you really willing to risk your life for your brother, Amazon?" A'toha inquired, intrigued by the enigma that stood proudly in front of him, even though Drakknian chains bound her like a dog.

"I would gladly risk all that I am and all that I have for Seldar's freedom. I have already risked all as a youth. I educated him," Eldin felt the truth served her best in this instance.

A'toha raised an eyebrow. It was well known what the Yashor punishment for educating young boys entailed. Indeed, this woman was gaining respect in his eyes.

"I shall see to it that you are heard, Eldin of Three Rivers. You have proven yourself to me," A'toha replied honestly.

"Thank you, my Lord," Eldin responded with quiet dignity.

"Do not thank me yet, Eldin of Three Rivers. You know not what the House of Elders will rule. Perhaps I am just prolonging your death," A'toha reminded her before he turned and motioned for the soldiers to move out.

* * *

Romyl held up her hand. She signaled for the rest of the group to lay low and helped Kidak to the ground. Everyone dismounted quickly and made themselves as small as possible. They found places to hide from view as a patrol of Drakknians rode past their position. So far they had been lucky and none of the patrols had noticed the riderless beasts in the foliage. They had been tracking Kiya and Seldar for over a fortnight. It had proven to be quite difficult once they left Yashor territory. Many times the group had wondered if they had lost the trail that had now grown so cold.

Once the patrol had passed, Romyl motioned for the group to continue. They followed the tracks in relative silence for another candlemark before coming to a stream. Romyl once again motioned for them to hide. This time, she dismounted and left Kidak on the horse. Romyl then took a look around on foot. Once she was satisfied that all was well, she returned to the group.

"I think that this should make an excellent place for mid-meal. We can catch some fish in the stream, and I saw an area that I believe contains wild white root," Romyl reported.

"I shall help gather the roots and try to locate a ruha tree," Kidak commented.

"Good. Maric and I shall catch fish," Romyl decided aloud.

"Then Ry and I shall collect any wild herbs we can find. Anyone opposed to adding some spicy fungus?" Dedak inquired.

You are going to kill them if you continue to add spicy fungus to every meal, dear. Why do you not allow one meal without the potent kick? Rynar mentally teased Dedak.

What say you? Has the great Amazon nation become a bunch of soft male-children since I was a youth? Dedak shot back.

Dedak noticed that Romyl and Maric did not look too thrilled by the idea. She turned to look at Kidak, who was starting to look ill at the very mention of her favorite spice.

"General Elrik had been quite fond of Hades Revenge. I, however, can only take it in small doses. It does strange things to my stomach," Maric admitted.

"Ah, I see. How about if I add it to my bowl only? That way, none of you have to suffer," Dedak conceded.

"Take care; I do not wish you to burn off your tongue quite yet," Rynar teased out loud.

The group chuckled as crimson crept across Dedak's cheeks.

You are going to pay for that one, my love, Dedak lovingly threatened.

Promises, promises, Jahru. Perhaps someday you will actually ravish me instead of talking about it, Rynar shot back; never looking at the dumbfounded expression she placed on Dedak's face.

The group separated, and each went about their task. Rynar noticed Dedak looking around nervously. She watched her as she tried to double back toward the stream but make it appear as though she were still searching for fungus and herbs. Rynar knew better, but she allowed Dedak her privacy.

Dedak found Romyl at the stream casting a small net she had fashioned from tree bark twine which she had hand hewn the night before. She smiled at the former councilwoman.

"Yes, Dedak? What is it that you wish to speak to me about?" Romyl inquired. "I assume you are not just interested in my fishing technique."

"Quite right, Councilwoman; I wish to know if you will perform a declaration ceremony for Rynar and I? Once we have found Kiya, that is," Dedak amended her request so that Romyl understood that she was not attempting to be callous toward Kidak's feelings.

"You wish me to lead the ceremony and not Kidak?" Romyl wondered aloud.

"I love Kidak dearly. I wish for her to stand at my side and be my First Witness," Dedak explained the honor that she wished to bestow on her "cousin."

"Ah, I see. It would be an honor for me to join you and Rynar. I have seen the love and devotion the two of you share. You are indeed a lucky woman to have found and recognized this. I shall be happy to lead the ceremony for you. Now if you will excuse me, I am going to catch some fish for our meal," Romyl excused herself.

Dedak beamed. She was going to be joined with her love as soon as they found Kiya. She did not care if it was in Drakknia, Yashor, or Hades for that matter.

Wherever it happened, it was going to be a magical time for the two of them.

Dedak returned to Rynar. Together they harvested some herbs they found as well as a few of the fungus that Dedak preferred. The sun ducked behind a stray cloud and Dedak wiped sweat from her brow. Suddenly, her stomach gave loud protest to its empty state. Rynar giggled and playfully slapped Dedak's muscular belly.

Sounds as if we better feed you before your belly throws a coup, oh mighty Jahru, Rynar playfully mocked Dedak.

You are in trouble now, little girl, Dedak thought back as she reached for Rynar.

Rynar broke into a run, and Dedak missed her arm by a whisper. Dedak took off after her giggling committed. Rynar looked over her shoulder and pressed off of her left foot, suddenly changing direction and circling an old willow tree. Dedak anticipated this maneuver and cut off her angle of escape. She ran directly into Dedak's arms with a barely audible yelp. Dedak pulled her close and claimed Rynar's lips in a searing kiss. Rynar melted into the contact. Dedak had one last thought before she lost herself in the mounting passion: *Goddess, I am one lucky Amazon.*

"Do I need a bucket of cold water to separate you, or are the two of you coming to mid-meal?" Maric asked as she and Romyl carried four good-sized rainbow-colored trout toward the awaiting cooking stones.

Crimson invaded Rynar's cheeks and the tips of her ears as she and Dedak jumped away from each other, startled. Dedak grinned wolfishly at Rynar. She had a way to make even the worst places seem like the Great Feast. Perhaps the Goddess had sent her as a reward for Dedak's faith. Perhaps it was just the Fates. Dedak cared little the reason, just as long as she could see that smiling face every day for the rest of their lives.

"You are a big softie, you know that, right?" Rynar commented on Dedak's feelings.

"You make me what I am, and I thank you for it," Dedak replied in earnest.

* * *

Kidak had the cooking stones red hot by the time everyone had returned. The fish were cleaned, gutted, and stuffed with herbs and root vegetables before being wrapped in the wide, thick ruha leaves. Kidak had soaked the leaves in water to prevent the contents from being burned. Then they were surrounded by the cooking stones. The water from the leaves hissed into aromatic steam that prompted more than one mouth to water in anticipation.

After a torturous half-candlemark, Kidak declared mid-meal ready to eat. Everyone gathered around as large sticks were used to push the still-hot cooking stones away from the leaf pouches of food. Kidak looked at Dedak and Rynar. Dedak smiled and reached down for the pouches. She and Rynar were the only ones who had hands used to the heat of constant cooking. Dedak carefully unwrapped each fish so they would cool and be easily handled.

"Ry and I will share a fish. The rest of you go ahead and have a whole one," Dedak offered.

"Are you certain? I am not really all that hungry," Kidak replied.

"You need to eat, Cousin. Your heart is hurting, and that is what makes your hunger fade. You need to keep up your strength. Please, for your health, allow me to share a meal with my intended," Dedak held firm.

Kidak finally nodded her consent. She would make certain that they had extra even-feast. Everyone sat down and consumed their meal. The fish melted in

Maric's mouth as she savored its delicate flavor. It was very tender and was easily picked from the bone. Maric closed her eyes as the meal reminded her of the ones she used to share with Elrik and Dinyar. They had some fine cooks in their employ over the seasonmarks. Sadness threat-ened to creep into her heart and spoil the simple joy of the feast, so Maric pushed back the memories to the deepest regions of her soul. Those times would never come to be again, so there was no reason to dwell on it.

After the fish were reduced to small piles of bones, Romyl stood and stretched. A full stomach of fresh food always made life on the road more bearable. She excused herself and took a short walk toward the road to scout ahead and find a place to relieve herself in privacy. She found an area that was close to the well-used dirt road they had been following and was concealed on three sides. As Romyl untied the flap to her pants, she heard horses and ducked behind some thick foliage.

Romyl watched as a wagon containing prisoners rolled past. It was be-ing escorted by six soldiers on horseback. Squinting into the sunlight, she made out the occupants of the wagon. As soon as the soldiers were out of sight, Romyl leapt to her feet. She tied her pants as she ran back to the others.

"We have to hurry! Get everything together. I have just seen Captain Eldin! She is in a wagon being hauled off toward a prison somewhere, I am certain. We can ill-afford to lose her. I think that if we stick close, we shall find Kiya," Romyl explained excitedly.

"Thank the Goddess!" Kidak exclaimed.

Maric and Dedak ran for the grazing horses tethered close by. They untied the tethers one at a time. Once all of the horses were freed, they led them back to the others.

While Maric and Dedak went to gather the horses, the others cleaned up the area. They dug a shallow hole and buried the bones and cooking leaves. Then they filled the water skins and made certain that their tracks were obscured. They would not be able to erase all of the tracks in their haste, but if they were being followed, their numbers would not be known.

Kidak was nervous as they headed for the road. They would have to stay close to the road to track where Eldin was being taken. It would mean being in the open for most of the trip. Many things could go wrong when you traveled behind enemy lines out in the open. Goddess, protect us all from the evil *Drakknians. Veil us in Your grace. Please let me find my daughter alive.* Kidak wrapped her arms tighter around Romyl's waist. It was now in the hands of the Goddess.

25

Eldin looked at the surrounding forestland as the wagon she was riding in creaked along. Overall, she had no complaints. She had been treated with more respect than she had imagined. A sudden breeze chilled her. If only she could have access to her belongings. Her cape would cut the chill wind and keep her warm.

Movement in the tree line caught her attention and she squinted. Were they being followed? Eldin saw the movement again and focused her eyes. There were riders in the tree line! Did Drakknia have problems with marauders as well? Should she alert the soldiers?

"Excuse me, Lord A'toha. Do you have many brigands here?" Eldin inquired off-handedly.

A'toha turned to face his prisoner. She looked unconcerned. Perhaps it was simply an odd question.

"We have a few. Do you not have outlaws in Yashor? I believe every society has an element that they wish did not exist. Do you not agree, Amazon?" A'toha returned the question.

"I do. How bad are your outlaws?" Eldin persisted.

"Not verily bad at all. We have never had any attempt to attack a wag-onload of prisoners with a soldier guard. Are you frightened or perhaps just lonely and wish to make conversation?" A'toha inquired after Eldin's motivation.

"Perhaps it is too silent back here," Eldin lied, deciding to keep silent about the riders.

"See that? You are already turning into a Drakknian, wishing for the company of a man," A'toha teased, wanting to have some sport with the prisoner who was quickly becoming his favorite.

Eldin gave A'toha the "not verily likely" look and then broke into a grin. Despite his being a Drakknian, she did like the male-child. Eldin looked out at the mountain rising in the not-so-distant horizon. Plumes of smoke rose from its peak. She recognized this as one of the Mountains of Fire. She had never been this close to one before. The smoke smelled of rotten eggs. It was not too bad from this distance.

"My Lord, what is on the other side of those mountains?" Eldin inquired.

"Ah, the Mountains of Fire are forbidden. No one knows. The Priests say that they are the entrance to Hades. The Gods of Hades guard the entrance with that thick, yellow smoke. The smoke smells so bad that you would lose your stomach well before reaching the gates. It is also guarded by molten earth that is so hot, if you touch it, your flesh burns from your bones and your bones become dust." A'toha repeated the stories he had heard from birth.

"Not a verily pleasant place. Has anyone dared to explore it?" Eldin asked.

"A few have gone up, none have returned. Why do you ask, Eldin?" A'toha wondered aloud.

"I have grown up seeing these mountains from my home. They were always so far away. I have never been this close to them, and I was simply curious," Eldin replied.

A'toha nodded and then they settled back into the journey. Eldin's thoughts turned to Kiya as the landscape melted into the background of her mind. *She should be safe by now. I wonder if she is near Kidak? She would like that. Goddess, I want to see you again, Kiya! If only you could understand my heart.* Eldin fell asleep with visions of flowing flame-tinged hair framing the most beautiful face she had ever seen.

* * *

When Eldin woke, darkness had consumed the day. She looked around and spotted Lord A'toha sitting near a campfire. The tantalizing smell of roasting meat reached her as a gentle breeze blew through the campsite. Eldin's stomach stirred to life and rumbled its displeasure at being empty.

"Having visions of sharing the Lord's meal? He only shares with those who warm his bed. Sorry to inform you that even if you weren't opposed to his affections, you would need to be a fair-looking man to turn A'toha's head," the blonde-haired prisoner sneered.

"You find that repulsive? Why? It is apparent from your own descriptions that the Lord A'toha would not be forcing his attentions on you," Eldin replied, disgusted at the tone in the prisoner's voice.

"I should have known that a filthy Amazon would not understand," the prisoner redirected his repulsion.

"Ah, I do understand now. You secretly desire Lord A'toha to mount you. That is why you protest so loudly," Eldin mocked the prisoner.

Suddenly, the blonde prisoner jumped to his feet. He attacked Eldin. As the prisoner fell toward her, she wrapped the chains that bound her wrists together around his neck and used her feet to flip him over her. The blonde prisoner reached up and tried to pull at the chain that was squeezing the life from him. The guards started beating Eldin to force her to release the man from her chain's death grip.

Lord A'toha looked up at the commotion. He found his feet quickly and ran to the wagon. The blonde prisoner was turning a reddish-blue in the face as he struggled against the chains.

"What is the meaning of this, Amazon?! You have given me your word that you would not do anything to warrant receiving abuse. Hold!" A'toha demanded.

Eldin grimaced as she strained her leg muscles to the limit. She arched her back and was barely able to complete the backflip out of the wagon and over the choking prisoner. Eldin now stood facing him, her eyes burning a warning into his. She unwrapped the chain from his neck. The prisoner collapsed at her feet, his lungs gasping desperately for air.

Lord A'toha grabbed the guard's hand and did not allow him to strike Eldin.

"Explain yourself, Amazon. I thought you were honorable," A'toha spat.

"This male-child attacked me. I was only defending myself," Eldin replied calmly.

"What would provoke such an attack?" A'toha felt there was more to the story than Eldin was telling.

"After slandering your sexual desires, he did not like hearing me tell him that I thought he secretly desired you to mount him," Eldin confessed.

Lord A'toha looked at Eldin. She was telling him the blunt and honest truth. Suddenly, A'toha laughed.

"Put that piece of scum back into the wagon. Although I could place him on half rations, I think he has learned his lesson. Remove the chains from Eldin of Three Rivers," A'toha ordered.

"But, Lord!" the guard started to protest.

"Are you questioning my orders, soldier? Would you like to join the brigands in the wagon? I seem to have a spare set of shackles," A'toha threatened.

"No, Lord. Your will be done," the soldier quickly backed down.

A'toha turned toward Eldin. "Would you join me? I am certain that there is enough food for both of us."

Eldin rubbed her wrists. That lout had placed a great deal of strain on them while she was choking him.

"I would be honored, my Lord," Eldin replied.

Eldin followed Lord A'toha to the campfire. The night air was crisp, and the heat from the fire was welcoming. Eldin sat down next to A'toha. He handed her an empty trail plate and mug. Eldin smiled at him.

"Thank you, my Lord. I must admit that the smell from your even-feast woke my stomach," Eldin sincerely thanked the male-child.

"I have plenty; please fill your plate. Besides, I would like to ask you a few questions. Would that be agreeable to you, Eldin of Three Rivers?" A'toha inquired.

"I have nothing but time for you, my Lord," Eldin replied as she tore a big hunk off of the roasted boar.

Eldin placed the hunk of boar meat on her plate and grinned as A'toha signaled for her to continue to fill the plate. Eldin took the lid off of a small pot that hung over the fire. A purplish-blue gooey substance bubbled. Eldin eyed it warily.

"It is edible, I assure you. My mother claims it is actually good for you. However, it may take some getting used to since the flavor is rather like chewing on your scabbard," A'toha chuckled.

Eldin did not want to seem ungrateful, so she placed a small dip of the goo on her plate and moved on. There was a pot sitting next to the fire to stay warm, and inside was a mixture of stalk vegetables. Eldin added a scoop to her plate and finished it off with a large hunk of molasses oat bread.

After securing her feast, Eldin returned to sit next to A'toha. He looked at her plate and smiled.

"You are brave, I see," A'toha teased.

"Well, if it be good for me, how can I resist such a tempting flavor?" Eldin responded as she stuck her finger into the warm goo and brought it to her lips.

A'toha watched her face scrunch as she sucked the goo from her fingertip.

"Mmm hm. Yes, my Lord, that is one mean scabbard you cooked there," Eldin agreed.

"It is usually better if you dip your meat into it," A'toha confided.

"I shall try that. Now, what was it that your Lordship wished to discuss with me?" Eldin asked, curious.

A'toha broke off a piece of his bread and chewed it slowly, while his mind worked to phrase his thoughts correctly.

"Do you believe that there is a correct way to love, Eldin of Three Rivers?" A'toha asked at last.

"I do not know, my Lord. I was raised on the tenants of the Great Goddess. The only true love that is acceptable is that between two women. I have known women who desire male-chil...uh, men, but they are usually stoned to death or shunned. I know that my greatest wish for my sib would be for him to live free and love completely," Eldin replied honestly.

"You are indeed an unusual Amazon, Eldin," A'toha replied with respect. "What of two men together? Does that seem wrong to you?"

"If the Goddess can deem that two women belong together...how could I then deny two men if they are in love? In Yashor, many of the eunuchs fall in love with one another. Many stay with one another until their deaths, working for the same family for their entire lives," Eldin responded.

"Eunuchs? You keep eunuchs in Yashor? How barbaric!" A'toha exclaimed.

"Yes, my Lord, you shall get no quarrel from me. It is equally as barbaric as keeping women as uneducated slaves to men. What is it that a Drakknian soldier once told me? Ah yes, 'It is impossible to savage a slave, since they are your property. My cows have greater value than my wife.' Seems equally cruel to me," Eldin retorted.

A'toha stared at Eldin. Could this Amazon truly be comparing women to men? What really was the difference?

"So you truly believe that women and men are...are equal?" A'toha questioned.

"Besides our obvious advantage in strength and endurance, I see not a big difference in ability," Eldin replied.

"Perhaps you are right, Eldin of Three Rivers. I must admit, you have a certain intelligence that is hard to refute. You should eat now, before your food gets cold," A'toha stated, effectively ending the debate.

"As you wish, my Lord," Eldin replied, and returned her attention to the mound of food on her plate.

Eldin felt as though she were gaining an ally in Lord A'toha. She smiled and shook her head slightly at the irony. Captain Eldin of Three Rivers and Lord A'toha of Drakknia; she had to admit they made the oddest of allies. What was it that her mother had told her when she was commissioned? *Keep your friends close and your enemies closer.*

Eldin felt her eyelids grow heavy. She was tired and needed to get some rest. The guards had been staring at her since she had broken bread with Lord A'toha.

She could see the contempt in their eyes. Given half a chance, they would like nothing better than to use her, gut her, and leave her as food for the carrion. This was what made sleep elusive.

Eldin walked over to the prisoners' wagon and climbed in. She sat down opposite from the male-child who had attacked her earlier. Perhaps sleep would find her if she leaned against the headboard and relaxed. Eldin closed her eyes. She slowed her breathing. It was several candledrips before sleep finally claimed her.

* * *

Eldin's eyelids fluttered open. She looked around, disoriented. The wagon had been on the move, and nothing looked familiar. Her head felt heavy, and she felt sluggish. Had she been given a sleeping powder? Her head felt as if a dozen Drakknians were dancing a jig on her skull. It must have been a strong sleeping powder.

Eldin tried to suck any hint of moisture from the inside of her mouth. It was as dry as a sun-bleached pile of bones from a carcass in the sand lands. Eldin reached up and rubbed her eyes.

"Lord A'toha?" Eldin squeaked the noise from her parched larynx.

A'toha turned to face her. He wore a worried expression on his face.

"Do you think you could keep down some water?" A'toha asked gently.

Eldin nodded, for her throat was too dry to speak anymore. A'toha handed Eldin his waterskin, and she pulled deeply from it. Cool water flooded Eldin's mouth and washed the road dust from her throat. Goddess, it felt like a healer's touch.

After a few more draughts of water, Eldin tried to find her bearings. She found the mountain rising almost on top of them. They had to be less than a day's journey from the base of the great Mountain of Fire. Lord A'toha had been right about the smell. Even from this distance, she could smell the acrid yellow plumes of smoke.

Eldin saw a village in the distance. It appeared that they were heading for it.

"Lord A'toha, is that our destination?" Eldin inquired, pointing at the village.

"Yes. It is where I must leave you in the care of our leaders. Do you still wish to petition them? You could always come and work for me. I could use a sword as skilled as yours," A'toha offered.

"I am flattered; however, I must petition for my sib," Eldin remained firm.

"As you wish, brave Eldin," A'toha replied, turning from her.

"Why was I given sleeping powders, my Lord? Did I not swear to you that I would be no trouble?" Eldin wondered aloud.

"I slipped you the sleeping powders because my guards wished to provoke you. If they had succeeded, I would not have been able to keep them off of you. I chose to have you docile. It was in your best interests, really," A'toha responded.

"Humph, I would rather think it saved them, my Lord," Eldin replied, indignant.

"That may be true. I did not want to risk it, and I am your keeper, Eldin of Three Rivers. You chose that," A'toha reminded Eldin.

Eldin preferred silence. She was angry with Lord A'toha for the deception. However, she could not allow her anger to ruin the fledgling allegiance no matter how tenuous it might be. She sat silently and watched the village rise with each passing klig.

Eldin's nerves were raw as they passed through the great gates to the village. The village was surrounded by a huge wooden wall. She could see that the wooden wall was actually a cast for the more permanent stone wall under construction.

Houses lined one side of the village, and shops lined the other. In the center was a huge courtyard. Eldin shivered. The courtyard had a gallows. It was for public display. She counted three women who had their lives cut short at the end of a rope, swinging in the breeze.

The wagon slowed to a stop. Guards once again surrounded the wagon. Lord A'toha climbed down from his perch. He motioned for the prisoners to be brought with him. Eldin was hustled down. Once out of the wagon, the guards poked at her with a pike.

Eldin flashed a feral grin. The guard who had been poking her paled. He had witnessed her prowess with the other prisoner, and he was certain that he did not want her deadly attentions focused on him. He gruffly ordered her to move.

Eldin walked behind Lord A'toha. Her chains had not been replaced, so she enjoyed walking with a measure of dignity. Eldin watched Lord A'toha disappear into a large house. It was made from a rich, dark wood with a thatched roof. Many large windows speckled the side and allowed the interior to be flooded with sunlight. Heartbeats later, a servant came out and relayed the order for Eldin to be brought inside as well.

Eldin entered into the house of Lord A'toha. Large elaborate tapestries hung from the walls. They told the family history. As Eldin passed through the main hallway, she noticed that the majority of the tapestries were battle scenes. These glorified the killing of Amazons. *How like the tapestries we have in our households. Just from the Drakknian point of view. We really are not all that different from them.*

Eldin paused at the base of a tapestry that was much different than the rest. It depicted a single male-child. He was almost roguishly handsome with shoulder-length chestnut hair and intense hazel eyes. She traced his jaw, and the fabric was like silk beneath her fingertips.

"Lord A'toha waits for you. You must not keep him waiting," the voice from behind prompted her to keep moving.

Eldin remembered her manners and stepped lively. She did not want to lose her best ally. She paused near the open large double doors at the end of the hallway.

* * *

Lord A'toha looked up, and a smile lit up his face. He motioned for Eldin to enter. She entered the room. It was a formal dining room. A long table occupied the center of the room. Lord A'toha sat at the head. Eldin strode purposefully toward the table and stopped short. She would wait for an invitation before sitting.

"Please sit down, Eldin of Three Rivers. I have some things to discuss with you," A'toha stated as he gestured for her to take a seat close to his.

Eldin sat down and returned her gaze to Lord A'toha.

"Who is the mal…man in the tapestry? He looks so different from the rest of the men," Eldin inquired.

"Ah, that is Barron F'azik. He is the man who has always held my heart. I wish that the laws were different in Drakknia. Perhaps we would have been properly declared," A'toha lamented.

"I think that I would take my chances with the Mountain of Fire. I would take my love and find a new home," Eldin commented.

"I do not know if I should think you brave or a madwoman? Is that really what you would do if you lived in my boots?" A'toha asked.

"I believe so. If I could not get the laws to change, I would have to do something in order to be together. Love is the most powerful force I know. It drives us to be greater than we ever dreamed we could be. It drives a young Amazon...or Drakknian, to learn a trade well. It drives them to save to purchase a home and land. Love drives a soldier away from their sword. It drives a poet to prose. Love drives an elder's heart to continue to beat. Love is quite possibly the only thing that will stop this war between Drakknia and Yashor. I do not know when that will happen, yet I can think of no other force great enough to cause a victory to be had by both nations," Eldin explained her position.

A'toha was enraptured with Eldin's speech. Her words flowed through his soul to ease his suffering. There was no greater elixir for heartache than hope. A'toha cleared the lump from his throat and graced Eldin with a genuine smile.

"I wish for you to be certain of your path, Eldin of Three Rivers. I will write you a village permit. That will allow you to go anywhere inside the walls of T'elkatoha. I want you to go to the shops on the other side of the village. Be observant. Watch what life is like for the women of Drakknia. I will give you a list of things to buy for my household. You will be under my protection, but some men choose to ignore that. It is illegal for a woman to carry a weapon, so you will have only your hands to defend yourself with. If you choose to attack a man, even in self defense, you will be arrested. I will have no authority to release you. Do you understand?" A'toha explained some of the Drakknian laws.

"I understand, my Lord. I gave you my word that I would do nothing to provoke you to treat me unkindly. I will abide by my word," Eldin reassured A'toha.

Lord A'toha rose to his feet. He strode to the fireplace, where Eldin's sword had been placed earlier. Gripping the hilt reverently, A'toha turned to face Eldin.

"I shall keep your kinsman blade safe. If you are indeed successful with your petition, I shall release it to your brother," A'toha remarked as he laid Eldin's sword on the mantle.

"Thank you, my Lord. I shall never forget your kindness," Eldin remarked in earnest.

* * *

It took a candlemark for Lord A'toha to prepare his list. Eldin waited for her trip into the village inside a small room off the kitchen. It was the room designed for a slave and was small, cramped, and bare except for a pallet stuffed with old hay. Eldin was certain that the pallet contained body bugs from the previous occupants, so she chose to stand instead.

A small crone with a head full of white hair and a body broken and hunched over brought a small bag of coins along with the list to Eldin. Eldin's heart broke from the sight of the woman. Her eyes were clouded, and Eldin could tell she was in poor health. Her skin, wrinkled like a roadmap of harsh treatment, fairly hung off of her bones.

"Excuse me, dear elder," Eldin began.

The slip of a woman looked up and she held her hands up as if to ward off an evil spirit. "I be no elder. Have you no eyes, girl? I am a she-devil, same as you."

"Who are you; Lord A'toha's slave?" Eldin persisted.

A low chuckle started from the woman but quickly turned into a cough. Once the woman was able to speak again, she addressed Eldin's silly question.

"I am Lord A'toha's doorway into this world," the woman replied.

"Lord A'toha would allow his mother to be in such ill health? What kind of monster would do that?!" Eldin replied, indignantly.

"You listen, she-devil. I am but a doorway for the greatness to enter into our world. I deserve no respect, nor pity. I ask for none. You be wise to shut your mouth and listen with both ears. You are nothin' without a man. You serve him well, and perhaps he will be kind to you and keeps you fed. You serve a man well, and perhaps God will favor you with receivin' his seed. That is all the worth you have. Go on and get to the list. If you should hurry, might be you won't feel the whip bite you this eve," the old woman scolded Eldin.

Eldin accepted the bag of coins and list from the woman and hurried out the door. She was in Hades; she knew it now. This was madness! The whole world was backward here. How would she be able to finish her mission? *Goddess, send me a sign.*

Eldin felt the cold stares from the villagers. Did she look any different than the other women here? Eldin looked around. She saw women shuffling from one place to the next not drawing any attention.

"You there! Show me your scrolls!" a male-child challenged.

Eldin handed over the small scroll that contained her village permit to the male-child. Eldin watched as his forehead wrinkled while he concentrated on the document. He kept looking at the scroll then back up at Eldin. Finally, he seemed satisfied, and he handed the scroll back to Eldin.

"Just see to it that you mind your manners, Amazon. I'll be watching you," the male-child threatened.

Eldin did not want to argue with the first male-child to taunt her, so she continued down the road. She would have to swallow her pride to make this mission work. Eldin noticed that the majority of the women walked hunched over. They always kept their eyes cast downward. None of them walked with their shoulders back and head erect. Perhaps that is why she was getting the strange stares from the locals. She tried to slump her shoulders and keep from looking at anyone in the eye.

Eldin spotted a large tower beside the stables, and she decided to have a closer look. As the road narrowed, the houses on either side of the street gave way to open grassland. At the end of the street, a large, stone, windowless tower stood in stark contrast to the small wooden stables. There were plenty of soldiers guarding whatever the tower contained. Eldin was still about twenty paces away when she first noticed the unmistakable odor of wheat. As she drew closer, the smell grew stronger. Eldin watched as a wagon loaded with wheat kernels pulled away from the tower.

I have you now! Eldin noticed the soldiers from the tower were beginning to pay attention to her, so she changed direction and spotted a wildflower growing in the grass. Eldin bent over and plucked the fragrant bloom. She brought it up to her nose and inhaled its sweetness. Out of the corner of her eye, she noticed that the soldiers had dismissed her as no threat and returned to their pacing. She counted twenty that patrolled in pairs. That was smart. It would make it more difficult for one shadow to take them out without raising an alarm.

Eldin walked back toward the center of town. She had seen all that she dared on this day. Her mind whirled around what she had noticed. The tower must be where the Drakknian Army kept its supply of wheat for this area. Unfortunately, it was made of stone, so it would not be easy to plant the poison. She would have to get inside somehow, past all of the guards. Fortunately, she did not have to make her move right away.

Eldin's attention was captured by the young male-children playing in the courtyard. They were playing with stick swords and having a grand time in mock battle. She smiled sadly; too bad that when they grew up, most of them would be dying at the end of an Amazon blade or taking the life of an Amazon with theirs.

As Eldin took a shortcut across the village square, she heard her name whispered on the wind. She turned toward the sound and saw long tendrils of hair touched by flame dancing in the breeze. Eldin froze. It couldn't be. How in Hades could it be her? *Kiya!*

Eldin turned toward the small holding cell, and her long strides covered the distance in a few heartbeats. Eldin reached the barred window and her breath caught in her throat. Kiya stood just on the other side of the bars. Another breeze blew through the holding cell. Kiya's eyes met Eldin's.

"Eldin, by the Goddess, I have found you," Kiya blurted out.

Kiya's eyes reflected the fear in her soul, and it burdened Eldin's heart. Eldin reached out and captured the rose-petal-soft strands of Kiya's hair that played in the breeze.

"What in Hades are you doing here?" Eldin inquired trying to dislodge the lump in her throat.

"I came to rescue you," Kiya replied, leaning into Eldin's touch.

"And you are doing a fine job of it," Eldin joked to ease the intense feelings that threatened to overwhelm her.

"Do not joke at my expense, Captain. There is too much pain. I came here because I felt that you deserved better than to die for a Council that no longer exists. I came because I…" Kiya tried to explain her heart.

"What say you?! The Council of Nine no longer exists? Have the Drakknians…" Eldin started.

"No, it was not the Drakknians. Keep your voice down, Captain, or we shall both be hung in morning," Kiya admonished.

Eldin looked around at the Drakknians. None seemed to be interested in her.

"Kiya, what happened? How did you get here?" Eldin inquired as her fingers tingled at the contact with Kiya's face.

"Not long after you left, someone attacked the Council. It was a coup. Eldin, many people in Yashor are dead. Many people were killed as a warning to obey this new ruler. My other mother was one of them. Your parents…were targeted as well," Kiya reluctantly relayed the horror.

Eldin felt as if a league of soldiers had just taken turns kicking her in the stomach. This had to be what she felt earlier. It had to be. Were her parents both dead? *Goddess, what madness have You allowed?*

"Eldin, I beg you to get away from here. Save yourself. It is too late for me and Seldar. We have already been sentenced to hang in the morning," Kiya warned.

Eldin looked past Kiya for the first time and spotted Seldar sitting by the wall next to a fine-looking young Drakknian woman, lost in conversation with her. Had he followed Kiya? How did Seldar get involved in this? *Goddess, I cannot mourn for my mothers now. Please help me be strong. I must save Kiya and Seldar, or I shall truly lose everything.*

"Worry not. I shall be back for you both. I will not leave you, Kiya. Goddess knows I would sooner cut my beating heart from my chest than to leave you behind to die. I will come for you! Be ready," Eldin promised as she tore herself away from Kiya and quickly retreated across the village square.

Eldin noticed the village's defenses. A high wooden wall enclosed the village where soldiers stood guard. In places, stones had already replaced the wood. The main gate was forged from steel and set into the massive solid stone wall. It would take a battering ram and at least twenty Amazon soldiers to break through that gate. Goddess! Where did the Drakknians learn how to fortify their villages? This was going to be one difficult rescue.

Eldin watched as the soldiers paced across the front of the wall, met in the middle, turned, and paced back. She counted the heartbeats it took for them to finish a complete cycle. Then she counted over again, and again. It was fairly regular. They would have forty-seven heartbeats in order for them to slip unseen past the guards. Not much time for mistakes.

Eldin walked toward the village's main gate. She noticed that outside of the gate the land was open for at least a quarter-klig. That was not good. If they were being followed, there would be no place to hide for quite a long stretch of time. She would have to check the landscape all around the village. It was certain that they could not leave the way that they had come.

Eldin turned and walked along the perimeter of the village. She noticed every small detail of the wall, the soldiers who patrolled it, and the layout of the village. It was certainly going to be a challenge to rescue Kiya and Seldar. Eldin was aware of the sun racing behind the mountain. Time was not on her side. She sighed and started back to Lord A'toha's home. Perhaps he could shed some light on the surroundings. Eldin smiled; she would just have to phrase the questions correctly.

* * *

Kiya watched as Eldin disappeared into the crowded market square. She sighed. She had found Eldin at last. Hopefully Eldin would make it out of this alive, even if it meant her own death.

Kiya turned around and watched Seldar speaking with the Drakknian woman. His eyes sparkled, and she positively glowed. *Ah, there are definitely sparks there.* She could just barely hear their conversation.

"You will see; my sib is the captain of the Three Rivers District Sword Corps. Eldin is the best fighter in all of Yashor! She will save you. I promise. Afterwards, if you so desire, I will attend you." Seldar eagerly offered his services to the beautiful woman.

"Seldar, you are a man. I must attend you. I be not worthy of your rescue but am quite fond of you. If you would have me, I would like nothing more than to go wherever you go and to lodge with you. If we really are rescued; otherwise, I shall follow you into the afterlife. We shall lay in the Great Meadow, and I will make myself a vessel for your seed for all eternity," the girl dreamed aloud, not noticing the crimson that had invaded Seldar's cheeks.

Kiya had heard more than she cared of their conversation. She moved over to a corner away from the direct draft and sat. She closed her eyes. Whatever the outcome for herself, at least she had been able to find and warn the captain.

Kiya yawned; somehow she thought that Eldin would be happy seeing Seldar and this girl together. Even as exhausted as Kiya was, sleep proved elusive. She leaned against the wall of the cell and rested her eyes. Her mind refused to give in to sleep, however. Her thoughts turned to Eldin. She envisioned Eldin's lips caressing her own. It was a pity that she had never actually gotten to know that feeling, and if Eldin failed tonight she would be hanging by the end of a rope in the morning. *I would have liked to have known just one kiss.*

* * *

"Let me see if I understand you, Eldin of Three Rivers. You came back with not one item from my list? Instead, you want me to help you figure out a way to sneak out of this city. Have I understood you correctly?" Lord A'toha boomed.

"Yes, my Lord. You understand exactly correct," Eldin replied, not backing down one iota.

A'toha shook his head and chuckled. He had to admit that the Amazon was either brave or extremely crazy, and most likely a little of both.

"Where is it that you wish to go, Amazon? Back to Yashor so you can wield a sword against my brothers-in-arms, against my F'azik?" Lord A'toha inquired after Eldin's change of heart.

"No. I only wish to travel over the Mountain of Fire. I wish to create a new society, one that accepts differences. You could come with us. You and Barron F'azik could start a life together," Eldin started.

A deep rumbling laughter rang through the great room. Lord A'toha wiped the tears of laughter from the corners of his eyes with the back of his fist.

"You amuse me, Amazon. I have already told you that there is nothing on the other side of the Mountains of Fire. You will be walking up to the gates of Hades.

How could I ask my beloved F'azik to follow you to our deaths? Why do you have this sudden desire to enter Hades?" A'toha wondered aloud.

"You have my beloved healer and my equally beloved sib in your holding cell. They are to be executed in the morning," Eldin truthfully explained.

"Ah, I see. You play the fool for love. When I was young, I also played the fool. I am older now, and wiser. Yet, I do have a weak spot for you. What can I say? You amuse me greatly," A'toha started.

"Listen to me carefully, Lord A'toha. I gave you my word that I would do nothing to warrant your ill treatment. I now have to respectfully eat those words. If you plan to stand between me and my blade, I shall be forced to deal with you the only way I know how. My heart aches for only one, and she is waiting her death at the hands of your elders. I will tell you that I will do anything...*anything*...to assure that her heart continues to beat. I am desperate to rescue her, and I am certain that you can understand the depths of desperation," Eldin eloquently threatened Lord A'toha.

"Do you love this healer above all others? Would you give your life for hers? Tell me, Amazon, would you die in her place?" Lord A'toha questioned.

Eldin's hands involuntarily balled into fists as her body prepared for a fight. "Yes, my Lord. I would gladly die for Kiya."

Lord A'toha chuckled and then stepped away from the fireplace. He turned his back to Eldin.

"I expect you to honor me by not stabbing me in the back, Amazon. However, I cannot actually see you take the blade. If I were you, I would not jump from the south wall. It may look like the best place to jump because of the pond underneath it, but the pond has wooden spikes jutting up just below the surface of the water there. The north wall has too many soldiers. The west wall is too far from any hiding place, and I guess that means you should take the east wall. Go to the south wall and then make your way around to the eastern edge of the pond. Once there, you will see the tree line. That is the best place to jump. If you do not break your legs, you should be fine," Lord A'toha explained as he waited for Eldin to take possession of her kinsman blade.

"The south wall to the east wall, I shall remember. Thank you, my Lord. I shall not forget your kindness," Eldin stressed as she started toward the doorway.

"Eldin of Three Rivers!" A'toha called after her, "If you find a paradise on the other side, come back for us. In truth I would like to live with my F'azik and love him without suffering the judgment of fools," Lord A'toha beseeched Eldin.

"If we find paradise, I shall be back for you. This I swear on my life!" Eldin replied before she tucked the blade under her cape, swung open the heavy oak door, and slipped into the darkness outside.

"May God help speed you on your journey, Eldin of Three Rivers," Lord A'toha spoke to the open doorway.

* * *

Eldin made her way stealthily down an alleyway. She kept in the shadows as she made her way toward the market square. Eldin did not want to raise the alarm too early, or she would never be able to get Kiya and Seldar out of that holding cell. At the end of the alleyway, she waited until the guard had turned. Eldin started counting the heartbeats while she bolted from the alley and sprinted for the back of the holding cell.

With her back against the wall, Eldin crept alongside the holding cell toward the guard in the front. She needed to hurry…she only had twenty-seven heartbeats left before the guard would return. Sweat beaded on her forehead and started to trickle down her face.

Eldin pulled her sword from underneath her cloak. She reached out and clasped her hand over the guard's mouth at the same time that she ran him through. The sharp blade easily slid through the soft flesh. The guard's scream of pain and terror muffled against Eldin's hand. She slowly took the body to the ground as the male-child died. Eldin snatched the key to the holding cell and opened the door. She reached for the dead guard and flung him through the door.

Kiya and the small group of prisoners looked up at her in surprise. Eldin brought her fingers to her lips to silence their unasked questions… fifteen heartbeats to go. Eldin quickly took the guard's cap and pike. She shut the door…seven heartbeats left. Eldin stationed herself in the guard's position.

"You need to be shorter, Eldin," Kiya whispered from the barred window in the door.

Eldin bent her knees slightly. She couldn't bend them too much or it would show underneath her draped cape.

"Just a little shorter," Kiya prompted once more.

Eldin bent her knees even more until she heard Kiya's approval. One heartbeat! The guard along the wall signaled down to the guard stationed at the holding cell.

"Lift the pike," Kiya instructed, after having watched the same routine exchanges for two days.

Eldin lifted the pike, and the guard on the wall turned. Eldin released the breath that she had involuntarily been holding. She started counting as she opened the door once more.

"Follow me, quickly!" Eldin asserted.

"What did I tell you, R'uneh? Eldin would come for us!" Seldar exclaimed as he helped the young woman to her feet.

Everyone in the cell fled. Eldin sprinted for an alleyway to the south. The alley led to the stairs that the guards used to climb to the top of the wall. Eldin had found them when she had scouted the village earlier. She looked over her shoulder; the rest of the group were doing a good job of keeping pace with her. Ten more heartbeats until the alarms were raised. They had to make it to those steps!

It seemed like an eternity before the stairway came into view. Eldin pushed even harder.

"Just where do you think you are going?" a voice behind them taunted.

Seldar looked back to see a Drakknian guard holding a sword to R'uneh. In a heartbeat, Seldar's rage was all-consuming. He leapt at the

Drakknian and grabbed the male-child's wrist. Seldar twisted the hand until the wrist broke and the blade fell from his grip.

"Do not worry, R'uneh. Eldin will save us!" Seldar stated as he punched the Drakknian guard.

They both fell to the ground, and Seldar reached for the dropped sword. The Drakknian also saw the abandoned blade and made a grab for it. Seldar smashed the Drakknian's nose with his elbow and then dove for the blade. The Drakknian was right behind him. Seldar rolled onto his back, holding the sword out in front of him. The Drakknian could not stop his forward momentum, and he fell onto the blade. The doomed soldier made a gurgling noise as he died.

Seldar rolled over and stood just as the alarm bell tolled. He quickly placed his foot on the body and pulled the sword from the corpse. He would need it. Seldar and R'uneh rejoined the group as they reached the staircase.

Eldin led the group up. Each stair seemed to take an eternity. Eldin could see that the wall guards were converging on them. She looked down and saw the village soldiers pouring out into the streets from their barracks.

"Great...just what we needed...a bunch of uninvited guests," Eldin mumbled as she turned her attention back to the guards who were just reaching the top of the stairs.

Eldin's sword clanged as it stopped the Drakknian's blade. Eldin continued to exchange blows with the guard as she steadily advanced. The guard's face was contorted by his effort at blocking her strikes. Eldin smiled a feral grin, his face showed his fear. That look proved that he was already defeated in his mind, admitting that she had superior skills. Eldin pressed her advantage, and in one fatal misstep by her opponent, she plunged her sword deep into his midsection. Using all of her wrist strength, Eldin twisted the blade inside his gut and pulled it back out, trailing entrails. The doomed male-child fell from the stairs and landed in a heap of mangled flesh. The dry ground greedily licked up the blood as it flowed from his corpse.

Eldin moved on to her sword's next challenge. She reached the top of the stairs and loomed large against the other guard. Eldin resembled a demon from his childhood stories. The wetness spread down his leg as he lost control of his fear. Eldin noticed the look in his eyes, and she realized that he was barely old enough to hold a sword.

"Jump and you may live, male-child. Fight me…and I guarantee that you shall die," Eldin gave him a choice.

He took one look at her sword dripping in gore, and it did not take long for the male-child to reach a decision. He threw himself over the wall into the village courtyard, out of her reach.

"Quickly!" Eldin needlessly reminded her group.

Eldin helped Kiya and the rest up the final steps. She turned and grabbed onto Kiya's arm just as she prepared to jump.

"No! Not here. There are spikes in the water. Come this way," Eldin instructed as she led the group to the east.

Eldin saw the soldiers reaching the bottom of the stairs. They had only heartbeats before the male-children would reach the top of the wall. When Eldin refocused on the surroundings outside the wall, she saw in the moonlight a wagon full of hay on the eastern edge of the pond. Eldin smiled. *Thank you, Lord A'toha.*

"That's it! Jump into the wagon. Go…go…go!" Eldin ordered as she practically threw Kiya off the top.

Kiya's scream suddenly stopped as she landed in the soft hay. She got up a little confused and jumped from the wagon. Eldin didn't even pause to consider who the young woman was that she tossed next. Seldar grinned at Eldin and jumped on his own. He would prove his bravery to his sib if it was the last thing he did! After everyone else was safe, Eldin took one last look over her shoulder at the advancing soldiers and then leapt for the wagon.

Eldin landed with a thud and quickly found her feet. She fled the wagon.

"Quickly, push the wagon so the soldiers cannot follow us!" Eldin shouted as she pushed her shoulder into the back of the wagon.

Seldar, Kiya, and R'uneh quickly joined, and the old wagon creaked as the wheels began to turn. It gained a little momentum, and soon it was taken by the hill into the water below. Eldin turned and led the group into the woods.

"Where are we going?" Kiya asked.

"We are going away from this village that wanted to kill you, if it pleases you," Eldin replied a tad sarcastically, not used to her orders being questioned.

Kiya resisted the urge to reply to Eldin's verbal bashing. She realized that they were all under pressure with the escape. She would, however, be bringing this up at a more opportune time for discussion.

As soon as they reached the tree line, Kiya watched in horror as Eldin was ambushed and struck in the head with a heavy blow. Eldin crumpled to the ground. Kiya screamed.

"Hold! Is that you, daughter?" Kidak called out from the nearby bushes.

"Mother?" Kiya replied uncertainly.

"By the Goddess, it is them!" Romyl stated as she stepped from her hiding spot and looked at Eldin on the ground.

Kiya and Romyl bent down to inspect Eldin for damages. She opened her eyes slowly. Eldin looked at Kiya and then to Romyl. Suddenly Eldin remembered the ambush and punched Romyl in the face. Romyl's head snapped back and she staggered backward a step as her body absorbed the blow.

"She is definitely alright. Come, Eldin, it is my mother and the rest of our group," Kiya explained as she helped a still-woozy Eldin to her feet.

"They are with us? Then who did I just strike?" Eldin inquired.

"Councilwoman Romyl," Kiya replied as she patted Eldin's shoulder.

"I struck a councilwoman?! Oh, Goddess, this day just keeps getting better and better," Eldin mumbled as she shook the cobwebs from her brain.

"Come on, Amazons, we need to move. It looks like you brought soldiers with you!" Maric stated as she raced over to the group.

"Which way should we go?" Kidak asked.

"We need to get up the side of any of the Mountains of Fire. It is a forbidden place. The Drakknians will not follow us there," Eldin replied decisively.

"Aye. This way!" Romyl called as she took off for the base of the mountain that lay ahead of them.

The group broke into a run. Seldar helped R'uneh keep pace. She was weaker than anyone else in the group after a lifetime of malnourishment. R'uneh ran as fast as her legs could carry her. When she stumbled she was surprised to find Seldar reaching out to steady her with total disregard for his status. R'uneh absolutely adored him.

After a quarter-candlemark, the group reached the bottom of the mountain. The ground started to incline. A noticeable stench of rotten eggs permeated the area. Romyl looked to Eldin.

"Are you certain about this? It does not seem a verily inviting place," Romyl double-checked with Eldin as she surveyed the strange carvings in the trees and involuntarily wrinkled her nose at the odor.

"I was warned about the smell. We have to ignore it. We have no choice. Those soldiers are going to be here any candledrip now. If we do not start climbing, we are as good as dead," Eldin quickly assessed the situation for them.

"I believe in you, Captain. I will follow where you lead," Kiya remarked and took a step forward.

Eldin took the point position and led the group past the trees with the carvings. It was still thickly wooded, and Eldin made certain to pick her path carefully. Pine needles, wet leaves, and deadfall provided hazards to the weary escapees. Suddenly, voices were behind them. Eldin motioned for everyone to hide. The small group dove for cover and listened to their pursuers.

"They have gone into the forbidden territory. Shall we continue to give chase, Field Marshal?" a deep voice questioned.

"No. If they are foolish enough to walk through the gates of Hades, let them! Come, let us report back to Lord A'toha. I only hope that he is in a pleasant mood. I would hate for you to lose your head over the matter," another voice answered.

Eldin slowly released her breath. She waited until the area was silent once more. Eldin signaled to the group to remain hidden as she carefully scouted the area for Drakknian soldiers. Finding the area void of enemy troops, Eldin made her way back to the others.

"We can keep going now. The soldiers are gone," Eldin told the small group as she once again took the lead.

The tired group resumed their climb up the incline. After a candlemark of constant climbing, the terrain started to change. The woods thinned noticeably, and the lush grass started to be overtaken with patches of barren rock. The rock itself was a blue-black, like the heart of a demon. Seldar helped R'uneh to her feet for the third time in a quarter-candlemark.

"Wait here. This has gone on long enough. I shall see to it that you can get some rest, dear R'uneh," Seldar instructed as he turned back toward the still-moving group ahead of them.

Seldar broke into a sprint and passed up surprised woman after surprised woman until he caught up to Eldin. Eldin looked over and smiled at her sib. He had great intestinal fortitude for a male-child.

"Eldin, we need to rest, please. I think you were correct. I do not fear that any Drakknians have followed us. We are safe, and it is the middle of the night. I am weary, and so is R'uneh. Please," Seldar quietly petitioned Eldin.

Eldin looked back at the group. Kiya was slipping a little further behind, Romyl seemed to be helping Kidak to keep pace, and Maric was slowing as well. The two women that Eldin was not familiar with were struggling just a bit to keep pace. Eldin looked up at the dual moons just visible through an ominous cloud cover. Night was indeed quickly being chased away.

"I suppose I have pushed you far enough for this night. See if you can find some wood for a fire. I want to be able to chase the night chills from my bones. Besides, I fear not the Drakknians will come for us, even if they do spot our fire," Eldin instructed.

Seldar bent his head forward and placed his hand over his heart. He looked up in shock as he felt Eldin grasp his hand and place it back at his side.

"No, Seldar. I am no longer a captain. You are no longer an expendable male-child loyal to the Amazon Sword Corps of Yashor. We have no councilwomen, nor do we have a country. We are free from any titles. From this day forward, you are equal to any one of us. Have you ears…do you hear me?" Eldin explained.

Seldar's eyes grew wide at the implications for his life. He licked his lips nervously and looked around at the other women. Would they also feel this way? *Great Goddess, what form of madness had possessed Eldin?*

"I am not worthy of being treated as an equal, Eldin. I am but a lowly male-child," Seldar replied.

"Go find us some firewood, Seldar. I shall speak with you more on this later. Right now, we have some cold, trail-weary women who could use a warm fire." Eldin decided to put off this conversation until they were both well rested.

Seldar gratefully accepted the chore of finding firewood. After all, that was his place in the world. It was his lot in life. It made him feel secure.

"I think we should make camp and try to get some rest. I will scout around to see if there is any water nearby. In the meantime, perhaps some of you would be willing to start digging a fire pit," Eldin announced.

Eldin found the women more than willing to take a break from the arduous climbing. Maric, Dedak, and Romyl started searching for food. Kidak, Kiya, and Rynar started digging a fire pit. Rynar found a sharp rock and used it to break through the hardened surface. Once the surface was turned, the rest of the pit could be dug by hand. R'uneh sat nervously to the side. She did not understand these women. How could they order a man around? What was going on? R'uneh realized that life as she knew it was over.

26

Eldin finished gnawing the meat off of the leg bone she had claimed. She snapped the bone in half and sucked out the tender marrow. Satisfied that she had not missed the tiniest scrap, Eldin tossed the empty bones away from the campfire. The hunting party had been successful, finding and killing a wild boar. Seldar and R'uneh had roasted the beast to perfection. The mood had certainly gotten lighter after their bellies had been fed. Eldin leaned back against the log and watched the group laughing in the firelight. Dedak had her arms wrapped around Rynar. It was easy to see that they were a young couple in love. Then there was Romyl and Kidak. They seemed genuinely in love, yet reserved with each other. Maric was sitting next to Seldar and the Drakknian girl. Seldar seemed positively smitten. Then there was Kiya...beautiful as ever, with her long fire-touched hair playing gently in the night breeze. Suddenly, Eldin remembered a question she had been meaning to ask Kiya and Seldar.

"Excuse me, Kiya, but I have one question for you. How did you get yourself sentenced to death?" Eldin inquired, as a hush fell over the group.

"Well, I had been searching for you. You are a hard Amazon to track, you know," Kiya started.

"It helps if you have been taught how to track," Eldin bantered back in a teasing defense of her skills.

"As I was saying, I had been searching for you. I was dirty and needed a bath. I felt as though I would never find you. I did find a deep, slow-moving stream so I decided to wash off the trail dirt. As I was bathing, two Drakknian male-children found me. Luckily, Seldar had been shadowing me. He stopped them from abusing me. Seldar convinced them that I was his "wife" or whatever they call it. Well, they discovered that I was not," Kiya abruptly finished.

"Oh, do not stop with the story half-told!" Seldar exclaimed quickly.

Seldar waited for the buzz to die down before he continued. "You see, we had them fooled…until Kiya burned the stew I helped her to prepare. The Drakknians ate it anyway. I told them that what she lacked in cooking skills she made up for in "wife" skills. Unfortunately for us, they later became ill from the cooking and had us arrested as assassins. They claimed we tried to poison them. Since they were some high-ranking runaway-collectors, we were sentenced to hang for the crime of attempted poisoning," Seldar finished.

The women around the fire burst into laughter. Kiya's cheeks burned.

"To think that I went through all of that to save you!" Kiya blurted before running away from the fire pit.

"I shall go get her," Eldin told a concerned Kidak, and rose to her feet.

Eldin found Kiya underneath a moss-covered tree. She closed the distance quickly.

"I am sorry, Kiya. I meant not to hurt your feelings. I only wished to know how you came to be in that holding cell," Eldin apologized.

"I risked my life to save you. I know that I am not a great warrior like you, but I felt like I had to save you," Kiya started to lay on the guilt.

"Hold, Kiya! I know that you were verily brave. I never questioned that. We were only jesting and releasing the feelings of almost being killed. Laughter is great medicine. Our intent was not to disrespect you, honorable Healer," Eldin explained.

Kiya kept her back turned toward Eldin. Her long hair danced in the gentle night breeze, and Eldin felt drawn to her. Slowly she stepped closer... heartbeat by heartbeat...until she stood close enough to feel Kiya's energy radiating from her body.

"I have something to confess to you. You are the reason that I survived. Many times I felt alone and outnumbered. I felt as if I would not live through this mission. I actually prayed to the Great Goddess to send me a sign. Do you know what I saw?" Eldin asked as she reached out and turned Kiya toward her.

Kiya's deep green eyes were flooded with unshed tears. Eldin wiped away the tears forming in the corners of Kiya's eyes.

"I saw you. You were the answer to my prayers, Kiya. You were the one thing that I thought about day after day. No one else even crossed my mind. I had to live to see you again. That is the only thing that kept me alive," Eldin laid her heart bare.

"Goddess, I have been such a fool. Eldin, I came after you because I gravely misjudged you. You are the only Amazon I have ever loved, yet I feared your intentions. I feared loving you because when I give my heart, it shall be for all eternity," Kiya admitted.

"I can abide by that," Eldin pledged as she bent forward, searching out Kiya's inviting lips.

Every nerve ending tingled at the first contact of the warrior's lips on the healer's. Softness on softness. Eldin wrapped her arms loosely around Kiya's waist as Kiya reached up and grabbed handfuls of Eldin's silky blonde mane. Time stood still as Eldin was assaulted by wave after wave of Kiya's intensity. Her heart beat fast and hard in her chest as though it meant to beat life into both of them. Eldin felt Kiya's soul intertwine with her own. She felt Kiya surrender to her, and a whimper escaped Eldin's throat. Their lips continued to dance in a more fevered rhythm. Eldin was losing herself to a passion she had never before known.

When Kiya parted her lips inviting Eldin to explore her further, Eldin responded like a moth drawn to an open flame. She tasted Kiya's sweet mouth for the first time and felt suddenly intoxicated by it. Their passion deepening, Eldin drew Kiya to her in a strong embrace and backed her up against the trunk of the tree. Eldin's hands began to map out Kiya's generous hip swells.

Kiya's eyes flew open. Delyn was holding her down. She was touching her...forcing her. Kiya's mind screamed.

"Get off me!" the words tumbled from Kiya's mouth as the power surged through her body.

Eldin's body flew through the air and she landed with a heavy thud. She felt like she had been kicked by a horse in the rib cage. What the Hades was going on? She could not catch her breath. Eldin looked up and watched in horror as Kiya fled the area. What had she done wrong?

* * *

Oh Great Goddess, Kiya has experienced her Awakening. We must find her quickly! Dedak silently explained to a visibly shaken Rynar.

That was Kiya? Goddess, I have never felt such rage, and fear, mixed with such love. How can that be? Rynar wondered.

No time to explain now. We need to find Kiya, before she hurts some-one, or herself. Dedak tried to keep Rynar focused on the task at hand.

Dedak helped Rynar to her feet, and they calmly walked away from the fire. Rynar followed Dedak. She knew that Kiya must have a lot of power, because she could "feel" her. It was something close to the way she "felt" Dedak. Only Dedak had made that connection. This was something wild...untamed...and definitely dangerous.

It did not take long for Dedak to follow her internal map to Kiya. They found Kiya crumpled beside a small pool of bubbling water. She was crying.

"What is wrong, Kiya?" Dedak gently inquired.

Kiya looked up and immediately choked down her sobs. She quickly wiped away evidence of her tears with the back of her hand before looking back at her cousin.

"I know not what is happening to me. You would not believe me if I told you," Kiya lamented.

"I will believe you. I have had my own Awakening, and it is scary as a Hades Hound chewing on your leg," Dedak replied.

"Awakening? What say you? I have never heard of such a thing. All I know is that one moment I was kissing Eldin and the next I had thrown her through the air… with…my mind. Only, it was not Eldin. In my mind it was Delyn. I am losing my soul to some demon!" Kiya relayed her fears.

"Panther piss. You are a Jahru, Kiya. You come from a long line of Jahru. What you are feeling, we have all felt. It is called the Awakening. It is when your soul disturbs your powers, and awakens them. The power floods your bloodlines, and you feel this incredible sense of the world around you. You can hear what others cannot even see. You can feel a heartbeat a klig away. You can enter the minds of others and know what they think. You can see every fiber in their bodies and repair the damage that you find. You can force your will upon them. You have become one with the fabric of the world and the heavens above. You are Jahru… embrace it!" Dedak explained to a stunned Kiya.

"Jahru?! You are a Jahru?" Eldin exclaimed in terror as she overheard the exchange.

"Eldin, wait! Kiya is still the woman you love. She is merely more connected with the world around her. It can be such a wonderful thing. I know because I fell in love with this Jahru." Rynar pointed at Dedak, then continued, "She has treated me with nothing but respect and love. Do not believe the old lies. The Jahru are our Amazon Sisters."

Eldin felt torn. She loved Kiya still, but this was nearly too much to bear. Kiya looked as though she were having a hard time dealing with the news herself. *Poor Kiya, Goddess, how alone she must feel.*

Only if you leave me. Eldin jumped. She had heard Kiya's words, yet Kiya's lips had not moved.

"It is important that you do not place your will upon anything or anyone during this time. I will have to teach you how to control your power. For now, just concentrate on keeping the power locked up deep inside you. During the awakening, if you will something, your will shall become real. It is a funny quirk, but once the powers are awakened at full strength, they somehow become less active," Dedak warned.

Eldin wanted to talk with Kiya privately. She turned to Dedak and Rynar.

"Many thanks for explaining all of this to us. If it is safe, I wish to speak with Kiya alone," Eldin petitioned for their privacy.

"We shall leave as you desire, Eldin. Please come back to the camp soon. When Kiya is weary, she will have less control over her thoughts. She needs to sleep for the safe completion of the Awakening," Dedak warned once again.

"I shall keep her but a few candledrips. I promise," Eldin replied.

Kiya and Eldin watched Dedak and Rynar get swallowed by the darkness as they returned to the fire pit.

Eldin turned to Kiya. Kiya refused to look at her. She reached out and took hold of Kiya's chin, forcing her to look up. Eldin's steady ice-blue gaze lovingly caressed Kiya's face.

"What happened back there? Did I do something to upset you?" Eldin wondered aloud.

"I…I do not deserve your love, Eldin. I am unclean. I am a…a whore," Kiya broke down as the sobs wracked her body once more with the memory of Delyn's words echoing in her mind.

"What say you? I do not believe that at all. Why would such a thing cross your lips?" Eldin demanded.

"I have no gift to give you. It has already been taken," Kiya spat out.

Eldin placed her arms around a protesting Kiya. She held her firmly in a loving embrace, despite Kiya's attempts to break free. Eldin sat down with her back against the trunk of a tree and held Kiya in her lap.

"No…I shall not allow you to run from my heart. I am not worthy of you either. I have no gift as well. You say that your gift was "taken." Did you give it willingly as I did, or was it stolen?" Eldin attempted to understand what Kiya truly meant.

Kiya's sobs deepened, and although Eldin was no Jahru, she did not need Kiya's words to tell her the answer. Eldin drew Kiya into her breast, and Kiya could hear Eldin's heart beating beneath her head. It was comforting. Kiya closed her eyes and relaxed into Eldin's embrace. She felt Eldin kiss the top of her head.

"So where do we go from here?" Kiya asked meekly.

Eldin's mind whirled around the events of the last two moon cycles. She felt lost and afraid, yet with Kiya in her arms those feelings paled compared with the love that bathed her soul. Eldin tilted Kiya's chin upward, and she placed a delicate kiss on those intoxicating lips.

"The only place we can go. We shall journey beyond the Mountains of Fire." Eldin's words brought strange comfort to Kiya, who melted into her embrace.

Kiya looked up at Eldin. She was terrified of the power that she felt surging through her body. She was terrified of this mountain. She was terrified that she would lose her mother. Most of all, she was terrified that she would lose her Eldin. Kiya relaxed and closed her eyes as the power quickly drained her. She knew that her life was forever changed. She knew the truth deep inside.

"Mmmm. Beyond the mountains of fire," Kiya echoed, fear evident in her voice.

"My life and my sword for you, Kiya," Eldin pledged, to ease Kiya's fears.

Kiya looked deeply into Eldin's ice-blue eyes. Why was it so difficult for the captain to say what she truly meant?

"Can you not say the words from your heart, Eldin? A soldier's pledge of fealty is not the same as a soul declaration," Kiya gently reminded her.

Eldin nodded. It was time to lay J'min's ghost to rest and to lay claim to the heart that had broken down all of her walls.

"I...I...love you, Kiya. Goddess, I have loved you since I first felt your touch so many moons ago. You make me more than I could ever hope to be without you. Please, Kiya do not ever leave my side again. You make my heart dance," Eldin poured out her soul.

Tears threatened to fall from her eyes. Kiya had never heard anything quite as sweet as this great warrior becoming vulnerable to love...her love.

"I shall never leave your side, Eldin. Your heart claimed mine long ago. I tried to deny it, but the Goddess would not allow me to abandon what She willed to be. I am now and for always yours...and yours alone," Kiya laid her soul bare in return.

Eldin quickly claimed Kiya's lips in a kiss that seared their souls together. She felt Kiya deep within her, coursing through her bloodlines. Kiya opened her mouth slightly, inviting Eldin to explore her more thoroughly. Passion swept away conscious thought as their tongues danced a rhythm that was both ancient and new...forever joining their souls. Breathless, they reluctantly had to relinquish the kiss.

* * *

Eldin gazed at the earthly goddess in her arms. She had lost her mothers...her country... her way of life, and yet gained the other half of her soul. They could not go back, they could not pretend; the only way left was over the forbidden mountain. Eldin looked out at the strange forest and remembered the night she had shared with Kiya by the waterfall; the water of the falls rushing and plunging over the edge into that calm pool at the bottom. *Goddess, let there be a pool on the other side of this mountain, for we have just stepped off the edge...*

"Beyond the mountains of fire..." Kiya mumbled in her sleep.

Eldin suddenly felt a strange sensation come over her body. It was like being stung by a swarm of bees, tingling all over. She looked down at Kiya and watched in horror as the healer's body became transparent. Eldin held up her hand as her own flesh became translucent. It was as if they were simply melting from existence.

"What the Hades?!" Eldin blurted out.